THE RIVER BELOW

FRANÇOIS CHENG

The River Below

Translated by Julia Shirek Smith

WELCOME RAIN

New York

THE RIVER BELOW by François Cheng
Originally published in France as *Le dit de Tianyi*.
Copyright © 1998 Editions Albin Michel.
Translation © 2000 Welcome Rain Publishers LLC.
All rights reserved.
Printed in the United States of America.

Welcome Rain Publishers would like to thank
the French Ministry of Culture for its assistance with this translation.

Library of Congress Cataloging-in-Publication Data
Cheng, François, 1929–
[Dit de Tiyani, English]
The river below / François Cheng ; [translated by Julia Shirek Smith].—1. ed.
p. cm.
ISBN 1-56649-100-2
I. Smith, Julia Shirek. II. Title.
PQ2663.H3913 D5713 2000
843'.914—dc21   00-063417

Direct any inquiries to
Welcome Rain Publishers LLC,
225 West 35th Street, Suite 1100
New York, NY 10001.

ISBN 1-56649-100-2
Manufactured in the United States
of America by BLAZE I.P.I.

First Edition October 2000
1 3 5 7 9 10 8 6 4 2

CONTENTS

F OREWORD

DURING THE FIRST HALF of the fifties, I often ran into Tianyi. I had been struck by his anxiously open face and by his painting. His art depended on a strange alchemy, blending density of detail with the most ethereal lightness. I had met Véronique, too, there in his almost empty studio. It was she who told me, in late 1956, of Tianyi's sudden return to China. Although sorry at the time, I was not unduly surprised by his departure. Many a student, studies finished, had gone home through choice or lack of funds.

I too was serving a harsh apprenticeship of exile with its second chance at life, and over the next decades I forgot most of the figures from my early days in France, including Tianyi and Véronique. They faded from memory like a random snapshot stuck away in a drawer.

Nearly a quarter of a century later, in 1979, I received a brief and totally unexpected letter from Tianyi. He asked me to contact him and, specifically, to give him news of Véronique. China had just emerged from the Cultural Revolution and was trying, in one way or another, to bind up its wounds. The country was witnessing a period of "repentance" and "openness." Half-opened doors and windows let the breeze blow in. Millions of individual dramas came to light, intertwined with details of the national drama.

After several inquiries, I learned that Véronique had died in an automobile accident about ten years earlier. Something made me hesitate, and I dared not pass the tragic news on to Tianyi just yet. I had not failed to note from his address that he was living in a home of some kind, and his agitated handwriting probably indicated a precarious mental state. But my mind was made up: I would go see him in person. Because he had beckoned to me, there was no resisting the desire to respond to his appeal and to learn what had happened to him.

I had to wait until 1982, however, to undertake the journey. I took advantage of an invitation from a Chinese university, which gave me an official excuse for a lengthy stay in China. After fulfilling my professional commitments, in the summer I traveled to the north-eastern city of S. I found the home from which he had written, a catch-all institution whose residents included those without families, the physically handicapped, and individuals considered mentally disturbed but not violent in behavior. The dusty waiting room was stifling; they showed me to a bench on the gallery that faced a central courtyard alive with abandoned humanity. After a short wait I saw coming from the other end of the gallery a white-haired person with a shuffling gait. As he approached, he stared at me with large, slightly bulging eyes which seemed out of proportion in his emaciated face. But my shock could hardly be compared to his when I had to tell him he would never see Véronique again. Stunned for a few minutes, he finally turned and, even more stooped than before, led me to his cramped room, where an ordinary table was covered with little heaps of paper. When he pulled out one of the piles to show me, I saw that it was actually one very long band, accordion-pleated, fashioned from coarse sheets glued together. Offhand, I estimated there to be about forty such piles. This collection of writings, which Tianyi characterized as rough and unfinished, had been meant for Véronique. Since she was no more, he entrusted them to me in their helter-skelter state, claiming that if left in China, they would more than likely be thrown in the garbage or used as fuel.

But how heavily did these writings weigh when compared to what a voice can convey? The voice buried deep within him for so many years, how could it not affect someone who had come from afar to listen to him? And so began the most intense days of my life. For hours at time, without a break, Tianyi spoke. As he spoke, I would write down everything that reached my ears. I did have a simple recording device, of course, but I feared that the tapes I made might be of poor quality or would be confiscated upon my leaving China.

In the evening, in spite of my fatigue I could not aspire to rest: I endeavored to devote myself to Tianyi's written tale. The story of his life—lived or imagined?—was extremely difficult to decipher because of the impatient and uncoordinated hand, with so many characters crossed out. There were also several gaps in the narrative and numerous inconsistencies. Yet across the choppy waves sometimes there would appear veritable beaches, bright and lucid. But then, in the eyes of Tianyi himself, these pages were only a sketch, a means of tracing the main thread and establishing points of reference. He insisted I ask specific questions to fill in the gaps. With me there as interlocutor, he ardently desired to end up telling everything, insofar as it was possible.

Listening to Tianyi, I had more than enough time to observe him. And yet I could not help but ask myself the question: "Is he crazy, as they claim?" I was not unaware of why he had been brought to that place. While undergoing treatment for serious intestinal problems, he periodically escaped from the hospital, going off to fill his pockets with horse dung he would find on the road. He claimed these pieces of dung reminded him of a type of cardboard he used for painting and which bore the name, appropriately enough, "horse-dung cardboard." Besides this peculiar habit, there was the fact that his speech and his drawings showed evidence of mental disturbance. Thus there was ample justification for sending him to the home. According to Tianyi himself, he continued to have alternate periods of agitation and prostration. "Is he crazy?" Knowing nothing about insanity, I just found his dual state upsetting: on the one hand, his consciousness of the uncontrollable side of himself; on the other, his lucidity when telling his life story. As I listened to him, from time to time I would notice his hands nervously fingering some object or his eyes flashing with the look of a madman. And yet he never lost the thread of his discourse; he entered patiently into the details. As the days went by, his mastery increased, although he did manifest some confusion—confusion respected in my transcription—over verb tenses. As he told the story of his past, he would break into the present tense when recalling certain scenes and episodes that must have affected him profoundly. In particular, when he arrived at the period of his return to China, he began speaking entirely in the present, as if the events related were surging up at the very moment he spoke of them. No more was he the lost creature begging for a listener so he might gather up the shreds of the past. Rising above the fatigue and physical suffering that afflicted him, he became a man of renewed dignity, almost soothed, transfigured. A sovereign strength seemed in the air, born of his mouth and presiding in turn over the birth of a destiny created anew. The face glowing with innocence and fervor in that half-lit room reminded me of the portrait of young Hölderin I had seen in Germany.

Once back in France, I, in turn, had to face the ordeal of illness. I was immobilized much of the time, and when I heard the news of that worn-out man's death I could not even consider a trip to China. He had wanted a portion of his ashes scattered in the waters of the Loire. . . . Then, long months of worry and suffering slipped through my fingers like sand. But I certainly did not forget Tianyi; his image gave me strength, at the same time fueling an unquenchable remorse over my inability to do anything for him. In 1993, I awoke from a surgical operation surprised to rediscover myself . . . living. And so, as if to repay a debt, I took on the arduous task of putting together the story entrusted to me and rendering it into French. I present it here.

Before all is lost, before the century is over, from deep in the unfathomable clay someone—by virtue of words alone—has made us a gift of treasures amassed over a lifetime filled with furors and savors.

PART ONE: EPIC OF DEPARTURE

I

I N THE BEGINNING there was the cry in the night. Autumn 1930. China with its five thousand years of history, and I with almost six years of life on earth, for I was born in January 1925. My parents had just taken me to the country for the first time, fleeing the city of Nanchang, its heat still oppressive, its streets tumultuous with the spectacle of executions. My little sister and I were in the bedroom our family would share; although it was late, my parents lingered in an adjoining room chatting with the aunt we were visiting. We had been entertaining ourselves with the rustic objects beside the only bed when suddenly we heard a long cry. Plaintive at first, distant, then closer and closer; strident, soon it had turned into a kind of repetitive chant, an insistent monotone, but infinitely soothing. The voice was a woman's, so resonant with immemorial echoes that it seemed to spring from her entrails or from the bowels of the earth. Words could now be distinguished: "Wandering soul, where are you, where are you? . . . Wandering soul, come here, come here . . .Wandering soul . . ." Truly spellbound by the voice and the words, and perhaps to calm my sister, who was speechless with fright, I replied in an almost playful tone: "Yes, I'm coming, I'm coming . . ."

And as the voice outside was growing louder, I raised my own in response. That was when the adults burst noisily into the room, my aunt first, followed by my parents. They all shouted: "Be quiet, child, be quiet!" then without a break: "You two, get to bed now! We thought you were already asleep!" Given without explanation and accompanied by distraught looks, the abrupt, brutal order left me shocked and unable to speak. After the candle had been blown out, I lay awake in the dark. I managed to catch some of the adults' conversation, and from it I understood more or less what was at stake. The woman crying out had just lost her husband. That night she called to his wandering soul so it would not go astray. According to the ritual, after burning paper money for the dead, the widow calls out just as the third watch begins. If by chance someone among the living answers her cry with a yes, he loses his body, which is quickly entered by the dead man's wandering soul that then returns to the world of the living. And the soul of the one thus losing his body becomes in turn the wanderer and wanders until finding another body for its reincarnation. Soon I heard the voices of the adults again, reassuring one another: "But an innocent reply does not count!" "How can they feel reassured?" I wondered. As for me, I saw myself already dead, losing my body!

I knew what death was, for an unthinking servant had taken me to watch the execution of a revolutionary bandit. Perched on the servant's shoulder, I had a clear view across the excited crowd. There was a cry that day, too, from the executioner who stood behind the kneeling prisoner. A brief, sharp cry, followed at once by the flash of a raised saber cutting through the air, a fountain of blood spurting from the condemned man's neck, a body sinking and a head rolling in the sand. Murmurs of admiration rose from the crowd. So this was death, a thing men inflicted on one another with a tried and true technique. On that occasion I had learned that one must at all costs avoid being bitten by a freshly severed head. For anyone so bitten replaces the deceased and will die, while the dead man shall rejoin the living.

Now that I had answered "yes" to the woman's call, I did not doubt the wandering soul had attached itself to me. Was there still a way to escape fate? While ruminating on this, I drifted off to sleep, a sleep disturbed by terrifying, nightmarish visions. My family's vague anxiety turned out to be well founded. All night I was delirious, gripped by a high fever. I awoke late the next morning exhausted and extremely pale. Extricating myself from the soaked sheet wrapped around me like a shroud, I discovered I was still alive. But suddenly I felt a stranger to myself. I was aware that my previous body had been taken by someone; what lay on the bed nearly inert—and could perhaps be felt with my hand—was another person's body, to which my soul had attached itself, come what may.

From then on, I could not get the idea out of my head that, contrary to the commonsense notion of people being bodies endowed with souls, a human being was—for me at least—a stray soul dwelling in any body it could borrow. I was convinced that from then on everything in me would be perpetually out of joint. Things would never match up perfectly. In my view, therein lay the essence of my life, or of life in general.

2

T WO AND A HALF YEARS had passed since the night of the cry. I now lived with my parents in our home for years to come, a humble cottage at the base of Mount Lu, in northern Jianxi Province, not far from the Yangzi River. In the meantime my little sister had died in a meningitis epidemic. One morning this sister, this playmate, this companion who slept beside me every night, did not open her eyes, or smile at me, or answer me. Just like that she was gone forever, leaving a great emptiness inside the house and out. As heavy as my parents' grief and my own heartbreak may have been, I remained convinced that my sister was somewhere, that she was playing hide and seek with me. How many times did I not turn around at the creaking of a chair or the crunching of leaves on the path.

My father, his own health deteriorating—he had always suffered from asthma and chronic bronchitis and eventually contracted tuberculosis—decided one day to leave the city and retreat to a secluded village in the verdant countryside of a tea-growing region. The thatched cottage occupied by our little family adjoined the village's run-down temple, which my father converted into a classroom. There he provided elementary instruction for the children of the village and the surrounding area. He also served as public scribe, a role which turned out to be as beneficial as that of schoolmaster. Besides writing letters and drawing up contracts, he was called upon to do calligraphy for the local people. For many of life's special occasions—festivals, marriages, funerals, birthdays, the building of a house, the opening of a shop—he turned his hand to all kinds of formulas, sayings, epigrams, mantras, steles, and signs. To my surprise I discovered that the illiteracy of the villagers did not preclude their revering ideograms; unconsciously but profoundly, they were molded by these written signs, showing as much sensitivity to the emblematic power as to the formal beauty. Sometimes the requests proved too many for my father, especially when his asthma was severe, and I would be obliged to assist him. I had something of a natural gift for brushwork, and I began the serious study of calligraphy. Following my father, I learned not only to copy the various styles from models left by the ancient masters but also to observe the living models afforded by omnipresent nature: the grasses, the trees, and soon the terraced tea fields. These last I observed so often that eventually I knew by heart their configuration: they were indeed skillful, complex creations. I marked how their regular and rhythmic lines, seemingly established by man, followed closely the endlessly varied contours of the terrain, thereby revealing a deeper structure, "the veins of the Dragon." Thus imbued with a vision nurtured by my apprenticeship in calligraphy, I began to experience a physical communion with the landscape.

Beyond the shapes, I had gradually become the companion, the accomplice almost, of the odors and colors emanating from the thick clumps of tea leaves. These plants broke the monotony of my rather lonely life (for the most part, the village children were obliged to work alongside their parents; they attended school only during their relatively few free months), for their nuances and tones changed constantly according to the season, the day, and even the hour. Such variation was not caused by temperature and light alone—fickle as they are in that locale—but was elicited by the mists and clouds forming an integral part of Mount Lu. These conferred on the landscape an atmosphere at times diaphanous and tinged with blue, at times heavy and close, like the engraved or sculpted images on folding screens.

"Mists and clouds of Mount Lu," so famous they had become proverbial, referring to something elusive and mysterious, a beauty hidden yet bewitching. With their capricious, unpredictable movements and their never-fixed hues—pink or purple, jade green or silver gray—they turned the mountain magical. They developed amid Mount Lu's countless peaks and hills; then, lingering in the valleys or rising toward the heights, they maintained a constant state of mystery. At times they dissipated abruptly, revealing to the human eye the mountain in all its splendor. With their silkiness and their scent of moist sandalwood, these clouds and mists resembled a being both fleshly and unreal, a messenger come from elsewhere, who might converse with the earth for a minute or for hours, depending on his mood. Some bright mornings they stole silently through shutters and entered the dwellings of men, caressing them, surrounding them, gentle and intimate. Should anyone try to grab hold of them, they would move off as silently as they had come, out of reach. Some evenings the heavy mists rose and met up with clouds in motion, producing moisture and bringing showers; the pure water would pour into jars and jugs the villagers set out under their walls. With this water they made the best tea around. Once the downpour had ended, the clouds broke up rapidly, and under clear skies the highest mountain would be briefly visible. The surrounding hills in no way detracted from the mysterious lofty beauty of this peak, which, unobstructed, reflected the diffuse evening light and displayed its fantastic, dangerously towering crags crowned with a vegetation no less fantastic. Meanwhile, the clouds, re-forming in the west, would turn into a wide, slack sea, on whose waves floated the setting sun like a dream ship gleaming with a thousand multicolored lights. And very soon the summit would be draped in a mauve mist, becoming invisible once more. As was indeed appropriate, since this was the hour for Mount Lu's daily journey westward to pay homage to the Taoists' Lady of the West and to greet Buddha. At that moment, the universe appeared to disclose its hidden reality: it was in perpetual transformation. What was apparently stable melted away into the moving; what was apparently finite sank into the infinite. There was no fixed, final state. And is that not the real truth, since all living things are but condensation of the breath?

Dating from then I had an intuition, although still rather vague, that my element would be the cloud—a thing immaterial yet substantial, an ethereal and almost palpable presence. I would understand later—when I was of an age to understand why the Chinese are so taken with clouds—why they use the expression "clouds and rain" to refer to the act of love and the state of ecstasy, why poets and Taoists speak of "eating mists and clouds," "caressing mists and clouds," and "sleeping among mists and clouds." What is a cloud, really? From whence does it come? Where does it go? I who had so much time to observe the cloud could see that it was born of the valley in the form of mists; then it rose toward the heights until reaching the sky where it could float in space and take on any number of forms, depending on the weather, depending on the wind. On occasion, as if not forgetting its origins, it consented to fall back to earth as rain, thus coming full circle. The cloud was always somewhere but it was from nowhere. What was it then? Nothing? But it seemed that without it the sky and the earth would have been monotonous.

My mother had it right. When she saw me with a faraway look, she would often say: "You're wandering in the clouds again," and invite me to step down from my carriage in the air. What she did not realize was that I did not float in a carriage borne by clouds; I was cloud. This identification with an evanescent element suggested, not for the first time, that I was destined to be a wanderer, one on the fringes, forever at the base of some elusive and inaccessible Mount Lu. I would not be rooted here, nor elsewhere, perhaps not even on the earth. With these thoughts, sadness would well up in me. A sadness accentuated by my sister's sudden departure, by my idea of the random nature of my body, and by my mother's everlasting Buddhist litanies punctuated with my father's fits of coughing. Crouched in the corner, in a house filled with the scent of incense and the odor of medicinal brews simmered for days on end, I would wonder: Will I leave my parents someday? Will they someday leave me? . . .

Even so, at times a lightness, a clarity, would pass over my spirit; with things as they are, I would say to myself, one might as well seize in passing what the earth can offer! For it is akin to the giant pumpkin that lies in the field and is so pleasant to touch and explore with the hands. There is no life too insignificant for seeking out what the earth has to divulge and display. Yes, all things seen or sensed, even ephemeral, appear miraculous. One must certainly take advantage of that. At such moments of exaltation, a confused sort of joy came over me, so pervasive as to be suffocating. One day I had a sudden revelation: everything the outside world aroused in me could find expression through an element within my reach. Ink. For, each morning before practicing calligraphy, I had to prepare my ink, patiently rotating the stick in the broad stone filled with water until I had a rich black mixture. How well I knew its fragrance. Once the liquid was ready there came the moment of which I never wearied, the testing of its flow. With bold strokes I would put my well-soaked brush to thin, translucent paper, which absorbed the black fluid quickly yet allowed it to flood slightly. Then, for several minutes longer the ink retained a fresh glossiness, as if pleased that a receptive and willing paper had consented to savor it. The Ancients compared this magic—paper receiving ink—to the young bamboo's powdery skin receiving drops of morning dew. I myself liked to compare it to the tongue after one has eaten a delicate rice-flour cake; a few morsels stick and melt, leaving a taste that seems in no hurry to disappear.

Thus, the day of my revelation, as I gazed deep into the shimmering, slightly iridescent liquid, the cloud-capped mountain appeared, the very view my eyes had taken in that morning. Without delay I sat down to draw the peak, trying to reproduce both its tangibility and its evanescence. The result, alas!, did not by any means correspond to what I had hoped. But I was won over by the magical power of brush and ink. I sensed it was to be a weapon for me. Maybe the only one I would have to protect me from the overwhelming presence of the Outside.

3

N OUR NEW SURROUNDINGS, I could see my mother almost blossom once the difficulties of getting settled had passed. When it came to the practicalities of life, it was she who kept our little family going. In face of hardship, this unassuming, barely literate woman exhibited a stubborn determination and a wisdom rooted in the soul of the common people. While my father's wisdom manifested itself in his fondness for reciting innumerable maxims from the classics and Tang poetry, my mother's had its basis in an immense reservoir of proverbs she too would quote in response to the most everyday situations. For example: "As long as the mountain is there, we shall have wood"; "He who plants a cabbage will not harvest a squash"; "Good medicine, bitter taste"; or those which revealed her Buddhist beliefs: "One good deed is worth more than ten pagodas"; "Men's eyes are often shut, but the eye of the heavens never"; "The candle of Buddha fears not the wind." There were still other Buddhist sayings, more enigmatic, which she uttered without always understanding, such as: "Nothing is lost, everything is given." "All is nothing, nothing is all." With patience and tenacity, she managed to create her own form of simple happiness. A vegetarian, now she could raise favorite vegetables in her own garden, and I helped her. I also learned from her where to find all sorts of edible wild fruits and vegetables and how to take away their toxicity. A skill from which I was to benefit much later (in the early sixties) when, as a camp resident, I experienced the harsh famine affecting the entire country in the wake of the human calamities.

Living next door to the temple, my mother could also practice charity according to Buddhist precepts. She regularly gave food and drink to those passing through who would ask for something. As the years went by, she even acquired a certain reputation in the countryside. It was surprising how many different kinds of people passed through this out-of-the way region: pilgrims, migrant workers, military deserters, runaway lovers, fugitive bandits on a country jaunt, scholars seeking solitude, wandering monks. . . . The China of old seemed perpetuated here, intact. Two among all the passersby have never faded from my memory: the wounded bandit and the wandering Taoist monk.

He arrived late one summer afternoon, the bandit. He made his presence known in a hoarse but resonant voice, and without waiting, entered the temple. I went in, too, behind my mother. Seated in the semi-darkness was an imposingly stout man with a haggard look, his hair standing on end. Despite a leathery complexion, he was deathly pale. Yet he exuded authority, ordering my mother to send her son outside. Obliged to leave, I nevertheless saw what occurred, watching from the doorway. With an agile swoop, the man pulled a gleaming dagger from his wide belt, and my mother jumped back. "Don't be frightened. I won't hurt you. But if you betray me, I shall be avenged, and it will be terrible for your family. Now, help me!" Thereupon he lifted one side of his black-cloth trousers to disclose an injured calf. A gaping wound, the flesh already gangrenous. My mother shrieked at the sight and drew back. But the man had no time to lose. A second order: "Pass my dagger through the fire and come back with a basin. But first, bring me a good-sized bowl of *gaoliang.** I shall be under the tree behind the temple. You will make sure no one goes there."

Despite my mother's efforts, she could not keep me inside, and I managed to cling to her as she whispered over and over: *"A-mi tuo-fo, a-mi-tuo-fo...."** I felt her hands tremble and her heart pound. For we could see from a distance the terrifying scene. Beneath the old tree the half-drugged bandit sat with his back to us, leaning forward as he worked at his wound, cutting away the gangrenous flesh with his dagger. Faint cries, becoming more and more like gasps, accompanied the movements of his arm. A haunting sight, this man alone in a desolate landscape, confronting the horror life had inflicted on him.

Aside from a few swallows fluttering in the distance, nothing moved. It was as if the awful sight had frozen the universe in place. On the horizon, the red round of the setting sun was another huge, bloody wound. Or it might have been a mouth, wide open and thirsty for blood, waiting for the wounded beast to expire. A wounded beast, crushed by pain and misery, that was the bandit. He aroused pity, as expressed in my mother's litany. For me, however, the dark silhouette outlined against the evening light was as impressive as a king on a throne performing some sacrificial rite. This shape imparted to the world around it a holy fear. Yes, a true king. The horrible task done, the man applied ointment and a dressing made from a kind of oiled paper that protected the wound yet peeled off

*Sorghum wine.
* "Buddha, have pity; Buddha, have pity."

easily—a material carried around by every bandit worthy of the
name. The man still had enough strength to drag himself inside the
temple. He stayed there ten days or so, and my mother brought him
food. Then one fine morning he was gone. The whole village had
known of his presence. No one betrayed him, for this was a bandit
who helped the poor. More than two months later, a little before the
Moon Festival, my mother found an armload of precious jewels on
the temple altar. She guessed their origin; she sold them at once and
bought offerings in abundance. The offerings were placed about the
altar, and villagers going by could take what they needed. Now the
long-neglected temple became a shrine. There was talk of miraculous
cures; pilgrims flocked to the place. At the time of the Moon Festival, a theater troupe came and stayed several days. Appropriately
enough, their play dealt with the wanderings of a man unjustly condemned and forced to become an outlaw. I, seeing a drama for the
first time, observed how freely the actor defied time and space! Leg
lifted, he crossed the threshold of his house. A crack of the whip and
he rode his horse. Back bent, there he was, twenty years later. In
short, neither space nor time, just a living creature moving about,
space-time originating with him. So it took no more than a bare surface, a few square feet, to portray all human dreams and passions.

During the performance, we snacked on toasted watermelon
seeds, lotus candies, and fruit fritters. The play ended, and a bright
moon shone high in the heavens. We were drawn to the river, which
sparkled with a silvery light. Using nets, we caught eel and shrimp
for the midnight soup. In the company of all the village children, I
spent the most beautiful Moon Festival of my life.

The other figure I am not likely to forget is the wandering Taoist
monk; he could be recognized from afar by his wide-brimmed straw
hat and flowing robe. He would come by at regular intervals, in
spring and in fall. When he arrived, he would sit on the temple steps
and wait for my mother to bring him a big bowl of hot rice covered
with vegetables. He ate in silence, slowly; the only sound would be
his chewing, for he savored every mouthful. At such times, these
dishes—so ordinary and boring because they were our daily fare—
took on a new flavor and inevitably made my mouth water. The

monk would finally stand up, hold out the empty bowl to my mother with both hands, as if making an offering, but he never thanked her. He would turn around, stroke his majestic beard, and depart. Except for his final visit: holding out the empty bowl to my mother, he said; "Thank you for your kindness. You will be rewarded." Then he added, pointing toward the hidden summit of the mountain, he continued: "I am going up there; I shall not return." Having spoken, he turned and off he went. As he walked, he began singing softly in a rather offhand way: "In the grotto of purity the immortals dwell. There a clear spring bubbles and never runs dry . . .!" Farther down the road, his flowing robe vanished into the mists with the lightness of a crane in flight.

Later, as an adult, during my stay in Europe especially, I would be forced to reflect on that China where I happened to have been born, since everywhere I ventured they would call me "the Chinese." I reflected on a nation whose flaws I knew, a nation nevertheless accorded a measure of greatness. Because of its sheer numbers, because it was so ancient and so enduring? But more, it seems, because of its pact of trust—or collusion—with the living universe, for the Chinese have always believed in the virtues of the rhythmic circulating forces which connect the Whole. And perhaps that explains their way of life, so unlike any other. In trying to fathom the Chinese, I would invariably confront the contrasting images of the bandit and the monk, two emblematic figures. Seemingly so different, they ended up for me more than complementary, becoming inextricably united.

The first has his feet firmly on the ground, just like the deeply rooted tree he leans against. Earth dweller to his fingertips, he demonstrates unbounded patience and vitality, much like the ground that supports him. No matter what calamity strikes, he does not give up. For he has a trust, naively fundamental—or fundamentally naïve—in his own desire to live, which he finds identical to that of the Universe. According to the situation, he can be gentle and kind (his natural disposition) or nasty and stubborn, all the while trying to model his behavior on an instinctive wisdom handed down through the millennia. His pace is slow and measured; he tries to maintain his dignity even when the burden weighs down his body. Questions of honor never leave him indifferent. Saving "face" in the eyes of the world is important to him. But, take note, in his code, "face" does not mean "surface." From turning over the soil once a year, he has become convinced that, in essence, the face is the bottom and the bottom is the face. Many a tyrant of the past has burned his fingers on this seemingly humble, docile creature, not suspecting him capable of rebellion. Too much tickling of his "face" and he rises up. And his rebellion is all the stronger because he is convinced that, while not being the equal of the Son of Heaven, he and everyone else have a share of the mandate of Heaven. Yes, living close to the earth, he does not forget that life here below is subject to the universal transformation, as is written in *The Book of Changes,* some of its maxims being known to him. Yet he does not feel a need to raise his head too high, or look too far, or lose himself in the clouds and jump into the unknown with both feet. Through the rising thunder, the blowing wind, the spreading mist, the falling rain, through the full moon that holds all the scattered fragments, is he not in constant communion with the beyond? Earth dweller he is, and earth dweller he remains. He neither doubts that the earth's yellow clay and his own flesh partake of the same substance, nor that his destiny depends on the earth and inversely that the destiny of the earth depends on him. Through him, indispensable link in the chain, the earth will be transformed. And with the transformation of the earth, he and those who come after him will themselves be transformed. Into what? He knows not, but he trusts. While waiting, he meticulously carries out his mandate. And if they seek to cut him down before his time, he will rise up and turn to violence. If he is captured and condemned to death, he will stand fast. At the supreme moment, he will prove worthy, saving face to the very end! Since destiny so decrees, he consents to abandon himself to the intoxication of the Great Return.

The other, the monk, is obsessed almost from birth by a longing for Heaven. He spends his whole life cultivating detachment, making himself light, stretching toward the regions of the air as toward an original dream. His usual posture resembles one of those Chinese roofs with four corners aimed toward the heavens as if it were a giant bird with wings eternally poised for flight. For the time being, he is making a stop on earth with a sly indifference and a calm detachment that enable him to smile at the blows of fate and stand up against the tyrant's oppression. And indeed it is this spirit of detachment that permits him to live his present life to the full, savoring the uncomplicated happiness offered by the earth. Able to live on grass and water, he owns little or nothing. From here below, he is one with the Whole.

4

AFTER THE DEPARTURE of the Taoist monk I dreamed of the peaks of Mount Lu, which revealed their dazzling beauty whenever the wind briefly tore aside their misty veil. My dream became more vivid after hearing my father talk of the highest peak and his plan to scale it in search of medicinal plants.

In the meantime I had become familiar with some of the areas halfway up, especially the Guling, which lay at the heart of the massif. A rounded mountain encircled by pleasant valleys, it was easily accessible and a fine site for dwellings. Long ago scholars, artists, and monks had elected it as an ideal retreat; and toward the end of the nineteenth century, Western missionaries fleeing the torrid summer heat of the cities of the Yangzi valley found the Guling cool and restful. Before long the mountain was dotted with cottages, bungalows, summer cabins, and at the center, a picturesque town of Chinese houses and Western shops. It was always a treat to tag along when my father journeyed to the town of Guling to shop or deliver calligraphy to customers. We liked to approach the top by different paths, for each route offered its own views. We walked past sites extolled by four-character sayings engraved right in the rock of the path; we walked amid the odor of majestic, welcoming pines, and to the murmur of springs and waterfalls, their sound punctuated by the crickets' song.

The day to climb the peak finally arrived. Taking time to look for plants on the way up, we did not reach the summit until late afternoon. Up to the last crest, thick vegetation hid everything from view. Then one more step and a magnificent sight lay before us. Beyond the tangle of crags and ageless trees with fantastic shapes, there stretched wave after wave of hills and mountains sloping toward the distant plain. At the far end of the plain newly washed by a heavy shower, a silvery ribbon glistened in the evening light: the Yangzi. I had often heard the grownups talk of the river but had not expected to see it so soon or in such an extraordinary setting. There it was, both call of the infinite and impassable barrier, peacefully carrying along the tiny junks that floated on its surface. I could not help but call the river by name, shouting out three times: "Changjiang! Chiangjiang! Chiangjiang!," as if to convince myself that what I saw was real and so as not to forget it. As if I could foresee the role the river was to play in the life of my imagination. While I stood concentrating on the progress of the junks, an invisible hand placed above the river a perfect rainbow, its top grazing a bank of fleecy clouds. But a moment later, I was sad to see the clouds at work dismantling the arch stone by stone in a surprisingly methodical way, as nimbly as those skillful acrobats of the traditional theater clear great stacks of precariously piled furniture from the stage. Nothing was left on the horizon but the setting sun, a giant gong emitting the final echo of a strange, unfamiliar melody. Lost in these heights, I stood beside my father, transfixed before the singular landscape about to disappear in the mist.

On the way down we thought we had taken a shortcut, and we found ourselves lost. Since the mist was rising fast, we feared going further astray and had to spend the night on the mountain. We headed for a small belvedere, a sort of open kiosk consisting of posts and a roof. Hurriedly we gathered branches and tree trunks to fill in the openings between the posts and to protect ourselves from possible attack by wild animals. There was moonlight. Despite the mournful cries of nocturnal birds, I was not really afraid; I felt almost in collusion with the summer night, so bright and clear. The starry sky—never before that close—sheltered me under its encompassing vault and at the same time swallowed me up. I took delight in identifying with each shooting star that flashed and glittered briefly before sinking into the Milky Way.

At one point in the night, when it had begun to turn cool, my father suddenly took me in his arms, held me tight, and began sobbing. Feeling his breath and his tears on my cheek, almost in spite of myself I had a moment of recoil, and even of annoyance. Recoil, because without admitting it to myself, deep down I had always feared catching my father's lung disease; annoyance, because I was not used to close physical contact with my mother or my father. In China, as soon as offspring reach a certain age, the parents rarely touch them unnecessarily and almost never hug them. Besides, like every Chinese child, I believed that an adult male did not cry and that it was a father's duty to be a model of good behavior, steeped in moderation, strength, and dignity. At that moment, there came to mind a long-forgotten scene: in Nanchang, I was walking with my father down a street with no sidewalk. A rickshaw approached from the opposite direction. The driver, obviously in a hurry, ran along sounding his horn. My father, probably busy with his own thoughts, was not paying attention and did not step aside. Nor was he obliged to do so; the street belonged to everyone and no part of it was restricted to a particular kind of vehicle. The driver had to brake, and the fat fellow sitting in the cart jumped out of his seat. He must have been some important person who thought the right of way was his. He rushed up to my father, grabbed him by the collar, shook him, and yelled. He let go finally, and my father stammered his excuses. Under the stares of the curious, my father adjusted his glasses, took my hand, and walked on. I was furious with the brutal man, but when I looked at my father I felt uncomfortable. Why such a feeling? Shame? Resentment toward his weakness? I had never tried to understand it. I only remembered the temptation to let go of my father's damp, slightly trembling hand. . . .

And that night on the mountain I fast escaped my father's grasp, claiming I had to relieve myself. Later, how I would berate myself for my instinctive reaction, my aversion! It was a wound inflicted by me, one that time would not heal. And I remember how in the hour before dawn he removed his own vest to place it over me, leaving himself exposed to the cold. Whatever the cause, that night of adventure marked the beginning of the final deterioration of my father's health. He died a year and a half later, early in 1935.

My father was not much for words. He seemed drained of energy by his various ailments and the care they required. And yet, when he would say: "It might be good to . . ." or "Some day we'll see that . . ."—expressions that he was fond of—or when instead of expressing his feelings directly he would quote lines from the Tang poets, wasn't that his way of seeking understanding and affection? Must the father-son relationship stem only from the father, as is the view of traditional upbringing? I, the son, couldn't have spoken innocently, spontaneously, and why not even disrespectfully, to break through the reserved silence in which my father had immured himself?

Afterward, from what my mother told me, I would learn how much my father had suffered in leading a life marked by inadequacy, a life doomed to humiliation and unfulfilled hopes, on the fringes of everything, including his own family.

5

MY FATHER WAS BORN into a large family. For as long as we lived at the foot of Mount Lu, he made it his duty to return home yearly in autumn or late spring with wife and children so he could "sweep the graves of the ancestors." This large family was like countless others in China, with its four generations under one roof, housed in multiple apartments distributed around a vast courtyard. That might mean as many as fifty people when everyone was present. Although his relatives had caused him much pain, the family was a sacred model for my father. As for me, growing up in a disrupted society that had gradually become more free, I always wondered how such a cumbersome, restrictive arrangement could have lasted so many centuries. At its best the Chinese family structure, the foundation of the old society, had its virtues. It was a living, self-contained unit, initiating its members very early into the basic dilemmas of human life. It taught them the value of tradition and the value of relations with others based on a spirit of cooperation and sharing that meant no one was ever left high and dry. It instilled in them the right degree of intimacy or distance in one's affections, a sense of individual and collective moral responsibility, and a feeling for celebrations and festivals as sacred rites. By offering a cross section of personalities and viewpoints in everlasting opposition, the family served as a crucible that forged the human being according to an ancient ideal. But if the family's foundation was undermined or it knew periods of division and decay, the same crucible would become a hothouse wherein flourished hypocrisy, egotism, power struggles, petty self-interest, vices, and one plot after another. That was the situation in my family. And it brought me pain, as it had my father. Yet in the end I was grateful to those people among whom I grew up, all of them—the depraved and the mediocre, the picturesque and the admirable. Through them I learned early to detect what is genuine and what is hollow in my fellow man.

There was my grandfather, a learned man and an important bureaucrat in the old regime, who had served as prefect in various departments of his province. After the republic had been established, he withdrew behind a wall of haughty silence, only visiting with a few surviving members of his generation. His only form of amusement was intoning ancient texts while the heavy odor of incense filled the air; occasionally he would test out his magnificent coffin, which stood on display in one of the rooms and was repainted yearly.

There was Second Uncle, ill-tempered and rapacious, who had seized financial power after the death of First Uncle. Aided by his spouse, he made strict order the rule in family affairs. The wife, who always went about with a water pipe in her hand and a teapot on her arm, never lost her deceptively placid smile as she sowed discord everywhere. When she was observed crossing the courtyard like a character on the Chinese stage, her quiet steps punctuated by little coughs and blinks, it was not hard to guess she was mulling over some malicious remark or thinking up some intrigue. Discord was the drug of her daily life; nothing else gave her such exquisite pleasure. When in the throes of withdrawal, she had to make do with a designated victim, her daughter-in-law, whom she mistreated with a refined cruelty. She too, however, was to have her share of pain. Her husband, so upright in his moral principles, would one day be caught red-handed, taking advantage of a young servant girl not yet sixteen. Outraged, in the end Second Aunt had to resign herself to finding him a concubine, but of her own choosing. Definitely not the servant girl. For she had been bought cheap when a child and had been so ill-treated that, made concubine, she might well seek vengeance or at the least not prove very submissive. The poor girl was later sold to a brothel.

There was Fourth Uncle, who grew exotic plants and raised small animals: birds, spiders, turtles, rabbits, et cetera. Very fond of games, he was unbeatable at chess and mahjongg. When not busy with his bureaucratic chores at the provincial ministry, he was forever seeking partners. He would wander from one apartment to the next, carrying the beautiful ivory-encrusted mahjongg box or a smaller box that held chessmen. He also went out frequently, either to the homes of friends or to tea houses. He did not need to let them know he was coming; his presence was announced by his booming foot steps and his sing-song voice intoning ritual phrases: "Here gather now heroes and sages" or "The Eight Immortals hail the Jade Emperor." Enthusiastic reader of historical novels and tales of cape and sword, he was so imbued with their spirit that he lived these olden times, identifying with the heroes, famous and obscure, loved by the common people. He imitated wonderfully the incisive rhythms of the ancient language that fit so well the actions of the characters. And in fact, the words and gestures of this colorful uncle were a marvel of elegance and precision. That would come out during games of mahjongg, in his way of lining up the tiles he had chosen, of selecting one, letting it resound between his fingers, and slapping it down on the table as he uttered some maxim with an appropriate image, such as: "Four flowered seasons!" "Three crowned stars!" Even when he reached the end of the game and noisily mixed the pieces together in his usual fashion was he responding instinctively to a concern for harmony and rhythm. Sometimes the mahjongg games at home would last late into the night. I enjoyed being lulled to sleep by the noise and commotion. Fourth Uncle had amazingly delicate hands, and everyone had to admire their skill. How easily his touch made precious the most ordinary object! Between his fingers, the fine porcelain of little household implements used for generations would tinkle and sparkle with new spirit. And how easily he learned to perform magic tricks, to wrest sweet sounds from a primitive Chinese violin, to carve a miniature flower from a piece of nondescript wood, to color old boxes! Before trips he was called upon to prepare the luggage, for he excelled at packing into a single suitcase a great mountain of things that should otherwise have required three or four bags; once done, his arrangement was so perfect that no one dared unpack the suitcase for fear of violating the harmonious whole or of being unable to put everything back. In the eyes of many, his innate sense of beauty and the agility of his hands came close to genius. Genius dedicated to little nothings, to the useless, as if just killing time like the rest of this family in decay.

Decay? They mentioned decadence and debauchery openly when talking of Seventh Uncle, whom Second Uncle could barely tolerate. An opium smoker, and always the victim of amorous passions even though he had a model wife who was well liked by everyone in the house. He could be smitten in rapid succession with an actor who interpreted female roles, a woman who played the *pipa,** and a cultured lady who led the life of a demimondaine and was famous for her beauty. Without daring to say so openly, the grown-ups kept their children from spending time with him. I felt drawn to him and to the odor of opium that drifted from the spacious bedchamber with its closed curtains. A magical atmosphere reigned in his room: in the semi-darkness, the glow of the long pipe, the lamp that blinked like an eye, the greedy sound when my uncle inhaled the stem, and the look of gratification and ecstasy that came over the face behind the smoke. Isolated within the family, Uncle was happy

A kind of xither.

to confide in me occasionally. After he had smoked, he would clear his throat until the little cough was gone; then he uttered plaintive sighs: "Oh . . . Oh . . . How bitter life is! So bitter!"

"Why bitter?" I once ventured to ask him.

"You do not understand yet. But remember this. In life, we don't really do what we want to do—and we do what we don't want to do. And when we don't do what we want to do, we are like this wooden pipe: it exists but is not alive. As soon as we do what we want to, well, we are nothing but flame. And very soon we turn into ashes. Yes, ashes, just like that. And ashes, they are bitter, aren't they?"

When he used the image of ashes, Uncle did not know how aptly he spoke. His own ashes would one day fertilize the land where he had spent a life that he characterized as bitter, although he had actually enjoyed it in his own way, just as he used to enjoy that vegetable he liked, appropriately named the "bitter vegetable," which becomes delicious when chewed. During the Sino-Japanese War, he fell seriously ill. All the doctors said it was hopeless. Moved to a convent and nursed by Christian nuns, he regained his health. He decided to remain with the sisters, and he became their handyman. In the early fifties, the Communist government brought the nuns to trial and accused them of stealing from the people, killing babies, and other awful crimes. The authorities asked Uncle to denounce them in return for his freedom. Refusing was not enough for him; he dared to testify as to their good works. When the nuns were sent away to a concentration camp, so was he; under the harsh conditions he soon died. After his cremation, they mixed his ashes with the manure for the camp vegetable garden, as he had requested.

And then there was Tenth Uncle, the closest to my father, and the one I can never forget. He liked to read modern novels, Chinese and foreign, and he often loaned his books to my father. He took an interest in my education, introduced me to the fairy tales of Grimm and Andersen, taught me a few words of English, and often took me on walks. He had some kind of job at a local bank but eventually decided to study architecture, first in Shanghai, then in Japan. Before he left, in my little memory book he wrote a line of verse in English, from Longfellow: "Life is brief, art is long."

6

BORN OF A CONCUBINE, my father was the last of grandfather's eleven sons. As the youngest, he always had an inferior position, made worse by his marriage to my mother, not a girl of good family, but the daughter of a nurse who had long served our family. Thus he saw himself always assigned the dampest, coldest part of that enormous house. Furthermore, whether it was their interior quarters or some other problem, he, sickly, and my mother, timid, had few defenses against the unfair, mean-spirited acts of those who consciously or unconsciously played the game of Second Uncle and his wife.

A follower of Buddha, my mother practiced the virtues of humility and compassion. Her patience earned her the sympathy of more of than one relative and made our living with the family bearable. I recall one significant episode. I see my mother going out the back gate and approaching a woman who had quietly loitered about the house for several days. The woman had just sold her three-year-old child to one of the members of our family, none other than Fourth Uncle, the lover of games. Their offspring consisting of three daughters, he and his wife had decided to buy the little boy. The woman, haggard, stood there hour after hour, presumably hoping to catch a glimpse of her son through the gate. I watched my mother hand the woman a handkerchief, which must have held a gift or money; then she assured her that the boy would be treated as well as a child born to the house. The woman left in tears but calmer than before. From that day on, it was as if I had a little brother, for my mother did indeed pay the boy much attention, especially since Fourth Aunt, often needed for long mahjongg sessions, was happy to turn the child over to her.

There was a woman who defended my parents whatever the circumstances, an unmarried aunt still living at home. A distinctive person with vivid coloring and a talent for story telling, she shone with an odd beauty that arose from her ugliness, and she never hesitated to stand up to Second Uncle and the others, telling them a thing or two in her hoarse voice.

The character of this unmarried aunt made me realize that the women in our extended family were not all alike. True, some of them, stifled and embittered by the constraints of their lives, did become petty or nasty, abusing any bit of power they acquired. But there were others who, like my aunt, were infinitely appealing. Many of these often proved more worthy, more noble, and more courageous than the men. And so it was with the aunt who had made a bad marriage and had dared to leave her husband, scandalizing both families. It took a long time for Second Uncle and others to accept her return under the paternal roof. She finally commanded their respect when she and a friend founded a school for orphans and abandoned children, a school soon renowned throughout the province. Apparently this aunt had been a lively child and adolescent, sometimes quite mischievous. Tested by life, she had become serious and thoughtful, speaking little, even to those who liked her. But when we ran into each other in the course of the day, she would place a hand on my shoulder and greet me with a silent, affectionate smile. At the time I did not know I would run into her again years later, at a crucial fork in the road of my life. Then a gesture and a smile were to prevent my being totally destroyed.

Yet another aunt, distantly related by marriage, made a lasting impression on me during her brief appearances. She was quite emancipated for her time. After successful studies in history, she had spent two years in France. I was unaware of her existence until one day at lunch I heard Second Uncle, indignant, announce to the table at large: "Do you know who I ran into? That girl from the Jiang family [in-laws of one of the aunts] who is back from France. And do you know what she did? Well, she put out her hand, like this! And what was I supposed to do? I put out my hand, like this, and I barely touched her fingers, and then I pulled it away quick!" In China the traditional greeting consists of joining one's hands without touching the hands of others; and in the old days a man was not allowed to take the hand of a young woman until they were engaged. Soon after, the family received a visit from the "Jiang family aunt." She spread out, helter skelter, a number of things she had brought back from France. My eyes rested on some cards of reproductions from the Louvre: Greek Venuses, paintings of nudes, in particular two in which the main figure was a woman seen from the back. But the grown-ups, surprised and offended, hurriedly gathered up the cards. Nothing, however, could undo their impact or my having seen them, those powerful images that shook me so, tracing indelible furrows in my imaginative world. Yes, I wouldn't soon forget these women with the magnificent bodies, my first nudes; as foreign and strange as they were, they stirred me to the very depths. And even stranger, the nudes seen from the front, while dazzling me with their anatomical perfection, their plump breasts like magnets, did not really make me feel out of my element, since mothers and wet nurses in China readily bared their breasts in public when suckling an infant. But painted from behind, the nude portrait—in which a woman surrendered herself, so to speak, unthinkingly—revealed the woman's entire body through the quivering rounds and sensitive hollows of the back alone, at the same time preserving the unknown obscure beauty of the woman herself.

Another female figure of whom I grew fond was someone long absent. My parents' apartment stood next to a shut-up dwelling, entry forbidden to all. According to the story, inside was the room of "the hanged woman." This image of a hanged woman was meant to be terrifying, but something about it aroused my curiosity. I was aware that every large family had dark corners where lurked secrets the grown-ups would try to keep quiet. As I began to spend more time with older cousins who did not hesitate to talk among themselves, I learned to notice things that were not as they should be. So-and-so had an ambiguous bond with his sister-in-law, such-and-such with his father's young concubine. And I was told that in the past strict family councils had imposed death sentences for such goings-on.

They did not go that far in my family. The hanged woman was the wife of a drunken great-uncle said to be inflexible: Had she committed suicide because of her unfortunate marriage or in the aftermath of some transgression? Whatever the reason, she had no longer wanted to live among this family. After her death, the relatives feared her ghost would haunt the premises, seeking vengeance. Naturally, the everlasting presence of the hanged woman reinforced the cousins' already strong liking for ghost stories. They strove to think up truly horrible tales with which to frighten one another. They usually chose night for these sessions, when the wind was howling outside. The smallest children, hanging on to every word and fascinated by the narrators' gestures and expressions, dared not turn around. They would end up sitting back to back in a tight little group. Along with the others, I listened to the stories eagerly; some of the terrifying details made me shiver, too. But to my surprise, deep down I was not altogether frightened. It was inevitable for the night to be inhabited by ghosts; that I knew from experience. I even thought it a good thing. Otherwise night would be disappointing, and as a result, so would day, for isn't day born from the night? Having strayed among the ghosts, I thought I could understand their way of speaking. And if one of them were ever to seize me, I would let myself be taken: it would just be another exchange of bodies! I was unwise enough to divulge these secret thoughts to the others. Thus I soon found myself obliged to prove my non-fear by going into the hanged woman's chamber alone and staying there awhile. And I accepted the challenge. One day I removed the padlock and ventured alone into the room, my heart pounding. Apprehensive at first, I soon recovered, adjusting to the oppressive odor of dust and mildew. Not much furniture other than a few chests, a bed and a table, their satin covers faded. On the table stood a photograph, probably from the turn of the century, a young woman with patrician features and a dreamy, sensitive look. But a will of iron shone in her eyes. Her gaze, full of everything she had never been able to say, seemed outside of time. Not having found the object of its love while on earth, apparently that gaze wanted to bore straight through the infinity of space and never stop, its only hope lying in some future reincarnation. In the complete silence of that room, while everywhere else in that large house human sounds and presence dominated at all hours, there came over me a peace of mind I had never felt before. I could not remember ever having had such intense communication with anyone among the living. I would have gladly lingered there but for the shouts of my cousins, who were becoming genuinely worried. When

I came out, I responded to their anxious questions with nothing more than the enigmatic comment, "It was strange, but really wonderful!" Oddly enough, following my adventure, I had in the eyes of others—pale and timid child though I was—an aura about me, a glamour, almost of the supernatural. Relatives nearly went so far as to ask me to intercede for them, particularly during the Double Seven Festival—the seventh day of the seventh moon. On that night, it was said, silver ropes descended from the Heavenly River (the Milky Way). Through a skillful mediator endowed with the power to grab one of these ropes, favors could be obtained. In any case, I did not doubt that I was in tune with the world of the dead, dating from the night of the woman's cry, and from my more recent encounter with "the hanged woman."

That other world was soon to welcome my father, who died in his very birthplace, from grave breathing problems suffered while visiting the family home. On his deathbed, the face lit up by his consoling smile was so serene that it wrenched from my mother and me tears of grief mixed with a vague feeling of gratitude. And after his passing, his soul, freed from its body, seemed to act with a new effectiveness to protect the survivors he had left on earth. No longer wanting to live with the family, my mother unburdened herself to Mr. Guo, my father's childhood friend, who had made a special trip from Nankin for the funeral. On the spot he offered her a housekeeping position. When fall came, mother and son embarked on their new destiny, setting out for Nankin, at that time China's capital.

7

1937. I had just turned thirteen when the Sino-Japanese War broke out. Surprised and infuriated by the unexpected resistance of a weary and poorly armed people on the verge of anarchy whom they expected to subdue within a few months, the invaders turned to the large-scale carnage that was to mark the first stage of the conflict. In Nankin alone, once they had taken the city, rampaging soldiers put more than three hundred thousand to death in the course of a few weeks, killing with cold steel, burying whole groups alive, and machine-gunning indiscriminately. Horrible scenes turned the stomachs of the Chinese, astonished into silence. These scenes were often captured by the Japanese themselves, either through official photographs of group scenes or more often by soldiers who wanted to show their merit, glorify their exploits, or simply preserve memories. These photos show soldiers advancing on live targets for bayonet practice or, sword in hand, posing surrounded by the corpses strewn on the ground. Other photos, not as frequent, but no less overwhelming, show undressed women, dead and alive, all rape victims. In some of the pictures, the victim is forced to stand next to her uniformed tormentor.

These women were delivered up naked to merciless stares in broad daylight, perhaps for the first time in their lives—many had never even stood naked before their husbands—perhaps also for the last time, since many killed themselves after the ordeal. How poignant their efforts to maintain their dignity so as to save face, leaving that as their only image to a blind world which had lost face.

The magazine photos that I had cut out and hidden in a secret corner horrified me every time I looked at them. But I was also aware that they attracted and haunted me, feeding in me a confused desire. Unavoidably, these pictures came to be superimposed on the earlier ones that my aunt had brought back from the Louvre. Together, they were the only naked women I had ever seen. What similarity and what contrast between the two sets of pictures! Same shapes standing there, soft, perfect, infinitely desirable. But the first group idealized, exalted, hiding an inexhaustible mystery worth pursuing all one's life; in the other, women dishonored, deeply humiliated, so much so that the very thought of desiring them became impossible, shameful.

I was thirteen then, the age of sexual awakening, and questions came up that embedded themselves like a knife in my flesh. The same beauty inspired the loftiest of feelings and the most despicable cruelty. Thus evil could nestle in the very heart of beauty. Beauty? Evil? I would have dealings with them. But right then I was still too young for questions. Nevertheless, I can remember my thoughts upon hearing some of the expressions widely used at the time to describe the scenes of horror: "Tales of blood and tears." "To wash themselves, they have only their tears." I told myself that the human body had far more blood than tears. That being so, all the tears of mankind could never wash away all the blood spilled.

During this period of total upheaval, my mother and I, following the Guo family, were part of the long procession of fleeing Chinese who went up the Yangzi by mountainside paths or in crowded makeshift boats to cross the famous and supposedly impassable gorges, heading for Sichuan, the vast western province. The relative peace we found in Tchounking, a city high above the Yangzi and its tributary, the Jialing, did not last. Overpopulated, crowded with new, hastily erected apartments and virtually without air defense—other than the countless shelters carved right into the rock—the city was soon devastated by heavy Japanese bombing. A new exodus of the population toward the countryside, an indescribably chaotic flight, added to the already staggering toll of enemy air-raid victims. The government institution employing Mr. Guo, the Center for Pedagogical and Curriculum Research, had to be evacuated to new quarters a two-days' walk from Tchounking.

Early in 1940, at the end of an exhausting journey through a rich and luxuriant countryside that contrasted with the poverty of its peasants, the twenty or so families that made up the staff of the Research Center arrived at their destination, a vast estate belonging to Lord Lu. That such an estate existed in this forgotten region seemed to the newcomers absurd, hard to believe. The imposing main house was old, with a large garden in front; similar in plan to our family house but on a much larger scale, it was composed of a series of apartments around a large central court. The new arrivals were to be housed in this structure. As for the Lu family, they now resided in a spacious modern house, behind the other and close against the mountain. The government had been able to obtain the older dwelling through an arrangement with Lord Lu: it agreed to close its eyes to his opium smoking—outlawed at that period—and to his arbitrary exercise of power in the region.

It did not take long for us to observe that Lord Lu's oldest son, accompanied by a dozen armed companions and seconded by a fair number of henchmen, had established a kind of reign of terror in the nearby towns and countryside, controlling gaming houses and occasionally going so far as to commit extortion and rape. The other sons had left to complete their studies, except for two in business and one youngster still at home. All the daughters were married except the last, who had just become engaged.

Shortly after moving in, we new arrivals witnessed the ceremony of the fiancée's departure for her new family, among whom the marriage would take place. After repeatedly prostrating herself before her parents and the altar of the ancestors, the young woman, dressed up like a doll and her face hidden, took a seat in a brightly painted palanquin, its predominant color blood-red. As soon as the cortege started off, I was amazed to see heartbreak instead of joy: the mother wept, the bride wept, and the entire household joined in with poignant cries. The bride knew she was about to face an unknown destiny; she was going to live with a man of whom she knew nothing, a man whom she had never seen. And, in fact, the high-pitched music accompanying the cortege was the same that was played at burials.

In the fall of 1940, I entered the newly opened high school in the main market town of the district, a half day's walk from the Lu estate. I was a boarder and returned home every weekend. One Sunday morning the following February, as I walked alone in the estate garden, at a turn in the path I suddenly caught sight of an unfamiliar young woman. She was walking hesitantly and seemed deep in thought. As soon as were next to each other, she looked up at me with her rather melancholy eyes, saying in a natural tone: "Look at the primroses. Spring is here!" With spring, she too was coming back to life. For I soon learned that she was none other than Lord Lu's third daughter, whose name I had sometimes heard whispered: Yumei (Jade Plum). At sixteen, while on a visit to her sister in F., she had fallen in love with a young air-force officer, although she was already betrothed to the son of a neighboring lord. The oldest son, who had never liked his sister's independence of spirit and who had often been jealous of her, followed their father's orders and kept her locked up in an isolated room overlooking the mountain for eighteen months.

From our first meeting, in my heart of hearts she was to me "the Lover." I had the strange feeling that I had always lived in her company, that she was an integral part of me, closer to me than my own body. I believed almost that she was somehow born of my desire itself, so much was her image the very one of which I had always dreamed, unless—as I found myself thinking—there lived again in her the young suicide whose memory was perpetually with me.

Thus our meeting did not arouse in me one of those sudden emotional upheavals that leave one defenseless, but instead that kind of vibration deep inside whereby something buried rises without haste and moves layer by layer toward the surface. From the depths of my being, I felt a serene sort of shudder, as if Yumei had been expected and as if from time immemorial she had been supposed to come; I was a little like a tree in winter greeting the spring breeze with mild surprise but never doubting that it would arrive.

These feelings I kept from the Lover. I was inconspicuous among the other young men who often surrounded her, attracted by her radiant beauty, her noble and elegant bearing, her graceful gestures, the captivating voice that recounted legends of the province and sang the heroines' arias from Sichuan opera. But her greatest attraction was an indefinable charm, blending reserve and spontaneity. In the company of others, she could remain silently attentive, or just as easily marvel over the unsuspected side of things with a fresh and communicative spirit. In her company, we had the impression of seeing the world for the first time while still standing firmly on familiar ground, that is, on our immemorial Chinese soil at its purest, its finest, its most genuine.

8

A T YUMEI'S SUGGESTION, one June day we decided to walk to the source of the river that flowed near the village. This all-day hike did not require extensive preparations. Besides our vacuum bottles of hot water, to sustain ourselves we simply packed eggs boiled in tea flavored with the "five perfumes," slices of glazed roast pork, sesame-seed cakes, not forgetting a few baskets of oranges and pomelos—all plain things adored by the young, tired of family meals too greasy and elaborate for their taste. There were about fifteen of us on the excursion. In the milky light of dawn, we set out single file on the narrow paths that wound along the river still immersed in mist. An indescribable joy seized our little group; invigorated by the cool breeze, we felt totally free. The grass wet with morning dew soon soaked feet clad in straw sandals or shoes of coarse fabric, but that did little to quell our high spirits.

Dressed in a light blue *qipao,* a *yulan* flower as her boutonniere, Yumei led the way, beaming. Ignoring the silly antics of some of the bigger boys escorting her, she strode along and kept us moving at a steady pace. In the course of that unforgettable day, I discovered a side of her I had already suspected: under that gentle, soothing exterior, a tenacious, almost savage force. She was indeed a daughter of this province of dazzling, contrasting colors. Land of mauve clay, dotted with azaleas and hibiscus, replete with red peppers and golden oranges. Land that has produced geniuses of proud and free spirit, the most famous of them the poets Li Bo and Su Dongpo.

Yumei would interrupt her walk from time to time and speak to those following her, the youngest of whom I was one. On each occasion, we were delighted. First, she would turn her head, tossing her jet black hair to one side and revealing ever so briefly the beauty mark on her neck, immediately eclipsed by her shining eyes. Then she would say in a joyful voice: "Do you see what I see, there?" or "Do you hear what I just heard?" And we were sure of discovering something we ourselves had not noticed. She might point to a site high on the other side of the river; she might draw our eyes to some brightly colored butterflies unfazed by our human presence; she might ask us to attend to the call of one bird answering another, or the echoes from a distant hill, echoes of the wild song a young peasant had been directing toward the hill opposite, perhaps the home of a girl he lusted after. Or, again—and here I recognized my mother's gestures—she might pull aside dense foliage or thick grass to pick aromatic plants or clusters of wild fruit. As she led others to discover a world throbbing with life, she was rediscovering herself, and with what passion, what greediness!, after long deprivation.

To those who saw her blue silhouette up ahead blending into the bluish air, she truly seemed the soul and voice of a natural world which was merely waiting to be revealed through her.

We passed through an occasional village. Yumei's presence invariably aroused sympathy. "Ah, Third Damsel!" "Here comes Third Damsel!" She was as much loved in the region as her brother was hated. That day she had only oranges and pomelos to give the peasants. It astonished the young people that such ordinary fruit, which after all grew abundantly in the province, should be a luxury in the eyes of the peasants. The hikers were still too young to know the extent of the destitution of the poorest peasants; those who owned no land and were obliged to give more than half of their meager yields to the "lords." And so many did not eat the oranges and pomelos, but saved them on the table or the altar, for a day when the whole family would be together. Others could not resist tasting them at once. How carefully they opened them—first stroking the surface with their rough hands—and how slowly they savored each section. The fruit acquired a nobility the young people had not suspected. The full baskets they had been carrying were soon empty. Proud, the peasants did not consent to receiving without giving. They offered the hikers red sweet potatoes and a kind of fruit that grows beneath the soil, called "earth squash." A seedless fruit, whitish and crisp, at the first taste it is earthy and rather pungent; once chewed, it gives off a cool, milky thirst-quenching juice. The more you eat, the more you want. The young people feasted on it the whole way.

Late in the afternoon we arrived at the source, which was channeled by a rudimentary canal conducting water to the center of a village: swift, clear water. We drank of it; we plunged into it. We were joyful, delighted we had seen this astonishing experience through, following that live, secret thing which is a river to come face-to-face with its origin. Fed by this beneficial water, the surrounding country was especially luxuriant. The village, which bore the name of the Qu clan, had a clean and prosperous look rarely seen in the province. There was a temple dedicated to the great poet Qu Yuan, the inhabitants of the village claiming to be his descendants. As such, they considered it their duty to welcome visitors in the manner of the ancient hospitality. The hungry, thirsty hikers were offered chrysanthemum tea served with jujubes and candied lotus seeds.

Seated in the shade of the willows near the temple, opposite rice fields that shone with a verdant grace, we could almost believe we were away from the world and away from time, or rather that we were in the time of High Antiquity, when nothing was yet fixed, when man first used the privilege of speech to name things—breeze, cloud, grass, water, the beloved and the wise man—and to order his words into song's primordial rhythms, which is precisely what Qu Yuan did.

Before leaving, we entered the temple. Yumei lit a stick of incense in front of a little statue of the poet framed by two tablets inscribed with two parallel verses he had written. We learned that the temple had been built during the Ming Dynasty, on the site of a stele erected during the Tang Dynasty. The villagers swore that the burning of incense had not ceased since the temple was built. We were struck by the feeling of strangeness here, not to call it anachronism, as we stood before this little uninterrupted fire in this obscure spot inhabited by illiterate peasants, a fire lit in honor of a poet who had lived more than two thousand years before—the first known poet of Chinese literature—and who had died in exile, drowned in a river.

By nightfall, the returning walkers had only gone halfway. Knowing there would be no meal for them at home, and in no hurry to arrive, they decided to stop and eat by the banks of the river. They built a fire and cooked the red sweet potatoes from the peasants, mixing in poppy stems and spicy vegetables gathered over the day.

Ah! Never again will I know the exquisite taste of the sweet potatoes roasted that night. Wherever I may be, I shall always love smoke, the smoke that recalls the plaintive voice of my uncle the opium smoker, the smoke that lets me hear the bright laugh of the Lover as she pokes the fire.

9

A FEW DAYS HAD PASSED since the hike. It was evening, and the heat kept people outdoors long after dinner. Holding their fans, they went on and on, dreaming under the starry sky, recounting legends, chatting. For amusement I had trapped some fireflies and put them in a little gauze bag, creating a portable lantern. I thought I would show it to Yumei.

Once inside the private courtyard her room faces, I come upon a sight so unexpected that I doubt its reality. The Lover, naked, stands washing herself in a wooden basin placed at the center of the courtyard. She laughs and talks with a young servant as the girl pours water from a small bucket over her shoulders and the water runs down her smooth, firm body. I know I should leave, but I cannot make myself go. I stay, heart pounding, unable to move. This is the first flesh-and-blood naked woman I have laid eyes on. From where I am standing I see her almost in profile; I make out part of her back and the swell of her breasts, glistening from the water and brushed by the light of the moon. The bath is over, then comes the drying, and she puts on her nightgown, carelessly leaving it half open. She stretches out on a bamboo bed placed near the door for the cool air. She refreshes herself with a straw fan, still talking to the servant girl momentarily busy in the courtyard; then Yumei grows silent, dozing perhaps. In the shadows, I too am silent, rooted to the spot. How long have I been here? A moment, a lifetime, I don't know. I finally return to the family quarters, like a tightrope walker or a thief.

Tormented by shame, in the days that followed I gave up visiting Yumei. Yet I did not stop asking myself whether the sight I had seen that night was real. Maybe I'd dreamed it. At least I tried to convince myself I had. And I almost succeeded. The image of her gleaming body had become engraved in my field of vision and was by now so lifelike that it seemed as if conceived and shaped by my imagination. Radiating through all my senses, it appeared more distinct, more tangible than if the Lover was standing before me in person. In spite of my efforts to stop thinking about it, the image returned, more insistent, more oppressive, turning into an obsession. Over and over I saw myself approaching her in secret by night to watch her undress, lie down, and go to sleep. But whenever I tried to touch her, to stroke the contours of her face, she would awaken and stare at me. And her innocent smile left me distraught.

I rose one morning with an overwhelming urge: an unknown force drove my hand to project onto paper the image that obsessed me. Taking a hard pencil and a softer one, I started sketching a half-length portrait of the Lover. With a kind of excitement, I rendered my inner vision feature by feature. The oval face, pure as jade, rarely touched by gloom; the flawless, sensitive mouth that revealed a controlled sensuality; the eyes, infinitely deep, with an astonished candor that only added to their mystery. As I gave birth to this image, I was being delivered of the burden suffocating me. And my heart beat faster at the sight of the miracle taking place under my hand. At one point, while drawing her hair, with a fortunate pencil stroke I hit exactly upon the way Yumei would toss back her tresses, ever so briefly letting the light fall on her whole face. Once that was down on paper, although the portrait remained unfinished, I felt my energy gone and sensed I should stop, that I ought add no more or risk spoiling the whole. I laid down my pencils and gave in to a feeling of release.

With my mind at ease, drawing in hand I had the courage to appear before Yumei again. Upon seeing the drawing, she was surprised, then delighted that someone could know by heart her face and her special expressions. Raising her head, intrigued, she looked straight into my eyes. And I realized she had just "seen" me for the first time.

From then on, she often accompanied me when I went out to draw. Our favorite spot: a forest pool we reached by various paths.

Without fail, each time I would be overcome by indescribable gratitude that the miracle was occurring again, that she was there, opposite me or beside me, talking or laughing with me, for an entire
afternoon. It was summer, 1941. China had been at war for four
years. I was approaching seventeen; she was nearly eighteen. In our
forgotten corner of the world, the long-ago stopping of time released
a savor of eternity, much like that of the pond, which reflected everything as incidental: a branch cracking, a cloud passing, a dragonfly
skimming the water, a kingfisher diving, vapor rising and from
within it the irrepressible cry of the lark . . .

Our conversation turned on things that came to mind, and was
proper. It was broken by silences when Yumei would concentrate on
a book, write letters, or become lost in thought. I never dared go so
far as to confide in her, nor did I ask the one who was in my company any questions I thought inappropriate. Once, as she watched
me draw a group of trees against a rather fanciful background, she
asked: "Do you often have dreams?"

"Yes, often."

"What do you dream about?"

"Oh! My dreams are more like nightmares."

"Nightmares . . . Aren't you happy?"

"Right now I'm happy. Usually, I'm not."

"You're not happy living with your mother?"

"Yes. But I only have her and she only has me. She's always afraid
something will happen to me. And I'm always afraid something will
happen to her. It's depressing."

After a brief silence, she said: "Look, I have a father, a mother,
brothers, sisters, yet no one really cares what happens to me. That's
awfully depressing, too!" Then with a bitter smile, she added: "As
far as that goes, we're even, aren't we?"

Before I could find words to answer her, she continued: "It's inex-
plicable, our human life. No one has a life of his own; we always live
for someone else. Look at this wildflower that doesn't even have a
name. How fully itself it is. Saying I like it, I pick it, and I put an end
to its destiny. In the same way, under this sky, on this earth, someone

is innocently living his life; others, claiming rights over him, nonchalantly make a gesture stopping that life before one day themselves disappearing, without any one ever knowing why. Yes, why?"

Following this conversation, I noticed Yumei silent more often. Deep in her eyes a shadow of melancholy flickered, like our pond before rain. At such moments, I would recall that above all she seemed to want to escape her destiny.

That fall, I arrived home from school one Friday afternoon and went to Yumei's house. Walking by the half-opened door of the Lu family's great drawing room, I witnessed, with others beside me, an astounding and appalling scene: the oldest son was once again imposing his tyrannical rule on his sister. Holding a short chain in one hand, with the other he had a tight grip on the girl's right arm, while she struggled energetically to free herself. Panting, eyes bulged out, the man leaned over his prey; surely he looked no different when committing rape. I was even convinced that the cruelty of the local tyrant found its pleasure in this act, myself having experienced a vague pleasure when I was playing with a little girl in the central courtyard and had abruptly grabbed her by the shoulders and pressed her against me, while the poor child struggled and moaned, biting my arm and gradually giving way beneath me. . . .

Suddenly the eldest son realized that people were watching and shouted at his men to shut the door and drive away the unwelcome visitors. By evening all the inhabitants of the estate had heard the news: the Lu third daughter was once again locked away. In the next few days they learned it was explicitly forbidden to venture into the mountainous region behind the estate. The eldest son's mercenaries were on patrol, for the air-force officer was known to be in the area and Yumei had been in contact with him. He was also accompanied by armed men. A possibly bloody confrontation loomed.

How can I forget that night of turmoil when the barking of dogs mingled with the shouts of men? The entire household was in an uproar. "Third Damsel has been abducted!" "Third Damsel is gone!" Meanwhile, we families from the Research Center held our breath. In tears, the women prayed that the fugitive would not be captured or wounded. And indeed, a few gunshots soon reverberated in the distance. I ran out into the night, frantic. I wanted to shout, too, but only a stifled sob escaped my throat. I tripped over a downed tree and fell to the ground. In the sky a myriad of stars shone. On earth, at the horizon, a confusion of lanterns and torches moved about.

And so for me the presence of the Lover was fated to last as long as the flowers in that garden where we first met: opening in the spring, at their peak in summer, they withered before the end of fall. Unless she did indeed have to fade away like the flowers so her image—henceforth beyond time and space—could be established forever in my heart as the Lover, at the very center of my desire.

IO

WITH THE WAR DRAGGING ON and life becoming more and more expensive, my mother could no longer pay for my studies. I was obliged to enter one of the so-called state high schools in a city a fair distance from home. The establishment had originally been a reception center for youth in exodus who wandered across China after fleeing their provinces or losing their families. Following its transformation into a pseudo high school—completely unlike any I had previously attended—inadequately funded by the government it offered a less than second-rate education and fast became the haunt of thick-headed and undisciplined schoolboys who, rejected elsewhere, came to join the indigent students.

This was the first time I had left my mother and our relatively benevolent surroundings. I found myself thrust into a brutal reality. Deplorable living conditions. Buildings of clay and straw, with foundations of bamboo latticework. Translucent paper for windowpanes. Pitiful shelter against the harsh continental climate of Sichuan Province! In summer the oppressive temperatures made classroom tables and chairs unbearably hot. In winter the cold turned students' fingers into chilblained sausages that could not hold a pencil. In noisy and overcrowded dormitories, the unsanitary conditions meant beds infested with fleas, bugs, and lice. Despite periodic group action, these formidable little beasts, who knew how to demoralize an entire regiment, multiplied still more, proliferated, nestled in humans' secret places, drinking their blood, gnawing at their bodies and spirits day and night, keeping them in a state of exasperation that bordered on despair.

The food consisted solely of vegetables—often spoiled—and partially husked rice, fare we gulped down hurriedly, standing. We hungered constantly for something better, and we were constantly hungry. The more affluent would visit the stalls that had begun to spring up around the school. From these stalls rose the pervasive smell of noodle soup with sautéed pork or stewed beef, a smell the very perfume of Nirvana to the nostrils of those who could not afford such treats. They had to be content to place at the bottom of their rice bowls a dab of lard, which would melt and impart enough creaminess to arouse an incipient ecstasy. Or again, at mealtime they might gnaw on a garlic clove or a dried pepper to help the rice go down.

Given this substandard environment, it should be no surprise that disease was rampant: tuberculosis, dysentery, typhus, malaria, appendicitis. Inevitably, I fell victim to these scourges. First dysentery, which brought me close to death. I recovered, or thought I had; ever after I was to experience terrible, unexpected attacks of stomach and intestinal pain, twisting and turning in my bed, although no doctor had a name for the condition. Then it was malaria that set upon me, and I was far too weak to resist. The most perverse of all diseases, it blasts the sufferer with extremes of heat and cold simultaneously, splitting him in two, all the while swaddling him in a suffocating bandage and making him turn round and round like a living mummy.

It was during this illness that I became once and for all afraid of my body, a body not entirely mine, capable of terrible treachery. Capable of letting the most hostile forces from the outside come to crouch inside me and become, before I knew it, my innermost being. Feverish and shaking, I watched my body rip apart from inside and escape my control entirely; it was like witnessing a scene of shocking domestic violence without the power to intervene. Alone in the gloom of a dormitory deserted all day, my companions a chipped thermos for hot water and a few rats that scratched at the legs of the bed, I was driven to examine myself and to reexamine my whole life. Cloistered and paralyzed as I was, that was about all I could do. And for the time being, the following was my life. Since my malaria had apparently come to stay and an attack now occurred regularly every morning around eleven, long before the appointed hour I would be dreading the "visit." To my surprise, it manifested itself in the form of a visitor. A visitor whose very face disturbed me. For I had the distinct impression I had always known him, and yet I could see that he was fundamentally different from the someone I knew. His presence produced that same hallucinatory confusion we feel upon thinking we recognize someone in a crowd and are about to approach him when a few minute particulars tell us he has to be someone else. Yes, it only takes a minute discrepancy for the familiar to become strange, for the almost true to become the completely false.

At first glance, the Visitor's face was thoroughly pleasant. He would look at me with his shining eyes, and I was hypnotized. As fever overtook me, I would sink into a black abyss. From the bottom of the abyss, I could see a single gleam of light above: the gaze of the other. Risking death by suffocation, I would climb toward that gleam. And I did so with my hands, my arms, my chest, my legs clinging to the face of the abyss, which seemed to bristle with sharp bamboo stakes for gouging out pieces of my flesh. I was thus reliving in my own flesh the unbearable pain of the bandit who had cleaned out his wound with a knife. To rise above the pain a little, I hung on to the idea that for once at least I was proving myself heroic. For once at least I had the chance to know something of what the legendary figure of the bandit had done, the chance to experience the physical suffering that a man could inflict on himself and, with all the more reason, visit on others. Whenever I neared the top of the abyss I took heart, encouraged by the ever brighter eyes of the one who stood above me, his face now illuminated by a barely contained smile. And finally I would see the other reach out tentatively to catch me.

Unfortunately his movements always lacked precision and determination. There would go my fingers, slipping between his outstretched hands, as my battered body fell into the black hole once again. Were it not for the light still drawing me upward I would never have had the willpower to make the infernal trek yet another time.

The day after, my body riddled with wounds, I would await the hour of the attack with even greater dread. The arrival of the Visitor was then gratefully welcomed, and once again I would receive him as a savior. And indeed, by focusing on his sparkling eyes I managed to summon up the resources to make the upward climb. But once again, despite apparent good will, the Visitor's rescuing hands did not move with great precision. And, once again, I would be driven to make the upward trek at the cost of unimaginable suffering.

After several days of that veritable descent into hell, the torture victim's body was a mere skeleton hung with a few paltry ribbons of flesh, as ridiculous as the shredded banner of an army that has seen every campaign. I had been reduced to a pitiful state in which nothing mattered any longer and there was no difference between accepting all and destroying all. And at that juncture, I reacted. They were making a fool of me! Who were the "they"? The Visitor, of course! All those days, he had reveled in my suffering. If, every day, he pretended to save me, it was only so as to amuse himself anew the following day. Then and there I decided to remain at the bottom of the abyss that very day, either giving in to suffocation or—should I have the strength—playing my entire hand. I waited in total darkness. A long time, I waited, until . . . Oh, surprise, the other, the one above, had vanished in the mist.

Who was he, the other? An unknown evil spirit, no question about it, from a region faraway, from the vast Outside. But it was my guess that he also came from a never-explored, hidden corner of my own body. In that case, who was I? Was I still master of myself? What was I doing here. What could I do on this earth?

During those days of thorough deprivation and total desertion, when even the smell of a squashed bug seemed friendly, I began to look at myself for the first time. Up until then there had been no cause for reflection; I was carried along by events: my father's death, the war, the exodus . . . I had to go to school because everyone went, because my mother scrimped and saved to pay for my schooling, telling me over and over that education was my only way out. And precisely because of events, I lagged behind: almost eighteen, I still hung about this sordid breeding ground, the pseudo high school. Nothing really excited me except a few literary works, ancient and modern, and drawing, of course. And even when it came to drawing, which I considered my strong point, the teacher, while acknowledging in me a certain gift and a very personal vision, criticized my lack of a sense of proportion and perspective, and even wondered whether I might not have defective eyesight. How could I not have doubts about a possible future as a painter? Besides, one could not make a living from drawing. I had a clear view of the destiny lying ahead: it was inevitable that I would be "good for nothing," and inevitable that my life, were I to live, should be spent on the fringes of everything. I thought of two lines I had learned not long before, by the poet Du Fu:

When I sing, gods and demons are present, I know;
If I die of hunger, my corpse filling a ditch, what does it matter.

After all I had just experienced, I felt certain that I too was to undergo extreme deprivation, the Terrible. At the thought of the Terrible, a reserve of obstinacy, rebellion rose up in me. What, give in to the blackmail of unbearable pain? Well, with death all pain would cease. And yes, I had connections with death, or rather, the dead. While I, like the rest of the world, steeled my body at the thought of death, at the same time I had a profound conviction that I would be protected by the dead.

Strangely enough, as soon as I had accepted being a "good for nothing" and had agreed to pay the price for being this "good for nothing," I immediately felt free of the wish to die, which had been nagging at me insidiously since the Lover's departure. Chills and fever faded away, a surge of desire took hold and whispered in my ear to remain in the world, precisely to *see*.

II

T O SUPPLEMENT the regular menu and to concoct remedies, a few students had for a time resorted to snake flesh and dog meat, which, according to traditional belief, are strongly *yang*, therefore "hot" and a good cure for "cold" diseases, such as the tuberculosis and malaria found at the school.

After an edict forbidding dogs to wander, there was nothing to hunt, and many directed their violent tendencies toward humans. For several months students had been enduring the loss of possessions pompously characterized as "objects of great value." In an era of extreme poverty, a pair of leather shoes, a wool sweater, flannel trousers, a dictionary, or an atlas, belonged in that category. The roughly built dormitories offered poor protection against thievery from outside. One day the residents finally came upon a thief in the act. The sounding of the alarm, then the manhunt. To the completely uninformed spectator, an absurd, if not comical, sight: on a narrow path between rice fields ran a lone man, gasping for breath; some distance behind him, like the tail of a comet, trailed a long line of maybe fifty persons, running, also out of breath. For a good while this undulating dragon slithered on the horizon of the countryside. While the energy propelling the tail constantly recharged itself, that which sustained the head wound down. Soon the head disappeared, devoured by the endless tail it had unwisely engendered.

Unknown to the school authorities, by night the boys set up a tribunal to judge the thief. In a tense atmosphere, under menacing glares, the thief—well worked-over since his arrest—made a confession, taking responsibility for all the thefts of which he had been accused, although it was obvious he could not have been the only culprit. In a quavering voice he obligingly explained when and how he operated. As it would have been impossible to restore the stolen items, long since sold, his judges imposed corporal punishment. They tied his wrists together with a rope, by which he was suspended from a beam. They were careful to provide the condemned man with a support from below that he could just graze with his toes. They hurriedly assembled a team of guards to keep watch. Late in the night, with the poor devil choking more and frequently, they feared he might end up dead and agreed to free him, not without informing him that he would receive the "supreme" punishment should he or his associates get it into their heads to repeat such crimes. During the trial, which in some ways prefigured the "people's tribunals" that China was to see a decade later, a whole race of budding defenders of justice came to light. This was in addition to the already existing phenomenon of clans or gangs whereby the strong exercised power over the weak, a phenomenon that would one day cause me suffering.

Along with the instinct for brutality unleashed on occasion, for some another element served as an outlet: sex. There too, the older boys, the initiated, did not hesitate to upset the ignorant, the younger ones, so as to exploit them. It would start with words. In a dark corner of the dormitory, everyone seated in a circle, the big boys would delight in recounting their sexual experiences, leaving out no detail. How they visited brothels. How in summer they would arrange to meet the women outdoors to make love on tombstones, something the women really liked, for the hot, slightly rough surface of the stones added to their excitement. The boys themselves, intoxicated by the images their detailed descriptions conjured up, would become increasingly excited, all the more so when they saw that the younger boys—who hung onto their every word, eyes feverish—were starting to pant. I believe it was not unusual that in the night some of the latter, still agitated, would submit to sexual abuse.

This debauchery did not involve more than a very few. Still, it contributed to a general ambiance of crudeness. Each student thought himself obliged to use "dirty" language in every conversation, to flaunt his vices, and boast of exploits that were for the most part non-existent. The weakened physique caused by malnutrition delayed in many the awakening of sexuality; in the older boys, it led to a lessening of desire. Nevertheless, a muted excitement was there, often artificially sustained by the need for compensation, and always exacerbated by imagination. A few young women teachers, whom we could look at all through class, opened wide the floodgates of carnal dreams. For example, the headmaster's wife, who taught English. In spite of an ordinary face, she was endowed with a firm, fleshy body, in which the protuberances, far from making her look ill proportioned, contributed to a harmonious whole. From her body and her spontaneity there emanated a candid sensuality, an effect she herself probably did not notice. Some of the boys wondered to what extent the husband, a stern, morose man, appreciated his wife's hidden charms. Nasty tongues could not resist applying to the couple the popular expression: "A peony growing in buffalo dung!" On summer days, when she taught in a sleeveless Chinese dress, a few of the boys would brazenly seat themselves in the front row like serious students, on the alert for moments when by some gesture, either routine or unexpected, she might provide a better view of her charms. At such times, a certain tall, skinny boy who did not hide his fondness for the solitary pleasure would take a seat in the last row so he could enjoy himself undisturbed. One day, noting his faraway, distracted look, the teacher asked him point-blank a question on the assignment. He could do no more than stammer a few "uh, uhs." The class choked with laughter. But, to the next question: "You're wandering in the clouds, then?" he replied, quite spontaneously: "Yes, yes, I'm in the clouds!" That provoked general hilarity, for we all thought of the expression "cloud-rain," in Chinese the metaphorical way of saying "make love." Amid the bursts of laughter however, we heard the teacher—who had no idea what went on in the back row—compliment him on the appropriateness of his response. For our lesson was Wordsworth's poem "The Daffodils": "I wandered lonely as a cloud . . ."

When it came to sex, I was more than confused. As well as being aware that in me was an alien body with needs not entirely mine, I could not get used to the anatomical or bestial view of woman. Was it possible for a woman, the other, to be something ordinary that could be gotten casually? Necessarily, she was an object to be pursued at length, and at long intervals even. I realized how strongly I was conditioned by the images of nude women I had come across. Those from the Louvre, so real, so carnal, and yet so far away, inaccessible; that of the Lover, the being to whom I had come so near but seen from so far, image that had been suddenly snatched from me, leaving no tangible trace.

And then there were the pictures of violated women, which frequently returned to haunt me. I could not help imagining the act of rape in various forms and the pleasure a man could derive from it. But such fantasies would come to be mixed with self-loathing when I was consumed by the silent reproach in the anguished eyes of those women so crushingly humiliated.

Thus, when it came to sex, I had a foreboding that there too I would have a life on the fringes, that I would never have a real opportunity to "penetrate" a woman. Not that I was not, just like all the other boys, swept with waves of desire, assailed by erotic thoughts, or that my wet dreams were not experienced as a shameful ailment. At times, however, a kind of exasperation would step in between my body and my self. Then with an unbidden ironic detachment I would contemplate my erection, which made me think of the skinny, rearing horse I had seen in the middle of a field, alone under a livid sky, his male organ hanging like a useless leg, ridiculous and pathetic, seemingly unable to find anything to satisfy it, a true emblem of cosmic impotence.

To relieve my loneliness I liked to go to the town near the school; one day, after the market closed I found myself following a peasant woman who carried at either end of a yoke two large empty baskets still spotted with feathers from the poultry she had sold. I could not take my eyes off the rhythmic swinging of the woman's hips, her tanned, shining legs, and the hollows by her ankles that seemed to cast smiles behind her at every step. Soon it was country, and there was no longer anyone about. As if hypnotized, I continued to follow her. At a bend where the road began to climb, there stood a grove of bamboo and acacia. The woman stopped suddenly and, turning around, shouted, "Shame, shame, following a woman this way! Aren't you ashamed? Aren't you ashamed?" Ashamed, certainly, and

I could only stare, unable to say a word. I was about to scurry off like a dog, when I heard the woman call me: "Come on, boy, come on!" As she spoke, she went behind the trees to a place where the ground sloped down to a sandbank. In a grass-covered hollow hidden from all eyes, she nimbly removed her trousers, which consisted of a single wide piece of fabric. Just as nimbly she spread out the fabric and lay down on it. It was in no way grotesque—the scene was totally enchanting. In the middle of that piece of faded blue cloth surrounded by a thick carpet of leaves, the plump ivory-colored body resembled an immense lotus in full bloom. I gave in to the invitation of her body. But compared with the instinctive nature of the woman's movements, my own—hampered as I was by anxiety to get it right—were clumsy and uncoordinated. In my hurry I saw the act, so often imagined, end in fiasco. And there was the woman, already dressed. The ambiguous laugh after she had turned to leave added to my confusion. I stood there, ridiculous. The next market day, however, I met the woman again. At the same spot, we repeated our experience. Gradually, I came to follow the rhythm of the woman, who uttered moans and proffered words thoroughly innocent and thoroughly obscene. Those words stirred up my blood and led me to pleasure.

The day came when I no longer saw the woman at the market. I concluded that her husband must have recovered. Taking over his tasks while he was ill, she had been able to go abroad freely.

12

IN MY CLASS there was a little gang of Sichuanese, all sons of prosperous landowners. They were a band of do-nothings, in school merely to kill time while awaiting a hypothetical diploma. Their only interest was martial arts, which satisfied a need for power. They had found a punching bag in a rather simpleminded boy called Harelip. The latter was forced to submit to their authority as the result of an innocently committed crime. Some upperclassmen had bribed a clerk at the mimeograph office to supply them with a set of exam questions, and they sent Harelip to fetch the printed sheet. Thinking it was a simple errand, he had set out fearlessly. Unfortunately, the authorities discovered the leak and immediately changed the questions, without finding the culprits. Subsequently, living in fear of denunciation, the poor errand boy became the object of ongoing blackmail. In the structure of the gang, which bent him to its whims, he played the role of "royal dwarf." On one occasion, after classes were over for the day, just for fun the members of the gang removed his trousers and shorts and left him in the classroom half-naked. He would have stayed there until dark had I not been so bold as to bring him a pair of trousers, greatly displeasing his tormentors. I, who did not usually attract much attention, was now treated to their hostile looks. I did not regret my act. For it was during a clash with the group that I met Haolang, who brought me out of my longtime solitude.

A native of Manchuria, Haolang at nineteen already had a history. Orphaned first by his mother's death, then his father's, he had been raised by an uncle. Two years before the war began, he had taken a job in a metal-tool factory in Tientsin. After an argument with the foreman, he left the factory without any particular plans. There ensued a series of inconsequential jobs until he lapsed into semi-delinquency. At the same time, the then-sixteen-year-old adolescent had sufficient clarity of mind to know that there was more to him than mere brute force, that an uncompromising inner flame consumed him. Attracted by a posted notice, he enrolled in evening courses organized by some obscure progressive intellectuals. And there, miraculously, the war gathered him up. Enlisting in one of the artists' groups, "Resistance to the Japanese and Salvation of the Homeland," he experienced the itinerant life, then life at the front. One of the "youngsters," but surrounded by seasoned artists, he discovered poetry and himself a poet. Unfortunately, in less than two years these groups, dominated by Communists and increasingly frowned upon by the government, would be disbanded. It was then that Haolang ended up at the high school. A man of the North, he was taller than average. His skin was dark, as if he had been cast in bronze. By his mere presence, solemn and quiet, he inspired respect. When seeing an American film after the war, I was struck by Haolang's resemblance to Marlon Brando. During the fight with the gang, doubled over to protect myself from my adversaries' determined assault against the stomach, I received a rain of blows on the head and shoulders. Haolang, passing by, intervened and managed to free me. In the melee, a book slipped out of his pocket and landed in a patch of wild grass. Before going off with my savior, I picked up the volume. Handing it back to him, I noticed that it was a collection of poetry entitled *Leaves of Grass*. We both laughed heartily at the connection between the title and the spot from which the book had just been retrieved.

Then began impassioned exchanges with my new friend, exchanges we both experienced like explorers in the desert who have suddenly come upon an oasis. In the early stages, as if to make up for lost time and banish once and for all the specter of solitude, we missed no chance to get together. Cutting class, neglecting homework and sleep, not to mention meals—Haolang went so far as to have to repeat the year so he could be in my class—we spent long hours comparing our life experiences, each telling the other his innermost aspirations. Thoroughly a poet, devoted to literature, Haolang brought to our exchanges the vast culture he had acquired through reading. Guided by him, I entered a kingdom whose splendor dazzled me, moved me deeply. Far poorer in learning than he, nonetheless I think I contributed my share of enlightenment. Through my sensibility, more secret, more unhealthy than his, and also through my experience as a painter, I thought myself better prepared to see beyond the appearance of things to the cracks and chinks that infiltrate them.

The fervor of our friendship made me aware that the passion of friendship can be as intense as that of love when the circumstances are out of the ordinary. I did not fail to compare my encounter with Haolang to my encounter with Yumei. She had moved me to the very roots of my being, but the tears of longing and gratitude aroused were like a sure and gentle spring gushing from one's own earth. Seen through the Lover's eyes, all the elements composing the universe proved tangible, connected by a light that was diffused, but unique and thus unifying. In contrast, the encounter with my friend was a veritable irruption, jolting me fiercely, carrying me toward the unknown, toward continual challenges. Our vaguely felt physical attraction was not the main force that compelled our pressing hunger and thirst. What the other opened up to me was an unsuspected, unfathomable universe, that of the mind. Alongside untouched nature, there was another reality, that of language. The young poet's impassioned words and writings made me realize that, for the man who thinks and creates, all remains not closed but boundlessly open. In the Friend's company, the self in me that had literally exploded would henceforth march toward a horizon which itself had exploded.

Haolang knew both classical and modern Chinese literature. Further, he had come into contact with a group of young poets, the generation following the July poets discovered and promoted by Hu Fung. These writers were establishing their reputation in the capital of Yunnan Province, Kunming, the new home of several prestigious universities. Haolang was in touch with Mu Dan in particular, whom he considered the best. I knew a little about modern literature, having read the famous authors, starting with Lu Xun, of course. Through my friend I became familiar with lesser known works that explored Chinese reality as a truly inexhaustible mine of dreams and tragedies. Yet, with my fondness for more radical questioning and more astounding revelations, I was left unsatisfied by descriptions that repeated ad nauseam accounts of injustices suffered and destinies thwarted. Already I knew that the human soul harbored terrible passions which the language of literature was still too timorous to express.

As for Haolang, just when I met him his interests had begun to shift. He was systematically devouring everything that came out on Western literature. And the contemporary literary climate encouraged his pursuit. It is true that Western literature had not been totally unknown in China. In the twenties, and all through the thirties, the Chinese had translated prodigiously, "right and left" so to speak, chaotically, and with mixed results, for many translators worked not from original texts, but from Japanese or English versions. All the same, a trend had begun. Hadn't Lu Xun, in 1925, with all the weight of his authority, advised a young reader to forge ahead and read "as few Chinese books as possible and as many foreign books as possible?" During the forties, years of upheaval and an intense need for openness, a combination of favorable circumstances brought in more literature from abroad. The war had brought a great concentration of intellectuals to the Southwest's major cities—Tchoungking, Kunming, Guiyang, Guilin, among others. Also, increasingly heavy political censorship and a temporary exhaustion of creative energy led many writers to turn to translating, their efforts further stimulated by the presence of representatives from the allied nations. The British and the Russians had come first, then the Americans arrived with foodstuffs, tons of equipment, and their magnificent collections of pocket books. We pounced on everything that appeared, poetry and novels, plays, essays, without neglecting any author, including those from northern and central Europe. Never in a million years did I imagine that I would one day have a special tie with France. Yet two twentieth-century French writers were to exercise a decisive influence on us, as on all Chinese youth: Romain Rolland and Gide. They made their presence felt through two incomparable translators, Fu Lei and Sheng Chenghua, both of whom had studied in France and had been acquainted with the authors in question. Ah, the mystery of human language! Do those who claim that cultures are mutually irreducible ever find it rather astonishing that a particular body of words, leaving its place of origin, overcomes all obstacles and reaches the other end of the world, to be understood there? The more a body of words is the bearer of human truth, the more rapidly it is understood. Where we were, at the other end of the world, opening one of those books printed on rough paper was enough to plunge us immediately into a different but soon familiar universe. At the time, we were living in a state of total deprivation. There was sickness. There was bombing. Our lives hung by a thread. Yet, through imagination, they were filled with rich experience. Sunny days invariably meant an alert. Enemy planes hummed overhead, swooping down on the capital, sowing death as they passed. We did not take much notice. All classes canceled, we would take refuge near the shelters dug into the mountainside. For us it was a godsend. Over long hours, amid the scent of humus and resin, the breeze ruffled the pages of the books we held in our hands. We were in the company of Jean-Christophe, Prometheus, the Prodigal Son. We nourished ourselves on *The Fruits of the Earth*.Were these works the greatest of literature? The question had little importance. They had spoken to us directly. With all its dramatic events, the tumultuous history of Jean-Christophe, seeking fulfillment through three cultures—German, French, and Italian—inspired every one of us at a time when we too aspired to metamorphoses. We knew that, after its long dialogue with India and Islam, Chinese culture had reached a point where the West was an essential voice and could not be ignored. Gide, for example, spoke to a Chinese youth like the returning prodigal confiding in his young brother. He exhorted him to draw on his inner resources, to regain his enthusiasm, to expand the scope of his desires, to free himself from the bondage of social and family tradition—precisely the source of difficulty for every idealistic young Chinese in that ancient country in decline.

To escape its predicament that ancient country would, alas, have to go through many a shock and torment. Neither of the two distinguished translators would reach the age of the man who said: "I am determined to be happy," nor of he who extolled "the belated serenity of a hero." Almost a quarter of a century was to go by; then, during the Cultural Revolution, at the height of the savage campaign against Western bourgeois tendencies, Fu Lei saw all his books and manuscripts scattered or burned before his eyes. Once his house had been searched, he and his wife were forced to live in one cramped room. Now an "enemy of the people," he was dragged before the Red Guards night and day to undergo endless interrogations as well as physical abuse. The couple finally decided to die together so as not to leave a survivor. As for Sheng Chenghua, he was sent to a labor camp. Despite his poor health, he was assigned every type of work. First, construction, which included the erecting of the camp, then work in the fields, where all day long he would stand knee-deep in the muddy water of rice paddies, his sixty-year-old body so brutally exposed to the assaults of insects. One day, under a fiery sun, he collapsed in the middle of the field and sank into the water, without a word.

13

T HE CALL OF the West. Or Europe, to be exact. In spite of the dreadful tragedy being played out there, we could not help idealizing that continent, seeing in it a soil blessed by the gods. We familiarized ourselves with the Rhine and the Danube, the Alps and the Pyrenees. And from the mere name "Mediterranean" reverberated a heavy load of myth and legends. Yes, Baudelaire's "exotic perfume" did not make us dream of some tropical isle but evoked instead the far western reaches of the old Eurasian continent. And Baudelaire's magical phrase awoke in my memory a whole string of sensations that I had first experienced when still a child living at Mount Lu, the mountain "colonized" by Western missionaries. That whole past surged up, very much present.

Among all the perfumes, inaugural in a way was the perfume of the book. It had impressed itself on me when the British missionary opened a dark wood chest, a long low chest that stood against the wall of his living room, its flat cushion-covered top serving as a seat. Enhanced by the scent of the chest's sandalwood, the odor rose from those blocks of paper that had crossed the seas to become patinated by time and touched by mildew. At the missionary's request, my father had come that day to deliver some calligraphic renderings of parallel sayings for an upcoming parish celebration. While as my father translated and explained at length the phrases he had prepared, I had an opportunity to plunge into the fascinating universe of books whose texts in horizontal lines were sprinkled with brightly colored illustrations. Some of the pictures showed human figures which were almost terrifying because they looked diabolically realistic—a realism that Chinese painting had always resisted; the fingers did not touch them, for fear they would jump out of the book.

But, rather than their content—which completely escaped me—it was the very materiality of the books that struck me from the first. These volumes of so many sizes were heavy in the hand and made their corporeal solidity felt, offering a remarkable contrast to the limp, light Chinese book with its thin, nearly translucent paper, its old ink that gleamed iridescent, and the indefinable perfume it exuded, a blend of fresh grass and dried branches. If the Chinese book was of the vegetable kingdom, for me the Western book was of the mineral or the animal. Some of the works had heavy cardboard covers and stiff paper whose whiteness was marred in places by the brownish rings of old stains. Those particular volumes reminded me of "dreaming stones" (stones of marble or jade with tortuous veins evoking imaginary landscapes), stones of a magical sort, which one could open as one wished, page by page. Other books, leather bound, were somewhat more flexible, yet resistant, that is not to say rough, to the touch. One might almost have been stroking the coat of a wild animal that smelled of musk: a deer or a boar.

Afterward, in my memory the odor of the book came to be mingled as if naturally with that of the Western body. The odor alerts the nostrils of every Chinese person who encounters Westerners by themselves or in groups on those narrow Chinese city streets. An odor hard to characterize (which Westerners themselves do not know exists and which we Chinese stop smelling if we live among them), it comes mainly from ingesting dairy products. In spite of the way some Chinese put it, "They smell like milk," there is not necessarily a pejorative implication in the statement, which is primarily a physiological observation. Our old race of farmers, pig and poultry raisers, from time immemorial has been ignorant of animal milk. Besides mother's milk, the Chinese child knows only soy milk. So, when a Chinese tastes cow's or goat's milk for the first time, he is sure to gag and may even want to vomit. In my case, the connection between the smell of milk and that of the Western body, far from bothering me, aroused instead a kind of complicity. For I first came upon it one bright summer morning on Mount Lu when a group of bare-shouldered young women—living incarnations of the nude pictures from the Louvre—passed me on their way to bathe in a little lake at the base of a waterfall.

Around the same time, my father often took me with him on his journeys to sell medicinal plants and buy new ones; we would go into the heart of Mount Lu, to Guling, a gently sloping hill developed into a town and surrounded by gardens and country houses. On the main street stood many office buildings, hotels, restaurants, and shops, both Chinese and Western. One day, passing a shop, I was truly bowled over by the intoxicating aromas escaping from the ventilator. At first, knowing little of the subject, I was quite incapable of distinguishing the odor of butter from that of vanilla, or the perfume of cream from that of chocolate mousse. All I could pick out among the aromas was that basic ingredient, which once again made my heart beat faster: milk. The bright, gleaming facade of the shop confirmed that it was a newly opened Western bakery. On subsequent visits, while my father did business with the Chinese pharmacists, I would invariably go and station myself in front of the ventilator. A moment of pure delight for me! Enveloped in the warm odor rediscovered, I was all eyes as I stood before the luminous items in the display cases. How could I not sense I had stepped into a new, exotic world? How could I not see the difference between that to which I was accustomed and that which kindled my desire? Color for example. Chinese pastries, cereal or vegetable based, generally had a dull, pastel surface. The steamed ones even retained the natural ecru of the flour used. Other cakes and crackers, crisp, fried in sesame oil or lard, were covered with a brown crust so dark they appeared to have been roasted with soy sauce. While the Western pastries in the display case did include cakes with pastel tints, the truly striking items had a golden luster—often with magnificent gradations—which could only have been imparted by the effect of baking on cream, butter, and milk. There were also cakes covered with brightly colored fruit. The delicate, rounded form of the fruit provided a harmonious contrast to the tart shells that held it, which had been carefully cut out or fitted into a tin. Yes, the very shape of Western pastries evoked something other. There was an opposition between Chinese cakes, plump and soft as if they were natural growths, and these with their clean, geometric lines, miniature pieces of sculpture or tiny works of architecture. And looking through the window at the young women clerks, whose cleavage with its delicate furrow seemed a replica of those blonde rolls with the shallow slash down the center, I noticed how the pastries were in harmony with their bodies, with the tints of their hair and their eyes, with their milky skin verging on pink and imperceptibly blue veined. Their very bone structure, sturdy and angular, was echoed in those appetizing products. It looked as though the Westerners had projected themselves fully into the cakes they had invented, seeking a mirror image. In a sense, they were eternally eating and savoring their own image.

As for me, there was no question about my desire to taste such cakes. During that whole period, I was truly obsessed with the word *milk* and with Chinese expressions using the word: "milk room" to indicate a woman's breast, "milk oil" for butter, et cetera. And along with that, I had just read in a children's magazine a story about a man becoming invisible. Imagining that I myself had become invisible, I had but one idea: to enter the bakery by night. Free to stand in the brightly lit room, I could then watch the milk spurt from the swollen teats of the young women and stream into crystal bowls. And while they were preparing fresh pastries with their milk, I could go into the store and sample unhurriedly, one by one, the entire gamut of pastries on display. . . . It did not take my father long to notice the desire nagging at me. He, who was always poorly dressed and never went into a "chic" shop, decided one day when his plants had sold well that he would buy his son one of the least expensive cakes. It was a custard-filled horn. With what gratitude I received the gift. With what cautious greed my mouth shaped itself to the conical roundness and my teeth crunched the crumbly pastry, before my tongue finally melted into the smoothness of the long dreamed-of custard! I could not have described the exotic flavor with words from my mother tongue, which had not provided for anything like that; yet, I did have the satisfaction of discovering that the flavor was indeed just as I had so vividly imagined it. In short, the satisfaction of any desire is in the desire itself. Now that I had reached the age of nineteen, I no longer possessed the fresh soul of my childhood; but that mild little experience, my first contact with the West, had prepared me to welcome everything coming from afar.

To give expression to the earth that had nurtured me, I would one day be a painter; inevitably I would encounter Western painting. I would uncover the secrets of Gauguin and Monet, Rembrandt and Vermeer, Giorgione and Tintoretto, all the great masters who have exalted form through the use of color. I would understand—with the strange feeling that I had already understood it long before—that the Far East, by ever greater reduction, strives to reach an insipid essence in which the inward self meets the inward universe, while the Far West, by letting the physical abound, exalts matter, glorifies the visible, and in so doing glorifies its own most secret, most insane dream.

14

THE WORKS OF Romain Rolland and Gide—*Jean-Christophe, La Vie de Beethoven, La Symphonie pastorale*—had whetted our appetite for Western classical music. Although literature and painting were accessible to us through translations and reproductions, music remained virtually unknown, except for what was picked up at random here and there from American films and old phonograph records. A feverish excitement gripped us the day we saw an ordinary poster announcing a symphony concert, which featured, appropriately enough, *The Pastoral Symphony*, at the National Conservatory in a city nearly twenty miles away. To get there, we had to walk all day. Arriving at night, we asked the Conservatory to put us up. They allowed us to sleep on the tables in a classroom since the concert was scheduled for the afternoon of the following day, a Sunday.

This, the first concert of our lives, was all the more memorable for its being marked by the unexpected—or miraculously opportune—intrusion of the Outside. In the middle of the third movement of *The*

Pastoral Symphony, the timpani creating the thunderstorm were drowned out by the blast of the air-raid siren. The conductor did not interrupt the performance, for the first warning was supposed to be followed by a second announcing the imminent arrival of the Japanese planes. In fact, between the two warnings, the audience had time to follow the third movement to the end, then reach the shelters in an orderly manner. When the concert resumed two hours later, it was in an intensely contemplative mood tinged by smiles of joy that everyone communed with the fourth movement's melody of calm restored.

After the concert, armed with a lantern, we walked all night to return to our school. Sleep was out of the question anyway; we were too elated. Chinese music, discreet and confidential, often plaintive, had hardly accustomed us to a song with tones so sovereign, so conquering—one which did not accompany nature but tore open its skin, pierced its flesh, to become its very pulse. What that symphony evoked of course were the wheat fields and pastures of far-off Europe. Yet how akin it was to the heartbeat of two walkers lost in the Chinese night! Responding to the measure of our footsteps, the terraced rice fields, bathed in moonlight and noisy with the croaking of frogs, seemed to spread out in ever-widening circles with a formidable, rhythmic expansion. To a man at last awakened, does not any land, old as it may be, become eternally virgin?

We had to wait several months before a second concert was announced, with an American orchestra and a Chinese soloist; we would not have missed it for anything. The program consisted of two works by Dvořák: *Concerto for Cello* and *The New World Symphony.* With the first notes of the concerto, the magic distilled by the music began its work. On the previous occasion, I had been impressed; the music of Beethoven had swept me away. This time, the feeling was deeper, visceral. When the slow movement began, a friendly hand came to lead me into a melody which rose, which intensified into something other but constantly came back to itself, following different twists and turns each time. Strangely, for me this music from afar, so foreign, was immediately close, as close as some ancient Chinese pieces. If there was indeed a difference, it was probably that in the playing of the slow movement, before each return of the motif there was the sense of a terrible parting, an inconsolable moan. The idea of parting and return gave rise to the image of a traveler returning home after a long absence, such as is so often described in Chinese poetry. As he nears the village, his step grows heavy, for he is gripped by fear of what he will find: an accident or a death in the household during his absence. As soon as he encounters someone from the village and the latter reassures him without his asking, on he goes, his step lighter, almost airy. He feels filled with supreme power, for it is he whom they await, now it is for him to bring comfort to those who remained at home and know naught of his adventures. As long as the melody lasted, my native region seemed within reach. Listening, I was carried on the music's wave of emotion, which made me feel that at any moment I would be reunited with the loved ones who waited: my mother, my sister, the Lover . . .

During the concert I was fascinated by the musician and his instrument. It was the first time I had seen a cello. I was immediately struck by the disproportion between this impressively large instrument and the soloist, a pale, puny young man—undernourished, like all Chinese youth in those days—seemingly not of sufficient bulk to control the sound. When he began to play, he devoted himself to the execution so earnestly that any possible disharmony was no longer noticed, just as if he had been a sorcerer in a trance whose gestures even if awkward were perceived as natural, indeed absolutely necessary. After a touching combat at close quarters in which he squeezed with his legs and encircled with his right arm the bulging body of the instrument, by turns assaulting and caressing it, in the end he became one with that mysterious creation, the cello, as appealing as it is impenetrable. So inseparable were the two that now one feared the player could never break away. Accentuating this fear was the constant reiteration of the melody's theme. For a moment I wondered whether the interpreter, captive of his playing and forced to prolong it, had forgotten the score. But the orchestra continued, unperturbed, and I was reassured. In the golden light of late afternoon, carried away I watched that solid block on the stage, a living block composed of two united, hostile beings involved in an internal to-and-fro where misery and exaltation, pain and ecstasy, confronted each other then intermingled.

And with the theme recurring yet another time, I was suddenly deluded by the mad hope that it would not stop and that I would sink once and for all into the matrix soil where all the feminine presences were joined together. But the movement was already coming to an end. The wrench of a sudden parting, such as I had known when the Lover left without good-byes. And the same taste of tears and ashes choking me, except this time I felt less alone perhaps, because of the Friend there beside me and because of the new conviction that germinated within me. I found myself whispering to the dear ones who had been gradually receding in the distance: "All is lost, all is found. I cannot touch you, but I shall meet you in some other way. In some other way we shall be together. Yes, I shall not forget the promise made this evening, on May 30, 1943."

On the way home that night, for the first time I talked to the Friend about the Lover, and at length. So acute were my words that she seemed to be there walking beside us. Since we had met, wrapped up in the excitement of our friendship and our discoveries, Haolang and I had scarcely found time to take up the subject of women. I only knew that his love life had been complicated, especially during the period when he lived with the artists' group "Resistance to the Japanese and Salvation of the Homeland," whose young members did not have strict morals. At the high school, he had made two or three easy and disappointing conquests. I on the other hand was poor in experience but had a fertile imagination. Because of that nocturnal walk, I was able to confide in him fully. Among my poet friend's responses to my story, the following is engraved in my memory. "It is surprising that this old degenerate world is still capable of producing figures like her! This may be just what a Dante or a Goethe was thinking: we shall be saved by Woman."

15

HEARING THE MUSIC of Dvořák, a native of central Europe, had made the far West less distant; now the land of Russia seemed almost close by. It became land of more importance than ever because of the decisive battles taking place there. We avidly read Russian literature, which we already knew slightly from translations of the twenties and thirties. Now, in the forties, new translations were appearing one after another and of better quality. Reading these works, we made our own the fate of that country heavy with chains and a wish for deliverance, heavy with torments and dreams. We learned to love those vast expanses so marked by the seasons, desolate or burning. We even loved Siberia, land of the damned, which Tolstoy would have liked to see a place of resurrection. From where we were, on the hot clay of our remote corner of China, we thought with incredible yearning of that far country peopled by so many beloved literary characters, not knowing that one day we would find ourselves at its border, separated only by a great river.

In the meantime, a whole series of questions crossed our minds, triggered by the expression "Russian soul" or "Slavic soul," which Dostoyevsky liked to use. Who are we? What is this very old, moribund country called China? Where is its soul? What is its destiny? And for us what is the proper creative path? By turning our eyes in another direction, won't we go astray? Unless we are already lost, and lost with us all inner voice and all true worth? These questions bothered me less than they did my friend, inclined as I was to believe in restlessness of spirit and the peculiar adventure of each soul. He with his desire to revitalize the language of poetry felt more concern than I. After several days of reflection, he expressed his opinion in a firm voice: "No, there is not much to argue about. I am strongly on the side of Lu Xun. The soul, we have it or we do not have it. If we have it, then we shall not lose it. Or else, it is at the moment we realize we are looking for it that we lose it. If we are to be reborn, we shall be reborn. If we are to disappear, let us accept becoming ashes; perhaps from them something else will be born of which we know nothing now. For the moment, salvation comes from elsewhere, from abroad. And first, from the West. There they have formulated questions and accomplished creative work that we have not and which we cannot circumvent. But, careful here—it is not the West as such that we shall blindly take for our model. The excessive rationalism and the desire for power, which in their exaggerated form isolate Western man from the living universe and from the rest of the world (viewed only as an object of conquest) have brought us physical suffering for over a century, through all the disastrous wars and suffocating occupations that they have imposed on us without respite. And they suffer, too, for when they have conquered the whole world and have no more conquests to make or when their own interests are at stake, they tear each other apart. See how in our time beautiful Europe has been turned into a battlefield, destroyed! What I'm talking about are the true creators, those who are trying to unveil the truth. Their shouts and songs, created within the freedom they have won, are for us absolutely unprecedented and are rending our horizon. Yes, we must have this drastically different other, to shake us up, to tear out the degenerate, rotten part of our roots. Without the enrichment of new blood and new knowledge, how do you expect us to arrive at an authentic life, the only life that will allow us to recognize properly amid the great hodgepodge of our heritage the values that must be retained? Strangely enough, it is after reading all those Western works that I am beginning to see our own culture more clearly. I can distinguish in it a hundred or so great creators, indomitable, indispensable, whom we shall never abandon. You may say that for a five-thousand-year-old culture, that's not many. It is enough to forge a soul, if there is a soul." Then, as though to break with the very solemn tone of his speech, he smiled and, with a slight wave of his arm, said: "As long as we practice Tai chi chuan every day, we shall not lose ourselves. As the master says: 'In the center of the Great Void we shall capture the Breath that connects Heaven and Earth, here and elsewhere, and why not, past and future.'"

The day after his declaration, the inspired poet showed me these lines he had just composed:

When nostalgia overwhelms you
Drive it off, to the far horizon.
Wild goose cleaving the clouds
You carry in you the dead season
Frozen rushes, charred trees
Bent low beneath the hurricane.
Wild goose that need not tarry
Free now for flight, or death . . .
Between natal soil and welcoming sky
Your sole kingdom: your own call!

I learned the poem by heart, never to forget it. I knew that with those lines my friend had once and for all embarked on his path.

I realized that for me too the hour of decision was at hand. The turning point came when I saw some reproductions of Impressionist paintings in the American magazine *Life,* new to China. How strongly I sensed even then the extraordinary painterly quality of artists like Monet, Cézanne, Gauguin; but I felt a special kinship with Van Gogh, with those fragmented shapes, with that bold alchemy of color, and with a personal vision captured from the very heart of real life! His work echoed in me like a fraternal call. The world below, fleeting as it may be, always demands expression. I was going to express it through painting, despite my having nothing. I did not need to search elsewhere. Was it a question of vocation? No. Of destiny.

16

WHILE WE DEVOTED ourselves to personal creative endeavors, day by day the situation in the country was growing worse. With the war dragging on, misery was rampant; yet there were profiteers, numerous among those holding power, and they grew shamefully rich. Corruption was found at every level and reigned supreme. Over the India and Burma Roads—built during the war at the cost of enormous sacrifice so China could communicate with the outside world—some were bringing in essential commodities to sell on the black market, making indecently large fortunes. Champagne flowed freely in the dancehalls; meanwhile, the ordinary people and the refugees who flocked to the wartime capital were starving to death. Faced with the brewing discontent among the population, the government had no recourse but to step up police repression. Abuses combined with general social disruption led to further abuses, ending in the absurd and the tragic. The newspapers were full of scandals. In my own locality I witnessed appalling scenes. In a neighboring market town, near the site of a famous hot springs stood a villa owned by a leading dignitary, the powerful finance minister, who had amassed a colossal fortune kept safe in American banks. The villa's outbuildings housed a contingent of guards, responsible for security and commanded by an officer. Modeling themselves on their superior, the soldiers exacted greater and greater tributes from the local population. When riots threatened, the commander was obliged to punish one soldier as a warning to all. The public beating administered is still a vivid memory. The condemned man lies face-down on the ground, between two lines of soldiers. Two men step out, one from each row, and strike the victim's buttocks with a long stick like the ones coolies use for carrying loads. "Harder, harder," orders the commander, for they are hitting a comrade and try to go easy at first. After the requisite number of blows, the two step back, replaced by two others. For a time the scapegoat endures the thrashing stoically, repressing his moans. Only a few muffled sounds are heard. But as the session goes on, he realizes that his leader intends to put him to death. His cries, loud and clear now, are accompanied by pleas: "Have pity, Commander! Spare my life, Commander!" His appeals gradually grow weaker; he is about to lose consciousness. They pick him up and drag him around the field. He has been revived, and the torture resumes. At the end, it is a dying man they take away rolled up in a mat, his backside larded with bloody strips and his insides probably shattered.

Far from appeasing public opinion, that punishment-made-theater resulted in a protest demonstration, with students joining in. The demonstrators demanded the commander be tried for his illegal act, straight out of feudal barbarism. The minister's response was to close up his villa and transfer the guards elsewhere. It did not grieve him to stop sojourning in those parts, for he had acquired another villa, at a new spa open only to the privileged.

Once again, the youth of China were on the alert, idealistic, young people still concerned about their country's destiny; who since the beginning of the century had been in the vanguard each time the country was in danger of suffocation and death; who at the beginning of the war had not hesitated to participate en masse in every resistance activity. Many of them had taken up the revolutionary cause, crossing the demarcation lines to reach Yan'an or other zones occupied by the Communist army. And now, in these dark years, the lava flow of revolution had surfaced anew, spreading stealthily but surely over the land, setting hearts ablaze.

In the streets and tea houses of towns near our school and the local university, there was a noticeable presence of young Communists and other young people newly won over to their cause. They were recognizable—and this is how the secret police spotted them—by their serious and dignified demeanor, and by the clear, serene, and determined conscience that showed in their eyes. Their appearance and their speech stood out against the surrounding coarseness and social decline. This impression of sharp contrast I was to remember when, after the war, I happened to see an American movie on the life of Christ, a film for the most part mediocre but with one impressive scene: the arrival of the first Christians, whose faces shining with purity were a radical contrast to those of the Romans, replete with fat and lust. Later, I would chance upon some old photographs of Chinese Christians from the end of the last century, whose gaze stood out against the surrounding world even more strikingly.

These young people thirsting for justice and ready to sacrifice themselves—and later they would do just that—passed around forbidden books. Such works soon fell into Haolang's hands. He began reading—and had me read—the writings of Marx, Engels, Lenin, all published in Moscow; and those of Mao Zedong, Liu Shaoqi, and Ai Siqi, the philosopher of the Communist Party; and various literary journals. One day, looking back to his experience with collective action early in the war, he announced: "We shall be revolutionaries. We shall labor by the side of the Communists, and if need be we shall enter their ranks. Not that I am taking up to their doctrine—except for some historical analyses that seem valid—but we don't have a choice. At present they are the only effective revolutionary force. In these days when we see around us so much misery and injustice, when something must be done to rescue China, can we think only of accomplishing something for ourselves?" Although I was fully behind any action against injustice and ready to do my part, I had a fundamental resistance to being recruited into a discipline said to be implacable, one that demanded absolute obedience and the renunciation of all individual thinking. On a deeper level, I neither believed in the destiny of man as being definable in advance nor in the destiny of this earth as an end in itself. There was also Evil, ever-present, which I could not root out of my imagined world. Given all that, how could one group, no matter how large, expect to "build" so rationally an "ideal" society for its members, and beyond that, for everyone else? Instinctively close to the Taoist spirit, I preferred the concept of the continuous creation or transformation of a Universe where the Earth was only a temporary stopping place. Haolang advanced the idea that for the time being it behooved us to help destroy the old order; once the yoke was lifted, we would be entering a new context, and we could strive to develop our society in a different direction. I pointed out that the organizing force of the revolutionaries, long established and with branches everywhere, would not withdraw on its own once power had been won. My arguments rattled him. Nevertheless, he was preparing himself mentally for possible direct involvement in the cause, should it come to that. To be ready for physical ordeals, including torture, he went so far as to ask the doctor about to remove his appendix with little or no anesthesia.

Summer 1944. Haolang and I, set back in our studies because of the war, finally finished high school. We were asking ourselves what to do and where to go, when destiny knocked. My mother had heard from Yumei, who very much wanted to see me. After her dramatic escape, she had lived in Tchoungking with the air-force officer, but eventually she had broken up with him. She was now living in the port city of N., where she had joined a Sichuan opera company. Without hesitation we decided to join her, crossing the immense province on foot. We did not suspect that we were committing ourselves to our life's real adventure—with no turning back.

17

IRST AND FOREMOST, how could we resist the call of the big city? We had been deprived too long. The name *Tchoungking* (Double Celebration) echoed in us like a popular song whose words we hardly knew, but whose tune we could not help humming at idle moments. Greedily, feverishly we plunged into a metropolis swarming with people and congested with vehicles of every sort. We were not put off by any of its discomforts. We reveled in the din and the dust, the furnacelike heat of late August, the strong odors of the heavily spiced foods sold in the streets. We even found delight in the stench issuing from the garbage trucks.

The city is still fresh in my memory. The site is superb, framed by two rivers—the Jialang to the north and the Yangzi to the south. Tchoungking rises high above them, a peninsula composed of a series of flat-topped hills ending in a large rocky spur that dominates the confluence of the two rivers. Atop the cliffs and at various levels along their sides sprawl great jumbles of low hovels and towering apartments, which could be thousands of seashells solidly encrusted in the rock. Everywhere countless stairs connect the streets and passageways.

On the heights the avenues stretch out, wide or narrow depending on the terrain; they converge at crossroads jammed with stores, restaurants, theaters, and movie houses, dancehalls, tea houses, and American-style bars.

Spots full of trees and rock gardens have been developed into parks, their terraces providing magnificent views of the kind that only the long scrolls of Chinese painting can capture.

On either side of the promontory, both of them flowing from west to east, the emerald Jialing, although swift, appears more graceful, more feminine than the wide Yangzi, red with the silt it carries down from the plateaus of far-off Tibet. The two rivers mingle their waters at the point of the peninsula, creating resounding, multicolored eddies before forming a single majestic stream, which goes forth to disrupt everything it passes, sweeping aside terraced fields with the back of the hand, with a shrug of the shoulders breaking up the mountains that stretch out downstream as far as the eye can see.

Much closer is an arresting colorful sight that never grows stale, especially when the hot lights of evening shine down. Whether the stroller turns north or south, on the far shore of the each river his eyes are drawn to a profusion of variously shaped hills which, even while trying to outdo each other in beauty, appear to communicate across the waters to make of their very contrast a panorama of audacious harmony. The hills to the north are dressed in tall and somber trees interspersed with great rocks in which inaccessible temples lie coiled; the hills to the south, their already delicate green further softened by pink mists, appear more pleasant and are dotted with picturesque houses and gardens in full bloom. The static quality of this picture is broken by the endless movement of the two flowing rivers and the intense human activity they sustain. Crossing from one shore to the other or coming from afar, countless boats of all kinds, all sizes, from steamers confident of their power to sampans fighting the waves, meet each other, avoid each other the best they can as they strive to pinpoint their destinations. Not far from the tip of the peninsula is the port, constantly bustling. Men embark and disembark, weighed down with burdens and merchandise. When night falls the only sounds heard on the hill are the shouts of men and the lapping of waves. Surrounded by the lights glowing on both sides of the river, the stroller can fancy himself a divinity contemplating the world below from the Milky Way.

In that year, 1944, seven years after the start of the war, the city kept growing, an excrescence taking on monstrous dimensions. In spite of the poverty engendered by seven years of war, in spite of the refugees flocking there, the city, many times destroyed and many times rebuilt, maintained a facade of prosperity, to the benefit of a class of nouveau riche. While waiting for the war's outcome, so long in coming, the city exuded an end-of-empire odor, similar to the stale, musty smell of corpses left to lie under burned ruins.

In the entertainment districts, restaurants and tea houses were packed night and day. To the sounds of music nauseatingly vapid and vulgar, customers with swollen, wine-flushed faces fell upon the collection of dishes spread over the tables, seeking a little forgetfulness. Among the crowd could be seen American soldiers on leave, a head taller than everyone else, drifting from bar to bar accompanied by *jeep girls*.

For us, American films were the greatest attraction. Excitedly we walked along the downtown streets lined with movie houses. Not at all discouraged by the endless lines, we would run from one theater to another. Once inside, what a leap into elsewhere, what a new and exotic world! Another space, another rhythm of life, an overflowing physical force emanating from nature and men. How could we not be struck by the never-failing vitality and the direct, head-on way those men approached life and unleashed their excess energy; by the casual self-confidence and by that material opulence almost unbearable for Chinese in our wartime era. We entered a universe with another type of environment and another form of architecture. The inhabitants of that universe had another kind of relationship with their surroundings as well as with one another. Their needs were other, as were their satisfactions, their thrills and pleasures, living as they did in a state of perpetual, frenzied motion. The stars, male and female, were too glossy, too made-up to be real. It was as if they were not of this earth, as if they had come from another planet.

While a world new and exotic emerged from the shift in space, there was also a shift in time. The Chinese were living in one century and the Americans in another. Centuries are not crossed and mores are not changed that easily. The lengthy kisses and the love scenes where the women boldly showed their charms pierced the armor of

Chinese modesty to the point of pain. In the dark, the moviegoers first submitted to the shock with embarrassment and wonder, then with delight; they felt the blood boil in their veins, and the repressed luvidness of their fantasies rose to the surface. The plots of the films were often grandiloquent or melodramatic. We did not really care. Across the scenery and the characters, we could re-create in imagination the American novels we had read, the works of Hawthorne, Jack London, Steinbeck. . . .

Downtown, near the movie houses, were many theaters. As a prelude to joining Yumei in the world of the traditional opera, we enthusiastically discovered plays. Here it was "spoken theater," Western style, different from the ancient theater, which not only has spoken dialogue but also song, pantomime, and acrobatics. Modern theater does without the masks, the accessories, and the ensemble of symbolic movements through which an actor on an almost empty stage draws space and time to himself and triumphs over them. The modern drama is acted out in a realistic setting, and within strict time limits. The plot gains thereby in intensity, and the theme is closer to life, more contemporary. In Tchoungking, works by a few foreign writers were staged, Anglo-Saxons and Russians, but most were by Chinese playwrights. A whole generation of dramatists was creating prolifically, encouraged by an enthusiastic public. For the times were more than favorable, with an extraordinary concentration of talent gathered in one small area. The war had driven writers, artists, and actors from all parts of China to a few cities behind the lines: Kunming, Guiyang, and most notably, Tchoungking. The majority were leftists or had "progressive" tendencies; their purpose was not to entertain. Some attacked contemporary problems directly in their work, others took up the great enduring themes; all were conscious of participating in an unusual moment and of paving the way for the renaissance of Chinese culture.

That artistic ferment contrasted sharply with the strict control exercised by censorship and with the vast network of surveillance and repression set up by the secret police. Strange situation, strange age! Tchoungking was the wartime capital of the Nationalist Chinese government, the country's lawful government. While carrying out a war of resistance against the Japanese, the Nationalists also massed troops around the Yan'an region, where the Communists had established themselves after the Long March. Early in the war, for the sake of national unity in face of the foreign invader, Nationalists and Communists had come together temporarily. The respite had allowed the Communists to spread out into the countryside in Japanese-occupied zones. Scenting danger, the head of the government had decided to break off with the Communists, while maintaining a facade of unity. Thus, paradoxically, he tolerated the capital's Communist contingent, which was very energetic throughout the war years. It published a newspaper, opened a bookstore, and organized a network of clandestine cells. It formed close ties with intellectuals, artistic circles, and American journalists, many of whom were quick to show sympathy for the cause. That sympathy assured the Communists international prestige and therefore some measure of protection. The result was a paradoxical situation for China: a government enjoying absolute power was obliged to carry out its anti-Communist repression with cunning. A large budget was allocated to the secret police, who had interrogation centers, detention camps, extremely sophisticated weapons, and countless agents. These watched and tracked suspects day and night, arrested them whenever possible, sent them to camps, or saw that they disappeared. But none of this activity could curb the aspirations of those who dreamed of change and renewal. Despite the secret reign of terror, the men won over to the revolutionary cause, armed with patience and eaten up with impatience, found ways to communicate in the shadows. Even if they were total strangers, through unmistakable signals they recognized one another. Looks exchanged, smiles of complicity always seemed to say: "Ah, you're one of us." And each would let himself be drawn into the vast underground movement. Later, much later, I would realize that those short years before the end of the war had constituted a precious time of freedom. And indeed the history of China, a country where imperial order was once the rule, is studded with moments of relative freedom, when one dynasty was ending and another had not yet imposed a new order. In these transition periods, men of valor and outstanding heroes would rise up almost everywhere. They plied the vast empire, meeting other men of their kind, and together they would experience unfailing comradeship, unlimited sharing. Modeling themselves after characters in the popular novels of ancient times, the revolutionaries of the forties braved all dangers and savored their underground life: clandestine meetings, secret messages, mute embraces. And the repression itself intensified their emotion, as with lovers having a forbidden affair. The threat of punishment only added to the shudder of delight.

In our own way we felt the shudder brought on by terror, when we went into the "progressive" bookstores or into Xinhua, "New China," run by the Communists. The secret police liked to rent apartments opposite such establishments. Inside the bookstores, agents in civilian clothes mingled with the customers and would follow them outside. The police were easy to spot by their lackadaisical way of skimming through the books and their inquisitive stare. Many readers were aware of the danger; that did not stop them from seeking books, so great was their thirst for reading material and for the sight of other faces. The danger was less for those content to read on the premises; it was greater for those who made purchases, since a "red" book provided the agents more than enough incriminating evidence. In spite of the risk, one day we both left Xinhua with books.

Once outside, we walked fast. In a low voice, Haolang advised me not to look back. We turned down a bustling avenue and stopped briefly to look at a movie poster. That was when we noticed the *tewu** following us. Although he kept a fair distance behind, he did not really try to hide.

"I'm going to get him," Haolang said as he walked.

"Watch out, he must be armed."

"I'll be careful." Then he went on in a cheerful tone: "Ah, this takes me back to the good old days when I was in the Artists' Group. We had dealings with those characters."

*Secret police agent.

"Let's go into this alley," said my bold friend. "Fine, right here. I'll stand behind the big doorway. And you go on your way, faster, as though nothing is wrong."

It was too late to object, and in spite of a back suddenly stiff and a pair of wobbly legs, I tried to speed up. The already gloomy alley was made even darker by the famous Tchoungking fog, which had been hovering over the city since early September.

A few minutes later, I heard a stifled cry and the sound of a body falling. I had barely turned around when I saw my friend running toward me. We both exited the alley quickly, hurried down some steps, and came upon on another avenue, where we melted into the crowd. Muffled by the fog and the hum of vehicles, two belated gunshots saluted our deliverance.

Laughing, Haolang recited the martial arts rule as if it were a haiku: "A punch in the kidneys, a punch in the jaw, a kick in the stomach, and that's it."

The next day we left that beloved, accursed city behind.

18

AFTER TCHOUNGKING, it was deep into the far reaches of Sichuan. Our journey would last over a month. With very little money—the State did not renew our student stipends past high school—we often had to stop and take on odd jobs for food and lodging. Aside from a few times when circumstances required boarding a bus or a boat, we traveled on foot, under very trying conditions. Nothing could have discouraged us however. The joyful expectation of soon seeing Yumei and the discovery of the vast province lent an appropriate pace to our trek and created a unique experience for us, a true initiation. Our whole life long we would pause and remember, with the realization that it had been the same in the back country as in Tchoungking: despite government control and the weight of incomprehensible tradition, for both China and us those days could not have been more unsettled or more exciting.

Except for the Mount Lu of my childhood, I knew nothing of the Chinese countryside other than areas close to the big cities. My friend, however, had knocked about all over China. He knew the yellow loess plains of the north as well as the regions of the lower Yangzi crisscrossed with canals and dotted with lakes. Nevertheless, he was impressed by the haughty aspect and flamboyant beauty of this inland landscape of continental climate and strong contrasts.

No need to seek out the well-known sites, such as Mount Emei or Mount Erlang. The most insignificant little corner of this land bears bold witness to its carnality. Deep valleys, with their delicate blood-red clay and their network of paths, evoke the open entrails of a primeval soil. Zigzag paths scale the valley slopes, wind through the terraced fields, and climb toward peaks crowned with dense vegetation or flanked with great overhanging rocks. Once above the rocks, seated in the shade of leafy trees, the hiker is treated to the panorama of a multicolored valley and its towering shapes, a scene often enveloped in a haze that rises from the water sparkling in the rice fields.

From time immemorial thought to be endowed with "heavenly favor," Sichuan fed those who had taken refuge there during the long years of war—half of China. Visitors from elsewhere have always been impressed by the varied and abundant produce of this fertile land. Extraordinarily juicy fruits: oranges, pomelos, and mandarins, as well as peaches, kakis, plums, jujubes, and sugar cane. And there are vegetables, brightly colored, odorous. These often have an insolently sensual look. The bamboo shoots stripped of their leaves and the giant turnips covered with rootlets resemble erect penises. Cabbages enveloped in long smooth leaves, jade or emerald colored, evoke the plump arms of well-to-do women, while eggplants and squash, round and shiny, bring up irresistible memories of the tanned thighs of washerwomen squatting at a bend in the river.

The riches of nature made it that much harder to accept the poverty of the peasants, victims of an unjust landowning system, although they were better off than those in other regions of China. To a certain extent the war had been good to them: agricultural products had become infinitely precious commodities, but even the most privileged among them were not that well off. Whatever their living conditions, they all respected the tradition of hospitality, readily sharing their meals with honest travelers who knocked at their doors. There would be a corner to sleep in for those who offered to help in the fields, especially if it was harvest season.

Once again I observed how the people of this land, sustained by its bountiful crops, had themselves been formed by them. The peasants were rarely coarse or vulgar. The work of setting out rice plants, which requires patience and meticulousness, had generated a race hardened by work but refined in spirit. They spoke rhythmically, resonantly, their persuasive intonation adding a special flavor to the words, which were dotted with imagery as piquant as the roasted peppers that accompanied every meal.

We would not forget one family in particular, whom we had asked for hot water to go with our noon rations. Hearing our knock, an aged peasant with a long pipe in his hand opened the door.

"*Lao-fu**, might we have a little hot water?" Haolang asked. Then, to reassure the man, he pointed to the bag we had placed under the only tree: "We're having a little rest there, in the shade."

It was the tired but cheerful look of the two travelers that reassured him, and he answered kindly: "My son and daughter-in-law are working in the fields. I shall ask my granddaughter to prepare water and bring it to you." And he called to someone inside: "Big sister, boil a little water!"

Soon the old peasant, accompanied by his granddaughter—a girl of fifteen or sixteen—came out with a container of hot water. Seeing us take our noon meal from the bag, he issued a spontaneous invitation: "But it's hot here. Come inside and eat. We have already had lunch: you can use the table."

We sat down to eat, but when the girl saw our lunch of cold *mantou*† and *shaobing*,‡ she rushed to the kitchen, returning with a dish of sautéed rice and eggs, to which she had added green peas and a sprinkling of chives. The rice mixed with the yellow slivers of egg

*Old father.
†Steamed rolls.
‡Sesame crackers.

yolk and the green vegetables gave off an exquisite odor, enhanced by a harmony of color that could not have been more pleasing. Touched by the ferocious appetite of the two strangers devouring the rice, she disappeared again and reappeared with a plate of vegetables marinated in salted, seasoned water, the famous Sichuan *paocai*. These vegetables are treated to retain their original freshness and their color, which turns even brighter as they soak in their crocks, big earthenware vessels with blue decorations. Each mouthful of sautéed rice, accompanied by wonderfully crisp cabbage and turnips, had an unusual earthy taste. The meal ended with a *doufu** soup. Frugal though it was, this hastily assembled meal remained memorable.

As we ate, the master of the house overcame his reserve to ask, "What do you do?"

"We are students. We've just finished high school."

"So you're *dushuren*.† Very good, very good. 'In books, there is a house of gold.'"

Then he continued with a mischievous smile: "'In books, there is jade beauty.'" Here the old man was drawing from the rich reservoir of proverbs that form the basis of colloquial wisdom. The two proverbs he quoted meant that success in studies assured one good fortune and a beautiful wife.

"Nothing is less certain! Look at us, we are living like two vagabonds."

"It will come. In our family, we've always hoped that somebody could go to school. But our life is hard, there is so much work. And how can we pay for schooling? My grandfather couldn't read, nor could my father, and it is the same with me and my son."

We thought we saw in his eyes a glimmer of regret for the possibility of another life.

After a pause, he asked: "Where are you going?"

Without going into detail, I answered that we were heading for the city of N. to see someone who worked in a theater.

"But that is quite far. It's fine, it's fine. As they say: 'Traveling ten thousand *li* equals reading ten thousand books.' Ah, the theater! Not

*Tofu.
†Men who know how to read.

long ago we had a real downpour. Afterward our villages brought an itinerant theater troupe here. Two years ago, you see, we had a terrible drought; we emptied all our storage lofts and we nearly starved to death. This year began the same, with drought. We had the monks say prayers. I don't know how many times we performed rites of entreaty. Men stayed out in the sun for hours, prostrate, hitting their heads against the cracked soil covered with dead grasshoppers, appealing to heaven, beating their torsos bloody with sharp reeds. Rain finally came; a good rain, a heavy rain. That is when we had the troupe perform. No better way to thank the rain god. It was nice, wasn't it, big sister?"

Suddenly included in the conversation, the girl blushed and nodded, while her grandfather went on: "The next day they took down their stage and left. These are special people, they don't lead an ordinary life. But they bring much enjoyment to our villages. . . ."

Again we thought we saw in his eyes a gleam of regret for the possibility of another life. But he had repressed such longing for many years. Having come from the land, he would remain faithful to the land, and to that piece of it his ancestors had passed down from generation to generation. To maintain at all costs the continuity of human occupation, so he could be there to offer hot water and sautéed rice to passersby on a scorching summer day.

Won over by the family's friendliness, we decided to stay a few days. There was plenty of work in those early weeks of fall. Haolang felt quite at home; he did not find physical work repugnant. Barechested, he plunged readily into laboring with the family. Beside him, I struggled. I had to limit my participation in the heavy tasks and I spent most of the day with the girl and her little brothers, cutting grass for the pigs. The chores all done, everyone, the two newcomers included, sat around an immense basin of hot water after supper, laughing and chattering as we washed our feet. We would linger there for a long while, remembering to feed the bath more hot water from time to time.

We two migrant workers slept in a little room adjoining the pigsty. It took us awhile to grow accustomed to the sickening heavy odor. Fortunately, the room overlooked a rear courtyard from which wafted the fresh scent of vegetables and fruits drying in the open air. The girl had carefully laid out the fruit and vegetables on large flat baskets: eggplants, corn, lotus roots, jujubes, plums, and more. All those hues and shapes massed together created a veritable flowerbed. The rear courtyard was the girl's special space; she passed through it often when caring for the pigs. As our little room was stifling and our bed full of fleas, we soon decided to spend our nights in the courtyard, under the stars.

The day arrived when we had to return to the road. The family was almost sorry to see us leave. After walking nearly an hour, as we rounded a hill there reached us one of those *shange** which is sung, according to tradition, by a woman's high-pitched voice. Through that voice, with its note of age-old longing, we seemed to hear all the buried sensibility and all the frustration of the Chinese woman, the peasant fated to spend her life in her enclosed valley, the city lady condemned to live in a house tight with doors. Deeply touched by the increasingly poignant song, we were even more moved when we raised our heads and saw atop the hill the peasant girl in silhouette. We knew that our exotic presence had aroused in her a longing for faraway places.

19

ALTHOUGH WE WOULD have rather spent every night in peasant dwellings, we could not always avoid the towns. Once there, instead of staying at inns—usually filthy and squalid—we sought out schools or temples. Unwrapping the blankets we kept in waterproof canvas, we were happy to sleep on the hard surfaces of tables pushed together or on doors removed for the occasion. We spent little. For our evening meal, we bought heavy, filling flatbreads and waited in a corner of the restaurant until the crowd was gone. Then, in exchange for a tip, the now-idle waiter

*Mountain songs.

would gladly serve us a soup made of boiling water poured into the skillet used for sautéing the entrées; the cook added a sprinkling of chives and vegetables in season. After dark we would get the famous *dandan mian* sold by strolling vendors. This consisted of a kind of thin noodle prepared right before the customer, who could choose a sauce from among a dozen tasty offerings. Sometimes we would be pleasantly surprised with an invitation to a private home. Since I made it a habit to take out my sketch pad and draw portraits in the tea houses, my subjects were apt to approach us, with Haolang's conversational skills forging immediate bonds.

We sat in every tea house as long as we could. That gave us a chance to rest and, more important, to solve a major problem: thirst. Except at springs, the water was not safe to drink, and travelers were always looking for boiled water. In a tea house we were well off, for one order of tea meant we could stay there for hours, stretched out in chairs, undisturbed. The waiter was armed with an immense kettle and circulated among the tables, filling each teapot as soon as it was empty. With flawless technique, he would lean over the patron's shoulder and pour a long stream of boiling water into the pot or fill a cup to the very brim with never a splash or an overflow.

In the wild, far from towns, thirst can be a cruel ordeal for the traveler. In that inland province with its continental climate, the uncompromising summer sun scorches everything. And besides climate, there is geography. Capricious roads climb toward the highlands then hurry down to the deep valleys. (When a peasant is asked how far it is from one village to the next, he always replies: to get there, it's this many *li,* to come back it's that many *li.* For his figures take into account the layout of the land, one *li* on an uphill stretch counting as two!) In the desert thirst may be a matter of course, but here it hits hard without warning. The traveler sweats, dries himself off, sweats again until suddenly he feels emptied of all his water, and is prepared to melt into the red clay. In Sichuan everything tends toward the extreme: overwhelming sweat, overwhelming thirst.

But overwhelming satisfaction, too. Nature seems to send the oppressed traveler a signal by placing on all the high slopes little groves of *huanggo,* a tree whose dense foliage and spreading branches provide ample, beneficial shade. A cooling breeze blows through these trees and beneath them vendors have set up with their wares, great piles of oranges, watermelons, sugar cane. And, there is the hot chrysanthemum tea that makes sweat pour off the traveler before it quenches his thirst.

The traveler passing through as summer draws to a close will find that the weather is not always uniform, and there are a few delightful moments in store for him. Suddenly, unpredictably, clouds can cover the incandescent sky. Then, while the atmosphere turns heavy beneath the blinding luminosity of the heavens, the greens of an abundant nature grow increasingly faint and transparent. At a certain point, all comes to a stop, waiting. The valley holds its breath to listen as the song of the *dujuan** echoes through the countryside. Then comes the shower. A generous shower, equally kind to all. Grateful travelers let it wash them head to toe. Soaked too is the countryside, which now glistens emerald and hosts a myriad of red and violet blooms bearing the same name as the bird, *dujuan*. For it is said that these flowers with the vivid dazzling colors are the blood spit out by the *dujuan* as they sing. The birds, according to legend, are the reincarnation of the soul of the Emperor Wang, a sovereign of Antiquity eternally seeking the soul of his deceased beloved. At this season divided between sorrow and expectation, the whole region inhabited by the legend rings with the echo of the supernatural.

In those days, we were under the influence of the Gide we had read. We were experiencing physically the writer's favorite expression, "thirst slaked." Later, I would read Rimbaud. Rather than his most well-known poems, what I immediately took to was "The Comedy of Thirst." Reading Rimbaud, I was also to remember a thought I had entertained in the valleys of Sichuan: man may be an animal with an eternal thirst, but nature has the water to satisfy his desire. It would seem that creation does not create any desires it cannot satisfy. In other words, man is thirsty because water exists. Man is of course at liberty to desire but can desire no more than what

*Turtledove.

reality has to offer, hidden deep inside itself. Even when he goes so far as to desire the infinite, it is because the infinite is already there, provided for him. In the course of events it is as if what man desires the most was there beforehand, contained in the desire; if not, how could he have desired it? Once again, I was convinced, as with the Western cakes of my childhood, that fulfillment of a human desire was to be found in the very desire itself.

This conditional freedom of human desires, far from demeaning or narrowing human existence, raises it, expands it, putting it at the heart of a vast mystery. And the human adventure is thereby rendered less chimerical. As I walked with the Friend to meet Yumei, I persisted in this strong but perhaps naive conviction. I told myself that if wandering was my earthly destiny, at least I was transforming that fate into a passionate quest whose purpose was bound to be disclosed to me one day.

As for Haolang, thirst awakened in him an old passion, dormant during his high school years: alcohol. All along the way, off the main roads there were little establishments that made alcoholic beverages from sorghum or rice; the fermenting grain could be smelled for ten leagues around, attracting lovers of drink like a magnet. To keep Haolang company as he enjoyed his jug, I too took up sampling the pungent brews.

Upon leaving an alcohol establishment one day, I was seized with violent stomach and intestinal pains. Unable to take another step, I collapsed and lay curled up at the foot of a tree. Seeing my state, Haolang ran to a nearby town and found a chair and bearers. They transported me to a larger town where there was a hotel, a noisy place built in traditional style. The room's walls, of finely carved wood inlaid with tiles, did little to keep out the hubbub and the music issuing from the corridors and the neighboring rooms. And at first we had to defend ourselves against the visits of a persistent floor attendant, who with the best of intentions brought hot towels and tea, offered snacks and cakes, and discreetly mentioned prostitutes. Finally the room returned to its role as a room shutting out the world. Meanwhile, my pain had not let up. But I did not call for a doctor, knowing from past experience that medicine had no power against an illness that came from deep inside; only patience and endurance could overcome it. To ease the pain a little, Haolang held my hand for a long while, silently. Then, tired himself, he stretched out next to me. Sensing the powerful muscular body and the peaceful breathing of my friend, I was soothed. The creature sleeping beside me was blessed with a country body. Like the Chinese peasant, he could drink water from the rice fields without falling ill, and he could endure the onslaughts of bugs and mosquitoes without flinching. That sturdy but supple body seemed to drain from my own puny body all the bad blood and all the bitter secretions, leaving only the traces of alcohol intoxication, now an intoxication purified. After midnight, nestled against the sleeping body of my companion, there came over me a feeling of deliverance and well-being such as I had rarely known.

20

N O TOLERANCE FOR alcohol—what a handicap! Quite simply, it cut me off from the reality of Chinese life. Eventually I came to see that. Isn't our reality soaked in rice wine, that yellow liquid warmed before it's drunk, whose fumes transport one to another world; and in sorghum wine, too, a strong liquid that floods the body, making it resound from head to toe like a violently struck gong? Intoxicating drink is an everlasting spring that irrigates daily life across every stratum. Since Antiquity, haven't thousands of our poets glorified wine and sung its virtues? Fortunately, during the long trek the Friend was there to save our honor and to handle some unexpected encounters.

In a market town's tavern one day, we watched from our obscure corner as a man entered, an imposing and disturbing figure. It was not hard to guess he was one of those petty chieftains who headed secret societies and liked to exercise the powers of a local tyrant. He sat down at the most centrally located table. To the waiter who had stopped everything to hurry over, he uttered his order in a few words. The waiter quickly brought several jugs of wine and a variety of snacks: crunchy gizzards, marinated tripe, roasted peanuts, thousand-year-old eggs, et cetera.

The noise and commotion in the room came to a halt. The only sounds were those made by the man: he poured the liquid into his bowl, drank with his thick lips, and emitted satisfied "ah, ahs."

"So nobody wants to keep me company?"

No one moved. Everyone knew his reputation as a drinker and the humiliation he could inflict on those who couldn't keep up with him.

"You're all cowards!" And he went back to his bowl.

"Here, for sure, they're all wimps!" He laughed heartily. Then he pounded a raging fist on the table and shouted: "I'm going to get mad!"

Looking toward our corner and seeing unfamiliar faces, he added, "What's going on over there?"

Haolang rose and approached him. Mildly surprised by the height of the young man who was obviously not from the province, the man asked, "Where are you from?"

"I'm from a land beyond the Walls."

Did that impress a man to whom Manchuria was another world? Or did Haolang's faraway origins pose a challenge to the petty tyrant, who wanted to control everything within his fief? Whatever his thoughts, he filled a bowl and proffered it to Haolang: "Drink up!"

My friend emptied the bowl in one gulp. The act brought a "very good" from the man; nonetheless, he did not stop there. He filled Haolang's bowl again and again, all the while quaffing his own.

The session lasted a long time. Haolang did not slow down nor did his color change. The Chinese love alcohol but get drunk easily; they have always admired those who can drink heavily without getting drunk, a sign of virility. The man soon realized he had found his equal in the man from Manchuria. Abruptly he asked; "What do you do for a living?"

"I've just finished high school."

"And later?"

"I shall be a poet."

The man was somewhat disconcerted by this incongruous answer. To show that he had a bit of learning, he recited, haltingly, one of the Tang quatrains all Chinese know my heart. Finished, he ordered: "Sing me something."

Now it was the poet who appeared disconcerted: he had not seen this coming. After momentary hesitation, he began declaiming long poems by Qu Yuan, written more than two thousand years ago. Being drunk helped, and he entered more and more into the intoning of the verses, with a strong northern accent that impressed his listeners. He ended with the lines:

Lifting my gaze, I scan the horizon:
The longed-for return, when will it come?
The bird takes flight to regain its nest:
And the fox, dying, turns to its lair,
Upright and loyal, yet I live in exile,
When shall I forget my fate, what day, what night?

That drew a ringing "Hao!"* from his drinking companion. As the man delivered the accolade, he took from his pocket a paper covered with cabalistic signs. Handing it to Haolang, he explained: "It is Lord Bao who gives you this, and it will protect you."

The first impulse of the two beneficiaries was to toss out the crumpled sheet, a carelessly sketched talisman bearing the signature of Lord Bao. We certainly did not foresee that there would be a moment on the journey when it was to serve as our identity card. The moment came when the chief of police, followed by two recruiters, seized us in a market town sleazier than most. A little earlier we had had the misfortune to catch his eye. Suspicious of our appearance and our accents, without preliminaries he had asked: "What are you doing, you two?" "As you can see, we're not doing anything. We're just walking." That answer, simple and truthful, had probably sounded insolent. At the time the inquisitor had said nothing. He had been content to spit on the ground, then spit out an

*Bravo!

insult: "Go on and walk then, son of a bitch." Now, escorted by the two recruiters, he was on the road hunting down the two "vagabonds." Weapons in hand, the three representatives of "law and order" were ready to shave our heads on the spot. Had we not quickly shown the talisman they would have put a rope around our necks and sent us to the army, that corrupt army, by then composed solely of unfortunates conscripted by force.

And so we confirmed the hard way what we already knew: this countryside laboriously tamed by the peasants, this bountiful, dazzling natural world was controlled by dark and powerful forces. Behind the bureaucrats, ferocious themselves, there moved hidden powers: secret police, secret societies . . . Honest folk were forced to maneuver skillfully not to be caught in their nets. One always had to avoid "tickling the tiger's mustache," as the old saying goes. But what else could we have done that day at the little temple of the Sun Gods? There, near the bridge, a group of good-for-nothings, members of the local militia, were trying to rob a drunk old landlady. Knowing nothing of banks, safes, or other hiding places, the woman had sewn her meager savings inside her threadbare garment. When Haolang interfered, they pinned him down and pointed a dagger at his face, intending to leave a mark in blood. The only defense possible was to utter the magical name once again: "Beware! Lord Bao will not be happy when I see him!"

Freed, we two intruders in that cruel and murky world could hardly feel proud. We owed our not being disfigured to that Lord Bao who without batting an eyelid had probably disfigured, deflowered, or whipped to death more than one innocent person. And who was still innocent? Was there anyone left who was not contaminated? The second drinker we met, perhaps?

While ordering wine in a dingy little establishment we had noticed a man seated in a corner a few tables away. He was middle aged, fairly tall, and strikingly thin, with a piercing stare that wine only accentuated. Haolang easily emptied his jug and asked the waiter to bring another. Following suit, the man requested a second jug for himself. "Here we go, it's a contest again!" I thought, worried. In the middle of the second jug I was relieved when my friend and the man exchanged smiles of complicity. The waiter had just brought us a serving of marinated tripe, and Haolang gestured to the man, inviting him to our table. It was a gesture of conventional politeness and the other was under no obligation to accept. He did not have to be urged, however, and came to join us. He was obviously looking for conversation.

Once at our table, he took a look around and was reassured as to our intentions. He lost no time in spotting the sketch pad in my bag, and in Haolang's, the collection of Esenin's poems and the collection of Chekhov stories. After several bowls, thoroughly drunk, he grew bold and told us things.

He had been a teacher. When the war started, having taken up the revolutionary cause, he left for Yan'an, but before he could reach his destination, he was arrested and sent to a camp. Following three years of internment and reeducation, they decided he wasn't that dangerous, and he was released. Returning to Tchoungking, he had worked as a cashier in a store. He was obliged to furnish the secret police with regular reports on his whereabouts and activities. Thanks to connections, he managed to escape from police surveillance. Hidden in the country, he made a living from odd jobs and, as my father had once done, from lessons and writing for others, all the while running the risk of being caught.

One day he suffered an attack of appendicitis and was taken to one of those primitive hospitals found in isolated country places. The operation went badly, and he was given up for dead. But in the morgue he was saved in extremis by his weak moans. The doctors adopted him, and ever since he had worked at the hospital as a nurse.

He spent his days struggling with the people's woes, physical and otherwise. Dressing gangrenous flesh, emptying waste, aiding peasants bitten by rabid dogs, treating the infected vaginas of raped children, enduring cries that broke the heart and wails for which there was no response.

He had but one means to fight his loneliness and depression: alcohol. "It helps protect against disease, and it helps me sleep." Coughing a little, his eyes feverish, he added: "I think I'm in the early stages of tuberculosis."

Pulling himself together, looking his two interlocutors straight in the eye, he spoke firmly: "The battle will be hard, but deliverance is near. The rest has no importance—it's all going to be swept away. Everything will be new, you'll see."

When we said good-bye, the poet took the two books from his bag and gave them to that man who, having miraculously escaped death, no longer feared it.

My happiest encounter was with an old painter-hermit. As I sat under a *huanggo* sketching the landscape, I heard a clear voice in back of me: "Young man, I see you are a painter. Would you two like to have a cup of tea at my house?" I turned around and thought I was seeing the Taoist monk of my childhood; there was the same serene and impassive face, but in this case lit up by a kindly smile tinged with irony. We followed him to his dwelling, a thatched cottage shielded by wild grass, behind it a vegetable garden. The old man showed us his amazing collection of ancient Chinese paintings as well as his own work. Some of his pictures were ethereal, others vibrated with density; all exhibited a superb mastery of brush and ink that breathed new life into pure Chinese tradition. He told us that in his own youth, back at the beginning of the century, the family fortune had allowed him to travel extensively in Japan and Europe. In the twenties and thirties, throughout the Yangzi valley he had enjoyed something of a reputation as a painter. He had been acquainted with all the great artists of his generation. But ten years ago he had given up mingling with society and had retired to this remote place to dedicate himself entirely to his art.

21

T RAVELING BY BOAT, we ended our journey in the city of N., a port on a major tributary of the Yangzi. N. was a prosperous city that bustled with business activity and the transit of goods. After an hour spent clearing a path through the countless sampans and barges that jammed the port, our boat finally docked. The port district swarmed with people shouting loudly and moving briskly; despite this feverish excitement, the ambiance was relaxed and good-natured. Merchants, haulers, and boatmen tried to outdo one another's salty expressions, provoking general laughter. All around there was nothing but tea houses, stalls, restaurants, and shops whose merchandise spilled out into the street. The air was saturated with odors: oil, wine, salt, rice, marinated vegetables, and spices of every sort.

Beyond the port quarter began the city proper; through it ran many streets, the major ones unusually wide for a provincial city. On these streets very old houses rubbed elbows with modern apartments. The two new arrivals were directed to the theater, which stood near the main intersection. Since it was already late afternoon, lodging was our first concern. We made some inquiries and were delighted to find a YMCA hostel. After a month of peregrination under appalling conditions, this clean and quiet place seemed an unhoped-for paradise, a good omen. The room was bare, with two single beds, between them a night table on which sat two Bibles in Chinese. Seeing the white sheets made us realize that a bath was imperative.

Once clean, we were as good as new, so to speak, and we set out for the theater. A gigantic sign announced the evening's program: *The White Serpent*, with Yumei in the leading role. So as not to interrupt her preparations, we decided we would see her after the performance. We went to sit in a tea house near the theater. Not surprisingly, this was a meeting place for actors and theater lovers. The atmosphere was out of the ordinary, a mixture of liveliness and unpretentious geniality. Here and there distinctive sounds rose above the general commotion: joyous laughter, a few strains of a familiar air, an unobtrusive melody played on the *erhu*.*

When we began to make out the faces more clearly, we could not help noticing a strikingly corpulent individual ensconced in a corner of the large room next to a wooden post. His body, comfortably settled in the rattan armchair, was topped by an immense head, square

*Chinese violin.

except for the gentle curve of the double chin. He sat there, sparing of gesture, barely moving. Yet there was an aura of great liveliness about him, mainly because of his expressive face, no component of which could be missed. At first he seemed a little drowsy, as if awakening from a long nap, but when the waiter brought him a hot towel, he began to stir. Tilting his head back, the man spread the cloth over his face and with his fat fingers pressed it over all the cracks and crevices of his face so the steam could penetrate more deeply. He uttered a long, long sigh; then he removed the towel and sat up straight again. The waiter, who knew his habits, brought wine and food. We could not take our eyes off the man while he chewed with relish and concentration the things he had slowly and deliberately chosen from his plate. He would screw up his eyes as he savored each morsel to the fullest, as if he had all eternity before him. Eventually he had downed everything, with many a swig of wine. A few minutes later, the waiter, unbidden, brought him tea along with fruit and cakes. The fat man put his hand around an apple, brought it up under his nose, and sniffed it showily. Delicately, sensually, he rubbed it against his cheek until biting the fruit had become an absolute necessity. He bit off a piece determinedly, chewed it slowly but greedily, and swallowed it. While his jaw worked at full capacity, his wide-open eyes had become round with an indefinable kind of excitement and he uttered little grunts punctuated with "Hei, hei! . . . ho, ho! Hum." It was if there were in him two minor actors, each with his role: the one, totally absorbed in enjoyment; the other, watching that enjoyment with sounds of approval. When the whole apple had been devoured, he took a sip of tea. Sighs, silence.

And that was when people approached his table and engaged him in conversation. They started with trivialities, so it seemed. His face was already playing its lively game. In their sockets, his eyes rolled like marbles or showed only white when he raised his head to the heavens; by turns he made his fleshy nose look flat or pointed; his chin wobbled when he laughed, a muffled laugh which never rang out and which might lengthen into a staccato chuckle. Even his ears contributed to the overall effect, for he could make them shake at will like two little fans. Without hearing the words he spoke in his bass voice, we could imagine from a distance the feelings they expressed: astonishment, dread, pity, sadness, or joy, commiseration, sorrow, or anger. His joy, never seemed very genuine, because of the two huge eyebrows that turned down at either end, and because of the mouth, whose corners turned down, too. These four slanting parallel bars marking his face indicated a kind of fundamental disillusion or insurmountable scorn. His perpetual hangdog look was constantly at odds with his facial expressions, which so vividly suggested a never-ending flow of warm feelings. The contrast created something of a comic effect. And actually, almost in spite of himself, almost naturally, the man provoked laughter by everything he said. Obviously, he was a comedian: on stage, his job was to "take the blows," thereby taking upon himself all the scorn for human existence. Even when not on stage, he could not resist using his dramatic power. Even here, speaking with that sinuous, persuasive Sichuanese intonation, he had his audience in thrall.

In a different corner of the room, several people, including some beautiful women, were gathered around a distinguished-looking gentleman. He was dressed simply, in a turquoise blue robe adorned with a long white silk scarf falling from his shoulders. There was something unreal about his appearance, as if he had stepped out of an old engraving. The almond eyes lit up when he smiled, and the delicate, aristocratic face radiated an indefinable charm that blended the masculine and the feminine. He spoke quietly, never raising his voice. At one point we saw him tap out a tune on the table with his fingers; then he hummed a melody. He was apparently describing or explaining a play. He paused occasionally, to pour his tea and raise the cup to his lips. All his gestures exuded elegance and grace. To my surprise, there was something familiar about the gestures. Yes, of course, Fourth Uncle with the nimble hands! Wasn't that his way of pouring tea and holding the cup? "Everything in the world changes," I told myself, "but some gestures have been passed down since Antiquity like a never-ending trickle of water."

As the room became more and more lively, turning into a veritable auditorium, we entertained ourselves assigning parts to everyone who arrived. They were all typed, actors as well as theater enthusiasts, for the latter unconsciously imitated favorite actors with whom they identified. There was one new arrival we did not have to cast, a man around seventy with white hair and goatee: he himself called attention to his role. At the door of the tea house, he noticed his shoelaces were undone. Instead of bending down to tie them, he raised his foot as high as his hands to stand on one leg like a crane, then took his time tying the laces. The task done, he bounded into the air with extraordinary lightness and came to rest in the posture of a general brandishing an invisible weapon, ready for single combat. A good many people gathered round him, and the applause was deafening. With clasped hands, he greeted them all, one by one. He was a retired *wusheng** who came regularly to visit the haunts of his youth and to encourage his juniors. His entrance electrified the room and served as a prelude to the performance, about to begin in the theater next door.

Announced by a brief flourish from the orchestra, the heroine made her slow and stately entrance, and I was overcome with emotion. "With the Lover, all is miracle," I said to myself, "unless it is all illusion."

In the warm ambiance of the theater and under the skillful lighting, everything appeared more than real and at the same time unreal. Are we here? Are we elsewhere? Are we in some fictional space dreamed by men? Might the tears and the pain only be ingredients to make more palatable a journey that goes nowhere, before it all sinks into the oblivion of sleep?

And yet miracle was the only word that all my inspiration could whisper just then. Miracle, my first meeting Yumei at the bend in the garden path. Miracle, finding her again. With my friend I had completed the journey, a long ordeal at whose end all suddenly seemed so easy, as if it had been arranged in advance. Then this performance on the very night of our arrival. She was here, undeniably here, within reach, out of reach. So much herself, so much someone else!

The audience, rowdy in other settings, listened in silence. It seemed purified somehow by the figure of the heroine, although she

---

*An actor-acrobat specializing in martial roles

was *a priori* impure: a serpent. This creature who comes from the depths of universal darkness, who through sincere desire and determined patience becomes a human being, a woman whose beauty is all the more fascinating for its animal origin.

She is initiated into love, a love entirely human but so great that it overcomes all the forces of tyranny and evil.

One of the forces of evil is the monk Fahai, endowed with the magical powers to which the White Serpent's lover, Xuxian, will surrender. Betrayed by all, forsaken even by her lover, the Serpent is to draw unsuspected strength from her unfailing love so she may pursue her earthly destiny. How moving to see the metamorphosis of a beast, in the beginning so humble and so close to the ground, meant to be crushed. She rises to such dignity that the nobility of her soul exceeds that of the man's; thus the drama goes beyond nature, radiating with the supernatural. Before her she finds nothing but a bare space that only the force of her desire can move, a space no human figure can ever fill.

Yumei was heavily made-up in the traditional theatrical manner, and she wore an ornate headdress. The painted face, which represented the Chinese ideal of feminine beauty, could not have been more impersonal; yet I did not fail to recognize all the features of her long-absent face, so often pictured in my dreams: the perfect oval, the delicate nose, the sensitive and sensual lips, the clear and penetrating gaze. Comparing her with the Yumei of old, I detected but a few changes: a more mature voice, a more confident bearing. At one time so wracked with doubts, this woman had striven long and hard to become a true artist in full possession of herself, capable of expressing a myriad of obscure passions.

Absorbed in her role, Yumei could not have noticed my presence. I was thankful for the darkness so that I too could become absorbed in the story, forgetting myself completely. Only at the end of the play did I turn to look at Haolang, who sat transfixed, almost hypnotized.

After the performance we went backstage. From a distance we could see the actress in profile as she lingered to chat with someone before going to her dressing room.

"Yumei!"

She turned around, only mildly surprised, as if she had been expecting me: "Ah, here you are!" Then, looking at my companion: "This is Haolang. Ah, Tianyi, what an artist you've become! He couldn't be more like the sketch you sent!"

And our first moments together ended in happy laughter.

We went to the tea house to wait for Yumei, who had to remove her makeup. I was speechless, overcome by gratitude for the destiny that had allowed me to see the flesh and blood Yumei again, now free and sovereign. To find the lover was like revisiting the land of my birth, like treading barefoot on that familiar clay, so soft and warm with its odor of moss and humus.

And finally, here she was again, sitting across from me now. Almost twenty-three, Yumei was a mature young woman. Under the long lashes, her lovely eyes expressed a cheer and astonishment no longer tinged with melancholy, but with a gravity and determination like those of the heroines she played. Formed by the theater, she was more graceful than ever. Her hands were plumper than before and dimpled.

"Where are you staying tonight?" She asked.

"We found a room at the YMCA."

"It's a good place. The hostel is run by a group of very likable young men; I sang for them at a New Year's party. When did you get here?"

"This afternoon."

"Why didn't you come and see me right away?"

"We didn't want to bother you. We sat in here to wait."

And I went on to describe some of the people we had seen earlier. When I mentioned the comical fat man, Yumei explained: "He is a most unusual fellow. Beneath that grumpy look there is a warm, compassionate person. In fact, he has taken me under his wing. In his youth, he suffered because of a thwarted love affair. He and his lover wanted to commit suicide by throwing themselves off a cliff. Jumping first, he broke a leg when he landed, and his terrified partner stayed at the top. That ended their romance, and he was left disabled. While recovering from the tragedy, he made up his mind to forget his troubles and enjoy life as it came. Early in his career, audiences who saw his terrible limp took him for a clown. But through his personality and his exceptional talent, he earned himself a reputation as a first-rate comic actor. Now he appears only rarely. When he does take on a role, people come from afar to applaud him."

Then, with so much to tell each other, we started chattering away. Midnight came and went, and Yumei showed signs of fatigue. We took our leave.

"You're going to stay around for a while, aren't you?"

"We have no special plans," I answered. "We'll stay until you've had enough of us."

"Yes, when I've had enough of you, I'll chase you away." With a mischievous smile, she continued, "Then, I'll chase after you like a hunter. I'll pursue you until I catch you."

22

FROM THE FIRST DAY, we were totally wrapped up in the life of the theater. We were in our element among performers completely devoted to their art; after all, they were our kind. We did our best to take part in everything, each of us employing his own particular skills. I tried to improve on the playbills; I also took an interest in the sets. Haolang volunteered to write the programs for upcoming productions. He was not satisfied with a mere plot summary; each time he took pains to put the play in its historical context. Sometimes he would even analyze the work and its main characters. He inaugurated the practice of hanging a vertical panel beside the stage with the words of the main songs. That enabled the audience to understand the music better and to appreciate each phrase, each word. Although such innovations may have annoyed the true connoisseurs who knew the plays through and through, they helped bring in a new audience, from the younger generation especially.

We newcomers felt all the more eager to suggest innovations

because the theater here bore the epithet "reformed." Its impresario belonged to one of the region's leading families, a family grown rich in the salt and oil trade. Passionate about the theater from an early age, he had moved to Shanghai in the thirties and had become familiar with all the traditional forms of dramatic art, especially those of Peking and Shanghai. Paradoxically, the war created exceptionally favorable conditions for his interests. The river port of N., his birthplace, became an important commercial center, with a growing population and an opening to the outside world. During the same period, thanks to the concentration of theater people in the Tchoungking area, the capital was witnessing a true renaissance of the dramatic arts. Accordingly, our drama devotee decided to found a theater in his own city, its announced goal the reformation of traditional Sichuan opera. His major reforms consisted of paring down the repertoire, removing a hodgepodge of useless complications from the scenery and the acting style, and cutting the plays to focus the plot and highlight the dramatic moments. An individual of wide-ranging abilities, this combination Maecenas and professional devoted his entire fortune to the project. He had a new auditorium built and opened his huge mansion to the troupe. Not burdened with a coterie, he would hire artists—even unknown ones—the minute he saw they had real talent. He sought out women to interpret female roles. That was how he came to rely on Yumei, whom he had spotted performing on some unimportant stage in Tchoungking. He encouraged new ideas and had no fear of offending the purists. Eventually he built up an outstanding reputation. Artists from Tchoungking came to consult him; from all around great crowds flocked to his plays.

This was my first experience working with a group. It was a community in all ways exceptional, a lively and colorful band of forceful and varied personalities. In the old Chinese society theater folk, like scholar-hermits, were among the freest of people, and also among the poorest. No different from the scholar-hermits who possessed nothing but the brushes for practicing their triple art of poetry-calligraphy-painting, the actors possessed nothing but their own bodies and a few meager props for exercising their particular form of art. Bodies utilized to the fullest, however, bodies adept at song, mime, dance, and acrobatics. Their wealth was in their bodies; they had no personal fortune, no permanent abode. The poorer they were the freer they were, and they lived in an atmosphere of solidarity and sharing.

Along with the scholar-hermits, it was actors who preserved the quintessence of Chinese culture, not only by transmitting it on the stage, but also in their everyday lives, in their slightest utterance, their slightest gesture. For these artists there was no gap between theater and life. By instinct and through discipline they mastered what was necessary for handling themselves properly on the stage; at the same time they mastered what was required to perform everyday actions. With them, everything took on that precision and elegance, that economy of gesture conferred by professionalism. As they moved about the stage and the world, waves of energy flowed from them.

Most of them had little or no education. Their speech was colloquial, never coarse; on the contrary, at times it appeared erudite. The rich theatrical repertoire, which used the classical language, furnished these artists words and expressions for many situations, utterances with a stylized and rhythmical quality that modern speakers of Chinese have lost.

The same sense of rhythm and style prevailed over the whole of their actions, even the most utilitarian. It was a pleasure to watch them walk, greet one another, take a chair, eat and drink, or even lift a bundle. It was as if they were accompanied at all times by an invisible orchestra, an orchestra that had taken up permanent residence inside them. And the things they touched acquired a solidity and a character unknown before, which only they could reveal. Even their way of buttoning a garment, of tying a ribbon, of lighting a pipe had a ritual aspect, as though nothing in real life was trifling and every detail had its significance.

Steeped in this dynamic spirit that conferred a dignity on everything and made it possible to face adversity with panache, I was sometimes ashamed of my own state, pessimistic overall. If I happened to stand before the big mirror backstage, I saw a brow creased with melancholy and a stooping, spiritless body that seemed to shrink into itself.

23

A T THE IMPRESARIO'S mansion, in a remote corner over-looking a little garden, Yumei lived in a spacious room she had divided with a screen. We visited her on days off. Someties she would cook something in the communal kitchen and we would eat with her instead of going to the theater canteen.

A room—a place of one's own. In my wandering life, had I ever really known such a thing? Would I ever, at some future time? Of course, if there is a paradise it is probably without dividers. But here on earth, needing shelter, the human being manages—when he is lucky—to enclose within four walls a chosen space no less pleasing than the abode of the gods. This place of one's own, this room of Yumei's, transforms everything inside into an expected presence and everything that comes from outside into an unexpected gift, doing so with a perfect simplicity. The oval mirror in its silver frame, the openwork porcelain cup, the yellow umbrella next to the green para-sol, the opera librettos piled by the incense burner . . . There just because they happen to be part of a life, these objects become pres-ences through the presence of the one who has gathered them. They are attracted to one another, creating a field of attraction that cannot do without any one of them. They have been taken over by their own silence, which is really an incessant muted hum responding to the song heard in the room. Sad song or happy song. Song of wait-ing. Song of welcome. Welcoming what comes during the course of the day. The brief morning rays and the twittering of birds, retelling each day the innocence of the world. The lingering rays of the after-noon, like a spool of silk unwinding or like echoes of light conversa-tion coming from the hall, from the courtyard, from those who sip tea and munch watermelon seeds while they talk of this and that,

bits of eternal human memory. Then, imperceptibly, the twilight fil-
ters in and touches those in the room. Within its confines they
become once more selves long divided between trust in sweet promise and despair at time's flight. Until the dear voice rings out in the
half-light: "But it's not late, we can still do something . . ."

When the weather was fine, we would enjoy excursions in the
area. Frequently I went off on my own to paint some scene suggested
by Yumei; meanwhile, my friends would go walking. One night after
the performance, Yumei was not tired and she surprised us: "The
moon is so beautiful tonight. It's off to my wood!" She had mentioned the wood innumerable times, but until that night she had not
offered to show it to us. It was several *li* from the city. An hour's
walk, and we were there. We had followed a path that took us to a
small lake surrounded by reeds and trees. Instantly, I recognized this
place as the far corner of the wood near the Lover's family estate, the
little spot where she and I had spent unforgettable moments. While
Haolang went for a swim, Yumei began to talk. "Isn't it true that life
is a mystery beyond our understanding? We were in the darkest of
nights where everything was denied us. Destiny guided us blindly,
without our knowing why we were walking or where we were
going. Now we have a bright night and everything has been given us.
I am here, you are here, we are here. Nothing is lost, everything is
found. Yes, we have found each other and this time we aren't going
to lose each other, are we?"

In response to this question, my whole being was one immense
yes, for these were words I had so much wanted to hear or which I
myself would like to have spoken. I was so moved that no sound
escaped from my throat. But nothing could have been more eloquent
than my whole body nodding in agreement.

The Lover went on: "In Tchoungking, I ended up alone, in the
depths of loneliness and despair. I took a job in a minor theater
singing minor roles. At night, so as not to sink into depression, I
would talk with the characters I was playing, characters whose fate
was like mine.

"One day, Mr. L. arrived and he noticed me. He had confidence in me, even though I had no professional stage training. Little by little, thanks to the patience and enthusiasm of all the members of his troupe, I learned, and I've found fulfillment in my art.

"You know that I lost my family. The troupe has become my new family. For anyone it is a piece of good fortune, having a real family, a cozy shelter where one never feels alone. But a family is made up of members of the same clan, of one's own people. And we know we can't live our whole lives among our own. I have an inescapable longing. I know deep down that I am drawn by something else, no, by someone else, from another place. One day, I realized that the someone else was you, Tianyi. Who are you? An angel dropped down from heaven? A creature born of the same soil from which I came? Wherever you sprang from, a creature infinitely myself and infinitely another. And most telling, you appeared at my family estate at a difficult moment in my life, bringing a face, a look, a voice, a sensibility unlike those of any person I had ever met. We forged a union, a blood union that we could not explain to ourselves much less to anyone else. I felt an overwhelming need to send for you. I thought I'd write to your mother, not at all sure the letter would ever reach you. Miraculously, you heard my call, and you came with Haolang.

"I don't know what will become of us, but I do know that our union, born at a decisive moment in both our lives, is sealed forever. . . ."

She could not go on. But she had said what she had to say, the words which could not have been said at any time other than that night, beside that lake. She seemed at peace now, as if she had made a confession. Under the moonlight filtering through the branches, the moment was crystallized into a piece of jade gleaming with dew.

24

AUTUMN WENT BY, then winter. In the second month of the lunar calendar, spring began to show its face. At the tips of tree branches, timid signs of a delicate green, a vague desire to send forth shoots. Our trio lived in total communion. Our relationship benefited from unusual circumstances: a favorable environment, the theatrical world; favorable times, also. As we had observed in Chungking and in our trek across Sichuan, we were witnesses to a moment in history when an old order struggled vainly to impose its laws, whatever the cost, a moment when conditions of near anarchy made every kind of freedom possible. That the end of the war was near only added to the climate of uncertainty. We asked ourselves about the future: civil war or national reconciliation? Much like the season, the era was heavy with death and the promise of the birth of something unknown. What was occurring at the national level the trio also experienced in its private life.

On a February day I shall never forget, our excursion took us to a forest clearing ten or twelve kilometers from the city. We spent the afternoon visiting a porcelain factory, where we watched the artisans: absorbed body and soul in their work, they operated the wheel with their feet while their hands shaped the soft, pliant clay. A whole afternoon spent in awe of their skillful, caressing motions, so precise and delicate. Motions passed down generation to generation from time immemorial, from the moment the Chinese country dweller first discovered the magic of modeling and firing matter to fashion utensils for household use. A whole afternoon watching shapers of bronze and porcelain. A tribe short on words but long on motion, little given to speeches, their talent lay in their hands and feet, hands and feet that came from clay and were the color of clay.

Artisans like these, repeating the same actions time and time again, perpetuate a circular movement that matches faithfully the rotation of the Universe. Movement seemingly always the same, but renewed each time, subtly different. That is the way the Universe must have begun, stirred by a necessity born of itself; that is probably how it will end.

It is indeed perfect and exhilarating, the spatial circle made by hands and clay, accomplices as the wheel turns; yet this circle fascinates me less than another, invisible, that has the power of a revelation. At some time in the past, the hands born of the originating clay, clay themselves, began kneading and shaping lumps of the same clay to make of it something other that had never before existed, the very emblem of real life. How to explain such a mystery? How could inert clay create skillful hands and inspire them to strive for a dream going far beyond clay? Unless the clay was not merely clay but retained, unawares, traces of an originating humus with incipient desires that would not rest until fulfilled?

Hands, human hands using as an instrument the clay from which they spring, not knowing that they themselves are merely the instrument of the clay. Mysterious circle, enchanting circle, endlessly turning round. And as it turns and turns, a shape appears, hesitant and trembling at first; then it declares itself with a conscious will, as if emerging because of a determination to be and to come into full existence. For everything has been there from the very first, like the fetus of an infant in the mother's womb. A body already constituted and not a succession of elements added one by one. Soaking up the daylight, seeking a balance between solidity and grace, taking on its final shape at last, blending joy and fear. Seeing the shape emerge from a lump of clay is akin to witnessing the miraculous first appearance of life or humankind on earth. For doesn't the Chinese myth say that the Creator mixed water and clay to fashion man and woman?

On the road back the trio proceeded at a slow, steady pace, a little tired but delighted by the rewarding hours spent together. I led the way along a path cutting through a narrow valley. I carried the little vase we had just acquired, and at one point I could not resist the pleasure of raising the object in both hands to feel its shape and enjoy its delicate luster. Walking behind me, my companions smiled at my resemblance to the officiant who carries the offering in front of the procession. I myself laughed at the thought, then silently pictured the exact spot in the Lover's room where I would put the vase in which I would keep an arrangement of fresh flowers. The first would be plum blossoms, for they were now opening. The plum blooms in the cold season; a tree of noble silhouette and soft colors that stand out against the snow, it symbolizes unfailing purity. It was the true emblem of Yumei: didn't her name mean "Jade Plum"? There had been no snow that year. In February, the wind could blow chill. But in that sheltered valley, the air was calm, transparent. Nature's components—the hills, the trees, even the soil—had long stood bare and now looked amazingly clean, smooth, and radiant. Like a piece of porcelain! Yes, the valley was itself an offering bowl fired to perfection, simply waiting for a god to pass over and reach down to consume the offering.

Then, as we walked on, the cry of a bird from on high. The voice of the bird was singularly clear and strong, with a fearsome note of determination—as though the bird had waited its whole life to utter that one wholehearted cry. The cry resounded high in the air, then came down to strike my head like a bolt of lightning. I turned around abruptly and said to my friends, "Hear that . . ." I did not finish my sentence and I saw. What I saw rooted me to the spot and truly destroyed me. Just as the lightning had struck my head and pierced my skull, what met my eyes shattered my heart. What did I see? Oh, almost nothing. A furtive movement. Probably the same furtive movement with which the Exterminating Angel strikes. Haolang held Yumei's hand in his, their fingers closely entwined. With my eyes on them, the two hands quickly drew apart, the friends still smiling. How I wish the hands had not drawn apart and that my two friends had simply been walking together in innocence! But the two hands had drawn apart abruptly, and I was aware of intruding on a private scene. Suddenly I felt in the way; I was excluded, excluded from all that had made up my dream. A reaction reinforced by my two friends' response: "What did you hear . . .?"

That night my heart pounded and my body shook from head to toe, with no respite in which to collect my wits. The world around me was collapsing; inside me, what supported my being had been taken away. Everything was crumbling. The gravitation of the universe had seemingly disintegrated, celestial bodies were falling free and with them, my body. A dizzying descent. I clung to the edge of the bed momentarily, and I lost consciousness.

In the days that followed, however, my friends did not notice the change in me. The blood pounding in my head made my eyes bulge but helped mask my pallor. I was tormented by feelings that horrified me. My need for purity and innocence led me to wish that our three persons had never existed or that we had never met. But since I could not refuse to accept the obvious, I came to desire the demise of the other two, whatever the consequences for me, even my own destruction. In short, I was obsessed by an irresistible urge to murder. One afternoon I recoiled in horror at my thoughts: I found myself lingering in front of a cutlery store, happily contemplating the whole display of useful scissors and knives, fascinated by the steel's dull sheen, which seemed to suggest oblivion by the cutting edges with their pitiless gleam. Ensnared by feelings of violence and hatred, I realized that if I did not wish to commit an irreparable act, my sole recourse was to run away. But one impulse kept me there. Quite certain that my two friends were having an affair, at the same time I could not rid myself of a flicker of doubt, and I wanted everything clarified.

In the days that followed, how did I to pretend to carry on with my life? How could I rise in the morning, repeat the appropriate actions, eat, even laugh when the others laughed? I do not know. Perhaps a certain energy arose from the smug satisfaction of analyzing myself, seeing myself as I really was. From instinct if not from experience, I had always known that the Two was not my destiny. That it would never be mine, the life of a twosome. A lasting one-on-one was foreign to my nature. On the other hand, how strongly I believed in the virtues of the Three! Not only did I believe in them, but I had found real fulfillment in the life of a threesome, and I could imagine no life more complete, no life closer to my dreams than mine beside Haolang and Yumei. And now I was back to being one, with no counterpart, back to my fate as the eternal outcast forced to snatch little bits of life from the sidelines, forced to live through the passion of others. Yes, during those atrocious days, I was tormented by carnal images from my long-ago secret look at Yumei; even as these fed the world of my imagination, they aroused in me feelings of horror and shame. I saw myself once again reduced to the pitiful role of thief, voyeur, and eternal spy.

Really, what could I do but spy? While I feared seeing for myself the cruel truth, I longed for concrete evidence of that truth, even were I to die of it like a moth flying into the flame.

So began some ghastly days: I tried to come upon proof of my misfortune even though I was furious with myself for being so petty, for stooping so low.

If I had to go off and leave the others alone at the tea house where we spent most of our free time, once outside I could not help looking through the window and past the lively clientele to study my friends' demeanor. And it broke my heart, the way the two looked at each other and smiled at each other in a sort of silent complicity, ignoring the people around them. I saw them as surprised by their own audacity, aware of their lack of awareness; but they were powerless to resist what appeared to be carnal floodwaters rushing from a broken dike.

We usually headed for the theater long before the performance. In the past, none of the three had paid much attention to the backstage comings and goings of the other two. But during those days of unbearable suspicion, I counted two occasions when I didn't see either of them for a few minutes. Once again, I pictured them embracing in some hidden corner. And I was irresistibly gripped by disturbing images.

But none of that constituted certain proof. Sometimes, with the strain unbearable, I would feel stirrings of affection and I would accept the intimacy of the other two; on those occasions, my pain was mixed with secret delight, a sharing in the sweetness of love. Their happiness became my own. Used to being torn apart, once again I was witnessing the division of my body into two halves: one rebelling in its pain; the other basking in its benevolence.

Would the torment ever end? Would I someday know the truth?

The day did come; the *coup de grâce* was delivered. The two friends suggested an excursion; resignedly, I agreed. On the pretext that I had to pick up a few things at the YMCA, I left them alone. Barely out the door, I dared to turn back. I saw the scene without much surprise, as though I had been expecting it, as though I were the director and the other two my docile actors. The scene I witnessed: Haolang and Yumei held hands, then they snuggled up close, Yumei nestling her head against Haolang's shoulder, all with no coarseness, with a touching propriety. The graceful scene is engraved in my memory forever.

I did not have the courage to rejoin the other two. I did have the strength to scrawl a note for my friend, which I left in our YMCA room. "I'm going away. Don't look for me. Farewell to you and Yumei."

25

ALKING BLINDLY, I came to a bridge. Long and fairly narrow, with no railing, it spanned a river whose current was swift. I could not cross just then, attracted as I was by the glistening surface of the water that flowed without a pause, without a hint of regret. The water did not attract me, it virtually sucked me into its ripples. How good it would be to face life no more, to let go, to be swept along by this liquid that seemed to know where it was going!

I sat on the edge of the bridge, my legs dangling in space, and I was soothed by the gurgle of the current against the stones of the bridge. Mechanically, my eyes scanned the pale horizon of an indifferent earth where I no longer had ties. Meanwhile, beneath my feet the river sparkled with a thousand eyes and seemed to whisper: "Just one movement and the whole burden of shame and fear will leave your body. Your soul will be a wanderer again, free." Free, really? A voice rose from the bank below, the song of a laundress as she pounded her washing:

Ice cold, ice cold the river,
But fair, fair the spring;
Ice cold, ice cold the river,
But soft, soft my white things...

Only then did I think of my mother, still on earth, the mother whose life consisted of patient resignation and endless waiting. I realized how unbelievably thoughtless I had been. Since arriving in N., I had only written her twice. Should I pass from this earth, no doubt I would be taking her with me. After that, how could I face my father?

In my total despair, I said to myself that if my father still watched over my mother and me, he ought to give a sign at this fateful hour. Yes, a sign. The laundress's song, wasn't that a sign? And wasn't that what providence meant—the good fortune to detect the sign at the right moment? Perhaps my father had never stopped giving me a sign. His voice, breathless from asthma, echoed in my ear: "Do not do anything stupid. Do not cause your mother grief; she could not be consoled, even in another life.

"Let's go off the marked path. Follow me." My father had turned to speak to me. We were climbing Mount Lu. "This way is harder and more dangerous—above all, no missteps—but it's under these overhanging rocks that the best plants are found. When I first came to Mount Lu for plants, I didn't find them. One day I met two old mountain men sitting under a tree. They taught me how to search for plants. Which proves that Confucius was right when he said: 'Among three men you meet by chance, there is at least one who can be your master.'" Hearing the word *master* as I sat lost on my bridge with the water rushing below, I recalled that I had never had a master. Other than my father. I thought of my father, who had shown me how to hold the brush, soak it in the ink, and make my first calligraphy character. That was my true birth into this world. And as I remembered my father, his image blended into that of the old painter-calligrapher I had met on my travels with Haolang.

Was I living a moment repeated so often in Chinese history? At a bend in a deserted road or in the recesses of an obscure valley, a young person encounters an old man who has been waiting for him.

If the young man cannot see what is there, he will proceed on his way; if he can see, he will enter into his real life. Before the old man disappears as mysteriously as he has appeared, he will deliver a crucial message through word or gesture. That is how the sign of the father is perpetuated, the sign through which China has survived for so many millennia.

At that point could there have been any father but the old calligrapher who had given me a sign even as he played innocent? He would take my hand, place in it a thick brush soaked with ink, and initiate me into the drawing of the true sign of life. It was the only thing I could do. A single brush is enough to remake a life, just as a thin plank is enough to save a drowning man.

Like the prodigal son, I retraced my steps on the road I had taken with Haolang as we went to Yumei.

26

FINDING THE ROAD to the old painter's dwelling was no easy task. Never dreaming I would see him again, I had not taken note of the way. A painful road, too, for it brought back memories of my hope-filled journey with Haolang. I searched, walking alone, all the while pondering the humble but edifying speech that would convince the hermit to accept me as his disciple. At long last I stood before the door of the hermitage. My heart pounding, I knocked. To my great surprise, when the master opened the door he did not appear astonished. "It is good you are back. I was expecting you," he said.

Once I was inside, he spoke plainly: "The great ancient tradition is what I can teach you. You are young, you live in a time open to all kinds of influences, some of them coming from afar. But it would be regrettable for you to remain ignorant of the living treasures of the past, which have proved their worth. So, to begin with, master the best of our tradition. How? Through the path you have already followed: start with calligraphy; go on to drawing, which teaches mastery of line. Then take up working in ink, the end being the creation of an organic composition in which the full embodies the substance of things and the empty ensures the circulation of the vital forces, thereby joining the finite to the infinite, as in Creation itself."

Later, after he had instructed me in the use of line and the techniques of organic composition, the master said: "Chinese painting is based on an apparent paradox: however it expresses visible or invisible life, it is always humbly obedient to the laws of the real; at the same time, it aims straight for the Vision. But there is no contradiction here. For true reality is more than the shimmering appearance of the exterior, it is vision. In no way does vision derive from the dream or the fantasy of the painter; it results from the great universal transformation set in motion by the breath-spirit. Being set in motion by the breath-spirit, vision can be captured by man only through the eyes of the spirit, what the Ancients called the third eye or the eye of Wisdom. How does one make that eye his own? Only through the way of the Chan masters, namely, the four stages of seeing: seeing; no longer seeing; profound non-seeing; re-seeing. When we finally re-see, we no longer see objects as outside ourselves. They are now an integral part of ourselves, and the work of art that comes from re-seeing is an exact projection of an enriched and transfigured interiority. So, it is essential to attain the Vision. You still hold things too tight. You cling to them. But living things are never fixed or isolated. They are caught up in the universal organic transformation. In the time it takes to paint them, they go on living, just as you yourself go on living. While you are painting, enter into your time and enter into their time, until your time and their time merge. Be patient and work slowly, deliberately."

My life with the master was not entirely devoted to the severity of lessons, however. Punctuated by walks and study outdoors, it was a life of constant celebration. There was not a moment we did not commune with the inexhaustible riches of nature, our eyes alert and our hearts joyful. The master led his disciple along secret paths to secluded places where the ideal China lived on. Most often it would be to a valley of sloping terrain studded with steep rock, not a good spot for farming. There were tiny fields, however, veritable jewels set in the rock, which brightened the countryside with their ever-changing colors. These fields were cultivated by peasant-hermits; when passing through the valley we never failed to stop at one house or another to sample new wine or taste freshly harvested vegetables. Then we would be on our way, penetrating deep into the valley, where resounded the cascade of a waterfall, where echoed the songs of orioles and turtledoves. Where, beyond a barrier of blackberry bushes and liana, we reached a kingdom that seemed to be waiting for us: a rounded hillock halfway up the mountain, sheltered by stands of ancient trees and composed of smooth steplike rocks. Unknown to all, we sat in contemplation.

It was as if we were sheltered in some cove, surrounded by grasses and plants of pungent aroma; by ageless pines whose song rose at the passing of the breeze; but mostly by rocks, some noble and stark, their faces displaying rhythmical folds, others craggy or calm, all of them playing a dangerous balancing game with the void. In the distance, the mountain opposite shone infinitely green and beneath a thousand changing facets revealed its one face. We would get down to drawing at last, sometimes with a brush, but more often with a plain reed or a sharpened bamboo stick. For, more than the minutiae of nature, the master demanded that I capture the inner thrusts, the lines of force moving things. And hasn't it always been true that through these things—rocks, trees, mountains, streams—and by affinities with them, the Chinese express their inner states, their carnal urges as well as their spiritual aspirations? In the master's company, I learned to observe the evolution of things and to sense behind their solid form the working of an invisible dynamic flow. And at rare moments, I did not doubt that my inner impulses were in perfect harmony with the pulsations of the Universe.

Working so intensely every day, I soon began to feel a new being emerge and grow in me. After some quick calculations I realized that only three months had passed since my arrival; but I had really forgotten time and was convinced I had lived three years or even thirty under the hermit's roof.

.　　　.　　　.

ONE DAY the master summoned me. Half solemn, half joyful, he said: "I know that you question yourself occasionally, and I know what it is you ask. What should I do now? How well I understand. In midlife, I too questioned myself. Success had come easily, and at thirty-five my earnings allowed me to travel in Japan and Europe. It was early in the century. At the time, the well-known, respected painters were from the nineteenth century: Delacroix, Ingres, Millet, Corot, Courbet, and others. The impressionists were being discovered, but their importance had not yet been recognized. While admiring its richness and its accomplishments, I was deeply distressed and disturbed by Western painting, whose techniques and vision were so different from what I knew. It seemed an extraordinary phenomenon, but outside my world. I visited the Louvre, of course. There I saw works by great painters of the past, the Italian Renaissance masters in particular. Awakening to a new ideal, they had devoted themselves passionately to all its possibilities but did not cast aside the exigencies of their craft. Those artists of the fourteenth, fifteenth, and sixteenth centuries sent me back to our own masters of the eighth, ninth, tenth, and eleventh centuries. I realized that I needed to look back to our own vital tradition rather than attempt some artificial syncretism that would make me a mere imitator or opportunist; I would have to find our own sources and revitalize them. You see, in my day the moment for encountering another tradition had not yet arrived. But a living tradition is not an iron collar, it is not confinement; it is liberty. It prepares us to meet face to face what is different without losing ourselves. Didn't our masters of the eighth through the eleventh centuries assimilate Indian art? Because they were steeped in their own living tradition, they could absorb outside influences without renouncing their own world. The more familiar they were with the finest in their own tradition the more easily they recognized the finest in another. I'm telling you this because you, you will have to face what is different. Once this war is over, I think it inevitable for China and the West to encounter each other on a deeper level, especially since the West is so free and so receptive to outside influences, even Asian. Accordingly, you must prepare yourself to confront the great art of another tradition and to find your own creativity as an artist. You might start by reliving the great adventure of our ancient masters. After assimilating the art of India, they went on to create their own forms."

The master's eyes began to shine, lit up by an almost boyish smile. He said: "You may have been offered an extraordinary opportunity. It is up to you to take advantage of it. A few days ago, I received a long letter from my friend, Professor C., a painter who studied in France and now teaches at the Academy of Fine Arts. He tells me that he and some other scholars have rediscovered the Dunhuang Caves of the far northwest—a vast region now being developed because of the war. These caves preserve intact countless frescoes embodying the whole adventure of Chinese painting's past, a panorama quite suitable—according to Professor C.—for inspiring today's artists and revitalizing modern Chinese painting."

It was the first time I had heard the name Dunhuang, and the master had to remedy my ignorance. Dunhuang was in the far western region of China, in the modern province of Gansu, on the old Silk Road. Around the fifth century the prosperous city of Dunhuang began serving as a place of exchange between China and the outside world as well as a stop for Buddhist pilgrims. Monasteries grew up all around. Not far from the city, at the foot of a long hill stood the openings of more than three hundred caves in which artists, inspired by Buddhism and encounters with other artistic traditions—the Indian and the Persian especially—had over several centuries painted frescoes of religious scenes and scenes of everyday life, for the edification of travelers.

Toward the fifteenth century, historical events led to the closing of the route; the region, soon overtaken by the desert, knew desolation then total abandonment. A few monks were the only inhabitants. At the end of the nineteenth century, Western sinologists discovered the manuscripts the monks had immured in the caves to protect from looters. The scholars carried off great numbers of documents, yet they did not touch the frescoes, which had been ignored ever since. "Now, because of the war, we Chinese have been forced by the enemy to retreat to the western regions, and we have begun to rediscover all these buried treasures."

The master could recommend me to Professor C., who was seeking recruits with the skills to assist him in his project, the copying of the frescoes. It would have been impossible to refuse such an offer: I accepted, and for the first time in my life I had committed myself to something concrete that was to lead somewhere.

The day I left, the master accompanied me to the crossroads. There he stopped and said: "What I could give you, I have given. From now on, follow the Way, keep to it, and forget me. Don't even bother to write. Anyway, I won't answer. I shall soon be going elsewhere." Those words, so painful to hear, were not spoken severely but with a gentleness and peace that illuminated and transfigured his whole face. After speaking, the old man turned in the direction of his hermitage. His robe billowed in the wind, and his step was light. I was suddenly taken back to the moment in my childhood when I saw the Taoist monk disappear in the distance for the last time.

The path of renunciation and detachment is a cruel path. It involves deprivation and the renouncing of immediate, facile pleasures. But that is how the torch of Chinese spirituality is passed on: a master exerts his influence on a disciple, gives him everything, then fades away so the disciple may become himself. For a long while I watched the master; he did not turn around. Eventually, his frail silhouette faded away completely. Tears came into my eyes and ran down my cheeks. There I was at a crossroads, once again lost and alone. I soon pulled myself together, knowing I was about to go forward resolutely, especially since the master had indicated the route to follow. Supplied with a letter of recommendation, I made my way to Chungking to meet with Professor C. He took me on immediately, and matters proceeded swiftly. It was early May, and we planned to leave for Dunhuang at the beginning of June. I had a month free to return to the Lu family estate at Douziba to see my mother.

·　　·　　·

AFTER OUR JOYFUL reunion, I had the task of explaining to my mother—prematurely aged from hard work and unexpressed grief— that I would soon have to leave again. What could she do but accept with resignation? Her whole life consisted of acquiescence and waiting, waiting for her only child, her unstable, elusive son. It did cheer her up that I had finally taken on real work, and with pay. I hardly dared tell her that Dunhuang was several thousand *li* away. I endeavored to explain that the first Buddhist missionaries had spread into China from the Dunhuang area, still the home of priceless sutra manuscripts. Coming of the people, my mother was excited by the idea of her son's going to the birthplace of Chinese Buddhism. At the mention of sutras, my mother grew sad, for she had begun to forget verses and passages of litanies learned long ago; she wished she had them in writing. As an act of piety, as if to redeem myself, I offered to transcribe the ones she could still recite. During the month I spent with her, I put the verses into an elegantly bound notebook, employing my best calligraphy and all the veneration my soul could muster.

During my hours of copying, I noticed my mother spent more and more time talking to herself. I became alarmed upon observing that her failing memory would sometimes lead her to mental confusion. She would forget the present and go back to a moment in the past. One day, as I was writing, she looked at me with the candid gaze of earlier years and said: "Go play with Xiao-mei [my little sister's name]. Watch out for scorpions. I am going to get medicine for Papa." Another time, she broke the silence by asking abruptly: "Papa isn't back yet?"

Another emotional ordeal awaited me: the torment of seeing Yumei's girlhood home. Every little spot reminded me of the innocent, dazzling moments spent in her company. Without my new resolve to commit myself to artistic creation, my sorrow would have been crushing. At first I hardly dared walk about the estate for fear of reopening the wound and feeling the blood drip from my very soul. But my mother became a calming influence. Knowing nothing of the drama that had occurred, she spoke of Yumei often and with deep affection. She remembered her simply as a daughter, and eventually I too learned to treasure the purity of my own memory of Yumei; I knew that my relationship with the Lover was no longer subject to the laws of time. The memory was fixed once and for all, like a solitary diamond. Neither Yumei nor I could alter its brilliance.

27

E ARLY JUNE, 1945. My face sunburned and my hair yellow with dust, I sat high above the bumpy road as our truck headed west toward an unfamiliar China, the faraway lands surrounded by the Gobi Desert. After our departure from Tchoung-king, we had passed through Chengdu, Xian, and Lansu, the capital of Gansu Province. This last-named city, bisected by the Yellow River and dotted with mosques, had provided our first glimpse of an elsewhere rich in history. Now we were traveling through a corridor more than a thousand kilometers long. Strung along it like so many pearls were ancient garrison cities, whose days of glory survived in their lovely names: Heavenly Waters, Fountain of Wine, Purple Gold, Gate of Jade, among others. The corridor, the first segment of the old Silk Road, ran the full length of the narrow province of Gansu. To the south, we could see the peaks of the Qilian range; north of us, the monotony of the desert was broken by hills and oases, and by the occasional ruins of citadels and fortifications. Our team, headed by Professor C., consisted of three painters, an historian, and a specialist in popular literature. We generally spent our nights at government stations that provided food and shelter. On occasion we camped. Stretched out in a trough in the sand still warm from the sun, I would gaze up at a starry sky almost unbearably bright and too vast, too close. I had not seen such a sky since that long-ago night my father and I lost our way on Mount Lu. As I had then, I now felt both fear and an intimate, bodily connection with the cosmos. Seeing the shooting stars that made lonely trails across the heavens then sank into the bottomless blue-black, I would be reminded of the singular path of my soul, the path of a wanderer. And I was overwhelmed by an indescribable nostalgia. The bright streak of an unusually red meteor made my heart bleed, reopened my poorly healed wound. Out of that amorphous, unpeopled vastness a whole people would march forth to haunt me, like insects emerging from the sand in the cool of the night. Among my loved ones the obsessive image of the Friend and the Lover came to the fore despite my efforts to drive it away.

·   ·   ·

AT THE END of a trying journey that took nearly a month, the little team reached Dunhuang, a midsized market town surviving in the heart of the desert. The sleepy little city pondered its days of past glory, when flocks of nomads, travelers, merchants, and pilgrims had mingled inside its gates. Welcomed by the local administrator, we spent two days in Dunhuang resting and attending to practical matters. Escorted by soldiers, we finally set off for the caves about thirty kilometers away.

A desert scene: scattered sand dunes, slabs of rock, a dried-up riverbed, a neglected oasis with a hill rising behind it like a wall or a screen. On the face of the hill an impressive number of caves had been hollowed out in the rock on three or four levels, paths and steps winding in their midst. With the patina of time, everything chaotic had been worn away, leaving an organic whole, reminiscent of a body born of some vital necessity, a giant beast that would remain ageless, forever in repose.

When we entered the body, which breathed through every pore, what an encounter! Once deep inside a cave chosen at random, we were stunned and stood motionless, speechless. We were enveloped, inhaled, by what came to life all around us: colors and shapes depicting scenes intimate or grandiose, which covered every wall and ceiling and had been there for over a millennium, their freshness intact.

Dunhuang would one day be world famous, but in the mid-1940s, the Chinese had just rediscovered it. We were there, just a few of us, living the simple life in an isolated spot forgotten by the world. Except for the sand hissing when the wind blew, we were surrounded by absolute silence. The echo of our voices and the unsteady flame of the fat candles my companions and I carried were the only signs of life. Yet it was life itself that revived and awakened upon being exposed to our eyes. A momentary miracle. Time had died; now it was reborn, proudly displaying all it held of memory and promise. Within that enclosed space was a beyond-the-world space, once inhabited by a race of worshippers who, before disappearing, had entrusted to these hidden shelters all their treasures: their pain and their joy, their experiences and their dreams, their loves, their truth, in a kind of inflamed yet serene glorification. An unbelievable song emanating from this space took the visitor, carried him, pushed him on to another cave, then another. But after three or four caves, we dared not continue, for the emotions aroused were too strong. And that was our first morning. For me it was the beginning of the first day of a new life.

When a visitor had learned his way around the caves and had acquired an overall view, he could see unfolding before his eyes, in panel after panel, the history of Chinese painting, not from its earliest days but from over a period of nearly a thousand years, beginning with the fourth century. That was when painters, encountering art from elsewhere, had become aware of their power and had turned their creations into an independent art. Sheltered from social upheaval and changes of dynasty, the cave locality had stayed protected. The spot was an ideal distance from the great road, the junction between China and neighboring small kingdoms, the route through which passed goods exported by China as well as those coming from India and later from Persia.

Surprising discovery: here, on the very edge of China, at the terminus of an endless semidesert corridor where the sea winds blew, in a place crossed countless times by border tribes riding wild, I felt for the first time the heartbeat of the enormous body that was China. This open "far west" may indeed have been on the periphery of the old country, but had it not been its nerve center for nearly two thousand years? It is no exaggeration to say that sedentary China, so rooted to its native soil, was always obsessed by this great open gap that could not be closed. Eventually, it was drawn into military adventures there, and finally into just plain adventures.

Fierce desert battles, countless corpses left unburied, burned by thirst or drunk on grape wine, dead from starvation or satiated with spicy grilled meats . . . China, monolithic, immutable? Nothing is less true. In the hinterlands of China there was already interaction between the North, with the Yellow River running through, and the South, crossed by the Yangzi. A known quantity. But with the "far west," the Middle Empire—protected to the north by the Great Wall and to the south by the Himalayas—found itself exposed to the arrows of a pitiless sun and the whiplashes of threatening but elusive forces come from elsewhere.

From the early days of the Empire, the frontier region was the scene of one expedition after another, with garrisons established to counter periodic invasions by neighboring tribes, whose dangerous horsemen were skilled in the art of war. A succession of brief victories and bitter defeats. Later, periods of relative peace saw opposing armies replaced by long lines of caravans. Along with merchandise these imported the stirrings of a religion, Buddhism; a faith declining in its own country, it was to bloom vigorously in China.

In Dunhuang, the spiritual adventure manifested itself as an extraordinary artistic adventure. That place's miracle: benefiting from the fervor of the devout and the pilgrims, an art had the time to ripen, to develop in successive stages. Already nourished by their own tradition and in full control of their technique, Chinese artists encountered an Indian art permeated by Buddhism and rich in exotic, fantastic images. These aroused echoes in the subconscious, leading the Dunhuang painters to bold inventiveness of form. Motivated by their fervent faith, they approached every theme with glad hearts.

Through their new expressive possibilities, these Chinese artists could give free rein to their fantasies, to their joys and their sorrows, to their sensual dreams and their repentance, to their needs for consolation and glorification. From their feverish creativity came a rich universe filled with scenes and legends of an infinite variety: scenes from the life of Buddha and the saints, scenes of angels in flight, scenes of celebration and everyday life, scenes of hunting and riding. . . .

As I entered this universe, observing it from within, I was struck by its special elements, these elements that had allowed Chinese artists to dig out from their native soil and take a dizzying leap into pictorial art.

The earliest painting, that of the Han Dynasty, was notably earthbound. In contrast, here on the walls of the caves an exploded and airy space took on a celestial dimension attested to in the magnificent flying asparas and in the rows of seated or standing dignitaries who seemed buoyed up by an invisible ascensional force. No longer concerned about chronology, narrative pictures upset the spatial-temporal order by arranging their episodes around a center, itself unfixed. Even in the most everyday scenes, the figures of peasants tilling the soil and artisans fashioning tools occupied space with a sense of ease, as if infinity were carrying them past the boundaries of their fields and the confines of their workshops. Such liberation of the painted space and such utter daring in composition, allowing the empty to play freely its role as structurer, were even more noticeable in the treatment of landscape and probably contributed to the elaborating of that very specific vision of landscape found in classical Chinese painting.

Plunged into the suspended space of the frescoes, into a universe bursting with force and inspiration, I felt my entire being crack under its rigid shell and felt my heart burst into a thousand fragments, into a thousand possibilities for creations and lives. Too many possibilities perhaps. I was aware that it would take a long, long time to find another center of gravity within myself. While waiting, making the rounds of the caves, I offered no resistance to the colors and shapes that took over my being. So as not to fall into a state of total confusion, I tried to view the works in chronological order. The frescoes of the first periods, painted with pale pink and deep ochre, had changed in hue, leaving only blackened outlines that seemed as if cut into the rock. The brush strokes, now revealed in all their boldness, reminded me of tree trunks at winter's end, when they are reduced to the essential and invincible, ready to bud at the slightest breeze. Then came the painting of the Tang Dynasty, with its edifying, sumptuous figures, as rigorous and rounded as the rumps of the horses so honored in the art of the era. When I came to the painting of much later times, of the Song and Yuan Dynasties, I grew calmer as the painting itself grew gradually calmer. A style of painting based on a technique of exquisite drawing and an exact science of color. Each patch of color had its separate existence—the blue, the green, the violet, the brown, et cetera. Immersing myself in those hues, I could disregard the content of the works and open myself completely to the brightly colored kingdom. When I approached a fresco, I melted into it little by little and I expanded into its mottled waves, such was the effect of the colors with their innate sense of measure. They did not try to outdo one another; each was conscious of its own value and at the same time careful to respond to the surrounding colors and to the overall harmony, not unlike the finely dressed ladies and devout worshippers depicted in the paintings. These figures wearing their best clothes appeared conscious both of their dignity and of the duty to be modest, seemingly ready to efface themselves to make way for the advancing divinities.

28

AFTER A PERIOD of preparation the team set to work, our task simply to copy the frescoes. For those of reasonable size, the method was to trace them onto wide pieces of fabric or paper stretched over the wall. Once the outlines of the figures had been traced, we would take down the fabric or paper and apply color. People nowadays, accustomed to color photography, might be tempted to laugh at such unsophisticated, archaic methods. But those copies reproduced the materiality and the freshness of the original works. Our efforts were later exhibited in major Chinese cities and proved a veritable revelation. In the act of copying, the copyist truly plunged into the space of the fresco and immersed himself in the invigorating current of lines and colors. He relived the moment lived by the artist who had created the work, adopted the painter's rhythm in his own movements, and felt the other's heart beating in hesitation or delight. Whatever else it might have achieved, that time-consuming, painstaking work constituted for me and my companions an experience more than enriching: it was unique.

With entire days spent deep in the caves—cradles or tombs— I forgot myself completely, devoting body and soul to the task. I was evolving outside time, in the zone where the living and the dead are one. My eyes were nothing but a horde of shapes and colors; my hands were nothing but a series of movements, more and more directed. Completion, followed by starting again, without a break. The universe was a smooth continuum. I could almost believe that life was a smooth-flowing stream, that my whole life would roll along in unison with the now peaceful rhythm of my blood.

Outside the caves, space stretched as far as the eye or the mind could see, inviting men to surrender to it. We became attuned to its indifference and its slowness, and to its simple components. To the nearby trees that offered a little shade, to the often dry river, to the more distant hill whose sands hissed when the wind blew, then on to the bumpy, subdued desert that went on and on until blocked at its very end by the snow-capped mountain range. An unsullied line of white mineral, scarcely disturbed by the rumble of storms or the fire of the setting sun. . . .

But a keen intuition came to me in the desert night: one may well be in exile and alone, but one is held by bonds forged more or less in spite of oneself. That is called destiny. During this whole time—an eternity? an instant?—when I thought I was unknown to all, forsaken by all, events were moving swiftly. They occurred on specific dates, almost as if prearranged, and some affected the world while others set my life on an *irrevocable* course.

.　　.　　.

ON AUGUST 15, 1945, barely two months after my arrival in Dunhuang, the war ended. In our isolated spot, there were only weak echoes of the jubilant crowds. The next day, the whole team went into the city, where a celebration had been organized around whole roast sheep. Amid the noise of firecrackers mixed with the sound of Uighur songs and dances, we passed around endless jugs of wine. After the strongly flavored meats and the vegetable cakes, we quenched our thirst by burying our heads in plump fruit that dripped with juice—watermelon, melons, grapes, *hami*. . . . On the way back, I told myself that what I had feared most about living in Dunhuang—stomach trouble—had not come to pass. Was the logical conclusion that my nature only did well in regions offering extreme thirst along with marvelous resources for quenching it?

But joy soon gave way to uneasiness. Before the year ended, vast numbers of people who had fled to the West during the war struggled frantically to return home. Means of transportation were sorely lacking, and anarchy reigned on the congested roads and on the sole river route, soon threatened with strangulation. It was a dreadful mess, and endless accidents ensued. Only the privileged and the well-off got through quickly and comfortably. Meanwhile, other worries beset the government. It had to face problems that were far more serious, problems posed by the threat from the Communists. The latter had resisted the Japanese during the war and presently occupied entire regions in northern China, areas they called "liberated zones." In spite of expressions of good will on both sides, in spite of so-called peace talks, the inevitable confrontations were leading the country toward civil war.

.　　.　　.

IN EARLY 1946, a letter from my mother told me she was in Tchoungking with the Guo family. The center that employed Mr. Guo was now there, awaiting its eventual return to Nankin. Before opening the letter, I saw with a shock the handwriting on the envelope. It was Yumei's. She had written at my mother's dictation, adding a few tactful lines of her own, to let me know that she too was living in Tchoungking, where her troupe had gone to take over from several closed theaters. Haolang, she said, had "moved away." It was not hard to figure out what that meant: he had joined the Communists in the "liberated zone."

Shortly afterward, a second letter from my mother, again in Yumei's hand, to let me know she had decided to stay in Tchoungking after the departure of the Guo family; she would be living with Yumei. The news was beyond all expectations and put my mind at ease. I even said to myself, "How very convenient for me." According to the schedule, our team would not be completing its work until early 1948. And Professor C. had mentioned that he could help me win a scholarship for two years of study in France.

How very convenient for me. All my life, I would reproach myself for whispering in my heart of hearts that egotistical phrase, which became so odious to me. More alert to the appeals, to the signs, might I have been less afflicted with blindness, and afterward, with regret? Yet I was merely asking for a little respite. But the fact is there. While men are bent over their petty calculations, making plans for the months and years to come, destiny is snickering quietly in the background. Its calendar is not that of men; it has its own perspectives, its own scale of values; it spurns human timetables, which obey immediate, visible interests. Destiny snatches men up as they stride along their precarious paths, setting them down on a road not anticipated, whose length and direction they know not.

In 1947, a scorching-hot summer descended over all of western China. Tchoungking became a hellish furnace. A telegram delayed in arriving brought the news that my mother was dangerously ill. I left Dunhuang hastily; my bus jolted along, rushing by cities whose names had delighted me but which now echoed ironically in my ears: Peace of the West, Gate of Jade, Purple Gold. In Fountain of Wine, I managed to board a military plane about to depart for Lanzhou. In Lanzhou, the capital of Gansu, I could finally send a telegram to Tchoungking, two weeks after the one I had received. Reply: "Mother passed on. Without suffering. Be brave. I am taking care of everything. Yumei." My journey from Lanzhou to Tchoungking in the heat and the dust was a long descent into the underworld. Throughout the trip, I was tormented by feelings of unworthiness and consumed with remorse. By failing to carry out my duty toward my father, I was somewhat responsible for his death. And how much more responsible I was for the passing of my mother, the only one left who cared about me—not to mention, the only one left who kept me in this world. Was all my brooding supposed to lighten the burden a little? Maybe not, but the fact remains that by dint of torturing myself I was finally convinced my mother felt it time to join my father since Yumei was there to take over; or else she had decided to depart for the Sky of the West, the Buddhist paradise, where her husband already was, and where her son was close by. Wasn't Dunhuang on the road that led there? I remembered a panorama I had painted at Dunhuang: it told the story of Mulian, the devout Buddhist who had descended to the underworld, facing a thousand trials to free his deceased mother's soul. Could I do the same, or did I still have too much life left in me?

In Tchoungking, the only trace of my mother was a box of ashes. Would I never see again that dear face so marked by hardship and yet so infinitely comforting? In the future could I summon up all the features of the face I had too often neglected in those last years, busy as I was with pursuing what interested me, only me? In another box I found all my letters, saved by my mother, and the very sight of them made me unbearably uncomfortable. Written at long intervals, they had often been scribbled in haste, without the concentration that truly loving words require. How good it would have been to talk to my mother one more time! One time, a good talk, long, endless, no reserve, no useless modesty—like a clear stream flowing, saying everything that came into my head and heart. Afterward, even death would be sweet. Why do people find it so difficult, so uncomfortable to talk? They talk more in absence than in presence. A whole life of words held in; then comes the supreme absence, with no going back to put things right. As long as my mother was alive, as long as I was sure I could go home and see that figure bent over in the dark kitchen whenever I so chose, I felt solidly rooted somewhere even when events tossed me hither and yon. After my sister, after my father, the one blood connection still left, the deepest, the most tenacious, the most nourishing, had suddenly been snatched away. Before me was an emptied world, a gaping void. The very universe was without roots. All its stars, in the manner of the human hordes bustling around me, turned relentlessly, pointlessly; all its stars clung to nothing but a blind gravitational force of boundless vanity. More than ever, the image of the shooting star seemed the only tangible reality.

My grief was moderated a little by Yumei's presence, a grieving presence, however. Deprived of my mother's affection, she too felt orphaned. And she was convinced she would never see Haolang again. Learning that I too was to leave her, she sank into despair.

Without being sure myself, I did my best to convince her that Haolang would return someday. As for my coming absence, I explained it was essential for me to seize the opportunity to go to

France; my scholarship would keep me away for no more than two years. While waiting, I extended my stay in Tchoungking as long as I could. In that postwar world of upheaval and uncertainty, almost three months of unadulterated, remarkable happiness, in spite of, or beyond, the ambiguous drama we had lived.

Being together, spending long moments talking or communing silently, we recaptured our earlier innocence. Words surged from the depths, words filled with questioning and affirmation, mostly from the Lover: "What is life? What is this life on earth? Isn't the gift of life uncomplicated, or shouldn't it be? A seed is planted in the ground, and soon it sprouts. Look out the window at the tree branches, how uncomplicated they are. They are there, always together, and that is that. Yes, basically we are asking very little: to stay together. It seems that is too much to ask. A strange world, and strange the human heart. And now here we are, alone. Each of us alone."

Then, emboldened, she spoke, breathlessly: "Do you believe me? Someday you will believe me. You are the one I love most in the world. You are my innocence, you are my dream. In my darkest moments, I dreamed of you, as of an eternal childhood. I am your sister, I am your lover. But we shall not be a couple in this life. Not in the present. Later perhaps, later surely. When we have survived a thousand deaths, I shall come to you, much as someone returns to his homeland . . . you came too late to my life, or too late to the world. After our first separation, you came to me with Haolang. Ah! how I loved our friendship; it was finer than love. Couldn't the three of us have stayed as we were, friends? It seems we lacked patience. If time had been ours, we would have succeeded. While waiting, as if driven by a blind force, as if in spite of ourselves, Haolang and I did what couples do, all the while knowing that our deed would exclude you and would mean a closing off, a withering away. Both he and I needed you; in a way, you give us strength. If only you knew how unhappy we were when you left. Not just because we were tormented by guilt. We realized that our fate was tied to yours, that without you we would not be fulfilled. And here it is: I cannot do without you or without him. Do not force me to choose. What a terrible egotist I am!" She could not keep from laughing through her tears.

Toward the end, knowing we had little time left, once again the Lover spoke frankly of the obsessive feelings she could not expunge: "To me, you are a native land, for I was born to real life with you, in you. He, he is the stranger who comes from afar; through his source, so different from ours, he enriches us, reveals to us our true nature. Both of you, you and he, have become essential to me. The two of you have entered my destiny, are my destiny, and I do not even know why. I do know that without you and Haolang, life is dull for me, neither here nor there, unimportant. But with you, everything takes on a glow, everything takes on meaning. And so you see, for human beings, living as a threesome, as three in one, is an unachievable dream. . . . Is it monstrous, what I've just said? I have said it, you have heard it. What is going to become of the world? Will we see each other again? But wherever you may be, hold on to what I have just said—it is our joint treasure!"

We were clinging to each other like a young brother and sister joined by blood, or like an old couple joined by tenderness, as if we were Fuxi and Nügua, the two mythical figures—brother and sister as well as husband and wife—who are, according to ancient legend, the founders of the Chinese race. They are depicted with human heads and bodies but fishlike tails. The tails, always intertwined, allowed them to survive the Flood.

It was the first time I had held Yumei in my arms. A strange sensation to have such a close, unhurried look at a face so familiar and yet so unknown. The mane of silky hair with its bluish glints; the mole, a black pearl adorning the delicate curve of her neck; the lashes whose flutter preceded an exclamation or a lament; the eyes with their special sidelong glance, the eyes that often flashed astonishment. Up close, those elements took on a peculiar relief; their scale was so increased they became the components of a vast landscape of which I, its viewer, formed an integral part.

My body was so close to the Lover's now, that I sensed it would take but little for us to be joined completely. If I moved my hands over her, she would yield to my caresses, opening herself to me wordlessly, and I could enter her. There was still time, and this was probably my only opportunity to accomplish the thing I so desired, the thing for which I had no doubt come into the world. But that thing, I would not do it, not yet, knowing full well that even if there was still time, the moment was not right. And hadn't my whole life been like that—in time, no; at the wrong time, yes? That thing would never be done in the seeable or foreseeable present. It would be postponed over and over, some hypothetical future fulfillment ahead. Hypothetical? Not entirely. Deep down, I was convinced of that. Always hapless and helpless, I had certainly learned not to be sure of anything; nevertheless I had a naive conviction, ineradicable, that whatever I sowed, if only in thought or through desire, would develop fully, irresistibly, almost independently of my will, flowering maybe sooner, maybe later—maybe in another life—when I least expected it. My main task lay in learning to identify those moments of flowering. If I could not, so much the worse for me: these things would happen anyway, but without me.

I absorbed the warmth of the Lover's body and the perfume of her hair, as if to store them up for the rest of my life. Taking the beloved's face in my hands, I gazed at it intensely, that face diaphanous from suffering and the golden October light. I whispered: "Yumei, Yumei, let us accept the terrible ordeal of separation. We shall find each other. We have already found each other, found each other for all time."

30

A T THE END OF 1947, I traveled to Nankin to prepare for the scholarship exam. Since I was the sole candidate in my specialty—wall painting—and had been warmly recommended by the professor on the selection committee, I knew that the competitive exam was merely a formality. All the same, I had to do it justice by studying the required subjects conscientiously.

I sailed down the famous Yangzi gorges that extended for several hundred kilometers, a route I had followed more than nine years earlier, coming to Sichuan. I had been a child then, still carefree, oblivious to everything. I remembered only being so overwhelmed by the magnificence of what we passed through that I had shouted at the top of my lungs; my voice had been drowned out by the deafening roar of the waves hitting the walls of the cliffs that rose up to touch the sky. And now here I was, a young man who had already been through too much, who knew too early the burden of his destiny.

This trip down the river was far more dizzying than my first, and fraught with peril. Rushed along by the current, the boat had to veer left or right constantly, avoiding reefs. Here and there would appear flotsam from the wrecks of sampans tossed about and torn to bits by the eddies.

I stood on deck with the other passengers, fascinated as much as terrified by the raging river. I could not help thinking that the river was the image of my fate. For what could I do but let myself by dragged along, carried away by the blind current until the final breaking up?

In spite of my fatalism, I couldn't help asking questions. What about this angry current hurling itself into nothingness with no regrets? Was it not a superb symbol of the vast universal perdition? If everything was only sheer destruction, why life rather than nothing? Why so much dreaming and desiring, why so much suffering and persevering? The water flowing continuously and roaring day and night conjured up an image that had frequently haunted my nightmares, the image of a young high school classmate who had been injured seriously. Despite tourniquets and bandages, his hemorrhaging would not stop. Then, someone had made a remark I shall never forget: "He is going to be drained of his blood and he will die." And under a blazing sun, on the way to a distant clinic, he did lose his life.

I was overcome with panic as I watched the people around me exclaiming, laughing excitedly, and trying to talk above the din of the wild waters beneath their feet. I wanted to shake my fellow passengers and cry out: "Danger!" They who thought themselves safely ensconced in a secure space, didn't they see that time was mocking them and carrying away their illusory foundation bit by bit, more surely than giant termites? And I, did I see more clearly than the others? What did it mean, the headlong flight of the river and time in one direction? What had the Ancients understood and said to make those who came after feel so reassured? Would I ever again see the Lover as I had known her, as I had dreamed her? Would I ever see my parents, in spite of everything, or beyond everything?

On board was a group of academics returning to Peking. It is easy to strike up shipboard conversations, and I accosted the scholars with my questions, taking the chance I might irritate some. But my rather perplexed countenance encountered a serious face that broke into a smile: "Very interesting question, vital even . . ." It was Professor F., renowned specialist in Chinese thought, whom some approached with a respectful timidity. I had gone to him with my naiveté, and without much embarrassment, for I asked nothing but to listen.

"Yes, the river as a symbol of time; what does it mean? Let's see, how can I answer that question?" He frowned behind his round silver spectacles. "We have to talk of the Way, don't we? . . . Well, what a coincidence! Tomorrow we sail through the native region of our beloved Laozi. As you know, he is the founder of Taoism. He developed the concept of the Way, the irresistible universal movement driven by the primal Breath. Until tomorrow then. We shall talk about it."

The scholar continued his discourse the next day, as if no night had intervened. "No doubt it was through the inspiration of this powerful, fertile river so like the Milky Way (See how wide the stream is here. Magnificent, isn't it?) that Laozi developed his vision of the Way. Like the river, the Way is linked with time. People say: "River of time," and the Way asserts: "There is no going without coming back." And yet, if we look at the river as we are now doing, it appears to be heading in a straight line toward its destruction, whereas the Taoists say the Way moves in a circle. Therefore, some will think there is a contradiction between the reality and the concept drawn from it. But they overlook the specific features of Chinese geography. China is a self-contained continent, with high

mountains to the west and wide seas to the east. The slope of
China's land mass is such that all the rivers, the two major ones in
particular, the Yellow and the Yangzi, flow without deviating from
west to east. These two rivers, the one rough and virile, cradle of
Confucianism, the other luxuriant and feminine, cradle of Taoism,
have the same source and they flow in the same direction, leading
the Chinese to believe that the temporal order has a point of origin
and a point of destination.

"So what has given us the idea that the irreversibility of time's
imperious order can be disrupted? Enter the middle Voids inherent
in the Way. Breaths themselves, they impart to the Way its rhythm,
its respiration; most important, they allow it to effect the mutation
of things and to return to the Origin, the very source of the primal
Breath. For the river, the middle Voids take the form of clouds. The
river, with its origin in the Way, takes its appropriate place in the
earthly order as well as in the heavenly. Water evaporates from the
river, condenses into cloud, falls back into the river as rain, feeding
it. By this vertical circular movement, the river, while assuring the
connection between earth and heaven, disrupts the fatality of its own
frenzied course. By the same token, at its two extremities, the river
transmits the same kind of circle between sea and mountain, *yin* and
yang. Because of the river, the two entities enter into the process of
reciprocity: the sea evaporates into the sky and falls as rain on the
mountain, which sees that the source never runs dry. Termination
going back to germination.

"We might say then that time proceeds in concentric circles, or if
you prefer, in spiraling circles. But one moment—This circle is not
the wheel of Indian thought, spinning endlessly around the same
things, nor is it what is known as the eternal return. The cloud con-
densed into rain is no longer river water, and the rain does not fall
back into the same water. The circle is completed only by passage
through the Void and the Exchange. Yes, the idea of mutation and
transformation is essential to Chinese thought, and is the very law of
the Way. Laozi's "return," of course, implies the coming back of all
things, but most important, the changing of one thing into another,
which results in constant return; the more return, the more frequent

the possibility of transformation, for the inspiration of the primal Breath is inexhaustible. Subtle and paradoxical perhaps, but that is how it is . . ." Behind the glasses, the flicker of a mischievous smile showed Professor F. was pleased at having closed the circle his words had traced.

I accepted his explanation gratefully, although many points were not clear to me. I did at least grasp the conclusion that nothing in real life is lost and that what is not leads into a future as continuous as it is unknown. An explanation I would remember in France upon reading *In Search of Lost Time*. Differing with Proust, I might have written: "In search of time to come." The law of time, for me at any rate, in keeping with what I had just experienced with the Lover, was not based on the accomplished, the finished, but on the postponed, the unfinished. I had to pass through the Void and the Exchange.

In Nankin, the exam took place as expected. As expected, I passed. The government immediately took the successful candidates in hand. We were given a chance to take classes and to study French intensively. It was not possible to return to Nanchang, my birthplace, to place my mother's ashes on my father's grave. I stuck the box in my luggage, with the firm intention of stopping in Nanchang upon my return to China.

Before sailing for France, I had was delighted to see in Hu Feng's journal, *Hope,* what seemed a providential sign: several poems by Haolang, sent secretly from his "new home." All the same, I was still worried about the Friend: the civil war that had begun two years earlier was now raging all over northern China.

PART TWO: A TURN IN THE ROAD

O N AN APRIL DAY IN 1948 I stepped off the train in Paris, my heart pounding. I had come from Marseille with a dozen other scholarship students, after a thirty-day sea voyage. I was struck by the contrast between the dreary hue of the streets of Paris and the City of Light glorified in my imagination. Most of the houses around the station were a tired gray darkened by decades of smoke and dust. The spring was still cool; passersby, squeezed into old dark garments not yet replaced in these first postwar years, had an air of indifference, gloom. I was not unaware that the Seine was here, with the famous spots over which tourists waxed ecstatic. But I was never one to embrace popular opinion. In the face of what the world saw, I always doubted my eyes. I would discover the charm of Paris later, in my own way.

A few Chinese who had come to study in France before the war and had endured the harsh years of the Occupation came out of the shadows to greet the new arrivals at the station. After helping us check our bags and before showing us to hotels in the Latin Quarter, they led us to a nearby dark and narrow street. This opened into a series of cul-de-sacs, darker and narrower still; the uneven pavement oozed dampness and was lined on both sides with low buildings, dilapidated and characterless. Here lived a number of Chinese who kept shops or restaurants. In one of the restaurants, not as badly lit as some, old hands and new arrivals celebrated our first meeting over lunch.

The lively conversation and the appetizing odors rising from noodle soups and colorful, spicy dishes (quite different from the unappealing shipboard fare) helped banish the smell of the moldy grease that filled the cracks in the walls, helped cast over us an ephemeral illusion of revisiting our native land.

Yes, I would learn to love this city where I was to live for a time. I would learn to love this country in the heart of Western Europe. But it would be a long initiation. While waiting—and I felt it, I knew it already—I would have to pass through purgatory, if not through hell.

I considered myself well acquainted with hell, since I had always been haunted by the phenomenon of Evil, leading to merciless death. There is another hell, however, more subtle, in which suffering and death are not evident, a hell I was to discover little by little. In China, I had not been fully aware of its existence. There, I was in a familiar world and knew down to the last detail the way of speaking and the customs. My face did not stand out from the crowd; it melted into the mass carrying me along like a wave since my birth. In Paris, for the first time I felt my strangeness, further accentuated by my status as a foreigner. I confronted a universe whose ABCs I was learning as diligently and as awkwardly as a newborn babe.

It was not the fear of being asked to show my papers. Everything was more or less in order. My body told me my deficiency was far more drastic; let us say I was deficient in legitimacy of being. Nothing seemed to guarantee my identity or justify my needing to be there. Worse than excluded, I felt separated. Separated from others, separated from self, separated from everything. I had come to France to learn painting. I confronted a trade that could not be learned: existing.

.   .   .

FOR THE TIME BEING, it was a friendly hell I faced. Too friendly to be genuinely friendly: that might be guessed. Too friendly to allow you to belong: that may come as a surprise. True, it is a strange hell that entices you toward its trap but keeps you from entering. On everybody's lips back then was one of those catchy phrases so loved in France: "Hell is other people." For me on the contrary, hell—as I learned to my sorrow—was in always being the other, to the point of being from nowhere.

At the end of the forties, not unlike the young so frantic to experience life, many well-off people hungered for a social whirl of festivities and frivolity as if they had to make up for the dark years.

Since Chinese artists were not yet legion in postwar Paris, I had the honor of being invited—in my capacity as a "rarity"—to dine in a drawing room that boasted of its open-mindedness. Introduced to the other guests, I was regaled with "so happy to meet you's" and

"I'm honored's" that boded well. I congratulated myself; at last, I could get to know "Parisian society." But the others were soon otherwise engaged, exchanging countless "Dears" and "Darlings." I had the distinct impression they considered me decoration, like the Ming vase in the corner.

At dinner I managed to hold my neighbors' attention briefly, and I even drew a few responses, such as "How interesting," or "How fascinating." If I tried to prolong the conversation by delving deeper into the subject, I would notice repressed yawns and an exchange of looks that seemed to mock my clumsiness. Then I recalled one of the golden rules of the French language: no repeating. Particularly in social conversation, let brio and lightness predominate. Above all, little witticisms, right on the mark, fatal!

Worn out by following the talk that whirled around me, I had begun to feel drowsy when the discussion turned to China. But I did not have to exhaust myself further, for several of the guests knew better than I what was or what should be a Chinese. As a matter of fact, one of them, after listening to me for a moment, proclaimed without preamble: "How odd, you aren't very Chinese!" Other fine minds, claiming expertise, issued pronouncements on Chinese thought, Chinese poetry, Chinese art. Listening to them I finally caught on to what it was they demanded of a Chinese. They wanted a creature with his head in the clouds, untroubled, unquestioning, his face smooth and flat, his smile beatific, a creature of a substance other than flesh and blood. He should be chatty, speaking naturally and without much forethought, avoiding carefully crafted phrases; his comments should be simple and rather naive, leading up to some amiable nugget of wisdom. In short, an unsophisticated being, destined to remain a bumpkin, condemned to a life with neither passion nor the desire to explore new worlds.

Once I had left the dinner party, I breathed in the cool, fresh air and swore they would never again catch me unawares. I told myself sternly that I would have to be more Chinese, that I would have to try to fit their idea of a Chinese.

2

HILE WAITING TO MOVE more easily in Parisian circles, the newly arrived, impecunious foreigner would seek out other foreigners.

The many foreigners were a heterogeneous lot and constituted a world grafted onto native society. Communicating in a sort of French, they helped one another as best they could, sharing addresses of cheap restaurants and hints on dealing with the bureaucracy, handing down their dismal lodgings, creating among themselves the illusion they were fully there, fully rooted.

They kept their enthusiasm. For example, the poorly washed and poorly housed artists of Montparnasse, who spent winter days clustered around smoky, noisy coal stoves in shabby studios, painting pale, wan models, happy nonetheless to be in the paradise of art.

After work the artists hung around in the cafés, exchanging countless hugs and hellos. They would reassure and encourage one another with a friendly pat, a shared croissant, a kind word about a picture. And that was how they fought off despair. The suicides acted with discretion; leaving abruptly, they were gracious enough not to upset the family. After all, perhaps such conditions were necessary to create a Modigliani or a Van Gogh.

As an artist, I ended up in Montparnasse, too, living at the end of a dark corridor in a little makeshift studio knocked together by the artists who had preceded me. Except for a few required classes in mural painting at Beaux-Arts, I spent most of my time at life-drawing sessions in the quarter. To look arty, I bought myself a pipe and for a time grew a mustache. Soon, however, I wanted to escape the constant bustle and a confusion of artificial influences, so I took advantage of an opportunity to quit the quarter. A Chinese sculptor returning home offered me his rooms, which included a much larger studio; but the place was in a distant quarter, in eastern Paris, on Rue de B. A hilly, roughly paved street that people found hard to stroll on, I found it smooth beneath my feet; I felt the same tacit accord I had felt with the streets of Tchoungking. After moving, I still spent most of the day in Montparnasse, where I had my routines: bistros and cheap restaurants, cafés where I occasionally sold a landscape in India ink, watercolor, or oils.

At the end of the day, I would return to my rooms on foot to save money. The long walk across Paris in the evening or late at night made me familiar with the great city, but did not rid me of the existential dread the metropolis caused me. I began to feel so tied to Paris that I could not imagine living elsewhere. It forced itself on me, heavy with past glory and unconfessed crimes like some great aristocratic family. From then on, I had no doubt that in my veins too flowed blood full of the perfumes and poisons of the prestigious line. I had become like the other members of the family: they would never dream of abandoning the ancestral home, although they knew all too well the defects that previous generations had accumulated in the mansion's nooks and crannies, in its dark closets, old beds, sealed chests, and other secret places.

Nor would I, the assimilated foreigner, abandon that house. At that time my scanty resources went for lodging and the purchase of art supplies, and there was no question of travel abroad or even in France. Except for a few escapes to places like Chatou and Bougival, in the footsteps of Monet and Van Gogh: a row of poplars quivering with light, a towpath with a grassy odor, and the waters of Seine catching errant clouds were enough to delight me. A caged beast briefly returned to its element, I felt the full scope of my powers, so often inhibited. At the easel, my eye sharp and my hand alert, I saw scenes of real life emerge from the strokes of a brush dipped in a diluted ink enhanced with colors mellowed to perfection. . . . The rest of the time I felt caught in the net of the city-labyrinth. My daily trek took me by a huge railroad station whose wide-open mouth sucked me in. I would inhale contentedly the feverish steam of departure until the last rumble of the wheels had carried off the always ridiculous waving of good-byes. Then the station became a deserted landscape, a ghostly greenish light hanging over it. I would linger awhile among those who never departed, the tramps, the homeless, the loiterers in search of a windfall, the folk who had ended up there like algae or shells on a beach after the receding of the tide.

Sometimes, on the way home I would take a different route, along the water, revisiting the indescribable sweetness of the maternal arm: the two arms of the Seine surrounding the isle that has always been the city's heartbeat. And my own heart would beat faster as I made my way from one to another of the bridges dotting the river. Suddenly I would have before me that rich architectural ensemble of the cathedral and the swarm of palaces, a view I no longer tried to sort out as I had in the first days. I was drawn by the stones amassed there over the centuries. An apparent lack of order, but an overall organizing principle and the majesty of a royal procession. Impossible to add or remove one stone and not alter the beauty of the whole. There is a mystery to the isle's great man-made creations, built one after another: born of the need of the moment, conceived without a global plan, even when fallen into ruin they present themselves to posterity as a single, coherent entity, powered by an imperious necessity. This harmonious jumble lives its present-day life on the isle's open palm. It is astonishingly changeable, exploiting the brightness of the sky and the reflections off the water. What animates it both inside and out is the weather. The weather of the day, a little different every hour, linked to a less visible weather encrusted in the stones, that experienced by men—joyously or tragically—since the stones were first laid. Passing from pale pink to silky gray during the course of the day, the weather wears purple at the hour of sunset. The light reflected off the stones gleams with the hues of the lilac or the lily, the gladiolus or the wild rose. Light seems to rush toward this mass of stones, which contracts then expands and will be tenderly cleansed by the caring river when night falls.

. . .

I RECALL ONE evening in particular when I walked along the river. Heading east toward home, I had already left Paris's lively center behind. A barge on the water reminded me I was going against the current. As the day faded I was not unhappy to be heading upstream, toward the river's distant initial promise. Where the horizon was already dark, a few hesitant clouds caught the last furtive ray of sun gleaming in the west like a wink or a sign.

Farther on, the river seemed deserted, and an odor of algae and heating oil rose from the banks. Piles of scrap iron and sand intensified the sense of desolation. I walked faster, fighting my melancholy, the melancholy that never went away; nocturnal in habit, it simply waited for an appropriate time to awaken. At that moment, an image loomed up and took over, the image of Haolang and Yumei, who were often in my thoughts, but never that vividly. I stopped short. I was strongly tempted to dive into the river, go upstream like a blind salmon, to the east, far to the east, until I reached the place from whence I had come. Not wanting to go on, I turned left near a bridge. There at the end of a shady street I had seen a silent church silhouetted against a sky dotted with the first stars. Forgotten by men, forgetful of itself, no longer knowing for what purpose it had been built, the structure was simply a presence, ready to receive the unexpected visitor.

On other days, trusting to intuition, I would leave the tediously direct thoroughfares and turn into unfamiliar narrow streets, taking a chance on getting lost. Drab streets inhabited by lives constricted and exhausted by everyday cares. Faded stationery stores, old-fashioned sewing shops, markets washed down with bleach at closing time and emitting smells of bloody meat, moistened bread, or curdled milk. Walking on, like a stray dog I would head instinctively toward light, sound, and odors. Odors of roast meat, marinated vegetables, and strong spices, mingled with heavily accented voices and women's high-pitched laughter. I would soon find myself deep in a neighborhood that seemed to have risen out of oblivion and yet was astonishingly real. I could almost imagine I was in one of those crowded Chinese streets that buzzed with activity and noise late into the night. A lump in my throat, I would start at the sound of a woman calling her child: the long-forgotten shouts of my mother calling me in the street at nightfall.

3

LIVING IN THE Rue de B. neighborhood, I gradually discovered that the great city harbored many loners. They were too self-effacing to show their solitude on their faces: it took time and skill to spot them. Past master in the subject, I could sniff them out at ten leagues. It was almost consoling to think I was not the only one of my ilk and that there were so many like me around. Then I had to laugh at myself: a loner who does not feel alone, that is too much!

There was the woman living in the room next door who invariably began her day with loud eruptions. She would cough and spit a long time, a very long time. Did she have chronic bronchitis? Was she a smoker or a drinker? Did she become choked up in the night and need relief? Whatever the cause, she had established this daily ritual, and thinking no one heard her, she would perform it wholeheartedly until she had reached a kind of painful ecstasy. She coughed angrily and spit peevishly, sometimes steadily, sometimes intermittently, at times faster and faster, almost with rage, as if she wanted to extirpate all her resentments and frustrations. And yet, since the session lasted a long time, not everything occurred with the same degree of intensity. She knew how to modulate her coughing and spitting by injecting some softer, almost tender notes into a noisy fit. Apparently, that was her way of singing: it was her own special song, usually sung near the end, when the irresistible impulse was slowing down and turning into hiccups, into gasps, then into spaced sighs, soft and plaintive as a lullaby. Then silence. She was finally soothed, I would tell myself, and oh, miracle of communion, I felt soothed, too.

Soothed she surely was when she left her room. If I met her on the landing or in the street, I was always amazed by the discrepancy between what I heard and what she provided to the eye. How could I attach to the person standing before me—quiet, modest, of no particular age—the image of the woman who minutes earlier had been unleashing such rage? She was once a cleaning woman, and piecework had taken its toll. Her life had been so marked by self-sacrifice that she gladly let others step ahead of her in line at the delicatessen. Off to the side, she would watch until she saw the clerk was not busy: "That bit of pâté will be fine," or "Just a little piece of liver." It was not hard to picture her back in her room unwrapping the bit of pâté on her plate, cutting it carefully, talking to herself while she ate it as slowly as possible, not to prolong the pleasure so much as to make her day seem shorter.

.   .   .

THERE WAS THE Armenian street peddler who had zigzagged across the Eurasian continent, wherever the winds of chance had taken him. Now he had his tool of the trade, a sort of cart that sat in a dark corner of the courtyard like a shipwreck washed up on the beach. In the morning, when he headed for that day's street corner of the day with his wares—peanuts, pistachios, nougat, and other delicacies—the squeaking of his cart on the courtyard cobblestones would carry me back to early childhood and my first trip to Mount Lu. We had to go part of the way in a mule-drawn cart; the squeaking of the merchant's cart as it hit the ruts was even more piercing. But the sound of jolting was pleasant to my ears; I associated it with the scent of the earth, the coolness of the mountain, and a feeling of deliverance, for my parents we had been fleeing the stifling heat of the city and the burdensome atmosphere of the extended family.

"Aha! You are Chinese! I know China well, that's a fact!" The Armenian would not let me go until I had heard the story of his Chinese travels. His China was the Xinjiang of the Uighurs, an area unfamiliar to me despite my stay in Dunhuang. But that did not let me off easily. Whenever I ran into him, the Armenian did not fail to improve on his initial version. And his desire to recount his travels was inexhaustible. I had the honors when it came to China, but anyone who happened his way—Iranian, Lebanese, or Greek—was treated to the epic tale of his trek through Iran, Lebanon, or Greece.

As volubile and approachable as he was, this humble man who had gone up and down the continent and had "been through the mill" was a loner, in a sense. For he had not told his whole life story to anyone; thus he had not told it to himself. He could never arrange end to end a life that consisted of a succession of expeditions. He could only hand over a fragment to each person he met, so that his life was truncated, with no possible way to link its episodes. And besides, he suffered the same fate as Marco Polo: people did not fully believe what he told them. "Tell us about Uruguay, you've been there, haven't you?" someone hazarded one day. He did not know where the country was and the name was a little like that of a tribe near the China-Iran border, so he answered without thinking: "Oh yes, I've been to Uruguay." Then and there, his reputation as a world traveler was launched! He was helpless against the great heap of disparate memories piling up inside him, crushing him. In the end, he dragged his life around like an animal dragging an overly long tail full of fleas. Feeding these parasites drained his energy, but he himself could not feed off them.

Not being able to connect one's previous and present lives, not being able to tell one's story in its entirety, even to oneself—that is loneliness. More than a few were oppressed by it, and I was among them.

Among them, too, was a violinist from India, who played at metro entrances in east Paris. He told me, "They're more generous in working-class neighborhoods, and they usually give out of friendship rather than charity." Especially since he was so good at playing nostalgic tunes that touched the people.

In his attic room, the bed took up more than half the space. Fortunately he had a skylight. Slender, he would stand on a chair, and with his torso outside, he could practice his violin in the open air; at least it kept him from disturbing the neighbors.

Emotional, always excited, his words came out in spurts, accompanied by sweeping gestures. I avoided talking to him while we were on the street because those waving hands were a nuisance to others. Once he knocked the hat off a woman passing by. But when he pressed his Buddha-like head to his instrument, his playing revealed an infinite gentleness.

Reemerging after a long period of intensive work, one day I realized I had not seen the musician for a while, either in the metro or the neighborhood cafés. I went to his lodgings where the concierge told me that he had been struck by a car. After a stay in the hospital, he had gone back to pick up his things, then had left with no forwarding address. One evening several months later I ran into him on the street. The man was almost unrecognizable. He had lost an eye, and he was dressed in the dirty garments of a semi-tramp. He told me he had not only lost his left eye in the accident but also the use of his left arm; there was no compensation, since the car had sped away and the driver couldn't be found. No question of continuing with his violin. Realizing how poverty-stricken he was, I tried to offer him a little money. The musician refused but accepted an invitation to eat in a little restaurant we had sometimes visited together. The dinner was an ordeal for both of us, since subjects once enthusiastically discussed had now become pointless, ridiculous. I ventured to ask if he might not be better off returning to his own country. "One does not return to one's country without having succeeded, otherwise one should not have left," replied the injured man, a terrible gleam in his remaining eye. "If I have to go back home, I'll die of shame."

Did he finally return to his far-off land, where he had dreamed of one day catching up to Mozart or Brahms? Had he sunk into the lower depths of the Parisian hell where, even reduced to total anonymity, he would forever remain a foreigner? I would never know, because I never saw him again.

.   .   .

BLENDING INTO THE shadows in the far corner of the café the silent, colorless man was just a pair of eyes blinking behind thick glasses. Those eyes took in the entire room as the man sat watching the café come to life or go back to sleep. The whole time he was there in the shadows, he did nothing but look; his eyes became the eyes of the café, like the old lamp above the tables, half on, half out, useful and useless. Was he taking note of something? Was he thinking about something? From his neutral, vacant air, he appeared to be letting images come to him rather than seeking them out. For him, the important thing was to look. At what, exactly? At the life of others, let's say, captured haphazardly. Following the life of others distantly, if not absentmindedly, is after all, a form of living.

On the way back to my lodgings after a day in Montparnasse, I would usually linger in that café awhile; I liked its relaxed atmosphere. But I was a little bothered by the man in the corner. Wherever I sat, I could feel the his gaze in my back. I escaped this stare only on the rare occasions when he was absorbed in reading. I realized he was extremely nearsighted; when he read, he would glue his eyes to the paper, and his rather prominent nose would literally plough the lines as he progressed through the text.

Lingering later than usual one day, I left the café at the same time he did. I followed him. It took patience to stay behind the stranger for he dawdled, stopping at every trash container on the street. He leafed through the discarded newspapers and journals methodically, taking what interested him; soon his arms were loaded with magazines. His final destination was an apartment building with a blank facade; he went in through a back door then started down a dark hall that smelled of mold. It was easy to imagine him sprawled on his bed, sniffing the insistent odor of ink, as he read late into the night, skipping no story—the amusing, the touching, the sordid, and the frankly horrifying.

Recognizing the man to be a true loner, I became fond of him. Every evening, I felt secure once I saw he was in the café. It was almost the same feeling I had back in Nankin or Tchoungking, when I would return from school and see my mother in her accustomed spot in the kitchen. Gradually it dawned on me that he was waiting for me, too. Eventually, inevitably, we struck up a conversation.

The man was a bachelor who had lived with his mother until her death. He had worked for an insurance company all his life, in a low-level position. Day in and day out, year in and year out, he had copied reports of accidents and every sort of dispute. When his superiors needed a substitute or someone to hold down the fort, they thought of the bachelor, always available, but when it was time for promotion, they forgot him. After long years of service, he had been given early retirement. Besides the errors attributable to his increasing nearsightedness, his way of skimming the files with his nose and drooling on them had bothered his colleagues. He did not complain, content to live on little. Apart from his small rent, he spent only for meals and his daily visit to the café. He went on wearing his old clothes, especially the jacket that his mother had patched when it gave out at the elbow. He no longer went to the doctor or even the dentist. He would treat himself when he was sick, delving into his memory for his mother's old remedies. He would endure toothache until the decayed tooth finally had to be pulled.

I was impressed by his resistance to physical suffering. A resistance born of a total forgetfulness of self that probably came from his way of living through others. He had received his training during the years he worked; in those days, the others were his colleagues, his superiors, and all the victims who rose from the pages of his insurance reports. At present, the others were the café patrons he watched every evening and the figures from the magazines he devoured before falling asleep. The man reminded me of one of those Taoist holy men who follow the precept: "For study, one seeks to be more and more all the time; for the Tao, one strives to be less and less each day. Becoming less and less leads to the state of non-activity." Without much effort, this man had reached the state of non-activity; so entrenched in it was he that his bodily woes no longer concerned him. They were incidents happening to someone else. I was sure that at the hour of his death he would be completely at peace, for he had already passed beyond, over to the side of oblivion. Then it would be up to the others, those who had ignored him all his life, to attend to him one last time: the little left of him would have to be put somewhere.

4

ALREADY FAMILIAR with the Chinese method of "three layers and five points," at Beaux-Arts I worked hard to learn the Western style of portraiture. After that, I became bold and tried out my skills in cafés, like so many others. I earned a fair amount, supplementing my scholarship, inadequate as the cost of living increased. During that whole period, I was fascinated, not to say obsessed, by faces, so much so that on the streets I no longer saw bodies. My eyes encountered only a swarm of heads floating in the air, avoiding each other or greeting each other with tics and grimaces, sometimes with smiles.

And what is this creation of so little bulk, probably the most changeable, the most uncertain, the most elusive thing in the universe? And, indeed, isn't the painting of a decent portrait the first sign of a true artist? What does a face consist of? A few dozen square centimeters of skin covering a skull and some bones, plus a small number of orifices. But it is the face, almost nothing, with no real thickness or depth, that points to the human being and makes each of us a separate entity; for of all signs the face is the most identifying. It is, no doubt about it, what allows us to say "I," and go on to "you," and "he." It allows a heart, a soul, to be revealed. Over a lifetime, a face is modeled by repressed desires, hidden torments, sustained lies, stifled screams, swallowed sobs, unexpressed grief, wounded pride, broken promises, fantasized revenge, suppressed anger, shameless acts, controlled hysteria, interrupted monologues, betrayed confidences, pleasures too soon over, ecstasy too soon vanished. As surely as tree rings, every wrinkle bears the marks of life. Unbeknownst to us, our experience is revealed in our faces, even while we make a daily superhuman effort to keep it hidden. Our faces are what we know the least about ourselves. Our faces are what we carry above our shoulders so that others may recognize us, attach a name to us, like us or despise us.

Was that all? Was that all I felt before a face? I knew full well it was not. For the universe to have started with nothing, only amorphous matter, and after so much blind groping to have produced a face, constantly renewed, each time unique, there must have been a secret hidden somewhere. For the face to have become that vessel concentrating all the essential sounds and senses, there had to exist at the start an immeasurable need to see, to hear, to feel, and to speak, and to collect the whole under a single mask without which seeing, hearing, feeling, and speaking would be no more than scattered fragments. And sometimes beauty—which is called "beauty"— will fasten itself to the mask, exerting its power.

A woman, whose face I did not see at first, just her legs. Through circumstance: I was in a crowded metro car. From my folding seat, I looked between the standing riders and spied on the seat across from me a pair of legs so marvelously framed that they formed a self-contained unit. I had the impression of seeing the legs of woman for the first time, and their beauty took my breath away. How true it is, I said to myself, that in painting it's all a question of framing. In the old times, didn't the Chinese artists like to isolate a flower in a hole to grasp its intrinsic reality?

At some of the stops I had ample opportunity, not to observe the legs, but to be bewitched by their harmonious curve and their full, rounded shape, like a ripe fruit. They were two of a kind despite appearances, neither their previous growth nor their pose making them symmetrical; they were complementary, engaged in a dialogue in which each understood the other's thoughts, a conversation no prying gaze could disturb.

That living unit, although perfectly proportioned, had an exaggerated, almost insolent quality that made it all the more fascinating. The cause? Perhaps the slightly excessive length, the pronounced hollow at the ankle, the boldly protuberant knee. What did it matter! Such tiny details are the mark of genius. The imperfect in the perfect, the unfinished in the established: how the Chinese calligrapher knows the secret alchemy of these things! It had taken millions of years of life's randomness to arrive at such a result. It had also taken the woman a lifetime of care and attention to arrive at such grace.

Could it be said that the woman is the holder of beauty, an asset she manages over the years the best she can? Actually, beauty is a profound mystery going far beyond the person of the woman and is a burden she carries only briefly. And while she carries it or puts up with it, sometimes awkwardly, the world clamors to feed off it. Doesn't the old Chinese proverb say "Beautiful woman, tragic fate"? She tries to make personal use of it, not knowing that the purpose and the laws of beauty do not come under the human order.

My delight was not to last. In the stifling metro, I had received it like manna from heaven. When I saw the face of the woman, my heart sank. I almost said *the face,* since from that day forward that was the face by which I would measure every woman's face. A scarred face that no eyes could stand facing for very long. The face to which the official lover had once sworn eternal vows and which would receive vows no more. What had happened? An automobile accident, that privilege of modern life? In a few brief seconds, the care of a lifetime wiped out. Her head was so unmatched with the rest of her body that an unconsciously cruel onlooker might have said that she was off to a masquerade, some grotesque sport with masks. Yet there was nothing more real in its completeness, just like the woman sitting there. Was she no longer a full-fledged person, not even to herself? Did she really have to be injured a second time, not by fate, but by the eyes of men . . . ? My observation, discreet as it was, had not escaped the woman. Her eyes—lovely, if one made a real effort to look at them—flashed angrily, directing scorn at the foreigner who took the liberty of "eyeing" her. Did she know that her face spoke more eloquently to the foreigner than did a Mona Lisa or a Fornarina, which said nothing to him? Did she know that the foreigner—at whom she would have barely glanced under other circumstances,—by looking long at her nose and her lips would come to love them like treasures? He whose profession it was to track down, as through a palimpsest, the earliest version, in which beauty is not yet a simple given to be preserved and fixed on glazed paper but is the impulse to strive for beauty, an impulse which by definition is not corruptible. Are human beings still capable of this impulse?

5

I WENT TO Holland. In Amsterdam I saw Rembrandt and in The Hague, Vermeer. In them I recognized two high points of Western painting: the passionate flame of the one and the silent music of the other.

How could their spirits have been produced in a country so small, so flat, spread out under a low sky and bathed in silvery light, a land almost colorless were it not for the tulips that foretell spring, their colors so dazzling that the eye cannot long behold them? Opening, these blooms reveal a contained, domesticated violence, so very like the calm and ordered country that had come into being after a long, fierce struggle. Unrewarding soil threatened by the sea, tenacious people forged by necessity.

My keen interest in boundaries of every kind led me to the Great Dike. There I saw the result of a hidden energy that could count on no support but itself. "Come hell or high water." No better expression to describe the gigantic bar men had valiantly planted in the heart of a hostile sea. The day of my visit, an unbelievably violent rainstorm, a veritable cosmic rage, pelted the dike, making an indistinct jumble of the sky, sea, and earth. At the end of the day, I waited at a bus stop, in a driving rain; a bus passed by without seeing me. Another would not be along until much later, and night was falling. I made my way to a nearby café. Dimly lit interior. Nobody paid me any attention; the barely audible conversations continued, sprinkled with occasional bursts of laughter. Wet clear through, I stayed by the heat and tried a cup of mulled wine to stop my teeth from chattering. An anonymous Chinese lost in the Far North, I was overcome by a sense of my physical fragility and by a feeling of such loneliness that I had to repress sobs.

Two hours later, climbing into the next bus, I was wetter than ever, like a drowning victim just pulled from the water. I stood facing the passengers, and I dripped so much that a little rivulet ran to the back of bus. Hair plastered to my face, dreadfully embarrassed, I looked for a commiserating smile to relieve my embarrassment. But nobody moved a muscle; I encountered only impassive, silent faces. In spite of wanting to stand because of the discomfort of sitting in wet clothes, I took a seat in the rear of the bus. My teeth chattered so fiercely that the man in front of me turned around. A long face spotted with freckles, piercing but markedly sympathetic eyes. Suddenly I thought wildly, desperately of Van Gogh. I saw him right beside me, and very like his drawing of the bare tree with the gnarled trunk. He whispered: "Don't despair, don't torture yourself. Let destiny drive in its point, right to the bone, for from that something significant emerges. Human life is impenetrable but full of meaning. Set your goal and head straight for it without wondering whether you will reach it. There is a time for everything, isn't there? A time for suffering, a time for joy, a time for turbulence, a time for peace. And above all, there is the overflowing force of life. There is the starry night of Arles. There is the sea laughing across the cottages of Saintes-Maries . . ."

The overflowing force of life, present in the radiant expressions captured in Frans Hals's incomparable portraits. Portraits I studied in Haarlem the next day, with a sense of peace. Discovering Hals's quick, dazzling art, I asked myself a question that had never before crossed my mind: "These canvasses I am admiring at this moment, are they any help to me in my state? Can they cure me of my fear, my thirst, my wounds, my loneliness? I had barely formulated the question when I was overcome by shame. What, judge art in terms of succor, support, comfort? Reduce the function of art to therapy? I held firm, however, refusing to renounce my question. And the feeling of shame gave way to one of deliverance. All at once, I was relieved of the burden encumbering me since I had begun to visit the museums of the West: lacking my own criteria, I had been following art history handbooks slavishly, submitting to their hierarchy of values. From now on I would have my own key. As I encountered each picture, I would bring forth my unhealthy state and ask myself whether or not that particular work cured me, fulfilled me, pulled me out of my rut of weariness, reconciled me with real life. From now on I could step lightly through interminable galleries that smelled oppressively of wax, wearing myself out as I pursued the legions of painters who had accomplished their common task: to fill space to the very edges, to lay on color until they'd had enough, to satisfy the eternal need for anecdote and illustration. I would treat myself to the luxury of admiring in this or that work of a bygone age, not the central panel with its overly edifying composition, but some small lower panel in which the artist dared give free rein to his inner vision.

But Rembrandt? If the handbook hadn't pointed out his importance, would I have approached him? I remembered saying to myself when I first saw his paintings in the Louvre: "Finally a painter for whom light does not shine; it simply radiates." At the time, I realized how strongly Chinese painting had conditioned me. In China, the Ancients rarely spoke of light (one might say they sought the bland essence of pure space). Western painters who played too wildly with the effects of light caused me physical discomfort. In Rembrandt I could see a mystical vision that went beyond the simple play of chiaroscuro, a light that came from some original darkness peopled with invisible creatures, a light intensely internalized by the painter. Quite early he must have understood that the true flame comes from man's inner being, that one must carve out a space in oneself so that human material can find its way in and be transformed. How old was he when he painted his mother's portrait, then his father's? Twenty-two? Twenty-three? Through his parents' faces, the imprint of humanity on them, Rembrandt was already sounding out the secrets of any life: the joys and the sorrows, the terrors and the consolations, the serene beaches tended, the gulfs to be crossed. His own life, so settled, so promising, would be woven of interludes of exceptional happiness and a succession of sorrows, resounding successes, and irrevocable repudiations. In the eyes of the world, his life would probably appear a veritable catastrophe. In the eyes of the Creator, perhaps his life had to be like that for him to become the unbelievable artist he was, the figure who lit up our poor planet with a gleam emerging from deep within its richest soil.

As I became better acquainted with Rembrandt the man and his works—those I had already seen in the Louvre and those I was discovering in Amsterdam, a city imbued with his presence—something occurred between me and the painter, a phenomenon akin to bewitchment and so powerful that at first I nearly recoiled from it. Mistrustful by nature, had I ever allowed myself to be so taken by another's vision? I had come with the simple purpose of studying the oeuvre of a great painter, and now this Dutchman with physique and habits far different from mine was breaking into my very being, invading me. Entering Rembrandt's private universe, I had hardly expected him to penetrate my own. Insidiously but surely, the creatures of the Dutchman were besieging the field of my fancy, laying bare the images of those desires and dreams that inhabited my unconscious. Now that my mother's image was fading, I could think of her only through the features of Rembrandt's second wife, Hendrickje, in whose eyes I recognized my mother's anxious gentleness and melancholy candor. And could my desire for a woman have been better incarnated than in Bathsheba, whose body exuded a calm sensuality in every detail and which, despite a hovering shadow of remorse, took humble delight in being so fully alive? Even the thought of my little sister (her laughing moon face at the Feast of Lanterns) would now be associated with the young girl slipping through the group of men in *The Night Watch.*

Faced with this progressive possession dispossessing me, it was natural that my first reaction should be negative. But I acquiesced quickly, resisting no more. My now awakened intuition told me that the hand of the great artist was the most fraternal I could encounter in the West, a rare healing hand capable of soothing my longings and regrets.

From that moment on, I embraced all the gazes emerging from the warm night. All became mine, as each in turn illuminated a patch of my buried sensibility, of my stifled reserve of humanity. The gaze of the painter himself of course. That of Saul, that of Christ, those of the evangelist, the conspirator, Lucretia plunging the dagger into her breast, blind Homer. And the non-gaze of the prodigal son, nothing visible but his neck. The non-gaze of one who, after turning away to look toward his own greater desire, no longer meets any gaze and has given up his own gaze. He is unaware that real life is a simple turning around, a simple face to face. Is not the prodigal son he who tried to go the longest way around and thus risked breaking forever the fragile circle of human love? Although the son in the painting is finally reunited with his father, I myself was condemned to wander. I had covered so much of the world that I had forgotten the way home. All my life, whenever I have heard voices in the wind crying to me: "While there is time, return, return . . . !" I could only answer: "There is no longer time. . . . It's too far, too late . . ."

      .   .   .

TOO LATE PROBABLY to find solace in the peaceful vision of Vermeer. Too late to return to the simple things around which women trustingly wait, sure that letters will bring good news and that the afternoon light refracted by the walls will transform each object, each look, into diamond. Sure that nothing in life will be scattered or lost and that in the face of the young woman with the parted lips all the colors of her turban, her collar, and her eyes—the blue, the yellow, the white—will flawlessly converge at the unbroken dream's point of light: a jangling pearl. Sure that a wandering god, remembering the human treasure, will pass silently through a narrow street in their good city of Delft, where between red brick walls the hues of wispy clouds and bright window panes join those of lilacs and where tasks are accomplished unhurriedly, amply filling lives.

6

I WENT TO Italy. My budget did not allow me to think of staying long, and I planned to pick up a fair idea of Renaissance painting by visiting Florence and Rome. Upon discovering the abundance of things to see, I nearly panicked; more frightening still was the number of styles or "schools," a proliferation favored by the heterogeneity of Italy's regions and the long duration of its artistic adventure. The country saw more than three centuries of feverish creativity in a few great centers that were far from one another but fierce rivals in invention nonetheless. To my mind, the only thing comparable was the China of the Tang and the Song Dynasties: for six hundred years, from the eighth through the thirteenth centuries, creativity had been continuous, carrying the artistic adventure to its highest point. When I at last came face to face with Italian art, I had been fortified by my own tradition and my experience at Dunhuang; without such a background, I would have been helpless.

In a few small cities I was the unwary victim of occasional hostility, fascist or racist in origin: everywhere else, I encountered the warmth and kindness of the Italians. In the Italy of the postwar era, I even found similarities to China in some working-class neighborhoods. People struck up conversations readily, asking questions in their direct manner.

"Cinese?"

"Si."

"Chiang Kai-shek or Mao Tse-tung?"

That question was usually the first on their lips: the Communists had just taken over in China. Called upon to choose, I was invariably perturbed. I would extricate myself with a question of my own: "De Gasperi or Togliatti?" The Italians often had a ready answer.

On the train to Rome, the conductor checked my ticket, then began to chat. After the inevitable questions, the man answered mine with a resounding "Togliatti!" I did not have to choose between Chiang or Mao, for my status as a Chinese had been enough to make the Italian friendly. He pointed out I could travel beyond my destination at no additional cost if I took slow night trains. His colleagues would look after me. And that is how, unshaven and unwashed, I ended up in Naples.

In that great meridional city whose gilded splendors shouted down the shadow of the plague, I sampled regional dishes at the *trattorie* and *rosticcerie* along the streets; I was drunk on the sounds and smells that carried me along. Seeking some respite from the bustle of the avenues, one day I walked into a monastery cloister, giving myself up to the coolness of the stonework around the fountain. At the end of a path, I came upon an elderly monk framed in the doorway of a little porch.

"Cinese?"

I nodded, awaiting the unavoidable question: "Tchang or Mao?" Nothing. Nothing but two shiny tears trickling down the monk's broad face, two tears trickling from eyes become almonds after long years in China, tears running down cheeks of a mat Asiatic pallor. With a northern Shandong accent, in an awkward Chinese both touching and comic, he told me of his nearly forty years as an overseas missionary. Driven from China abruptly, he felt out of place in his homeland, as though he had been destined to die in a foreign land. He showed me to the other end of the parlor, to a room where he had set up his own little museum. Religious objects, a copper censer from the Ming period, pious scenes hand-embroidered and now faded, missals and prayer books in Chinese, worn walkingsticks from his days in the countryside . . .

Tearing himself away from his memories, he said, "To know the real Italy, don't keep to the big cities. Go to Apulia; that's where I was born. One of my nephews has a farm there. He will put you up."

I traveled to that region, where I discovered fruits and vegetables—olives, artichokes, peppers—so fragrant and tasty they brought back memories of the Chinese earth. And the spontaneous hospitality of my hosts could not but bring back memories of the generosity of my countrymen. And like China, and even more than China, this southern territory openly displayed its true self, its opulence and its poverty, all the while concealing a buried side that no form of speech had yet learned to express. Determined to leave behind the grandiose and the flamboyant whereby human architecture attempts to defy the assaults of time, I took the opportunity offered me and explored a land divided between mountain and sea. Under a harsh light barely tempered by the sea breeze and the opaque shade of the pines, living things slowed the steps of the traveler, penetrated him with all the density of their presence, obliged him to ask their secrets. Capturing clouds and winds, taking in wounded birds and weary beasts, the ageless olive trees—felled dragons—had everywhere established savage sanctuaries no less authentic than the Byzantine chapels that adorned the region. Who were they, the olives? Emblems of the place? Banners of the infinite? One might wonder but could not explain. Their teachings seemed directed only to those who could attend their rustling silence. Were their dreads and agonies, forever mixed with those of the human world, of any help to that world? Why were the olives here, so obstinately here? And why were men here beside them, seemingly in harmony with the earth and yet so uncertain, so consumed by cares and expectations?

Away from the West's cities for the first time, at the very tip of the continent, far from everything, I was impelled as never before to look long and hard at the vain aspirations of human destiny. In this country where some still followed feudal practice, women did not dine at the communal table. And yet how visible was, the glimmer in their eyes, a blend of muzzled candor and stifled dreams; with no artifice, Apulian women could look at a stranger and reveal all their astonishment and solicitude. Behind a mask of words hopelessly day to day, I felt the pulse of passions happy and tragic, of short-lived loves and long-lived resentments. At the heart of the dreariness of days that even the singing language did not enliven, I saw the ever-wider secret lacerations: behind imperfectly closed shutters, bodies sweaty with lust and transfixed by an incandescent torpor; or the cat I came upon at the edge of the field, disemboweled with a pocketknife and eyes gouged out, lying between the dense grass and the lingering patch of blood where the intermittent rays of the sun tried out effects of ruby and jade. In short, everything had from time immemorial been broken and separated, without cries—cheerful or subdued—covering the secret wound. At the hour when the crows skimmed the ground, the traveler in search of lodging could see the mute mist rise behind human volubility. An old man on a doorstep, seated like a wooden statue screwed to its pedestal, did not open his mouth except to shout rudely at a group of children returning to their orphanage. One boy broke away from the group, caught up by who knows what in the distance. As he tried to stuff an overly long shirttail into outgrown trousers, with the eyes of a bewildered mole he stared at the stranger; or rather at the elongated shadow the stranger dragged behind him in the setting sun, perhaps the shadow of what had been snatched away in the beginning, which the stranger suspected was there still but forever out of reach. At that moment, in the declining Apulian light, I heard again the same old injunction, this time decisive: "Never again be a beggar on this earth. Be the one who receives all, even the unthinkable. And all the things of which you are the receptacle you shall carry to the very end, so that those who seek consolation in you will survive. . . ."

·   ·   ·

AND WHAT DID I get from the painting of the Renaissance? Coming from afar, many centuries later, could I really put myself in the shoes of Italian painters and see what they had seen, with all that had obsessed them in their time? Useless questions, probably. One thing was certain: however obvious the uniqueness of Western painting may appear at first sight, it had taken a visit to Italy for me to comprehend fully the true extent of the break with tradition, and to comprehend the place and the moment when the break had materialized. When exactly? And with whom? Considering the painters chronologically, which ones made me realize the balance had been tipped? Not the pre-Renaissance greats, like Cimabue, Duccio, Fra Angelico and Lorenzetti. Among them, I still felt in my element. I knew Buddhist art well enough, with its scenes of adoration and narration, to recognize in the figures here the same fervent piety, the same inward gaze born of pain and ecstasy. With Cimabue, the more the frescoes were faded by time, reduced to working drawings—the Assisi *Crucifixion,* for example—the more the figures, now taut as a bow, resembled those of Wei at Dunhuang. And Giotto? No, not even Giotto. Of course, in him the great dramaturgy had already been set in motion. But his space, boldly construed as it was, was still indeterminate, tied to the unknown.

The one who first stepped out of the ranks to proclaim haughtily, "After us, painting will be acted on a stage with flawless perspective!" was Masaccio, the painter I came to know from my stay in the monastery next to Santa Maria del Carmine. Every night before the bell announced supper, I would stand in the chapel a good while, in the shadow of his frescoes. It was not hard to see that when the time was ripe, this bold genius—here so briefly—had needed but a few years to rip apart the ancient curtain of space and nudge toward center stage not a creature of myth but man himself: man still taken with the sacred, and already too aware of his new power, man anxious to see himself in performance. Is it an exaggeration to say that, with Masaccio and those who were to follow, Western man had feverishly "staged" himself? His backdrop the objective universe, man now played the leading role. The universe, while participating in man's action, had been relegated to the role of stage set. And everything man had experienced in the company of the universe was now transmuted into nostalgia for a far-off past.(Ah, how nostalgically I would set out to track down the West's long line of painters who sought to restore the lost kingdom: Giorgione, Poussin, le Lorrain, Turner, Cézanne, Gauguin . . .). The beginning of greatness. The beginning of solitude. Later I would understand the West's obsession with the themes of the mirror and Narcissus. Snatched from the created world, setting himself up as the only subject, man loved to admire his reflection. After all, from then on it was his only way of seeing himself. Gazing at his reflection, he captured his own image, with its salient feature the power fed by a liberated spirit. Steadily contemplating and exalting himself, he soon acquired a practiced eye that would not stop until it had transformed all that was not he into object—more precisely into object of conquest. No longer acknowledging any other subject around him, he long deprived himself—willingly? in spite of himself?—of interlocutors and peers. Could he really escape a keen awareness of solitude and death?

I do not think I ever felt as much in harmony with the Chinese painters of the Sung and Yuan Dynasties as I did in the museums of Florence and Venice. Those artists believed in the virtues of the emptiness in which organic breaths move. They believed body and soul because their cosmological vision spoke to them of those virtues. Over the centuries this cosmology had reiterated—and here all the teachings of my master rang in my ears—that creation stems from the primal Breath, which derives from the original Void. By splitting into the vital breaths *yin* and *yang* among others, the primal Breath rendered possible the birth of the Multiple. Thus connected, the One and the Multiple are all of a piece. Drawing conclusions from that concept, the painters aimed not at imitating the infinite variations of the created world, but at participating in the very activity of Creation. Between the *yin* and the *yang*, between the Five Elements, between the Ten Thousand living entities, they strove to insert the middle Void, the sole guarantee of the smooth functioning of the organic breaths, which become spirit upon attaining rhythmic resonance. Not astonishing that for a goodly number of Chinese, a pictorial masterpiece uniting the slender beauty of a bamboo leaf and the endless flight of a crane is much more than an object of enjoyment; it is the sole locale of real life, a place immediately inhabitable.

In China I used to laugh at that, for I did not attribute such powers to art. But here I found myself thinking that if the art of painting had never existed, humanity would have been deprived of some of its most lofty, purified dreams. I, anyway, would have suffocated.

"You are right," said Mario. "I would gladly exchange one of these Titians for a Guo Xi or a Mi Fu!"

Mario was a painter I had met in the Galleria degli Uffizi. Working side by side with a German named Hans, copied painting in museums. He was not impressed by the overwhelming heritage. Born to it, he could run a finger over a work on display without excessive respect, like a child who dares to pull grandfather's beard. In the eyes of this young man born to wealth, the pictures his ancestors had willed him were there merely to provide him a living. Hadn't he mass-produced copies of Lippis and Del Sartos, copies that some of his clients, taken with their spanking newness, had found better than the originals?

Hans had greater qualms and asked himself pedantically, "How can one paint after all that? Why even try?"

"Life goes on!" was Mario's commonsense answer. "We must continue eating spaghetti," and he led his two comrades behind the museum to streets where the pasta was delicious and the Chianti as bright as the laughter of the girls.

In the middle of the meal, growing serious—his face suddenly handsome and poignant—Mario had something to say: "Don't get lost, Tianyi. Don't look as if you don't know which way to turn. Of course there are really too many paintings. Here's a bit of advice, words from a copyist. Stick to a few painters who speak to you, two, three, four, not more. Track them down. Get to know every one of their works. Eventually you will be a close friend. You'll understand what inspires them, what motivates them, and you'll even catch on to their tricks. Believe me, without being a genius yourself you can get to know a genius from the inside. When that happens, even Da Vinci, even Michelangelo will not appear so overwhelming. You'll chat with him like a friend, just as we are chatting with each other now."

Wise advice indeed. Why hadn't I thought of it? How could I have so quickly forgotten my experience with Rembrandt and my resolution to devote myself only to those artists who cured me?

I went to the great artists, looking for moments when they were not preoccupied with the showy and the monumental. And I discovered spaces full of listening and exchange. Giorgione's bolt of lightning that rents the radiantly blue-green air: is it a sign of threat or of a tacit accord? Bordering the clouds and echoing in the woman's rounded body, its luminous curve flashes swiftly over the rigidly geometric bridge and buildings at the center of painting, seeming to reestablish the invisible circle that moves between earth and sky. And, in the painting hung in Venice's Galleria dell' Academia, what of the angel Carpaccio introduces into Saint Ursula's bedchamber? Is he an intruder? He will not awaken nor frighten the young woman as she sleeps surrounded by familiar, orderly, protecting things. He will not take another step, he will refrain from speaking a single word. Although everything may have in fact already been accomplished, time stands still, contemplative and fulfilled, much like the little round window just below the ceiling. . . .

Then I came to know Piero della Francesca's unbounded universe, so amply filled by figures of an exceptional plasticity. These stern, haughty figures, spaced at a respectful distance from one another, their impassive expressions accentuating the dramatic scenes, reminded me oddly of the mountains in the scrolls of Fan Kuan. A strange parallel. Would the Chinese painter agree to leave his eleventh-century retreat to follow in the footsteps of the donor and converse with Saint Jerome? He would probably do so gladly, for in this intimate scene that hangs in the Academia, the unusual composition—the background is placed higher than the human figures and appears to support them and penetrate them—makes the tree, the rock, and the surrounding hills seem active participants in the conversation.

The Arezzo painter laid aside his impassivity when he painted his mother. At Monterchi, I stood a long while in tête-à-tête with the *Madonna del parto* in the cemetery chapel, a haven of coolness in the droning light and odor of a summer's day. A simple, human woman—so human that she was to produce a God?—standing in her sorrowful dignity. The hand placed on the stomach, where the dress opens, suggests both giving and protection. But the choice is not hers. The angels have already opened the curtain. Like any mother, she must give, and the folds of her blue dress will billow out, limited only by heaven's canopy.... Taking advantage of the attendant's momentary absence, I went up to the fresco and stroked the hand and the dress. I knew that someday—my mother had no tomb—I would paint my own fresco. That would be my way of connecting all.

7

HE ADVENT OF THE Communists, which they themselves called "Liberation," ushered in a completely new era for China.

Dreaming of just such an era, men and women—many of them quite young—had committed themselves to the revolutionary ranks in an exemplary spirit of self-denial and sacrifice. They had accepted all the hardships, endured all the ordeals, and given everything, including their lives. Several million young peasants recruited into the army had died in combat. Amid the ruins from long years of civil war and the eight years of the Sino-Japanese conflict, a beating of drums and a clashing of cymbals summoned an entire people to the construction of the society everyone longed for.

Throughout Chinese history, these vibrant forces had never failed to appear. Each time tyranny, corruption, and invasion had left the country teetering on the brink, with every truth violated and every human value trampled, it was they who saved our old race from complete annihilation. They furnished a long line of martyrs, a golden thread running through an endless tapestry woven of laughter and tears, dreams and fury. Most of these martyrs were imbued with the Confucian ethic, which so extolled the virtues of human dignity that it assigned man the privilege and duty of participating as a third in the work of Heaven and Earth. Others were moved by the

Taoist spirit with its inclination to oppose the established order, for it held that man could abide only by the Tao, the great universal Way. These two currents of belief came together in at least one basic notion, the concept of the incorruptible Breath—synonymous with the incorruptible Spirit—that moves the Universe.

In the twentieth century, backed by a whole generation of valiant men and women, Sun Yat-Sen had overthrown the corrupt Manchu Dynasty, founding the First Republic in 1912. He died before overcoming the feudal forces that reigned in all the provinces; they continued to have their way, for his successors could not contain them. More than twenty years later, another man, a born revolutionary, was the next to capture and channel the rising energy of men of conscience. Once the divisions and conflicts of the initial period had been settled, he came to the fore among the numerous revolutionary leaders because of his theoretical thinking and his tactical skills. At the head of his party, he led a lengthy struggle; through him, the common cause triumphed, but the sacrifices had been enormous. After the seizure of power, the new republic was proclaimed; on that occasion the uncontested leader appeared: contrary to his accustomed image—deliberately casual, sometimes disheveled—he was stuffed into a severe suit buttoned to the neck, his demeanor serious, hieratic, almost imperial, as if it were not that easy to divest oneself of the tried and true model of the old system, with its rituals, its language, its archetypal imagery; one slipped into it more or less unconsciously, as into a mold.

Was it conceivable that the revolutionaries might withdraw once the revolution was finished, instead of imposing a new order that would necessarily end up harsh and rigid? Definitely not. They would need to have been sages, not men dedicated to carrying their actions through, men bound to the desire for power. Inevitably, a new order was established. Just as in the past, leaders reiterated that the necessity for it had to be understood. A matter of revolution, wasn't it? It was essential "to clean up the remnants of counterrevolution"; it was essential to "pull out the roots of feudalism." How one wishes the revolutionary genius in charge had kept his lofty outlook, had remained loose and free, free in relation to the weight of history, in relation to his own obsessions. How one wishes the order he inaugurated had been different from those that came before. Apparently the human imagination was not yet ready to conceive of something else. And there was the historical reality. Besides the ancient imperial model, there was a more up-to-date model, more scientific, established a few decades earlier by the big brother next door. More than thirty years of armed struggle and increasingly tight organization had created a rigid system, which hardly allowed for flexibility or innovation. Inevitably, a country as vast as a continent was marked into little squares. Not a village that was not transformed into a production brigade; not a city dweller who was not made a member of a neighborhood committee. Through regular criticism and self-criticism sessions, everyone was encouraged to become aware of his ideological baggage, to bare his soul. Henceforth the country was inhabited by people asked to rid themselves of their ulterior motives, people always ready to serve the Cause. Maybe there was justification for enforcing such a strict regime on a society that had foundered in anarchy for nearly a century? But did the theoretical basis—that uncompromising collectivism born of a moment of excessive rationality in the Western world—really take into account the make-up of man, the flesh and blood creature driven by secret desires and drawn to unpredictable dreams? Nevertheless, in its rendezvous with destiny, that generation of Chinese was ready and all too willing to provide the effort needed to snatch the old nation out of its corruption.

In early 1950, a letter from Haolang and Yumei arrived, fairly short, written in a new language, rather clichéd. The gist of the message was that they were together, living in Shanghai. I answered immediately. Without being overly expansive, I told them that I looked forward to seeing them once my stay in Paris was over.

Having said that, was I really convinced deep down that I would see them soon? From my vantage point at the other end of the vast Eurasian continent, I had a vague sense of a solid, aggregate, increasingly unknown reality retreating from me, much like a ship that cleaved the waves as it carried away those most dear to me. Major things were underway in China, significant, of vast proportions, unprecedented in history. For he who presided over that reality, a man out of the ordinary, excited by the prospect of action that might affect the whole continent if not the whole world, could not stick to the humdrum, the routine, for long. He did not stop launching, one after another, movements and campaigns—"Spit out the bitter water," "Three against," "Five against," "Purification and rectification"—as a first step toward the visionary goals obsessing him. With a liking for grandiose statistics, he reasoned in massive terms: so many million people involved in such and such a campaign, such and such a percentage of the population dedicated to such and such an endeavor, . . .

These mass movements could be explained by the logic of revolution; in the domain of the spirit, however, the Leader was faced with a contradiction that would come out over the years. He had not had extensive schooling, but he had read widely. He was aware of the grandeur of certain traditional values of Chinese culture. Secretly, how he dreamed of an era worthy of the Tang and Song Dynasties, an era when geniuses would outdo each other in brilliance, when there would be an explosion of immortal works! But he had another side: with his voluntarist vision, he tended to a greatly oversimplified concept of human nature and creativity. Sure of the superiority of his ideas, anxious to become the beacon of humanity, he found it impossible not to impose a narrow path, his own, which led toward a single goal; and impossible not to stick to his hard line, which would inevitably stifle the spirit of all others.

With fear and trembling, over the months and years I followed what was happening on the ideological front in China. Back in 1942, in the Yan'an days, a harsh campaign had taken place in the wake of the Wang Shiwei affair and also in connection with the Yan'an Pronouncement on literary and artistic creation. In 1952, the film *The Life of Wu Yuan* was attacked in what was actually a campaign against all artists and intellectuals. Early in 1954, it was Hu Feng's turn: the distinguished literary critic dared express his reservations about the Yan'an Pronouncement. Always bold, Hu Feng sent the Chairman a long letter, explaining the literary situation in the country and suggesting conditions that would permit true creativity. Cut to the quick, the recipient of the letter took immediate action. All writers, artists, and other intellectuals were invited to write letters denouncing the errors of the guilty party. The campaign then took on a more radical turn; Hu Feng's close associates were forced to make his personal correspondence public. The authorities tried their best to show that famous writer Lu Xun's favorite critic had been a traitor since the thirties, not to mention an agent of the Nationalist Party. The news was frightening, and I knew there would be repercussions for Haolang. Since he had published poems in the journals started by Hu Feng, he was bound to be in police files as a member of the "clique."

Near the end of 1954, I was startled to see in the mail one day an envelope in Yumei's hand. Posted through an intermediary in Hong Kong, the letter informed me that Haolang had been sent to a "re-education" camp in a marshy region of northern Jianxi, my home province.

8

N THE DAYS that followed, I strayed through the streets of Paris like a wandering soul; the suffering and disgrace of the Friend and the Lover became my own. And I knew their ordeal would go on indefinitely, for there had been no formal trial or sentencing.

One morning I awakened in my dingy room and realized that China was henceforth closed to me, that I could not return, that I would never return. I was in exile, condemned without appeal.

The idea had never before crossed my mind and was earthshaking, comparable to the shock of learning one has an incurable disease. The sudden knowledge that one is in exile for good, no return possible, is like a death foretold. At that moment, an entire life with its memories and—even more painful—its hopes, has been snatched away, is out of reach. Nothing is the same; there was a before, there is an after. One still goes through the motions, pursuing the innumerable, tedious routines of everyday life, even breaking into a smile when politeness so requires. But a fleeting glimpse of oneself in the mirror or a fleeting memory of some past happiness is a nail through the heart. Parallel with the life unfolding in the here and now is a life between the lines, lived before, in another place, in a setting henceforth more and more hazy, more and more distant, inaccessible. When awareness comes, it is already too late; the possibility of revisiting the other setting, the other life, is forever denied, even for one last time.

Except in dreams. In dreams I would find myself happily stretched out on a bed improvised from school desks that smelled of dried ink and squashed bugs; or I might be tenderly stroking the rough wall of a Yangzi gorge as if it were a woman's smooth flank. And beloved faces, even those I thought I'd forgotten for good, would enter the very depths of my being, unannounced, as if it were the most natural thing in the world. The faces of my father, my sister, but mostly of my mother, whose box of ashes I could see on the shelf by my bed. Faces of other members of my family. The face of Haolang and the face of Yumei, separately or together. For a long period, they slipped into my dreams at almost regular intervals. Their presence was no longer connected with my past but with my present, in happy or tragic situations: strolls through Paris or its suburbs; lively conversations in a mixture of French and Chinese; a chase through a dark alley where the other does not hear my shouts but finally turns around, revealing the face of a stranger; the discovery that the curious gathered around the victims of a fatal accident are looking down at Haolang or Yumei. . . . These happy or tragic moments would end with my suddenly awakening in the night, gasping for breath. Once, however, I had no doubt the thing was real. The two who dwelled in me were telephoning from a hotel, telling me they had just arrived in Paris and asking me to come to them. I got up and dressed, the Friend's northern accent still ringing in my ear: "Don't forget your sketchbook!" and the voice of the Lover: "Don't keep us waiting. We're hungry!" On the way out, I stuck my hand in my pocket; the little slip of paper with the address of the hotel was no longer there.

How was I to survive in this foreign country? Through the understanding of an administrator, my scholarship had been extended; but now it had run out. There I was, without a degree, without a real profession. Painter, of course, but not having an arrangement with any gallery, I managed to sell paintings only rarely. Some of my compatriots were rapidly establishing reputations, however; they had mastered just the right combination of artistic elements. I had gone too far afield. I wanted to take the long way around; it was an agenda that would have required two or three lives. Could I have done otherwise? I was loaded down with baggage crammed full of disordered memories to digest and obscure meanings to elucidate. And in art I had followed the teachings of my old master and I had experienced Dunhuang; I had studied France, Holland, and Italy. Was it so easy to throw overboard what I had seen and amassed, to rid myself of it with a flick of the finger? Would consigning it all to oblivion excuse me from taking the roundabout way? I was Chinese, I lived in the twentieth century, and I had always been tossed about, challenged—challenged by China, challenged by the West, challenged by life. I would need one hell of a stomach to digest everything, me, the puny fellow with the sick insides! Perhaps I was not a painter after all, but an eternal questioner, a maladjusted creature clinging provisionally to life, clinging to a few invented forms, a few blended colors, a few instinctive gestures. Perhaps I would rid myself of all my burdens someday; I would be overtaken by lightness and— why not—nonchalance. Then, with no more than a nudge from me, the wall would tumble down, and I would resolutely pass over to the modern side. Having an affinity with Cézanne, Kandinsky, and Klee, I should not find it hard to slip in among my contemporaries, into the rapidly changing West, which swore by novelty. Their approach may not have always been fresh, but my contemporaries already seemed part of my artistic inheritance. But I didn't mind that; through them I too might well find the road to a true metamorphosis. But I was waiting. I was not ready, not yet. I needed to make haste slowly, very slowly, even if it meant dying of hunger.

9

DOING PORTRAITS in cafés and selling landscapes to private parties no longer provided enough to live on. I had to cut back on food. There were days when I just nibbled a crust of bread and sipped a glass of wine. The kind of hunger that makes one dizzy began to plague me in both mind and stomach. Was I to experience the same rapid physical decline as the Indian violinist? And more important, struggling with basic needs, would I lose my moral dignity? In the brasserie where I forced myself to sketch despite trembling fingers, the sound of plates filled then emptied grew more intolerable every passing day, and it was hard not to shout something at the sated diners who did not for a second dream of sharing. One day, after a customer had paid he stuffed his wallet into his pocket rather carelessly. As he walked by me, a little wad of bills fell to the floor. Fascinated by the hope the notes represented, I hesitated momentarily before alerting the man. . . .

A Korean friend convinced me to get a job at Les Halles, where I unloaded produce trucks. Long nights, feverish, flaying: shouts and laughter, coarse lamentations, the rubbing of shoulders, the mingling of sweat. Muscles were developed in that hot, crowded male atmosphere hardly softened by the few women present; they themselves frank, robust, and sometimes superb. As dawn broke, the ex-hausted crew could at last sit down to a steaming bowl of broth. . . .

Later I found work closer to home, in a student restaurant where I had sometimes eaten, one of those that had not been renovated after the war. The cleaning procedures were rudimentary and inappropriate, and the work more manual than mechanized.

The first task was to dispose of leftovers on hundreds of trays: scraps of meat chewed and rejected, bones of fish and fowl, driblets of grease and gravy. Touching the hard, cold metal of the trays and the tepid, slimy matter rejected by the human mouth, we could not help but shudder in disgust. It took some getting used to. At a pre-arranged hour, the world came to a halt, and in unison great masses of men ate, chewed, and swallowed. For them the task of digesting what they had gotten down one way or another; for us, that of dealing with mountains of vile-looking waste. I had looked for work to guarantee my daily bread; I had not expected to be playing a part, modest as it was, in a gigantic enterprise. In the great city, with the slaughterhouses—themselves gigantic—as background, the onetime slow and simple activity of eating had become a frenzied discipline, turning monstrous.

Once the trays had been cleared of food, we would put them in a dumbwaiter that creaked its way noisily to the basement. Downstairs, we hosed off the trays before they were washed in huge basins of chlorinated water. The washing was entrusted to a few burly fellows; to others, like me, fell the task of drying. My chore, I soon realized, was no less painful. The trays, made of an alloy, were heavy and awkward; once dried, they were to be stacked on a trolley, which then had to be pushed to its destination. Back bent under the load, I was storing up aches and stiffness for the night. With the drying, the dishtowel—soon soaking wet—took on the tinge of the aluminum and gave off an unpleasant greasy aroma. The cloth's cold dampness accentuated the humidity of the steam that rose from the cement floor and penetrated the air and our bodies.

About a dozen of us worked there, various nationalities: Hungarians, Poles, Tunisians, French, et cetera. A noisily cheerful ambiance was the ideal, with a smattering of crude jokes. I was slow at picking up student speech, I had trouble joining in. I was befriended by one of the two Frenchmen in the group, a pale young man with glasses. He tried to spare me from efforts that seemed beyond my physical capabilities. He was a Communist and did not try to hide it. In spite of his slightly oppressive seriousness, I enjoyed chatting with him since he had a wide range of interests. But after a few conversations, there was one subject I avoided: the Communist regime in China. He admired it unreservedly and thought that China's experiment represented a new hope for mankind. Ordinarily attentive and almost humble when I talked of things about which he knew nothing, here he barely listened, sure he knew more about the subject than I did, since he read *L'Humanité,* which often published articles on China. He even tried to convert me, arguing that sacrifices were necessary for such a revolution to succeed. When he spoke of politics, his pale face grew more wan but his cheeks turned pink, and behind the glasses his eyes would sparkle as if he were a lover transfixed. How could someone so perceptive, so concerned about humanity, let himself to be so blinded by passion? The man smitten with justice will proclaim it everywhere and will soon take it into his own hands.

The passionate pallor of the Communist rubbed off on me. I looked in a mirror one day and saw an ashen complexion. I blamed it less on the hard work in the basement than on the uninspiring and sometimes rotten food they would heap in front of us before the students arrived. I always had trouble swallowing my meal, since I knew only too well the standards of cleanliness in the kitchen; and I was put off by the fetid odor that lurked in the immense hostile dining room, penetrating walls, tables, utensils, clothes, and hair; the odor of countless meals served over the decades and of refuse too casually cleared away, a smell lovingly enhanced by the insistence of bleach. Before long I had a perpetually bloated stomach, and I often felt sharp twinges of pain. Every night, walking home alone, I said to myself: "It would be terrible to be sick in Paris. Do not, do not get sick!"

.   .   .

BUT I DID NOT have a choice. One winter night in 1954, I was stricken with a high fever and severe intestinal pain. The next day was a Sunday, and a good Samaritan neighbor called a substitute doctor. When the latter arrived, I did not feel saved, for I was looking upon a malevolent angel. The man had a gruff look, his ill-defined features distorted by a permanent scowl of disappointment. I remember word-for-word our conversation, based on confusion, if not contempt.

"You're Vietnamese?"

"I'm from China."

"Same thing . . . I know Indochina well, actually. I lived there a long time."

Silence on my part.

"Well, what seems to be the problem?"

"I have a fever and my stomach hurts terribly."

"No surprise, in this poorly heated room! Undress, I'm going to listen to your chest."

When he saw my bare torso, he remarked, "Not much fat on you, is there! You have to eat, sir!"

Then he listened to my chest, asking incongruously: "Where did you pick up that beautiful silk shirt?"

"I brought it from China." It had been a gift from the Lover.

"No wonder, can't find things like that here. Do you have chills?"

"Yes, from the cold maybe."

"Just as I thought, it's malaria. You have had it, of course?"

"Yes, but I was cured. I haven't had an attack for many years."

"It's one of those nasty things that doesn't go away. All Indochinese carry a touch of it around with them."

"I just said that—"

"Believe me, sir, it's your malaria acting up. You have to take quinine; it won't hurt you and it'll make you feel better."

Before he left, my visitor had some advice: "Eat more, do a better job of keeping warm." Then, as if driven by a sudden impulse, he said: "Do you know this line from Rilke: 'When men who hate each other must sleep in the same bed'?" Without waiting for an answer, he slipped out the door.

I had my doubts, but the pain was overwhelming, and I told myself the quinine certainly couldn't hurt me. So I decided to take it, in the strong dose recommended by the doctor. Result: instead of decreasing, my intestinal pain increased, and my gums began to swell, leading to mouth abscesses. I could no longer swallow anything; even drinking was an unbearable ordeal. A second doctor, responding to an emergency summons, sent me to the hospital.

In the immense public ward already crowded with the ailing victims of an especially harsh winter, the nurses squeezed in a bed for me at the end of a row, next to the door. Anyone entering or leaving had to walk around the end of my bed.

.   .   .

I FOUND MYSELF cast automatically into a universe where the

unwell, no longer their own masters, were reduced to poorly bathed, ill-smelling bodies delivered up to the unknown. I had to confront the borrowed body I hardly knew. Even the simple gesture of inserting a thermometer or a suppository became hesitant, awkward. Opening my mouth wide to medicate the abscesses, I would see, distorted in the chipped mirror, my throat and the mass of soft purplish flesh that was the underside of my tongue, and I would be as terrified as by a true image of hell.

The sick man's day was broken up with endless comings and goings: doctors and nurses, gurneys taking patients to X ray, carts bringing meals, families visiting, et cetera. Toward evening, after dinner and before bedtime, there was a brief lull at the changing of the nurses' shift. The patients strong enough took advantage of the momentary freedom to leave their beds and spend the time together. Even the seriously ill isolated behind glass at the end of the room would leave their cubicles like fish escaping an aquarium. Before night, the ordeal each of us feared, all felt the need for a little communication with others. Any conspiratorial smile, any encouraging word was received like an unexpected gift. Because the outside had become inaccessible, faraway, almost unreal—a place whose existence was attested to by nothing but the presence of the angels in white—the patients felt they could find solace only through one another and in their common suffering.

In the night, everyone's great concern was to find the energy to cross the deep abyss relatively unscathed while counting the minutes and the hours until the first glimmer of dawn, and to find the energy to conquer his demons and rise above the groans of the others. Groans and death rattles. For death prefers to strike by night, when the victim is without defense or resources. In the night, nurses would come to take the dead to the morgue, the homeless with limbs frozen stiff, the gravely ill struck down. Going by, the nurses would brush against my mattress while they passed corpses over my head.

My body riddled with sores, I met again the Visitor from long ago, whom I had not expected. Too exhausted by unremitting pain, too tormented by the fear of putrefaction, I was in no state to resist that presence (the only faithful one, after all) of him who came from afar and at the same time from inside me. Comforter with a bewitching gaze, he encouraged me to climb out of the abyss whatever the cost. My flesh burned by the bubbling lava, I managed to hoist myself to the top; then, just as in the past, pretending to help me, he let me fall back as if by accident. . . .

Except for the visitor's phosphorescent gaze, the only gleam in the dark was a night light whose blue glow watched over the cubicle where a young man with leukemia slept; by day it was the mother who watched over her only son. When I thought of the young man, I felt privileged. At least I could disappear from the earth and no one would know, no one would grieve. Wasn't I the only foreigner in the huge ward? Already, in this place of perdition, I no longer had a name—they simply called me "the Chinese"—and in the morgue where they would deposit my corpse, I would still be an element outside the mainstream, destined to be returned to an unknown origin. At the thought, I snickered almost as lugubriously as the Visitor, and in that hour before dawn I plunged into a nightmare.

Clinging to that blue glow on the following nights, I tried to master my fear. I communed with the suffering of the other, who now had a face. Meanwhile, the young man with the feverish eyes and sunken cheeks had become my companion. He had indicated through successive hints that his greatest regret was to leave this life never having known woman. How could I console him? I could tell him that any man born of a mother has already known woman. And his mother, if she knew it—and she would not—would gladly take him into her again, warming him with her flesh so he could be reborn. Night after night, lacking comfort myself, I forced myself to become a comforter in spirit. Before dying, the young man had thus been destined, in his own way, to make a sign of life to me. A sign for life.

10

IN THE PALE GRAY light of a Paris afternoon, a thin, post-illness shadow trailed behind me as I passed along a street of flaking walls very like those worn mattresses cast out on the sidewalk by night, mattresses stained with secretions of every sort, deformed in the center by living bodies, feverish and fevered, inert and restless; by dead bodies, abandoned or lovingly attended. I hugged other walls, too, these blind and silent, irrevocably gray with a despairing gray never seen on any palette, the color of that moment when real things go off at last and dissolve in the invisible wave of nothingness. Standing in my damp-walled room where the cracks had been stuffed with strips of yellowed newsprint, I inhaled the odor of moldy wood and rancid oil, and I heard the sound of saws and hammers, interrupted occasionally by the shouts of children and the scratching of rats.

One's private quarters, originally meant to provide shelter and warmth, have in our day become the privileged mirror of the solitude of a humanity that exists in an echoless universe, clinging somehow to an earth that nourishes but provides no light in spite of being a little beacon in the eyes of the other planets. Humanity is reduced to drawing its own melancholy brightness from within.

I knew my destiny was that of the wanderer. As long as I lived in China, I had the illusion of being rooted in a region, in a language, in a stream of life that went on whatever the cost. And now I was without roots in a Western land that enticed me, all the while remaining closed to me. Just as the faces at police headquarters remained closed, those official faces that threatened me with non-extension of my visa or immediate expulsion since I had no source of income. My existence was no longer marginal; it was illegal.

Illegality. Non-right to existence. The Europe to which I had entrusted my greatest dreams, was it a refuge for me? Now that I had nowhere else to go, fear took hold of me and crept into my flesh simply from my taking a good, hard look at the continent. Spoiled by nature, inclined toward thought, replete with artistic creation, it had been unable to form a crust thick enough to asphyxiate the monsters and keep a gulf of terror from opening wide within its borders. When delusion took over, the desire for power and domination that possessed so many was turned against themselves for lack of distant tribes on whom to exert their will. All-out wars where everyone on one side was driven to kill those on the other, organized carnage. The genius of technology dedicated to the cold-blooded extermination of an entire race, reducing it to ashes, leaving only mountains of the rings, wedding bands, gold teeth, and eyeglasses of which each individual had been stripped beforehand. . . .

It was the era of the Cold War. I knew that with the smallest new conflict I, among so many others, would be a sacrificial lamb; instantaneously, the yawning trap, the snare of violent death would open beneath my feet. Like dead leaves without branches or roots I would be trampled into decay, swept away, burned. . . .

In the mirror of my room, I saw myself totally alone, with no one else on earth.

My painter friends, although they suffered from their exile, did not ask themselves so many questions: Argentineans, Hungarians, Austrians, Spaniards, Lebanese, and others from Japan, Korea, Indonesia. "To know a country and love it, there is nothing like getting to know its women," one of them once said to me. Women? I had had a few sporadic encounters, with no dreams of anything permanent, convinced I would not find a person who would provide me the silent, trusting warmth of one's native soil. In the studios and the nearby cafés, relationships with women were not that hard to come by, subject only to the caprice of seasons. In spring and summer there prevailed a kind of excitement bordering on exasperation. In cold weather, with blasts of wind sweeping the boulevard, the most important thing was to keep warm. We took shelter in smoky cafés, and after sharing milky coffee and soft croissants, a pair would go back to the room of one or the other to crawl into a pathetic, ill-smelling bed. The flesh was sad and the speech shivering. Other than that, there was always the temptation to be drawn into a group orgy at the place of some upstart painter, where disguise and nudity, mandatory, strove to devise cruel and empty games in which a pitifully restricted desire would visibly sicken and decay.

.　　.　　.

WITHOUT MY expecting it, without my being on the lookout for it, a woman's face imposed itself on me one day, with a blinding clarity. In the Parisian hell, there had to be someone who could make me smile. It happened at a Pierre Fournier recital.

I knew of the famous cellist from some records I'd heard at an Austrian sculptor's place; among the pieces was the same Dvořák concerto that had impressed me so long ago. Thus, in my Paris days of hardship, strain, and uncertainty, seeing the name "Fournier" on a poster, I suddenly felt a nostalgic hunger, like someone long ill who, improved or cured, craves some ordinary thing beloved in childhood: hot chocolate, grape juice, marrons glacés, or, in my case, soy milk, marinated bamboo shoots, candied lotus seeds.

Failing that, I was hungry, physically hungry, for the sound of the cello, solemn and sensual, airy and sedate. I had no doubt that the sound would alleviate my fear and dismay more surely than a sleeping pill. I hungered for it as for a vital substance that would fill the ever-present hollow in a stomach never satisfied by the insipid food dutifully ingested day after day. In my precarious financial state, the concert was a luxury. I tried to justify the expense by telling myself that music was a form of therapy. Others, for a little solace, turned to alcohol and tobacco or consulted fortune tellers.

I was standing in line, still far from the box office, when a young woman approached with a ticket in her hand.

"Would you like a seat? I have a ticket from someone who couldn't come."

I hesitated briefly, for the price of the ticket was more than I had planned to pay, but I found myself answering, "Yes."

When I got to my seat, I was happy to see that I was fairly close to the stage: I could more easily commune with the interpreter and his instrument. The young woman was already in her place, next to mine. I nodded to her, then each of us retreated into a discreet silence, waiting for the concert to begin.

At the intermission, over the applause: "How beautiful!" my neighbor spontaneously remarked.

"Yes, what mastery and what purity in the playing!"

"Are you a musician?"

"No . . . and you?"

"I'm a clarinetist."

"You are giving your professional opinion!"

Finding my comment not particularly original, I added: "The clarinet and the cello have a lot in common, then?"

"Absolutely."

Not wanting to be obtrusive, I did not prolong the conversation. I concentrated on the program my neighbor had lent me and enjoyed learning something about the pieces: a Bach suite, a sonata by Schubert and one by Brahms.

After the concert, we walked part of the way together. When she said good-bye, she handed me an announcement for a chamber music concert in which she was to play.

On the long walk home, when I would put my hand in my pocket and touch the folded sheet, through my fingertips I felt a special sweetness, close to rapture, a delight so intense that it went through my heart like a burst of flame. On a more naive level, I felt like the player who strokes his winning lottery ticket every so often to make sure it is still there. In the Paris night, in the world night, I was alone no more; I was no longer a lost creature, cut off from everything, without family, without identity. But it all hung on a creased sheet of paper! In the darkest night, the spark from a match, a trembling flame, a firefly, was enough to keep the whole universe open.

Later that night I tried to recall the woman's face. At first, her smile and her eyes stood out. But the more I tried the more indistinct the face I sought became. I was no longer sure I would recognize her on the street. Fear gripped me, fear of seeing her go up in smoke.

I got out of bed and felt in my jacket; the paper was there.

My life seemed to me an uninterrupted string of anticipations, future accomplishments. My record of failures had resulted in my being like someone who walks through a desolate region, not daring to turn around for fear he might see phantoms pursuing him. What oppressed me was not a longing for the past that each of us tries to re-create in imagination. I did not like myself, I could not bear to gaze upon myself. Just as I avoided rereading my letters to my mother, I did not seek to take pleasure in reminiscence, for I knew that in remembering I would die of shame or anguish. Despite an unshakable pessimism, a certain confidence—it too unshakable—lay coiled in the obscurity of my deepest desires, which I had not yet deciphered. I was convinced that my life, deferred, would still come to fruition, in spite of myself and without my knowing.

I went to the concert. The clarinetist—she was accompanying a Schubert song, *Schäfers Klagelied*—I found different from my memory of her. There as a musician, she was somehow more real: her light brown hair with its glints of gold; her slightly nearsighted eyes, enchanting in their mixture of timid reserve and candid astonishment; the straight, delicate nose; the pale cheeks that blushed at the slightest emotion; the fine, sensitive lips, made for modulating sounds; the slender body that would have seemed frail to anyone unaware of the controlled, profound spirit moving it. She was really there; I would not lose sight of her; I would become close to her. Backstage, she welcomed me with a natural smile, as if she had been expecting me. From that day on, I would attend all her concerts and escort her home.

II

YOU COME FROM far away. . . . But I'm not asking who you are."

Véronique's words, spontaneous and full of good-natured trust, formed the basis of our relationship as friends and lovers. To the question: "Who are you?"—if she had asked it—I could not have replied. She had trusted me at once. Why? Was it enough that I was at a cello recital? Or that, even though I came from far away, I responded to a Brahms sonata as she did? I received her presence, her face, her body, like a gift; there emanated from her a blend of gentle patience and tense, almost painful willpower. And indeed, her presence had the power to transform everything. The world around me, once so oppressive, opened up, rich with meaning and resonance. It was as if through the image of Véronique I was seeing my surroundings for the first time. Especially since she and I were not always together; each time her form approached or retreated, I had a sense of novelty, a feeling that something unusual was occuring.

Véronique played in an orchestra based in the city of L. From time to time, she would go on tour in France or abroad. Besides having her professional obligations, she guarded her independence, which I learned to respect, but not without pain. Especially at the beginning of our relationship, when she would take leave of me on her doorstep after a walk or a concert: "Let me be alone, I need to pull myself together," or "Let's see each other in two days. I have to practice, I'm not pleased with myself right now." I learned to wait— pangs of waiting I eventually transmuted into something positive. In a state of tension both anxious and pleasurable, I would make myself work, often quite rewardingly. Sometimes, unexpected bonus: coming back from a tour, with no advance warning, she would stop by my rooms: "I'm here! Make me a noodle soup. I've developed a Chinese stomach!"

Later, seeing that the trial and error playing necessary to master a new score did not annoy me in the least, she would often come to practice in my studio. While the sounds of her clarinet echoed in the next room, I would work on my canvases. Can I ever forget those hours of competing and confiding? I went back to ink, encouraged by Véronique, who was fascinated by what she called its "velvety feel." Full strength or diluted just the right amount, ink brought my work to life, not through the effect of light but through some unsuspected essence. I was begininng to hear my voice, to find my way. Day after day there took shape on my canvases real-life landscapes purified by memory, landscapes where Véronique met me intuitively.

Or, more precisely, where she met the faraway land of my origins. And she was increasingly moved by the details of my past, delivered to her in little snippets.

One day, looking at a series of particularly serene pictures, she said: "Oh, can I keep these? They calm me, comfort me." The remark, in itself ordinary, astonished me. Did she need to be calmed, comforted? Beside my tortuous life, her existence seemed to me smooth, all in a straight line, like the simple dresses she wore, which suited her so well. Certainly Véronique's life was oriented toward a single goal: music. Unless, because of living in sounds and for sounds, a kind of tension dwelled within her. Or maybe even some secret torment. What do we know of the person with whom we seek to share our private life? How can the other tell us what is in his or her life? And how can we understand what the other is telling us? In my own urgent and rather egotistical need to confide, had I been able to listen to Véronique? In any case, she was too refined to pour out her feelings. "I'm not asking who you are," she had said. Yet I think she came to know my life better than I knew hers.

It took a coincidence for her to speak of a painful interlude in her past. I shall not forget the afternoon: during a break, a few words of mine brought up a time she had hitherto kept silent. I was telling her the legend of Boya, one of the greatest musicians of Chinese Antiquity. Boya learned the lute with the great master Chenglian. An exceptionally gifted pupil, he achieved mastery within three years. Even so, the master found fault with him for clinging too closely to his instrument. Since he could not detach himself from it, he could not express what was in his heart. Then came the day when master and disciple embarked on a sea voyage. They stopped at an island. And suddenly the master vanished. Left alone, surrounded by waves and the calls of birds, Boya began to play as a cry for help and as an expression of his terror and distress. Forgetting his instrument completely, he finally attained the true song.

"But what you are telling me is incredible. That's what happened to me!" Moved, blinded by tears, my friend told me she had contracted tuberculosis at nineteen, three years after beginning her clarinet studies. A mortal blow: the collapse of her dream, and several years to drag out in a sanitarium awaiting death. The war was just ending, so she hadn't had much of a life yet and was quite poor. What saved her was the miracle of medicine, of course: but to her mind, the cure lay in her internal melody—made up of the heartbreak and longing she never stopped breathing into it—against loss, against abandonment and despair. Stripped of everything, she had transformed her suffering body into a musical instrument; thus she had been able to continue with her music, "thinking" it according to all its strictures and techniques while imparting to it a new vitality and truth. So that, once past her illness, when she held a clarinet in her hand again, there was no sense of an interruption; even better, there was the heady feeling that she had mastered her instrument. After that, giving up her musical studies was out of the question, despite the advice of her parents, not to mention the doctors, all of them fearing she would wear out her lungs.

Unconsciously Véronique might have wanted to forget that past, that break in her life. She had told me about it inadvertently as it were. She would have been wrong to regret doing so; her story brought me closer to her. With enough time I might have gone deeper into her inner world. But can I be sure? In the light of that incident and of our life together, I could already gauge the difficulty of touching the real depths of another, a fortiori, another who is woman. Can a man connect with the utmost desire of a woman, when she herself cannot fathom it? Certainly there is infinite tenderness, which whisks away a man's prejudices and fantasies as if they were trifles. There are moments of ecstasy that keep alive the ephemeral dream of the One. The man—nagged by the finite—struggles to connect with the woman—assailed by the infinite—without ever succeeding. He remains an abandoned child weeping beside the sea. The man would be soothed were he willing to listen to the music echoing there, inside and outside him—to listen humbly to the woman become a song too nostalgic to be within reach.

12

ÉRONIQUE'S engagements took her to different places; I accompanied her sometimes, discovering cities and regions beyond Paris and becoming better acquainted with the French countryside. The time came when Véronique, with a slack period in her activities, decided to introduce me to her village on the banks of the Loire. Before we left Paris, she rented us each a bicycle so I could better explore the region.

From living within the confines of the city, I had forgotten the physical well-being occasioned by long walking tours, like the ones I had taken in China. Traveling by bicycle, quicker of course, put me in tune with the earth once more. I was drunk on the cool air, the scent of grass mixed with the odor of dust along the country roads.

As is expected of visitors, we saw the châteaux, those dwellings born of a fortunate encounter between the Italian and the French in the days of the Renaissance. The architecture, at times too mannered, too measured, is onetheless enchanting in its internal harmony and its perfect accord with the landscape, the trees, the hills, the streams, and the gentle clouds fringing the sky. I could not help but think of the Chinese tradition of *jiehua*,* whereby the painter strives to contrast the geometric lines of human habitations with the natural environment, all the while combining the two elements in a perfect symbiosis that denotes a rare moment of harmony.

How thrilled I was to find that Véronique was indeed the child of her land. So pale in Paris, here her face took on the pigmentation of the locale, a subdued radiance with a slight cast of pink and an occasional bluish glint. Her features and the lines of her body harmonized with the elegantly cut building stones animated by well-proportioned relief. For the stones were there to enhance, to ennoble the outlines of the those who dwelled in their midst, and to keep them from growing slack or flabby. Once the people here had perfected their style of building, the architecture must have then compelled them to resemble their building stones. Art did not imitate

---

*Painting with square and rule.

nature but compelled nature to imitate it. Véronique blossomed as she reentered the familiar landscape that had permeated her childhood and adolescence.

She knew the backroads, the paths that crisscrossed field and forest. Over the fields, over the plateaux covered with wild grass and wreathed in mist, invisible waves of a very special odor reached us.

"It smells of the river!" I exclaimed. Véronique was both disappointed and delighted. Disappointed, because she had intended to surprise me; delighted, however, to recognize in me a connoisseur ready to love this land of rivers.

"You are a real 'river person!'"

"How could I not be, good Chinese that I am!" And I remembered the lower Yangzi between Jiangsu and Zhejiang.

"Let's go see the Loire!"

We came upon the river at a spot where it was especially wide. Voices had grown distant. In midstream, eddies, mischievous or insidious, sported with sand banks as indolent as the reflections of the passing clouds. I thought I had entered one of those landscapes of antiquity so loved by the artists of the classical age. A landscape preserved in this isolated corner forgotten by time. We were there, the two of us, also forgotten, but perpetually discovering each other.

Véronique's village stood on a hill overlooking the Loire. Leaving our bikes below, we walked up a narrow path that cut through vegetable patches. Halfway to the top there were houses encrusted in the rock. One of these troglodyte dwellings was the home of my friend's parents, worthy artisans whose enduring simplicity harmonized with the river.

The Loire—in French a feminine word that rolls off the tongue with a clear and open sound—running wide and slow had fashioned an entire tribe of fine-featured, bright-eyed, levelheaded folk, so levelheaded there was always the danger they might become soft. But I knew from experience that one had to be on guard when dealing with a river. Under a peaceful, inoffensive surface lurked dangerous eddies, veritable spinning tops that could suck clumsy swimmers to the bottom.

Although a child of the river, had I ever been so deeply affected by

a flowing stream? Did I ever tire of the peace that came from stray-
ing along the levees where the Cher mixed its waters with those of
the Loire, where the Indre—feminine, too—succumbed to the attraction of the mighty river? Largely hidden by the wild vegetation, wide
stretches of water came into view here and there—faithful, sparkling,
unbroken mirrors of the morning of the world, with the herons'
flight barely marking the surface.

Just as in the days with my master, in Véronique's company I sat,
contemplated, and drew. Not so much the river itself as the surrounding landscape, a landscape of wooded hills, limestone rock,
open fields, to which the stone bridges and slate roofs added an
appropriate touch. Through its flowing movement, its reflections,
and the halo of moisture it conferred on all things, the river did not
let the landscape remain monotonous or closed in but drew it
toward the horizon and united it with the sky in a sweeping nuptial
gesture. In this little universe where all elements maintained their
proper distance and were (as my Chinese eye easily perceived) carefully ordered by the middle voids, I did not expect any spectacular
scenes. I simply went about fine-tuning my observations, sharpening
my senses, capturing intangible hues, all the varied tones that
changes weather would bring to the water and to the hills on the
opposite shore. Mercurial, indecisive, hesitant, these tones would
lead me unawares from one mood to another, without my losing any
of their nuances, like the child who, totally absorbed in his bedtime
story, drops off into a sleep in which the story continues to unfold.
When rain came, ever so stealthily, I would stay in my spot, as
motionless as the occasional fishermen whose silence was interrupted only by the sharp quacking of ducks. I would wait. In this
region of France where the river was in collusion with the clouds, I
knew the rain never lasted into night. In fact, I do not remember any
night when light did not keep its rendezvous in the west, spreading
far and wide, merging water and sky. With one exception. A storm,
contained for centuries perhaps, exploded angrily, downing trees,
raising waves, freeing a thousand wild things from their cages. Lightning crashed down, and it brushed my shoulder. No shelter near us,

we did not stir. Contrary to my experience at the Great Dike in Holland, in this place I was ready to die, with few regrets.

.   .   .

OUR STAY IN the region led us irresistibly upriver, to the source of the Loire. During our slow trek, the river never wearied of our steps and let us share its meandering secrets. On the last day, before the last bend, before Mount Gerbier-de-Jonc raised its mysterious outline, we stood a long while atop a hill that looked straight down into the emerald current, and we let the piercing brightness of evening hold us in its grip. And I understood that nothing in me was changed. The man in exile who contemplated the vast landscape, was he not the child of Asia who had gazed upon the River Yangzi with his father and who had gone up other rivers, to other sources? Then and now, it was the same discovery: a long, wide river begins as a tiny trickle of water buried under impenetrable grass. Drinking the clear water that spurted from a rock fountain designed for the thirsty traveler, my heart swelled with gratitude. Gratitude for the region that had welcomed me, and for the woman who had brought me to the river's source.

13

U PRIVER TO the source. Would it be the beginning of a new life? Or the end of another? That time is cyclical and that each new cycle brings changes both foreseen and unexpected was an old theme, an integral part of my vision, and I no longer doubted its validity. And if it were indeed so, couldn't I hope to be released from memories and ties? In this foreign country, now a new person, by an act of will couldn't I cut the roots of the past, untie the most inextricable knots? Cut the roots? Maybe. Since man is merely a creature gliding over the surface of the earth, an animal the culture hands a few tried and true ways, is he really so deeply rooted that he can't imagine being transplanted? To go beyond my past was tempting in spite of the difficulties, and I was trying to convince myself it could be done. But when it came to undoing the ties of the heart . . .

Two years after the journey to the Loire, another letter from Yumei, sent by way of Hong Kong again, and long in arriving: "Haolang died at the camp, from an illness, so the report said. We never exchanged a sign, all relations were forbidden. And you, don't write me either. But think of me from time to time, your Yumei." Without expecting an answer, the Lover had included her address.

Although fearing the worst, I had only expected long, trying years for Haolang, he who was so tough, he who had an unconquerable will to live—never did I foresee such a sudden end. My only friend, the brother hated for a moment and loved forever, that strong, bright figure was no more? Gone from the earth for good? Yumei's brief letter, written in a trembling hand, was now held in a no less trembling hand; and on that fateful Paris afternoon I was once again astonished, not so much by being where I was but by henceforth being from nowhere. The soil was giving way beneath my feet. The foundation of my being had suddenly split open. More precisely, all the soils I had trod during all my years of wandering were collapsing, one by one, leaving but one soil on the horizon, the faraway soil of my birth. Without it, nothing else to hold me up. On my native soil, I knew, someone awaited me like the weeping willow by the pond, someone whose mission was to watch over living and dead. That someone, with her strange yet familiar beauty, tossing back a lock of hair, smiling through her tears, seemed to cry out: "Return!" or even "Here you are at last! Here we are at last!" Beyond the empty horizon, I heard the call of a destiny that I could not escape. I heard the gentle voice of life itself, of my own life, which for all eternity had foretold what was to pass.

PART THREE: MYTH OF RETURN

I

N EARLY 1957 I return to China. I must overcome the pain of a double separation: I am being torn away from Véronique's affection and from creative endeavors barely begun. But I have no choice, and indeed, I am not making a choice. I am conscious of going straight toward what has merely been postponed and is my destiny: to rejoin the Lover! After all, is she not there, alive? Can I abandon her in her deep distress? I know that returning to an altered, unrecognizable China will be a veritable descent into hell. Am I afraid? Not really. Just as when my mother died, I think of the Buddhist legend of Mulian in hell. Mixed into it now is a European legend, that of Orpheus. I am ready to pay a heavy price, to sink into the mire if need be. A sort of excitement makes me brash enough to think that by rejoining Yumei I accomplish a great deed. Not that I imagine I go as a savior! Powerless, worn out by hardship and anguish, I have become what I am, someone on the fringes, more than disqualified. I am the one who needs to be saved. Let us put it this way: reunited, the Lover and I will be saved. Together, no adversity can touch us. At least I try to think so. Love, love. Through song, that word fills the Western air ad nauseam, like the smell of gasoline. Have I ever uttered it? I hardly dare assign a content to the word, for it is such a mixture of confused instincts, immediate needs, satisfaction with the self, demands on the other, and the hateful desire to possess and dominate. But at this turning point I have to take a close look at the passionate feeling I have always had reason to avoid. A feeling scarcely human—burning lava ready to melt the flesh and bones of those who throw themselves into it—that men apparently cannot yet truly experience. But I know full well it is the only treasure still left me. And with this scarcely human treasure I must face the inhuman.

On to tedious days of running back and forth to police headquarters, various consulates, and the Chinese embassy. Véronique remains clear-headed and dignified. Her dignity obliges me to regain my own. No giving in to tears and laments. Sadness will come later, much later. She embraces my longing and my hopefulness. Because of what I have told her of my past, Véronique understands my nature. She would even be happy to meet Yumei. Then, suddenly she is devastated by the idea that we shall never meet again on this earth although we shall both be still alive. And for several weeks she cannot breathe into her clarinet properly. She has always lived in a small world where every corner is easily reached. The idea of a permanent separation in this world—to the Chinese, not at all unusual—seems to her both appalling and unreal.

In Peking, I am put up at the Friendship Hotel, reserved for foreigners and returning overseas Chinese. People of every nationality, of every color and tongue, crowd into the lobby. We hail one another, we embrace one another. An atmosphere of gaiety prevails, artificially maintained but based on warm, friendly feelings.

Among the overseas Chinese, enthusiasm alternates with circumspection. Genuinely delighted to regain their homeland and share with others what they have studied in the West, they are somewhat apprehensive about living in this country: they will have few chances to go beyond its borders and they must adjust to a severe, disciplined lifestyle. Their apprehensiveness is justified when they meet with officials. Beneath their apparent amiability, those in charge give the newcomers a sense of the demands of a hierarchical society. Soon, usual styles of dress are discarded, "Mao" suits are donned, and stereotyped phrases are mouthed.

At my request, which coincides with the plans of the authorities, I am assigned to the School of Fine Arts in Hangzhou, not far from Shanghai, where Yumei lives. Another request receives an equally positive response: I want to visit my family in Nanchang before I start work. In China, the right to return to one's birthplace is sacred, and the authorities have not dared abolish it. And it is the only excuse the Chinese can use to travel within their country. To reach Nanchang, I have to go through Shanghai, where I shall probably spend several days—my opportunity to see her for whom I have returned.

I step off the train in Shanghai and am happy to have a little time to myself. Impossible. I am immediately taken in hand by the City's

Cultural Section; they put me up in an official establishment, and my roommate is a cadre.

2

I HEAD FOR Yumei's district the first chance I get, pretending I'm off to see the sights of the city. I am already acquainted with this mad, sprawling metropolis, having spent over a month here before I left for France. Unfortunately, Yumei's building is on the outskirts, far from downtown; I have to change busses several times, fighting my way through a crush of passengers at every transfer. Ah, the suppleness of the Chinese body, which I lost in Europe; it allows a vehicle to take on an incredible number of people, their overlapping bodies forming a magma so compact that water could not pass through it. In comparison, the Paris metro at rush hour would seem comfort itself. Out of breath and exhausted, I arrive in a bleak and rather squalid quarter: row after row of concrete apartments, hastily constructed, dilapidated. Inside these grimy structures families are packed together and every sound reverberates.

I arrive at the address that was on the envelope from Yumei. I climb the stairs to the third floor, and I knock on her door. A disheveled woman with a shrill voice appears. I speak the name and she shakes her head: "Don't know her." I persist, but she tells me she was assigned the apartment a year ago and has no idea who the previous tenant was. She adds: "You'll have to ask the neighborhood leader," and bangs the door shut. Other doors fly open briefly, letting escape the howls of children and the clatter of cooking pots. Completely at a loss, I walk downstairs thoughtfully. I must avoid running into the neighborhood leader at any cost. I assess the possible consequences of the authorities' learning that a Chinese just back from a long stay in the West has been snooping around. The slightest thoughtless act could compromise Yumei, who, as the consort of a "criminal," is bound to be under heavy surveillance. I walk away,

trying to think out what I should do. At a busy street corner, I collapse on a bench by the bus stop; a crowd is waiting. I am startled by
a woman's voice behind me. I turn around; I see a woman I do not
recognize. I stand up and face her, saying to myself: "Oh, no! . . .
The neighborhood leader!" But her look is concerned, not at all
inquisitive. I approach the stranger, and we stand off to the side; so
as not to attract attention, we pretend we are waiting for the bus.

"Yumei used to be my neighbor. You are Mr. Zhao, back from
France?"

"How did you know?"

"Your shoes aren't from here." She makes her astute comment
with a sad smile, then she continues: "You are looking for Yumei. I
don't know how to tell you. Don't look for her; she is gone . . ."

Seeing my bewildered look, her voice chokes with emotion. "I'm
going to tell you the whole story. I'm not afraid; I am a worker.
I'm from a good family; they don't dare do anything to me. Yumei
didn't always live in our neighborhood. After Mr. Sun was sent to
the camp they took away her apartment downtown; they gave her a
room next door to us; she shared our kitchen. Her life wasn't easy.
When she went to government offices, there was always more red
tape than usual, and the neighborhood leader used to come and
cause her trouble. But she was always beautiful and dignified, and so
kind . . . We knew she had been a famous actress in the Sichuan theater. Occasionally, we would ask her, and she would explain a role
and sing it for us. It was lovely! Then they gave her a two-room
apartment with her own kitchen, and the neighborhood leader didn't
come and bother her anymore; the local Party secretary had designs
on her. Then, one day they told her Mr. Sun had died in the camp. It
was horrible. We did our best to console her and help her. Finally,
she came out of it. But there was still the Party secretary making
advances and pressuring her. He wanted her to marry him. One day
she gave me this little package and told me: 'Keep this for me, it's
safer with you, because I don't know what will become of me. I have
a friend, Mr. Zhao, who lives in France. If he ever comes back—but
I don't think he will—and I'm not here, you can give it to him.' At
the time, I didn't understand why she was giving it to me. I just

agreed that the things would be safer with me. I didn't know she was
going to do what she did . . ." Again, her voice was choked with
emotion. Then, all in one breath, hurriedly, she told the rest: "Well,
she killed herself. She did it without warning anyone. You know that
suicide is considered a crime. They burned her remains right away.
That is the story. Don't be too sad; she is at peace now. Take this
package, and don't be too sad. And now, I have to go . . ."

When the woman turns to leave, I take a tentative step to detain
her, but she has already merged into the passing crowd. It is too
much for me. Where am I? Who am I? What am I to do at this
moment and in this place in the midst of eternity? Above all, I must
not go back to the bench or stay fixed like a piece of deadwood. Fly
away. Vanish in thin air. Turn into a cloud of oblivion, far from the
stench of earthly decay. The downtown bus arrives; like a robot, I
am carried along with the crowd rushing through the narrow door.
I get off at the last stop. A wide avenue, with a blind procession of
vehicles and pedestrians. No bench in sight. I take a few steps and
collapse against a metal bar serving as a bicycle stand. I know I cannot rest here for long without arousing suspicion; a man still
young—how old? barely thirty-three, already on his last legs—
loitering on the street in the middle of the day. Little do I care. My
grief gives way to rage, to a feeling of being taken in by some huge
prank. It is high time to halt the trickery; I should laugh my most
raucous laugh right in the face of a world as grotesque as it is
hideous. I have to end my days, yes, but not in any old way. At least
one time in my life—the ultimate time—do things in my own fashion. Otherwise, I will be playing the game of all the tyrants engendered by this monstrous life. No more fear; no more giving in to
despair. Despair, I know it only too well. Despair when, after leaving
Yumei and Haolang, I stood on the bridge at sunset; when, after
leaving the master, I stood at a crossroads under a livid sky. Back
then my mother was always on the horizon. Despair when, on learning of her death, I hurried along the endless road from Dunhuang;
when, on the banks of the Seine, at the bleakest hour, the image of
the Lover and the Friend loomed up before me. The Lover was
always on the horizon; now all I have left of her is this little package,

still unopened. Yet, at all costs I must not give in to despair. I have to try to think things through. End my life, but coolly, and with composure.

I straighten up and head toward the Bund, Shanghai's wharf on the shores of the Huangpu, with the not very strong hope of finding a more isolated spot. I shall have to accept the fact that in this vast country where the regime's net of surveillance spreads far and wide a corner to oneself is not likely to be found, especially in the big city. A simple truth comes to me: to live man needs some obscurity. I am beginning to miss the churches one comes across when strolling in a European city. Believer or not, one is always free to enter. While abroad, I got into the habit of seeking the silence that lay within their thick walls of hewn stone; there I could be by myself and face myself, yet not feel completely alone.

I stand on the Bund, looking at the ships in dry dock, and I work up the courage to reach into my pocket for the little envelope from the Lover. "Forgive me, Tianyi. Do not forget me. Do not forget us. We are with you, I am yours, you know that." Besides the letter, a handkerchief embroidered with a plum blossom as distinct as a burst of blood, and two sheets folded in half, one yellowed, the other more recent. I unfold them and recognize my first portrait of the Lover, done fifteen years before, and a forest sketch from our days in the city of N. On the back of the portrait, these penciled lines: "All of Haolang's works were taken from me and burned. I have nothing left but your two drawings, which I have kept always."

What do I have left of my dear ones? Rapidly, I tick off the meager inventory: a few letters from Yumei, the embroidered handkerchief, several of Haolang's poems committed to memory, and my mother's ashes. It is past time for me to join the dead. But the dead, more alive than the living, oblige the latter to tarry longer on earth, whether it be a few days or a few months. I know that before I make my last decision I have obligations to the dead.

Now I have to find my way back and return to my quarters before we line up for the evening meal. A leaden night sky hangs heavily over the bustling, smoky city. Depression takes hold; my strength gives way. What has substituted for energy through the day, my grief, my rebellious rage, my burst of willpower in face of the tragic and the absurd, all that collapses now. I stagger, choked by sorrow. Yumei is no more, Haolang is no more, the world is no more. How can I, all alone, handle everything ahead, the coming minutes, the endless avenue with its broken pavement . . . ?

Without knowing how I have arrived, I am back in the dormitory, where I fake an interest in the bland remarks of the cadre who shares my room, he of the nasal voice and the coarse laugh. I have to invent some things I might have done in the course of my day: visits to bookstores, to the Museum of Painting, the House of Lu Xun. And I have to endure the long night, punctuated by the satisfied snores of the fellow in charge of looking after me.

3

AFTER MY FATHER'S death in 1935 I did not keep in touch with the family. As I suspected, my father's grave is gone, along with everything else at the family burial plot, in keeping with the new regime's rules and regulations. The land has been turned into a pathetic cultivated field. The house was requisitioned and is occupied by many families, from different backgrounds. The only members of my family still living here are Second Uncle, he who once tyrannized everyone, and his descendants. His wife is dead; he is now blind; his only son—onetime terror of tutors and servants— his daughter-in-law, and their two children are crowded together in the north wing of the house in the cold, damp rooms he had once assigned my parents.

The uncle with the magic hands, he who played chess and mahjongg, has also died, from boredom and deprivation probably. His wife lives with their adopted son, the boy my mother used to look after. He works in a factory, as does his wife. They have a child.

The opium-smoker uncle, of whom the family used to say "That fellow has caused us nothing but trouble!," died a martyr's death in a camp. His wife, gone mad, stagnates in an asylum.

My trip to Nanchang also includes seeing many cousins, now spread about the city. Tedious visits, all alike, for every subject is taboo, and the conversation is always about "grub," which, besides work and political meetings is their main concern. Food takes up an exorbitant amount of time: they must stand in line at every shop; they must share kitchens with neighbors and cook on primitive stoves. Since meat is scarce, they fall back on not very exciting vegetables. Notwithstanding, from time to time they work miracles. Then, with a few successful dishes on the table, they will let themselves go and be free, noisily swallowing soups, rice, and sauces. That is the greatest compensation for what they endure silently night and day. Instead of comforting me, these reunions plunge me into the deepest distress. While everyone else is splashing about in the swamp of a futureless life, I, with the weight of my terrible tragedy, am actually sinking. I wonder how I can pull myself out and face what may be an even worse fate.

A sole figure stands out among the relatives: my maiden aunt. Deprived of her room under the family roof, with no real resources, she lives in an old people's home. In the immense ward, she stands up and breaks away from the mass of bent, shriveled folk who pass their days here. Walking up to me, she is straight, steady, her own person.

"Ah, it's been so long, so long. I recognize you, you are . . ."

"Tianyi."

"Your poor father died before the war, in 'thirty-six, I believe.

"No, in 'thirty-five."

"Your mother died, too, in Tchoungking, I heard. I was very fond of her. She was so good, so fair, so helpful. And you, Tianyi, where have you been?"

"I'm just back from France."

"France? Incredible! What did you do there?"

"I studied painting."

"Painting? How interesting. Do you have pictures to show me, landscapes of France?"

She says all that in a loud voice, ignoring the fact that people are listening. Other friends and relatives, who know I've come from France, have not asked any questions; not that they aren't interested, but the subject is too dangerous and too compromising. When I lower my voice to answer her, she deigns to lower hers. All the pictures from France have been sent directly to the School of Fine Arts in Hangzhou. So as not to disappoint my aunt, I decide to draw her portrait. The face always considered ugly has improved with age, gaining in nobility and dignity.

I sketch her features and she does not stop talking. She has preserved intact the frankness and loquaciousness once remarkable in the stuffy family atmosphere and even more noticeable now, an oddity in the stifling atmosphere of a country under lock and key. Her words flow out, spreading a veritable oasis between the cracked, damp walls of the huge ward. Several times I have the urge to confide to her my tragic tale. I restrain myself, knowing that, with her integrity, she would not comprehend the arcana of my tormented life.

The portrait finished, my aunt smiles broadly and all her wrinkles vanish. In passing, she mentions to the aunt who returned to the family home after a bad marriage and later started a school for homeless children. I confess, not without embarrassment, that I have not yet paid her a visit.

To be honest, I had completely forgotten that aunt, who kept to herself much of the time. I go to the school, where she still works. I have to wait a long while before she can see me, for she has a thousand tasks: watching the youngest children, housekeeping . . . Once we are together, she explains her situation. After the Liberation, the school passed under the control of local authority. She was given an assistant, a woman Party member, who knew nothing about education; her role was to oversee the functioning of the school on the ideological level. Since my aunt stuck to her pedagogical principles, conflict was inevitable. Taking advantage of a campaign, the assistant criticized her harshly and encouraged parents and colleagues to denounce the errors in her thinking. My aunt was then relieved of her duties as director; but they kept her on at the school to perform menial tasks. These she assumed in order to stay near the children; in spite of everything, she wanted to bring them, in silent fashion, her kind of enlightenment.

My aunt recounts these facts in an almost neutral tone, as if she were relating external events of little concern to her. It is not hard to guess that beneath her impassive air, there is an unshakable dignity, an uncommon high-mindedness. Suddenly, I feel certain it is to see her that I have returned to this country. I picture myself as a child, running into her in the courtyard of the family home. She used to place a hand on my shoulder with a smile silent but full of affection. We rarely exchanged a word, but it seemed as though many words were spoken between us. More than twenty years later, here we are again. The moment for confidences has come; I begin to tell her the story about to explode inside me. She listens carefully, not uttering a word. When I am done, she is silent so long that I think of indifference or disapproval. Finally she speaks, her voice solemn and steady.

"We have lived in spite of all that has gone against us, and we shall live, if life so allows. We have been stripped of everything; one thing alone is still ours, and no outside force, no tyrannical repression can take it from us: what you call love, what I name fellow feeling. It cannot be taken, for it comes from us and depends on us alone. You have experienced a terrible tragedy: the loss of two very dear ones. Have you really lost them, Tianyi? To me, those who have been worthy of arousing a genuine love and are forever after revivified by it will never pass away, will never be gone. You say you have lost any reason for living. What are you saying? The survivor, more than anyone else, must live. Your mother is no more. Is she no longer anything to you? All that she endured, all that she accomplished with such patience and affection, was it so you would no longer live . . . ?"

The next day, my aunt takes me to what used to be the family burial site. She helps me spread my mother's ashes over the ground, the ground that goes on nourishing the living.

4

THE CITY OF Hangzhou with its Lake of the West and surrounding hills is renowned for its typical southern charm. Never have I seen the contrast between carefree nature and the world of men more flagrant than in our autumn of 1957. The landscape seems to laugh at human beings in their mad fury. The campaign against the rightists is in full swing. It follows the Hundred Flowers movement. The Leader, trusting in his personal aura and confident of the effectiveness of earlier campaigns and purges, had thought he could make a gesture of openness, his ulterior motive the testing of the people's loyalty. All were encouraged to express their thoughts, holding nothing back. But the people took advantage of the newly opened breach to demand greater freedom of expression and to criticize more and more vehemently the abuse of power on every level. The country threatened to become uncontrollable. Additionally alarmed by events in Hungary, the leader was to stop the movement short by unleashing a campaign to hunt down "rightists" in all segments of society. Pursuing his obsession with numbers, he set a high figure, proposing between forty and fifty as the percentage of "corrupt" elements among intellectuals, artists, and university faculty.

The School of Fine Arts, directly involved, is plunged into an excitement that soon turns into madness. All day long, cadres hold denunciation meetings and criticism sessions, which uncover targets vulnerable to attack by all. Calligraphers are mobilized to cover every available wall with *dazibao* and painters are invited to make giant caricatures. While the campaign is at its height, no one is sure of his fate, for the quota of forty percent has to be reached. Along with acknowledged rightists they are hunting down problematical elements, and they resort to seeking out unmarried people, who are more "available." The latter, under duress, agree to sacrifice themselves in the place of others. With the promise that by making an effort to "mend their ways" they will soon be rehabilitated. At the start, in the overenthusiastic atmosphere, given that he or she is not the only one, the individual at whom the finger is pointed is not overcome by shame. With a certain gusto, people lend themselves to the collective excitement. And there is humor, too. For example, a sculptor admits he should be considered a rightist; now he understands why he has botched the left side of the statue he's been working on. For the time being, many are not assessing the consequences of being labeled "rightist." Before long it turns out that lengthy and sincere self-criticism is not enough to "mend one's ways"; it is necessary to undergo reeducation in a work camp, usually in a remote region. Further, the listed one, wherever he goes, is subject to ill-treatment and humiliation by the authorities. An odor of infamy clings to him, spreading to all the members of his family and driving away friends and relations. As time goes by the authorities may remove the label "rightist" from those whose cases are not considered serious; nevertheless, the fact of their having been so labeled is duly recorded and stays attached to them like a permanent tag. Should the need arise, during subsequent campaigns they can be reminded of their errors.

Although required to be present at all activities, I am not directly affected by the campaign. I have just arrived; since I don't know anyone yet and no one knows me, they have no reason to implicate me, even though my long stay in the West could constitute an error. All the others, eyes red, features drawn, are so traumatized that they no longer think about anything; they do not even dare think, for fear of being turned in. Each of them is wrapped up in avoiding the attack of the moment. I am almost the only one who looks at the outside world on occasion. Some mornings I indulge myself by contemplating the landscape, at its richest this time of year. The lake at the foot of the hills, veiled by an ethereal mist, stretches out, invisible, exuding the nostalgic aroma of the infinite. In its center, the dike is a thin line, a tracing of dried ink. The blurry outline of a boat fades into the faraway memory of eternal China. In the middle of this horizontal picture, one vertical is distinguishable, a tiny shape. As I approach it and my steps becomes audible, the shape stirs and comes toward me. It is someone from the school, but not an acquaintance. Passing me, the other furtively wipes the corner of his eye. He pulls himself together immediately, and for fear of being denounced, says, "That cold mist stings the eyes."

5

AT THE END of this turbulent period, the School of Fine Arts—short of staff because so many of our colleagues are in camps—tries to resume its activities. With this cold wind blowing across the country, we institute a kind of self-censorship. Accordingly, the curriculum undergoes some major changes. Now we study only those Western painters whose subjects seems safe, whose works have some social content: Le Nain, Millet, Delacroix because of an occasional revolutionary theme, Courbet for his participation in the Paris Commune. Besides traditional Chinese painting, we take up oil painting again. We are allowed to venture out of the classroom to paint from nature; we just have to remember to add a few busy workers to our landscapes. My students and I invariably go to the tea fields that cover the hills around Hangzhou. There I find anew the fragrance I remember from my childhood days at the foot of Mount Lu.

As I stand at the edge of the field to sketch the workers, I am especially intrigued by one old woman: like the others, she is wearing a straw hat and is picking the tiny tea leaves, but her movements are extremely slow and awkward. When she reaches the end of her row, I try to speak to her without the overseer's noticing. In China, through the force of circumstance we quickly learn the ventriloquist's art of uttering words without moving the lips.

"Your work is hard. We would like to help you."

"You can't. Here, each of us has to do what she is assigned to do."

Then she starts down the next row. But each time she comes back, we pick up our conversation:

"When people drink tea, our famous *longjing* tea, they never think about the work that goes into it."

"It's like the vineyards in France: they look so beautiful, but at harvest time, what a job!"

"You've been to France?"

"Yes, in the twenties."

"I myself came back from France last year."

"Imagine that!" the old woman seems to be thinking.

"Who are you?"

"My name is C."

When I hear who she is, my heart skips a beat. The name is familiar because I've read some of her prose works and translations. I knew that in her later years she had gone to Yan'an to join the ranks of the revolutionaries, all the while keeping her independence of spirit. Not long ago, she dared to criticize the Party; and so she too was condemned, probably even before the campaign against the rightists.

"You look like my mother."

Moved, the woman does not answer for a moment, then goes on: "I am the mother of those who show affection for me. But in the times we live in, there is little affection. I have a daughter. She has been sent to the other end of China because of me. Wherever I go, once my status is discovered, faces close up as if I had the plague. For a while, they gave me a room with no lights, next to the communal toilets. Even at the hospital, I must wait until everyone else has seen the doctor. Finally they favored me with a job in a dusty library where I filled out cards. My asthma got worse; they let me switch to outdoor work; so here I am. I have been pretty lucky. Others, even old people like me, are sent to camps. Here at least, I can drink *longjing,* a tea I have always loved." That last remark is accompanied by an impish smile.

During the fall of 1958, I see Mrs. C. from time to time, at irregular intervals. She is gone more and more frequently, for health reasons. Finally, one day at the end of September, she is gone for good; there is no trace of her other than what is at the center of my painting: a frail figure in a crudely woven straw hat who stands tall amid the tea plants, like a tree ruthlessly pruned down to nothing but a few scrawny branches bereft of leaves.

Before the year is out, some of our school's teachers and students are rehabilitated and return from the camps. A few have been in the Far North, the Chinese Siberia; their accounts focus on the incredibly harsh living conditions up there, caused by the cold of course, but also by a lack of the most basic facilities. These men from the mild climate of Hangzhou were suddenly plunged into the pioneering life, assigned to clear a region the inhabitants of neighboring provinces had never dared take on, even when fleeing famine. The few folk who did live there were hunters. Immense marshy stretches covered with high grass—some of it poisonous—and swept from mid-autumn by an icy wind out of Siberia. In winter, no one would think of sticking his head out the door; on the snow-crystallized plain, clothing becomes stiff as steel and the breath freezes solid. Yet the camp residents were forced to brave the elements. One of the teachers had a little piece of lip torn off when he was doubly foolish: first, he breathed on his saw, gluing his lip to the tool; then, trying to get free, he pulled hard. All of them, ill prepared, were plagued by chilblained hands and feet.

However, when spring finally arrives, the region passes from extreme cold to exceptional heat, and an explosion of nature contrasts with the awful monotony of the winter landscape. Wild plants appear everywhere, often rare species of brilliant color; and the animals awakening from hibernation offer a broad panoply of nature's diversity: wild geese, white swans, Mandarin ducks, deer, boar, wolves, to the great joy of the hunters. At the mention of wolves, one of the teachers recalls an old hand at the camp who had become something of a legend by fighting off a wolf. It was at the end of a day spent clearing land. Behind the others, he walked along the path dragging his long-handled spade. Suddenly he felt the breath of a wild beast on his neck. He had the presence of mind not to turn around; otherwise he would have had his throat torn to ribbons. With a forceful thrust of the shoulder, he managed to throw the animal to the ground and, turning around, he stunned it with the spade; the creature let out a howl before being subdued by the other workers, who had come running. Since the man's name was Haolang, "The man with the wide-ranging mind," they played with homophones and changed it into Haolang, "the howling wolf."

"Haolang, you say? Haolang, the poet?" I asked.

"Oh, yes, that's the one, the poet. He was one of the first sent to the Far North and he's in one of the strictest camps."

"Haolang, the poet. That's impossible. He died in a camp in southern China!"

"The story is that they reported him dead during an epidemic at his camp in the South. Then he was transferred to the North."

6

THE ABSURDITY of fate! How can I be in such a cruel, unexpected situation? I came back to China because Haolang was dead and Yumei had survived him. But Haolang lives and Yumei is dead, needlessly.

With the Friend alive, I can't contemplate my own demise just now. As long as I am alive in this world I shall have but one goal: to join him. Join him? From where I am, stuck in this part of southern China, as solidly fastened as a bolt in a massive machine, I have to find some ridiculous means to cross the continent and reach its farthest point. Could such a strange notion be anything but chimerical? And yet, henceforth this chimerical notion is my only reality.

When I calm down a little, I think things over and my crazy dream seems a little less unrealizable. I almost convince myself one day or another I shall achieve my goal. Like others, I am beginning to comprehend some of the peculiar workings of our collective life that have become everyday processes; which, although perhaps not ensuing from an all-embracing will, are nonetheless irrefutable facts of life; and which all of us, powerless, accept as natural laws. Yes, they are facts of life and might be summed up in a proverb: "Happiness separates; unhappiness unites."

Routine occurrences: young lovers in the same work brigade are subjected to harsh criticism for their "petty-bourgeois" sentimentality and a lack of devotion to work; married couples find themselves assigned to different places. In contrast, there are other sorts of togetherness: when a campaign is underway no one is surprised to find himself some fine morning in the same pickle as others of his kind. "Favorite places" are set aside for these folk: public squares, the scene of interminable criticism and self-criticism sessions; the country for lengthy farm-labor stays; the reeducation camps, et cetera. I am actually pleased that the Far North has become the region of choice for banishment. No matter what happens, my mind is made up: I shall go there. I simply have to arm myself with patience and not overlook a suitable opportunity.

My confidence does not spare me from anguish, however. Each week, each month that goes by seems lost time, endless.

In 1959, I have the feeling that this is it: destiny is winking at me, is giving me a rendezvous. The Leader has the Party launch a campaign with a fairly limited goal: to clean up "the residues" spotted during and after the previous campaign. This time the movement is directed "against opportunists with rightist tendencies." And immediately I am crying out to destiny: "Here's our chance! . . . Opportunist! But I have every right to call myself one! After all, am I not someone awaiting an opportunity?"

Mustering up my courage—and despair makes me rather rash—I lower my head and enter the fray. I hardly take the time to reflect for fear I might botch what could be my only chance. I unmask myself so energetically that I command the silent admiration of colleagues and students. Ordinarily modest and self-effacing, I don't know how I find the audacity to expound my ideas: I speak of the good in Western painting and of the great tradition embodied by the painters of the Renaissance and the Classical age, and I even praise a few modern artists. I do not have to wait long. Overnight I become a "key figure," honored with *dazibao* and endless criticism and self-criticism sessions. After a few of these, I begin to admit that perhaps I have gone astray; eventually I agree that I deserve the indignant disapproval of all. I would be untruthful were I to claim I am not racked by anxiety the entire time. But deep within me there dwells a tenacious, not to say cynical, peace. In the middle of one of these discussions, I can be seized abruptly with a kind of joy, happy that for once I am able to mock the hostile forces relentlessly hounding each of us.

As I expected, I am to be punished. In order to show the sincerity of my desire for reeducation, I myself request to be sent to the most distant region—the Far North, that is. As a result, I go up in the estimation of the authorities. My request is even noted in my file, a good mark for me.

Everything has gone more or less as anticipated. I am not overly surprised; I know the campaign mechanism, its disconcerting simplicity. But it is still a shock to be put on a train to the Far North, a long sinister train moving day and night, a veritable traveling tunnel that is designed to lead nowhere; we walk back and forth in the corridor, we relieve ourselves between the cars. Reality, harsh, inescapable, grasps me in its fists of steel and suddenly turns into nightmare. Yes, nightmare. For at the same time, everything seems unreal to the point of absurdity. Over long hours, I torture myself wondering if I have not merely constructed this whole chain of events in my head.

I find myself here, mesmerized by the train's rhythmic squeaking, lashed by the air filled with whistles and coal dust; among my companions in misfortune, people of all ages and from everywhere, whose attempts to maintain a positive air before the cadres ill-conceal their dismay and despondency. Also with us, a number of young people, restless and noisy. The latter are supposedly "volunteers"—I cannot help laughing to myself: when it comes to volunteers only I am the genuine article—heading out to develop the distant regions of the homeland. Constantly stirred up by the group's leaders, the youngsters sing edifying songs at the top of their lungs, interspersed with slogans shouted in unison. They end up exhausted and sprawl sleepily on the wooden benches, their demeanor like that of the train, which creeps along slower and slower as it begins to penetrate the Northeast, sometimes stopping altogether for hours at a time in the middle of nowhere. It is almost as if it shares the men's uneasiness about the final destination.

7

T HE TRAIN, panting, arrives at its last stop, a station lost in an immense yard overrun with cranes, equipment, and hastily erected buildings. Farther on, gigantic sheds shelter tractors, crates, and boxes piled ceiling-high. Parked around the sheds are vehicles of every kind. This is supply headquarters for the cities and the camps spread out over the region.

The new arrivals are piled into ancient trucks. Our convoy then heads single file down the wide dirt road toward a town, a sort of center from which other roads fan out, leading to various distant work camps.

Beidahuang! The sinister name rings in the ear, a synonym for implacable nature, exile without return, and defiance of destiny. And here it is, forbiddingly stark, unfolding before the eyes of the new arrivals. A vast, desolate expanse, its hugeness is unbearable. Endless swamps with blackish silt, surrounded by impenetrable high grass. Breaking the monotony, from time to time, higher terrain with dark woods. In the distance, as far as the eye can see, stretches rugged, arable land beyond which rise the ramparts of mountains eaten into by great white blotches. This geographical area, harmonious and dissonant, conjures up an infinity of wild beasts torn to pieces in some cataclysm and flaunting their putrefied flesh and tattered hides shamelessly under an indifferent sky. Cultivated fields loom up here and there, incongruous in this setting of inviolate nature. It is not hard to imagine all the hard work and sacrifices of the pioneers. Soldiers turned civilians, political prisoners, and common criminals, sent here en masse. The State, through its successive campaigns and its deportation policy, unceasingly extracts and renews human resources.

A squeaking pile of scrap iron, our truck wheezes and jolts its way along the dirt road. Except for the young, none of the passengers says a word: each is silently sizing up the unknown according to how much he can withstand. At last the camp appears: a jumble of hastily erected dwellings and other structures. We have arrived at one of those spots in the heart of desolation where a few men strive to impose their rule on nature and on other men. It is here that each deportee must try to survive.

Under what conditions? Contributing what work? Vital questions to men abruptly snatched from their hearths and assigned here for a term measured not in days, not in months, but in endless years. "What you have now, it's luxury!" the oldest hands enjoy telling us repeatedly. Just a few years back, these men—according to what they say anyway—knew a life worse than that of the cave dwellers. Our prehistoric ancestors at least got to choose where they would live, in milder climes and sheltered from the elements. Our modern-day convicts were set down amid wild grasses infested with insects and disease, in a land of glacial winters, this northern corner of the Far North deserted by humans and frequented only by wild animals.

Under what conditions? Providing what work? Directed at all levels by the military assisted by political commissars, the camps are organized on the model of the army. At the base are the production brigades, all more or less the same distance from one another. The brigades are joined into divisions, the whole making up a large collective farm, with a major in charge. By the years 1955–1956 there were ten large farms in the Far North with a total of more than one hundred thousand people. Most of these establishments could not be accurately described as camps. They are populated by former military men, soldiers, and non-commissioned officers, transferred in entire units and settled here for the rest of their days. Like other Chinese peasants, these former soldiers live collectively, setting up their households in villages. But other units of production exist that are, strictly speaking, work camps. From the early fifties, well before the large farms were set up, other State farms, few in number and much more primitive, were already in operation; to do the heavy work, they were supplied with cadres undergoing "reeducation" and prisoners subjected to "reform through work." All these cadres and prisoners, originally under the jurisdiction of the Ministry for Security, are at present under military authority; divided up into various divisions, they comprise the special camps. In recent years these installations have had their ranks swollen by new political prisoners and by common criminals. Men and women are kept separate in the camps, and alongside the official hierarchy there are other pecking orders that must be respected if one does not want to be bullied: soldiers over civilians, old-timers over newcomers, workers over intellectuals, et cetera. The military men never miss a chance to remind the intellectuals—most of them clumsy and puny—of all the ordeals endured by soldiers in past wars; they also claim there is good reason to be happy now because we live in a world of peace, assured of our daily rice, thanks to the struggles of the army. These uncouth men talk in stentorian tones, eat their reserved dishes with gusto, sleep soundly in warm beds, and are not burdened by emotional or metaphysical torments. Sure of their rights, they use their privileges to toy with the destinies of those under their command. Some of them parcel out favors so they can take advantage—secretly or openly—of women in their weakness. They are persuaded that a little physical effort and a bit of discipline will be good for all those wielders of the brush who constantly seek the intricate and the twisted when they should rely on simple, straight thinking.

Wielders of the brush turned into wielders of the mattock are housed in dormitories of rudimentary construction: rough boards combined with grass lathing, and buttressed in places by large mud blocks. Subject to the relentlessly intemperate weather, no sooner are the buildings up than they look dilapidated. Inside, their flimsiness is even more apparent. The roofs and walls cannot keep out fierce winds and heavy rains; the poorly leveled floors constantly ooze moisture and cold. Along the walls, *kang** have been built at ground level. On each of them ten or more people sleep each night, head to foot. No provision has been made for personal effects; down to a minimum, they are piled up in the corners. Daily discipline cannot erase the impression of dirt and disorder. With no place to store them, our individual bowls are scattered over the floor, awaiting their use as chamber pots or cooking utensils. Spread out every which way around the central stove are trousers soaked with water and sweat, shoes and socks covered with mud.

Except on a few midsummer days, not everyone gets a chance to take a real bath. We always wash on the run, in cold water from a large cement tub that sits on the damp ground in the backroom. The water is drawn from the well and brought here by the bucketful; we pay the price for it, especially in the dead of winter, when the carrying is done in blasts of wind that can fix one to the spot. Having become beasts of burden, we have quickly grown accustomed to

*Clay beds.

dirt; we accept the filth that sticks to the skin like scabies, attracting fleas and feeding lice. Along with the filth, there is degradation even more difficult to bear: bowing down before the stupidity of the leaders, having to efface every personal trait as if one had been born of the dust to exist without past or desire, and devoid of every bond of affection or any need to wear a name and a face. No private moment, no private place—except by night in dreams. But once night has come, the gloomy oil lamp extinguished, exhaustion casts each of us on the *kang,* amid other drained bodies, amid other dead stumps.

Improved housing and living conditions do not take priority; construction work is saved for the winter months and carried out slowly, heroically. Running water and wooden beds will come later. While waiting, there are many other tasks to confront.

8

EXCEPT FOR a few periods of rest determined by the season, there is work all the time and every task is deemed urgent. Projected production figures must be reached; to be "favorably regarded from on high," those figures must be surpassed. Orders and slogans from the leaders invariably include the qualifier *qiang.** Are these activities always justified, appropriate? Of the dams constructed and fields cleared without preliminary study or preestablished plan, a great many prove useless and unusable, simply the whims of ignorant leaders. And at the cost of superhuman effort and lives sacrificed: dead-tired workers collapse and, unseen in the grass, are done in by tractors; others are torn to bits by defective explosives. Countless are the men disfigured, those with hands and feet atrophied by cold, the women with ailments caused by standing too long in icy water during their periods.

The extremes of nature make every project brutal and lengthy. In the Far North, spring is usually only a prolongation of winter. Over

---

* "Race against the clock," "rescue operation."

many weeks, under a wind that lacerates the face and the body, we prepare the soil and sow the seed in wheat, sorghum, and soy fields so vast we cannot see to the end. With bare hands and chilblained fingers—vestiges of winter—we use our picks and spades to break open ground petrified by the frost; then we move aside for plows drawn by horse or tractor. We take out the *mantou* we've been softening up under our jackets. Nibbling, we do not stop our work for a minute, keeping pace with the seeder as we wield the huge sacks of grain, the fabric as sharp as sheet metal, so stiff is it from the cold. The pace of the seeder, imperious, shattering, is a harbinger of the coming year. After it truly thaws, we plunge into clearing other lands, more wild, more recalcitrant; we burn grass and brambles, by hand we pull out tough, thick roots that impede the march of the tractors. We fill marshy spaces with basket after basket of sand, carried on men's backs. Then summer is here, with its sudden, fierce heat. Now hoeing and weeding have to be done. Step by step we move along the endless furrows, our heads and torsos black with mosquitoes—engorged with blood, motionless, they stick to flesh gluey with sweat. We stir the soil, we remove the rye grass, we straighten up the seedlings. Others are consigned to tasks no less repetitive: plugging up faulty dams for the tenth time, reinforcing irrigation ditches . . .

Until autumn arrives, we have an obsessive fear: rain. If we are unfortunate and it comes, it will mean a real disaster. To the sky's sniveling countenance man responds with a grimace. An incessant, sticky rain falls, transforming everything into mud. Machines can no longer venture into the fields, and each of us knows what awaits: a sentence of one to two months' hard labor in a black and green hell. From three or four in the morning until eight at night, we work with our hands and feet sunk in the dark clay. Dripping wet, holding our sickles, we bend low and tens of thousands of times a day we complete the same sequence of movements: grab a handful wheat stalks, make one swift cut at root level, pull up the plants and place them in rows off to the side. The exhausting work finally comes to an end. Worn down by the dampness and the filth, the ranks reduced by sickness and accident, can the troops now hope for a little respite?

No. Between the end of the rains and the coming of the cold, the time is more than brief. Without waiting a day, without a night intervening, we have to shake the winnowing baskets set out in the main courtyard, dry the grain, put it in sacks, take it off to the barns. And indeed, by mid-October, there is a heavy white shroud over mountain and plain. Winter, impatient to confirm that its fearsome instrument—the cold—remains as efficient as ever. It is using it already without restraint, straining its capacity to the limit, lowering the temperature more each day. And arbitrarily, the season unleashes gusty winds or snowstorms that make earth and heaven spin and cause the wolves to howl in distress.

The vast, sealed landscape is silent testimony to how living beings are subject to the winter's merciless law; not a creature can be seen, except for a few bold convicts. Their helmeted heads sunk into their shoulders, their bodies wrapped in layers of threadbare jackets held tight with string and rope, these men try to clear a path through the snowdrifts. For this is the season chosen by the leaders to enforce another law, equally merciless, that of profitability. There is no longer any "urgent" work, so in good conscience they can devote their manpower to projects deferred: the building of roads and dwellings, the digging of canals and reservoirs. Can men work when it is freezing hard enough to split stone?

Freezing hard enough to split stone? An expression I picked up in France, it is not at all appropriate in the far reaches of Northern China. For the truth is, at minus forty degrees Celsius rock and ice form a single piece, a block as hard as concrete. Thus, the whole Far North forms a bloc, so to speak, against human effort. On the vast work site, each worker—a snowman to his very bones—is assigned a space; his job is to get through the block. With a steel pick and all his might, he strikes the icy surface. The point of his pick leaves not a mark, no more than a needle can mark a diamond. He strikes again. The rebounding pick makes his arms and hands vibrate, and his frozen skin is marbled with little bloody cracks. That does not stop him; his painful energy is soon dissipated. Give up? He does not have the right. Nor does he really want to. Even if it is wasted effort, he is at least warmed by the exertion. In this place where any exposed flesh is hatch-marked by a Siberian blizzard sharper than a dagger, where the whirling snow congeals everything in its wake, he knows that if he stops moving the sweat will turn to ice beneath his jacket. He will be given over to congestion of the lungs or death. Of course, if he feels up to it he can drag himself over to the center of the work site where a fire has been lit. Warming himself there, he will understand why they say in the Far North: "The chest, a burning coal; the back, a block of ice." But he is not ready to move away yet, and he keeps on striking. More intelligently now. He focuses on one spot with the point of his pick. About thirty blows later, a mark appears. A hairline crack in the block that has scoffed at him until now. Then a split. And the ice is broken. Now it is the turn of the rock below to suffer his assaults. This is the beginning of a long day's work, infinitely more bruising than what he has just accomplished. But he has the satisfaction of knowing his hand has not bled for nothing: his blood is victorious.

9

FOR NOW, the main thing is to endure, to survive amid others condemned to the same fate, people one doesn't know. During the large-scale campaigns, a whole group might be sentenced and sent off to the same camp. Prisoners generally found themselves among their own kind. The current campaign is a sort of mopping-up operation to collect the "residues" from the previous campaign. We form a disparate ensemble, we come from everywhere. The stagnant pond of old-timers is swollen by the flood of newcomers, who are divided randomly among the different dormitories. My own camp, initially composed of university faculty and people from the arts, now includes other elements, some of them surprising. During the trial-and-error stage when newcomers and old-timers are getting acquainted, all conversation is in connected with everyday practicalities and work. No one volunteers any information about himself. No questions are asked. But there is a total lack of privacy: several sleep on one *kang;* communal toilets have no partitions between the holes. In the so-called shower room, bathers carry their basins and jostle one another to get to the water container, improvising a gloomy ballet.

The lack of privacy creates too intimate a knowledge of one's fellows, through sound, smell, and touch. Rumblings of the stomach, expulsions of gas, hiccups, sneezes, coughing fits, words surfacing from nightmares, stench of sweat and urine. Skin touching skin, slimy skin, rough, and on occasion, covered with bloodstained bandages . . .

But the disgusting state of their bodies has nothing to do with the real personalities of the people I come to know here. My own camp and neighboring ones are less strict (if one can use that word) than the "reform through work" camps. In the latter, political prisoners are mixed in with common criminals, who have a higher status; bullies and informers are used to reinforce an already rigorous "discipline." Of course, my camp and others like it also house their inevitable share of toadies and sneaks. But, as I gradually discover, the rest of the "cons" are among the finest elements of China, often unjustly sentenced for just what makes them so admirable: uprightness, sincerity. Their presence makes it worthwhile to be in the Far North, despite the heavy price. An expression I learned in France comes to mind: "the *cream* of society." Then why does the regime methodically skim off the best minds of our country and exile them to out of the way places? Can moving people somewhere for years to work in degrading circumstances really reform them?

If by some strange chance the authorities suddenly decided that dissidents with creative abilities should be sentenced to live and work together, developing their special gifts and communicating freely with one another, what a vital community would be formed! What a workshop of creative activity! Unfortunately, such people are more vulnerable to the harsh winds of fate because they have been inspired by an ideal. And here they are, assembled in this place for having done the very minimum of what conscience dictated. Writers and artists, some of them still young, their creative drive struck down too soon. A civil servant, an honest, serene man, a practitioner of calligraphy and Tai chi chuan, punished for questioning a decision by his neighborhood leader. A humble university librarian, gentle and effeminate, too gentle not to stir up his bosses' and colleagues' love of persecution; they claimed he shook his head before a *dazibao*, although it was just his habit of nodding while he read. A learned philosopher, an expert on Chinese culture, also conversant with Plato and Kant, punished for defending the values of idealism. A historian who specialized in bronze mirrors and embroideries of ancient China, for questioning the belief that socioeconomic conditions determine the evolution of art forms. An apprentice engineer and Party member, a tall skinny fellow, for suggesting that the factory where he worked could be run better. They call him Don Quixote because he once removed a bee's nest from under the roof; he had covered his face with a gauze mask and had used a long bamboo stick, as if he were the helmeted knight armed with his lance. They say his wife left him when he received his sentence. And by his side, the inevitable Sancho Panza, a comic actor, who was deported for acting in a play the authorities took to be a satire of the regime. With a native optimism and an impish wit that betray his rural Chinese roots, he brings a ray of light to the camp. He is the only one of us who can shut up the guards, which he does by quoting the Chairman or saying something clever. If he dares stand up to them, it is because he is blessed with incredibly good health: as tireless as a buffalo, he does not cringe at the harsh tasks they inflict on him.

10

TWO MEN STAND out because they always stay in the background. Older than the others, they sleep at the very end of a *kang* off by itself in a corner. It is easy to understand why when one knows what they do. On them falls the most degrading task of all, the chore everyone else wants to avoid: cleaning out the latrines and transporting a portion of the excrement to a fertilizer processing tank. And yet this assignment is a privilege. The work is not at all exhausting; on the contrary it is in line with what they can handle physically. They can carry their buckets as empty or as full as they like; they can walk as fast or as slow as they wish, with no voice at their backs relentlessly haranguing them. They have ample time to complete their daily mission. There's just one thing. This privilege has turned them into "untouchables." Since it is so hard to bathe here, especially if one is old and feeble, these two always reek of the latrines. They cannot "clean up their act."

Although both are gray and wrinkled, they offer a contrast in physiognomy: one has a scowl he seems determined to maintain; the other a placid face across which flits an occasional slight smile. Who are they? The scowler is an economist, guilty of a crime of lèse-majesté: he expounded the theory of a mixed economy in which State enterprise would compete with private enterprise. He also advocated a Malthusian policy in total opposition to the idea extolled by the Chairman: "The more manpower we have, the stronger we are." The one who looks placid—or resigned rather—is a veteran of camp life. He was in the first contingent of prisoners, those sent from Henan in the early fifties. While a good number of his companions have passed on, he, the least likely to survive, remains, but at a price: an atrophied left hand that is practically useless and, from a stint in the mines, a damaged lung that makes him cough all winter long. Seniority, poor health, and good behavior probably explain how he ended up a less strict camp after many transfers. When it comes to his past, he is laconic. To the occasional new arrival who inquires about his origins, he invariably responds: "Landowner." And the crime for which he was sentenced? His only reply is a faint smile. But we know what it was: a supremely audacious act, the hiding of counterrevolutionaries in his house. That he was not shot along with them was something of a miracle. That he has ended up in this camp is something of an incongruity. But people are used to him and his odor. They are aware that beneath his plodding, ingenuous exterior there is a rather cultured man; he can hold his own among the intellectuals. His seniority is evident in his clothes: he has painstakingly patched them with scraps of fabric picked up here and there. I am reminded of certain cars I had seen in

Europe, plastered with insignia attesting to their owners' travels. He is called Lao Ding—"Old Ding." This epithet is due him naturally, but here it seems conferred through unanimous approval. Isn't it encouraging to have in our midst an old person who is not a burden, who is not a nuisance? We are grateful to him for maintaining his unassuming dignity. Beside him, we feel young and we nourish the hope that we shall not reach the end totally destroyed.

And is that why I have agreed to replace the economist, who was sent off to the division infirmary? Or is it because I have been impelled all my life by a need to be with people older than myself? Their very fragility seems to confer on them a kind of solid wisdom. Unless I really am inhabited by a masochism that constantly makes me want to do what repels me, makes me want to touch bottom. Then, too, there is that other wearying need—typical of the weak—to seek the reasons behind the behavior of others. What is it that motivates Lao Ding? Why does this old man stuck back in the corner say hello to me from time to time? Why does he take an interest in me? I ask myself. Is it my status as a newcomer, or as a painter, or as someone back from abroad? Though the last topic is taboo, once for no apparent reason, the gray-haired man whispered to me in the shower room, "you're pretty far from the ocean, aren't you! And even farther from the Mediterranean." Or finally, is it just that I need to step back a bit? But whatever my reasons, my volunteering to do the shit work is a great relief to everyone. Huang, our section leader, who usually bares his teeth and shouts and carries on, agrees without a fuss; as far as he is concerned, I am not much of a hand anyway when it comes to heavy work.

For several weeks, I serve my apprenticeship at the nasty job, a gauze mask over my nose to keep out the suffocating stench; then, when night comes, I sleep at the end of the *kang* next to Lao Ding. Following a general reorganization, we join six other workers in a separate dwelling, a kind of shack or hut at the very edge of the brigade's domain, and even more primitive than the other camp buildings. On stormy nights, our humble edifice is like a skiff buffeted by the wind. Inside, at the base of the walls, moss and mushrooms sprout, to the delight of the rats. Eight of us occupy this tight space. On us fall the chores of cleaning the latrines and tending the pigs, and the related task of tending the vast vegetable gardens enriched with human fertilizer. None of that excuses us from helping with collective projects when there is an emergency.

Adjoining our hut are covered pens sheltering around thirty pigs that the brigade is raising. A tough breed, some of them have protruding teeth and ferocious-looking snouts. Stubborn, grunters, these creatures wallow in their filth and require constant care. Because they are so filthy, we have to brush them, polish them, clean their litter and troughs, wash the buckets and basins they use. To ensure that they fatten up nicely, we provide them a varied diet and always heat their food. What's more, weather permitting, we have to herd them to the marshy places where their favorite grasses grow. We also assist the veterinarians during epidemics or births, which sometimes means staying up all night in the worst of winter.

Having such close dealings with hogs, supplying their favorite foods, handling slimy, viscous mixtures nearly as repugnant as excrement or manure—a swill that plashes into the troughs with a sound echoing the famished grunts—leaves our arms penetrated to the very marrow with a nauseating stench. When we ourselves come to eat, we feel like retching; the simple act of swallowing is impossible. This permanent nausea gives us herders a deep-seated aversion toward pigs in general.

Aversion? In spite of it, we shall transcend our loathing, we shall give in to these creatures so physically alive in their clumsy heaviness. To the hand of a man deprived of woman, the animal's rough hide will soon come to feel soft. And to ears deprived of soothing words, the grunts will take on a sweetness sufficient to touch the heart. What pleasure for such a man to feel his innocent companions thrash about in his arms or between his legs. What heartbreak too when one of them, fattened up, is to be pulled to the other side of the courtyard to have his throat cut. His angry cries will be the lament of love betrayed.

Autumn, ceaseless rain. To replace the machinery bogged down in the fields, in every camp several hundred men and women bow down and pick up their sickles, devoting themselves to the harvest salvage, sixteen to seventeen hours a day. Late at night, the mess hall, filled with steam from cooked noodles and the smell of wet hair and acrid sweat, rings with the hoarse voices of men and women worn down by fatigue and pain. In the dim light, I see the former librarian approach, more pale and thin than ever. Just to say something, he whispers: "I've seen you leading the pigs to the pond. They're being well cared for. They look kind of troublesome, but I know they're nice. . . ."

"It's really a lot of work."

"I think it would do me good to take care of them, even for a day!"

"A day or two, maybe that's possible. I'll talk to the leader. I'll offer to trade places and do your work in the fields."

The former librarian will not have the good fortune to stroke the pigs, those "nice" animals. Before I get a chance to substitute for him, he collapses in the field without a sound. That does not keep them from requisitioning me to help with the harvest.

II

WE MAY FEEL intense disgust, and we may miss seeing women about—a privilege of those who work in the fields—but not one of us, even for all the gold in the world, would trade his job in the latrines and the pigsty for the restrictive life of the big dormitories. Although we are visited and inspected regularly, here in the annex we are spared the military discipline that prevails elsewhere, especially during the long winter months when, except for outdoor projects and political meetings in the great hall, the prisoners live atop one another under the leaden supervision of leaders, minor and major. Our quarters are more than cramped, smelly in summer, ill-heated in winter, but we have a sense of belonging to a "private club" where something of a life of one's own is possible. Men from the big dormitories join us when they can slip away. In the shelter of a place almost as denuded as ourselves, what moments shared, moments snatched bit by bit from the absurd! Before a small audience, the historian, no pictures to rely on, describes with contagious enthusiasm the mirrors and fabrics of Chinese antiquity, their shapes, their hues, their workmanship, their discovery, their connection with some woman's life or some historical event. Young writers and poets read past or recent works. Musicians give recitals of silent music. Lacking a piano, the pianist has drawn the black and white keys of a keyboard on a long strip of paper. Here he exercises his fingers, playing Schumann, Chopin, or Rachmaninov, and humming along. The first moment of elation over, his face is streaked with tears; looking at the hands ruined by so much heavy work he knows he will never again be a real pianist. Sometimes he will accompany the singer in our group when the melody is one he knows: Beethoven's *Adelaide,* Schubert's *Der Lindenbaum* or *Das Wanderer,* or maybe a Schumann song for Clara . . . Far more poignant than any perfect rendition is the odd harmony emanating from the singer's deliberately muffled voice and the pianist's hummed accompaniment: a faint dirge of desperation.

At such moments, when the waste of these men's lives is apparent, Zhang the Mute imposes his silence. The broken human voices are succeeded by the cracked sounds of bamboo, sounds he draws from a sort of pipe he has had since they took away his brush, a pipe into which he blows as lightly as he can. Were it not for the instrument in his hand and his visible blowing, no ear would be alert to his music. For the sounds produced, barely audible, depend on imagination or vague desire. Yet, we hear. What we hear comes from beyond the thin partition between us and the outside, from far away, farther than the wind, farther than the hungry bear howling on the edge of the settlement. A gentle breeze touches the virgin beach, ruffling sands and reeds. From one moment to the next, we might expect to see at the horizon a boat floating on invisible waters. . . . Then, nothing. Nothing but a long silence, nothing but an immense heart beating. Zhang the Mute imposes his silence on all; he bids us enter his silence where we commune indefinitely, with pure feeling. I know this colleague well from Fine Arts, where he taught traditional painting. After the Liberation, he was one of the few to paint according to his own vision, refusing to introduce red flags and giant cranes into his landscapes. Similarly, in his calligraphy, lacking an awareness of correct edifying maxims, he still wrote mystical lines, such as:

> *Within; essence of things*
> *Define it? Already beyond words.*

And his muteness only made his case worse. When he was the object of criticism at political meetings, he would stay silent, absorbing the insults, accepting the rebukes without flinching. In the camp, he continues to merit his nickname "the Mute." But he is definitely not a shy loner, and he is a faithful member of the club. Ensconced in a corner, saying nothing, he has become our most attentive ear, or our most relentless; a smile or nod of approval from him is beyond price.

One day the camp carpenter arrives unannounced to repair the pigsty. There is an uncomfortable and circumspect silence; our discussion has been interrupted. The outsider acts as if he sees nothing. He goes to work and he whistles. To whistle while working: a sign of a comfortable, independent life!—a privilege reserved for those free craftsmen whose only worry is the quality of their work. After an hour, he comes to say good-bye to the group crowded into the little room.

"You're all *Zhishi fenzi.** You want to read some books?" he asks straight out.

Again we are silent, taken aback by this question as dangerous as it is incongruous.

"You want to read books, don't you?" The craftsman's smile is pleasant.

"Books? . . . Well, sure."

"I have a lot of books, you know. Over all the years I've been here, I've seen generations of people come, live here awhile, then go off. I like books, so when they leave, they always give me the ones they've brought in secretly. I have a whole library now, and unfortu-

---

*Intellectuals.

nately, I don't have time to read. Reading doesn't come easily to me, and there's always too much work around here. . . ."

"A whole library! What sort of books do you have?"

"Name a few. I'll see if I have them."

We make three selections at random: Tolstoy's *Resurrection,* the poems of Du Fu, the short stories of Shen Congwen. The next day no one can believe it when the carpenter proudly sets down the works we mentioned.

After that, thanks to steady contributions from the carpenter, our annex becomes a true Ali Baba's cave where the privileged members of the "club" come to draw out their treasures.

·   ·   ·

UNEXPECTED AND almost unbelievable, this good fortune goes on for some time. Then the most feared visitor of all shows up at the door one day. Teeth bared, smug with authority, Huang, the head of our section, shouts in a hoarse voice. Sometimes we feel sorry for this nit-picking, peremptory character; not as mean as some of the others, he feels the need to rant and rave constantly, beyond what his bosses require. "What's the meaning of this? You're forming cliques now? Are you plotting or what?" Since no one answers, he goes farther: "Well, you're going to get it!" Then Sancho Panza, good actor that he is, offers a response: "How could we dare plot? We all want to be model revolutionaries. That's why we are studying."

"Studying? But you're here to work!"

"Nevertheless, the Chairman says: 'Study, study some more, keep studying.'"

"Well, what do you know! You're forgetting that you're in re-education!"

"And that's just what we want, to educate ourselves and re-educate ourselves. We want to be both 'red and knowledgeable' as the Chairman recommends."

That does it. Thoroughly exasperated, the little leader barks orders: "Shut up, Oily Tongue! Break it up, everybody. Now! Don't try this again! Otherwise you'll find yourself locked in a cell. I'm going to be reasonable—I won't report you this time. As a warning—a small punishment—nobody gets a rest for two weeks. And you, Oily Tongue, no rests for a month!" Sancho has gotten off rather easily. The leader has not gone too far, for in fact he is afraid his superiors will accuse him of negligence. Is the gossip true, that his mind is elsewhere these days, that he's trying to put the make on one of the members of the women's brigade? Besides, he has a certain appreciation of the positive role the comic actor plays in the group; he defuses the atmosphere. As for being deprived of his afternoon nap, Sancho the Robust couldn't care less. That ritual has always bored him. But then there's a big difference between boredom and having to slave away in the hot sun during the siesta hour. . . .

12

NOT FOR A MINUTE do I forget my reason for coming to the Far North: to find the Friend. As time passes, I am paralyzed by anxiety. So near Haolang, I have never felt him so far away—beyond reach. I am practically convinced I shall not manage to see him again. The Far North is a continent in itself, an ocean with scattered isles that are the camps, isolated from one another. The only communication between them is through official channels. Of course, it has not taken long to find out which camp is Haolang's. He is not unknown in the Far North, both as an "old hand" and as a poet; some of his works circulate among the younger prisoners. From town, the road to his camp is much longer than the road to mine; according to my estimate, the distance from my camp to town then on to the Friend's camp is probably around 150 kilometers. A hundred and some kilometers . . . that's almost nothing, compared to separation by death, to oceans between continents, to mountains and rivers between the vast provinces of China. Short as the distance may be, the wall between us is insurmountable. It is a wall raised by men, by administrative barriers, by rigorous surveillance. We live in different camps. I know that I do not have a chance.

Along with my anxiety there is dread, and my deteriorating

health. Can I last long enough for that outcome too good to be true? I am haunted by the tale of the shipwreck survivor who swims for several days and nights, then finally spots the distant shore. Now totally exhausted, he can go no further and the final waves cast his corpse onto the beach.

Several times I arrange to join the crew going into town for supplies. I linger as long as possible in the shops and the cooperatives, hoping for a chance meeting with the Friend who could himself be a member of a similar crew.

Almost losing hope of seeing him again and a fortiori of living with him awhile—my dream before I arrived in the Far North—now I resign myself to getting a message to him. But I don't even have a way to do that. Maybe through the carpenter? Twice, I am on the verge of speaking to him, but I hesitate.

Camp life goes on, a life subject to the demands of each day, each hour, with no time for reflection. Just before summer, some poorly built canals overflow and some soy fields are flooded. While the bulk of the manpower is mobilized for canal repair, two companions and I are requisitioned to go into the fields: we drain water, lift up seedlings, etc. The hours spent under the scorching sun are sweetened only by the nearby presence of women. Lightly dressed, in this place of deprivation they have an unbelievable power to attract, even if some are gray or not at all good looking. I, with my head definitely elsewhere, am one of the few to pay them no heed.

Out in the field one day I raise my head and through the mosquito-saturated sweat running down my forehead and blurring my vision, I can make out an attentive observer preserving the image of our collective work. Not an official photographer aiming his lens at us—we would hardly make a convincing propaganda shot!—but a young man with a big sketchpad.

"Strange thing, destiny," I say to myself. "Things are repeated in this life and are never the same. In Hangzhou I sketched the labor of the tea harvesters, among them the writer, Mrs. C. Today someone else draws the damned as they slave away, and I am among them. Now the sketching painter has become the sketched! This is certainly cyclical time as our Ancients knew it. One cycle is ending; another is beginning and appears to follow the same path, but is opening into something else."

Just as with Mrs. C., when I reach the end of my row, I strike up a conversation with the young man, our voices low:

"You're a painter?"

"Not yet, but I like to draw."

"I am a painter."

That response brings a gleam to his eye. My interlocutor, visibly embarrassed, seems to want to apologize for not helping me with my work, but he knows the rules: everyone to his own task.

The conversation resumes each time I reach the end of my row. Finally the young man, to whom I've mentioned my unit number, invites himself to visit me in my quarters next to the pigsty.

Who is he that he can move freely within and without the camp?

On his first visit he reveals his identity; he is none other than the younger son of the camp commandant. Looking at his work, I take pains to be patient as I correct his beginner's mistakes, pointing out to him what should be avoided. The help I offer seems so precious to him that we end up becoming friends. While well aware of the risk of betrayal, I am tempted to ask him to get a message to the Friend.

I unburden myself to Lao Ding to whom I have long since confided my tale of the Friend and the Lover. He already knows the young man from seeing him in our annex so often, and he simply says: "Since you have trusted me, why not trust him, too?"

Trust, in our little universe ruled by mistrust and denunciation? But I do not forget the tradition that has kept Chinese culture alive for a thousand years against all odds: the respect a young person has for his elders, or a disciple for his master. With that tradition behind me, I decide to speak to the apprentice painter. Still young myself, I am already playing the role of the elder, passing on the torch of truth received from the Ancients, handing it on to the next generation. Will this new generation have enough comprehension and gratitude not to doom its predecessors to total oblivion?

The next time the commandant's son visits me, I take a good look at the smooth face raised toward who knows what ideal, and I feel a sudden thrill: I am certain I am on the providential path; the much desired goal is within my reach. A winged angel stands before me in this dilapidated room next to a pigsty. My intuition will soon be confirmed by events—unless, by some unlikely chance, the events have been caused by my desires alone! As soon as I speak the name Haolang—magical name, as this instance proves—my interlocutor begins to recite in a singsong voice: "So often have we drunk of the dew / in return for our blood / that the land burned a hundred times over / thanks us for our existence . . ."

Considering the messenger's privileged position, his mission would appear to present no difficulties. But that is not so. There is no regular transportation between the camps; he must wait to catch a ride on a truck. Every message means an all-day round trip. Worse, once in the other camp, how can he avoid attracting attention when seeking out Haolang? Despite his reputation, the poet remains a thorn in the side of the leaders, because of his special status and his uncompromising character.

And now that Haolang has learned I am here—the news is a shock indeed!—the essential is virtually completed. Communication through thought has been reestablished. I believe in its power; I already see my friend. If something should happen to me in the meantime, I would die with less regret. But as long as the young man is around, I am convinced I shall see Haolang in person someday. Yes, in person. Just as I am now accustomed to seeing Yumei. How many nights, a moonbeam, she comes to me as stealthily as a wolf— or a White Serpent—and inundates me with her surprised look. How many days when, in my idle moments, she is suddenly near me, very near, too near. Unaware that I am broken by despair, in a cheerful voice she speaks her favorite words: "But it's not late. We can still do something!" And certainly, there is still something left to do. Thus, I try to imagine the circumstances of a reunion with Haolang: a big meeting connected with some new political movement; a New Year's celebration, when several camps get together for entertainments . . .

13

ID-MAY. Arrival of the cursed thing the old-timers speak of with dread and resignation, the thing that is part of the "epic of the far North": fire. Already more likely in a natural environment where trees and grass are crackling dry in summer, this scourge is largely man's doing: the ignorance of many—beginning with those in charge—in matters of safety and the repeated use of fire in the flimsiest of structures. When the catastrophe does occur, the lenders can do little more than launch an attack with ill-trained men and shouts of "No fear of flame, no fear of death!"

The news arrives at the camp in late afternoon. General mobilization: except for kitchen workers, everyone to the front. In trucks, atop tractors, on horseback or on foot—using every available means of transport, we head for the scene of the disaster, twenty kilometers away. En route we run into groups from other camps, as panic-stricken, as unkempt as we are. In the atmosphere of tragedy and crisis those meeting, faces tense, merely exchange waves or shout the latest news. The fire, stirred up by the wind, threatens to destroy all the crops in the vicinity.

A group of burly fellows, the "musclemen," have been dispatched first in motorized vehicles. I am among those who have to get there on foot. It will take us nearly four hours, unless the trucks pick us up on their way back. Overcoming our breathlessness, we quicken our pace. In the distance smoke rises from the plain, announcing the drama being played out ahead. As we draw closer, the fire turns the clouds pink and lets its staggering heat reveal all the power of its dominion.

"No fear of flame, no fear of death!" Now, with no other thoughts in our heads, we must run toward the unleashed monster, across fields, not bothering to retrieve shoes lost during our race. Many pull off their jackets, tossing them by the side of the field, and are down to their already soaked undershirts.

The drama's setting, surrounded by night: beyond vast millet fields, a great stretch of wild grass, meeting in the distance a dense forest from where the fire has spread. A section of the edge of the fields has burned. Yet, between fields and forest, wild grass has been cleared away for a long firebreak. At what a cost! Just before our arrival, tragedy. Digging the break, the men did not watch out for the wind, which suddenly changed direction. Ten of them, overcome by smoke, have died in the flames; others are seriously burned. And now several hundred or maybe even a thousand men battle the blaze relentlessly, their weapons whatever is at hand: makeshift brooms fashioned from grass attached to branches, spades and picks of every size, buckets of water passed from hand to hand. Improvisation and disorder. Eyes bloodshot, leaders run from one group to another, shouting orders at the top of their lungs. Nobody listens to them. Torsos covered with soot-blackened sweat, undershirts tattered, the men strike at the flames as much in fury as in fear. The death of their comrades turns them into wounded beasts. They vow they will not retreat. . . .

Unbelievable arrogance of the flames. Gigantic Medusas escaped from their abyss, they constitute a force as monstrous as it is fascinating, a force devouring everything it passes, itself devoured by the necessity to satisfy a need that cannot be explained. In their strategy of conquest, the flames play with a thousand ruses, with paralyzing threats, with wily attacks. As soon as the prey is within reach, they begin by circling around it, charming it, bewitching it, grazing it, stroking it; then, sure and determined, they grasp it, embrace it to the point of suffocation, lick it from all sides, lengthily, lasciviously. When the victim is finally ripe, they tear it apart in one swoop, crush it, swallowing it with no mercy.

City fires are not like those of the wilderness: here, in nature, the impulses contained in the primeval lava seem to have no limits, no end. The whole universe of living things is hurled into the madness. Trees twisted in pain and rebellion splinter into fragments, explode into embers. The rabbit, the deer, the boar—all the animals torn away from their lairs speed away, bounding too high, falling straight into the flames. The sound of their flesh sizzling is drowned out by the deafening crackle that springs from everywhere. As for men, exhausted, coming apart, they continue to strike with rage. They cannot stop. Nothing will stop them, neither burning nor death. For once they are free to strike, and they will strike until the ultimate spasm. Cutting off the heads and tails of hydras and vipers perpetually reborn, they express all that has been held in day after day, their anger, their grief, their feelings about the death of others and their own death.

I feel the near uselessness of my activity in the gigantic battle, as I stand in the second line passing buckets of water, subduing firebrands with a pathetic broom. Dulled by the suffocating heat, my brain remains alert enough to think that the anarchy of this fiery night provides me my only chance to find the Friend. As we ran, I repeated to myself, "Haolang's brigade must be here! Haolang's brigade must be here!" Now I know for certain it is, and with it, Haolang is close by! I set about perusing a darkness torn to shreds by the fire. Between shadows and flashes of light, I try to get a good look at the faces of any tall firefighters heading to the front line. Arduous task, the smoke is so blinding. And worse, a foolish hope. In this moving throng how can one spot a particular person? And supposing Haolang does appears before me, would I even recognize him? I still picture his twenty-year-old face! I look, I keep looking. The only chance . . .

As the night passes and the flames recede, my hope fades. Suddenly I think of going to the area set up for the injured. Once there, I learn that three of my brigade were among the first victims, all evacuated by now. Of the three, the one I know best is Don Quixote, who had been stationed in a very dangerous position. Others with fairly serious burns still wait on the ground on stretchers, ready to be evacuated. Some are covered with sheets, only their heads showing. Hurriedly, I inspect each stretcher: a parade of faces, one blending into another. Almost at the end one stands out, and I see it clearly as can be; I recognize the powerful head of the man of the North; his face and hair are badly burned; other parts of his body probably are too. Tight-lipped, stifling cries of pain, eyes still red from combat with the fire, he looks with indifference at those bustling around him. To be sure I am not mistaken I call, "Haolang!"

The man's eyes turn toward me, he looks at me for a split second. Nothing comes from his mouth, but there is a touch of a smile on his swollen face. Before the stretcher bearers carry him away, he moves his head slightly, signaling me a second time.

14

H IS "HEROIC COURAGE" has earned Haolang the respect of the authorities; the commandant's son has done the rest by interceding with his father. What I no longer dared hope for, even in my dreams, will soon be a reality I can touch with my trembling hand. This one miracle is enough for me to think that in this life—as in others—over and above suffering and misfortune, nothing is in vain.

.   .   .

THE DAY arrives: I see before me a man of less than forty, who looks at least ten years older, hair graying, brow wrinkled and scarred, but cheekbones and chin still showing a determination confirmed by his penetrating gaze. A heavier man, with a heavier step, and a face weathered by hard outdoor work. Statue of stone or bronze eroded by every kind of storm, a solid block compacted into the essential. This man has known death, has been taken for dead, but his lifeforce and his creative force have banished all thought of giving up.

This man has known infamy and has been treated shamefully by his peers. First he sent to a camp in southern China, another marshy region, its summers extremely humid and scorchingly hot. Before those lands were drained, and even afterward, pestilential vapors rose from the ground. In the olden days, condemned men were dropped off there to be devoured in short order by leeches, mosquitoes, and even more fearsome small creatures. In the modern camp, one day some prisoners threw their bowls of bitter rice into the field. Inexcusable waste of State property: the military head sentenced the whole crew to work in the rice fields under a hot sun; they also had to eat the remains of the spoiled rice. They all became ill and several died. This man, counted among the deceased, narrowly escaped death and was subsequently dispatched to another camp in a region no less hostile, at the far end of China where he was born. By nature probably better suited to a northern climate, he managed to survive. Anyone else so severely punished and so often acting commendably would have been set free by now. But his case, especially serious because he refused to admit his errors, was one of many referred to the Chairman, who was to pronounce the final sentence. But the Great Leader either had other fish to fry or simply forgot, and Haolang's fate had never been decided. No one else dared take up the matter. And now this man, who has been through so much and has become like tempered steel, must face something that his willpower might not overcome, for it concerns his deepest feelings.

Before fall is over in our memorable year of 1960, the man I have come to the ends of the earth to find is transferred to my camp with its less strict regime. This occurs by an arrangement among the leaders, who know that a famine is in the offing and also that the various camps need to be consolidated.

No words can adequately express our feelings upon seeing each another; we do not even try to speak. We just let our tears flow; we cannot stop touching each other, to assure ourselves that this is real. Later, words will come spontaneously, forming twin rivers, which will flow day and night, joining in a common sea. We both have so many things to say, so many stories to tell. We have been part of each other's thoughts for so long we forget we parted nearly fifteen years ago, under unpleasant circumstances.

Let the words well up spontaneously? Not yet. First I have the immediate task of looking for the right way to tell the Friend that the Lover is dead. The right words—I must find them and speak them. When they echo in the Friend's ear, the story of the years of separation, that river about to overflow his breast, comes to an abrupt halt. Henceforth, not a single syllable from his throat. This man of such verbal brilliance is dazed and mute. For entire days he is a robot, consumed with grief and remorse—remorse for ruining the Lover's life as well as mine—and rebellion. Total destruction tempts him: he would like to destroy himself and the world around him. Probably only my presence keeps him from committing an irreversible act.

Can he allow himself to wound his only remaining loved one yet another time? I have no choice but to accept, alas, that there are people bound together to their very roots by bonds which, once forged, can never be sundered. Such connections have the power to overcome resentment, remorse, rebellion: it has nothing to do with the good will of each party or the events of their individual lives. Such connections compel people to abandon their plans and do things not of their own choosing. I, Tianyi, why am I here, instead of in France, where I would be free to pursue another path? What is it, this order? Blind destiny? Destiny, perhaps; blind, probably not. Since leaving the School of Fine Arts at Hangzhou, I have traveled many tortuous roads. From paving stone to paving stone, I was inching toward my mad dream. I am here, in this place of perdition. Haolang is here, in this place of reunion. . . .

·   ·   ·

OUT OF DESPAIR and from long years of deprivation and self-discipline—for he wanted to remain worthy of the Lover—the Friend now turns to alcohol and casual sex. Surprising as it may seem, in our rigorously controlled environment, it is possible for bold and wily men to have relations with women on the sly. During communal projects where joint men and women crews operate tractors or other machinery, or in the infirmary, to say nothing of—the height of perversity—encounters with wives and daughters of the ruling class. Don't some of the men of the ruling class themselves provide the example when they use their power to take advantage of the women cons?

Terror and fury predominate in our universe of tyrants, but even in the inhuman there are little cracks that leave openings for the human to germinate and grow.

15

NOW THAT Haolang is here—and I don't quite know how to admit this—everything seems pointless. When I was determined to find him, I felt anxiety and despair, then indescribable excitement as I came closer to my goal. Maybe my mission is over, since I've found him and I've told him about Yumei. Maybe that marks the end of the story of the trio. But it is not over for me—seeing the distress I have caused Haolang, I am almost numb, and my desire to live ebbs day by day. I knew he would take the news badly, but that doesn't help. Suddenly, I do not see what our reunion means. Do we have to look for meaning? Isn't being together enough? But what are we going to do? What will become of us?

While the Friend wallows in rebellion and remorse, I cannot stem his slide toward destruction but spend long hours pondering our situation, my thoughts and questions so involved that at times I don't understand them myself. What do we prisoners do? Continue to bow down, both of us, before this endless humiliation? Get it over with, our life of bottomless mediocrity? Who might help us sort things out? No one. Yumei, if she were alive, probably could help. But then, if she were alive, I wouldn't be here! Instead, I have Haolang. How does he feel about me? What role do I play in his life? That is the limit! Now I'm looking for proof of our friendship! Haven't we always been bound together "hand and foot?" Were we not as one when we walked across Sichuan? Soon after they had become lovers, didn't he tear himself away from Yumei because of me? The flesh-and-blood man here with me, isn't he the original Friend, the inalienable companion? Whatever he may have done, whatever he might do, isn't he part of me? Isn't he part of Yumei, too, since she loved him and made him happy? Is there any room for jealousy? Isn't my love for Yumei one more reason to love Haolang? All that is as inextricable as it is desperately clear! When I decided to go find him, what was I looking for? A bit of flotsam to cling to? Or something more? Didn't I hope to encounter the spirit that had awakened me in my youth, revealed me to myself, spurred me ever onward? Is that spirit of his still alive, or is it extinguished for good?

In mid-September, speech—long held back and heavy with the unsaid—suddenly flows freely again. It starts with a conversation unexpectedly initiated by Lao Ding. Yes, our companion Lao Ding, always a good listener but generally so reserved. (Thinking about it later, Lao Ding's part makes sense in the order of things: for where could a third voice, an outside voice, come from except from the one person—the only one—to know our story?) There is a day in mid-September when, between the end of the harvest and the arrival of blasts of snow and hail, all is suspended for a moment, a day when the air, carved out with a saber, is as hard and pure as crystal. While the animals huddle up for the long hibernation, men with no strength or sorrow left seek a little comfort: some retreat into their memories, others take refuge in forgetfulness. A few get ready to confront the truth of their lives, a truth always out of joint with what they imagine.

.   .   .

On this September afternoon, at the siesta hour, having no interest in sleep, Haolang leads me and Lao Ding beyond the vegetable gardens to a stand of scattered birch trees, the little wood some like to visit for the breeze and a bit of shade. No one is there at this time of day.

Haolang has been drinking. He is agitated, from the alcohol and from the rage inside him. Once in the wood, he shouts several times, which seems to calm him down a little. Then, silent, he collapses against a tree. After a few minutes, Lao Ding speaks up in a determined voice, a contrast to his usual placid tone.

"Let us ask forgiveness for everything that has happened to us."

"Ask forgiveness?" says the outraged man.

"Ask forgiveness and forgive those who have hurt us."

"Forgive . . . ?"

"Yes, forgive. I do believe that forgiveness is our only weapon; it is our only weapon against the absurd. Each of us has experienced terrible things. And now the three of us are here together. We know that we cannot act like those who have hurt us. With forgiveness, we can stem the chain of hate and vengeance. We can prove that in the Universe the incorruptible Breath endures. . . ."

We sense he has a great deal more to say, Perhaps too much for him to continue right away, but those few words are enough to start Haolang talking.

"Forgiveness . . . Break the chain of hate and vengeance . . . Let's talk about it, before it's too late. It was so I could be forgiven, wasn't it, that I went off to join the Communists, leaving Yumei on her own. . . ." He is choked up. But he does not give way. His mask hardens as he pulls himself together. "Our underground group was made up of about fifteen, well, seventeen, to be more precise, led by a Party member. To reach the liberated zone in northern Hubei, we had to cross an especially dangerous region. Six days' walk, broken up by alerts. We would hide in caves, or in 'safe' villages. We were so tired that we slept while we walked. On the last night, when shots rang out in the woods, we didn't know what was happening. Roused from sleep so abruptly, we thought it was a bad joke. Obviously, we had been betrayed. Someday they'd find the traitor. He would get his punishment: disfigurement, hanging. In the meantime, deep in the woods, in the moonlight, there was panic. A bullet went through my calf, and to make matters worse, I twisted my ankle running. I had the strength to drag myself to to a tree. Feeling a ditch under my feet, I lay down in it and covered myself with leaves. How many times did feet approach to the tune of shouts, then walk away, come back, step over me? I didn't breathe. I would have thought I was dead if it hadn't been for the blood gluing my pants to my skin and the terrible pain. Terrible pain? It was nothing compared to the cries that rent the night. The cries of bodies in torment, barely covering the cries of the executioners; the cries of one young woman, cries that the human ear would never have thought possible to endure and that will not fade for all eternity. These are China's finest children. They had uprooted themselves from the warm shelter of the family. They had left their soft beds to serve a cause they believed to be just. And here they were, delivered up to the most vile beasts of the Creator: men seeking revenge. At dawn, I gathered my strength and walked to a village. While I doubted whether anyone would dare take me in, I was counting on the fact that the militias did not risk maintaining a regular presence in a guerrilla region. I knocked at several doors, and was finally taken in by an elderly peasant couple. Well aware of what would happen if somebody reported them, they took care of me anyway, sharing their bowls of rice and their year's supply of bacon, a tiny slab hung above the stove. Under their taciturnity and their rough exterior, what consideration, what delicacy! Since there was no room for another bed, I slept on theirs. At night, once asleep next to me, they did not stir. I could hear only their peaceful breathing. In them I found the parents I never had. When I could walk again, the search for contacts began. How to find a friendly signal in a world of cruelty and mistrust? It turned out to be simple, however. One day at the market I looked across the stalls and saw a man with a dignified face smiling at me. He had been watching me for some days, of course. Experienced, he had no difficulty spotting the lost creature who wanted to rejoin the flock. There was another long walk, to the ends of the earth, in the company of three others. To a river, where a boatman waited for us in the wind-blown reeds. Then a hard crossing against a raging current. But on the other side, the promised land at last! We were finally among 'our own'! Were all the sacrifices worth it? We were ready to believe it was so.

"A whole people awakened, became industrious, traveled newly built roads, cultivated newly acquired lands. Fraternity was in fashion. China cannot remember having experienced that before. But could the Revolution be content with the simple happiness just within reach? Could it keep from making the number of victims the standard by which it measured its ambitions? The war was still on, and the Party was already setting up popular tribunals. I myself was caught in the trap. Appointed a war correspondent, I covered the frontlines, in Henan and Shandong. Struggles without respite, battles without mercy. Our men had to be heroic, ferocious—to kill so as not to be killed. They didn't mistreat prisoners, that's true. But first they exterminated on a massive scale to 'reduce the vital forces of the enemy.' But why I am telling you all this? I sought forgiveness by pursuing a more distant aim, a wider aim. And then it turns out I've led my beloved to her death . . . Chain of hate and vengeance, yes. Who among us can still claim the right to forgive? And you, Lao Ding, in the name of what, and whom, do you dare talk to us this way?'"

"In whose name? . . . Confucius's for one. Didn't he advise *xu,* mansuetude? But for me, it's in the name of something else . . ."

A heavy pause . . . then he resumes. "It's a long story. Oh! a simple story really, which I am not allowed to tell, on pain of death. But I'm going to trust you two with it.

"I was an unthinking young man. I come from a family of landowners and scholars in Anhui. Back in the early thirties I studied law, and I was destined for what they call a brilliant career. China was in the throes of disorder; me, I planned to lead a peaceful existence as a notable in our region spared by the war. I had postponed my marriage because of my studies. In the end I broke off the engagement, scandalizing my family and that of the young woman, who was deeply hurt. Thus began my life as an 'eccentric.' What had happened to me? Let's put it this way: I had received some shocks, and after that, I was sick of everything. What were the shocks? In the city of H., the provincial capital, I was walking on the street behind the courthouse one morning, and I came upon a scene of torture, the beating of a prisoner with a nail-studded whip. A piece of flesh flew into my face. Later, on the river at the edge of the same city, I saw a door floating downstream with a pair of adulterous lovers nailed to it. What animal would have done that? I realized that evil had penetrated my wretched people, that evil had permeated men. The life lived around me, with abuses of all sorts and acts of intentional and unintentional cruelty, no longer seemed possible for me. At that point I could have become a redresser of wrongs, or a revolutionary. Instead, I became . . . a Buddhist.

"That surprises you, doesn't it? I think I was obsessed by pity. My nature kept me from adding violence to violence. From then on everybody in my region regarded me as a local *jushi,* a respectable practitioner of charity. I enjoyed my respectability, which I 'bought' cheap; my family fortune allowed me such a life. Family fortune? As long as I spent it on wells, bridges, temple repair, the family put up with me. But they made a fuss when I turned to squandering large sums on the poor, or when I considered purchasing a press to distribute Buddhist texts. Since I appeared to have no interest in marriage, they even suggested I might pursue my path just as well in a monastery. I myself had been thinking along those lines. But it didn't happen, for in the meantime something else had occurred.

"During a cholera epidemic, I had met the members of a Protestant mission who were supplying vaccines and helping us care for the sick, including my own family. We managed to save many lives. Afterward, we became friends. That didn't keep us from having lively discussions on basic questions. I wanted to know how they, Chinese, had adopted a religion from so far way. They pointed out that Buddhism had been a foreign religion. As for the beliefs themselves, there was the puzzling and uncompromising way they envisaged suffering, death, love, life, all of it tied to the person of Christ. I reacted to their faith with disbelief and at the same time with a spirit of serious inquiry. One fine morning . . . I remember that the night before we had argued until we were quite red in the face; finally, to calm ourselves, we decided to forego further discussion and accept the fact that belief depended on temperament: some become Confucians, some Taoists, others Christians. . . . Anyway, that morning I called on Pastor Hong, who welcomed me, somewhat surprised. I asked if I could help him pass out his little brochures proclaiming the 'Good News.' To the indignation of many, to the laughter of nearly all. They pointed at me on the street: 'If it isn't Ding the Cripple. *Chi zhai** isn't enough for him anymore. Now he has to have *Chi jiao.*"† I stood firm. Wiping off spit did not disgust me. It seemed a necessary ordeal. Soon afterward they posted me to another city where I assisted a British pastor who thought that someone with my education should become a pastor. I would have to study in Shanghai or Hong Kong. Meanwhile, there was too much to do. The shadow of war hovered on the horizon, and our

*A vegetarian diet.
†A diet of religion.

parish hall had become a court of miracles: we received, we fed, we nursed, we consoled, indiscriminately. Everyone came through our doors, paupers and thieves, civilians and soldiers, even Communist soldiers en route elsewhere. (And that was why, when I was on trial after the Liberation, my life was spared.) But there were so many difficulties to iron out, so many problems to solve: material misery, physical misery, quarrels, dissension, sorrows . . . Did that mean an inhuman life, where toil was all? No, despite the obstacles, we lived in joy, a rough, tough joy. We reinvented our lives day by day. No one felt despised, neglected. No one felt alone. Dedicated body and soul to my work, there was no time to think of a personal life. It loomed on the horizon, however. Through a face, so human, too human: that of a widow. A look exchanged one afternoon between two passageways . . . We were to marry. The Liberation prevented that, fortunately; otherwise she would have dragged the ball and chain of infamy her whole life. Even before the 'cleansing' campaigns, we religious people were put on trial. Foreign pastors were deported. Pastor Hong, myself, and a few others were punished for hiding two coreligionists who had been naive enough to print tracts against the materialistic ideology. The tract writers were shot forthwith, in front of thousands. We spent three years in prison—in conditions more than harsh, you know about that, Haolang: fifteen of us slept on the floor in a room designed for eight; sitting next to the only slop bucket, we would eat our putrid food—before being sent to various camps for 'reform through work.' There we were forbidden to disclose our backgrounds, except to say we had been landowners. The mines in Shanxi, the dams in Henan. Finally, we were brought here at the army's request. Left in the wild grass, between earth and sky, exhausted, we had to start from zero. We lived in makeshift tents and in sheds made of branches and plaited grass, then in somewhat more substantial shelters. Injuries, bites, fevers, dysentery, and the terrible cold of those first winters got the better of many of our group, among them Pastor Hong. We dug a pit to bury our dead, with not even a sheet to wrap their bodies in. When the ice was too thick, we would pile the corpses outdoors, in a distant spot where they were soon entombed under the snow. When the thaw came, we would find only an inextricable magma of rotting corpses . . .

"What makes me bring up these things I have never told anyone? I was speaking of forgiveness. The revolutionaries so taken with justice are dispensing their justice more and more mercilessly. Who can stop the chain of hate and violence? We cannot. Only God can. Chinese history is studded with good, upright men, lovers of virtue and holiness; many of them died martyrs in the name of the scholarly ideal, in the name of the incorruptible Breath that moves the Universe. All that is magnificent and honors our country. For without these men of noble spirit, without these martyrs, our land would not exist. But can't it also welcome someone from another place and time who was willing to die in the name of love and forgiveness . . . ?"

Abruptly, he stops. He has said too much. He sees that his listeners are no longer attentive. Or rather, that they are finding him difficult to follow. The edifying speech of a believer always sounds preposterous or obscene to those who do not share his convictions. Though Haolang is aware of this aspect of Chinese life, He belongs to a generation that has never knelt. For the most part, matters of religion pass right by him. Because I have the examples of my mother and my uncle the opium smoker, I feel less out of my element, and I have been down a different road, to the West.

Haolang arises from his prostration, is now on his feet. He puts his arm around Lao Ding, as if to show the older man he can trust in his two confidants as surely as he trusts in his God.

16

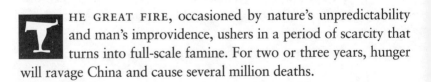HE GREAT FIRE, occasioned by nature's unpredictability and man's improvidence, ushers in a period of scarcity that turns into full-scale famine. For two or three years, hunger will ravage China and cause several million deaths.

Can natural disasters alone trigger a catastrophe of such magnitude and duration? Later the clearsighted leaders of the Party, along with the historians and the economists, will acknowledge that the direct cause was a series of monumental blunders by the Party, which was obeying the directives of its Head. By force of circumstance, he had gradually turned into an unbridled monster. After the campaign against the rightists, he was all the more impatient over the obvious failures as he went on pursuing his ambition: to mark history with his stamp, even if it were of sword and blood. Lacking sound knowledge of human nature or economics, he engaged in enormous and convulsive acts, sexual almost, which soon drained the nation's vital energy. Over a two to three year period he launched several outrageous endeavors one right after another: the Great Leap Forward, with its impossible objectives; all-out rural collectivization through "popular communes," where the peasants lost even the right to cook in their own homes; and to the detriment of agriculture, national mobilization to make steel in primitive local foundries, a steel that proved unusable. With such large-scale mistakes, not at all surprising for a country's means of production to fall rapidly into unbelievable negligence.

And the Far North is no exception. Three seasons in a row, we have had to neglect essential tasks to cast steel and craft tools by hand. As for the food we produce—much less than before—a sizable portion is set aside for shipment to regions more sorely affected.

The misfortune of all means the good fortune of some. The famine has made camp life more comfortable, if such a thing is possible. The first step is sending home those who have served their time. In principle, I have the right to be among them. I do everything in my power to stay, for the Friend's case is still pending; no one can decide it. Those remaining in the camp see a gradual letup in the iron discipline to which they have been subjected. Strict food rationing is instituted; before long, the command realizes that all are diminished by hunger and cannot cope with the essential work. The effects of malnutrition are felt as early as the first winter. Scheduled projects, even though reduced to a minimum—the construction of new, more substantial dormitories—cannot be pursued. It takes but little for the blizzard to sweep aside men deprived of calories and loaded down with rocks and lumber, leaving them in the snow, frozen and helpless. Their own health weakened, the leaders let each prisoner seek his subsistence outside of collective efforts. There is less work now all year round since some fields have been abandoned and no more land is being cleared. Resourcefulness is the rule. The more enterprising search the fields for kernels of wheat and millet missed during the harvest, or they venture forth to gather edible wild plants. With whatever tools are at hand, they fish, they hunt insects and small animals they would not think of consuming in normal times. Others, less skilled, are on the fringes. Their survival depends on the sporadic generosity of kitchen workers or on what strength they have left.

The famine leads Haolang to frequent a special breed of men: the hunters. Like them he is a native of Manchuria; with his northern accent and build, and bolstered by his reputation as the wolf killer, he has been readily adopted by this dwindling tribe of nomads. He has perhaps even been tempted to join them. Thanks to them he often has fresh meat, and more significant, he has rekindled his long dormant life force. These unkempt men, smelling of alcohol and wild things, spit out words as brief and rough as pebbles; they seem to have stepped straight out of some barbaric legend so ancient that no one can remember the details. Clad in skins, shod in plaited straw, rags around their feet and legs, they travel by dogsled in winter, in milder seasons on horseback or on foot.

When the hunters first showed up in our universe of iron discipline, the cons were astounded by their demeanor, all instinct and liberty. With what fierceness, what envy the men under the yoke pictured the primitive life, revisited through the proud figures of these intruders looming out of the grass! Intruders? But were they really? They were masters of this cursed region long before anyone else arrived. Fleeing their famine-ravaged provinces, they—or their fathers before them—abandoned meager plots of land and corpses rotting on the roadside. Stomachs filled with tree bark and moss, they reached this land from time immemorial destined to deal death. Slow-moving peasants became fanatical hunters in order to survive, hunting wild beasts with makeshift weapons: pikes, large knives, bows, rocks . . . How many fell victim to cold and hunger, bites, poisoning; how many sank into the marshes, their live flesh surrendered to ants and vultures before death came to free them? How many others, gone astray in mountains locked in snow, were frozen into blocks of ice that long preserved their lonely grimaces? The survivors have become a strong breed fearing nothing, not the gray wolf or the black bear, not the storms that blow through and carry everything away. Their huts and their caves remain, enough shelter for them, and their raucous laughter proof enough that they are very much alive and enjoying it. Knowing their geography and meteorology by heart, they offer tribute to gods and demons and accept their destiny without complaint, just as, without batting an eye, they stab swift and hard to slaughter and dismember their prey.

As long as the seasons permit, they hunt ceaselessly. When the weather decrees that they stop, they obey; or rather, they take advantage of the change to allow themselves a little pleasure, suddenly recalling that they are men among men. Then they climb down the other slope of the mountain and head for frontier towns and villages. For weeks and months, they trade skins and meat, bones and plants for essentials: salt and alcohol, rifles and ammunition. They expend their remaining energy in dives and brothels. Some are even tempted by the domestic life. Human passions are theirs. A mixture of gentleness and brutality. Living outside the law, on occasion these trigger-happy sorts confuse the animal kingdom with the human. Some of them forget that although slaying an animal out of necessity may be acceptable, killing a man or a woman out of jealousy or self-interest is considered a crime. And within their unofficial, unstructured tribe—which does exist as an authority, however, even if only to regulate territorial disputes—there circulate tales of bravery and vengeance, to the great delight of those who spend too many long nights in huts or caves. Contaminated by alcohol and crimes, is this tough breed threatened with extinction? Of course not. Instinctively, the hunters know just how far they can go. In their dealings with the animal world, they have learned moderation. Plunder? Necessary. But not to excess. Nature must be allowed to reproduce itself. And they know that it is the same in human affairs. All the more so because as their ranks thin out and their strength ebbs, there is no lack of young adventurers to join them. No, the danger does not come from within themselves, but from the outside. Seeing the military arrive and camp after camp set up, they sense vaguely that the slow process of their second death has begun. To them, the large-scale clearing of land is an enormous desecration, an unspeakable devastation. Through the force of circumstance, they have renounced their agricultural origins. From meadow to meadow, from marsh to marsh, they are retreating toward the mountains.

17

BENT OVER, racked by hunger, noses stuck to the ground as we glean kernels of millet and track grasshoppers or rats in an abandoned field on the road to the distant Great Mountain, Haolang and I don't notice the approach of a little band of those unkempt men, rifles on their backs, daggers in their belts. The leader, an imposing one-eyed fellow—a hunter becomes a chief only after suffering a bad wound—recognizes in Haolang a man of the North and asks him:

"Where are you from?"

"Harbin."

"What's your name?"

"Haolang. Sun Haolang."

"Ah, it's you! A 'howling wolf,' that's fine by me, it's good enough for us!"

The nomad's sparkling teeth have a cheering effect on Haolang. For the first time I see my friend's clouded look give way to laughter. In response, the hunter takes a brace of partridge from his basket. "Here. Don't bother with plucking. Roast them in clay. Then break the clay, and the feathers'll come off. And you just eat them!"

This simple recipe is enough: soon a thin plume of smoke rises on the steppe; soon, above the cooked flesh, I catch the aroma of the

rare moments of happiness in my life. Moments with the whispers
and smiles of the departed—did they ever exist?—slowly recognized
in the odor of incense, of opium, and of sweet potatoes roasted
beside a country path after a day of walking to our hearts'
delight. . . .

From this on, chance encounters, always near the mountains,
occasions when the hunters never fail to give Haolang part of their
game or roasted meat; he in turn shares it with me, of course, and
any other cons nearby. Sometimes the nomads linger, letting Haolang
fire a few shots, not without showing off their own skills: with a
sharp whistle, they can send wild geese into the air; with a rifle in
each hand, they can fire at two targets at once. Afterward, they sit in
a circle, passing flasks around and exchanging coarse remarks.
Haolang appears perfectly at ease on such occasions, almost radiant.
His weathered face, matching those around him, and yet truly
unique, reveals one aspect of a complex personality. And I say to
myself: "This orphan, after fleeing his uncle's guardianship might
have become an adventurer, or why not, an outlaw? What makes a
man, so open to all, a blank slate at the start, follow one road and
not another? Why did he, Haolang, with his wealth of possibilities,
hurry down such a narrow path?" To see him sitting there, among
men wrapped in skins and rags, in the heart of a vast and desolate
land, I have a sense of unreality, of absurdity. A feeling soon replaced
by a conviction. This violent landscape—where every blade of grass,
every rock is eternally tormented by the wind and proclaims hunger
and thirst, blood without echo and death without burial, broken
pledges and unfulfilled love—is the very site of an ancient promise
given for all time then betrayed a thousand times. An epic, buried
here for centuries, cries out for resurrection. By whom? Why not by
this man with the ruined, noble face of a fallen god? Yes, I am
gripped by the conviction that what moves Haolang comes from a
place much farther, more remote than he himself realizes. Somewhere, an undrawn breath seeks to turn into song. But first that
breath must gain possession of a few men who can endure its terrifying pressure, men with the tenacity to be pushed beyond themselves. Haolang has never been short of breath, has never denied

song. Accordingly, he should compose the epic our old Earth awaits. The thought startles me like a warning shot. How tempting to pass it on to the Friend at once! I resist. The poet, desperate to forget, is listening hard as the hunters explain the virtues of bear paws. . . .

When night falls, the shadow of the mountain overtakes the plain. The men rise as if snatched up, take their leave, depart. We see them stop farther on. They set two bowls on a flat rock. In one they place a piece of meat and in the other they pour a little alcohol mixed with the warm blood of a goose, its throat just cut. All bow down wordlessly, facing east. As a flame flickers in the wind, the chief utters loud, staccato phrases, echoed by the others. For a moment the vast steppe is nothing more than a heartrending cry of fear and solitude.

·   ·   ·

ON ONE SUCH night, the two of us left to ourselves in the wilderness, Haolang cannot resist saying: "If I had been alone, I would have left with them." That abrupt remark throws me into confusion. How can I respond? First, aren't I as enraged as he, still and always, over the ruin of his vocation, the calling that once made him feel kinship with Li Bo and Du Fu, with Whitman and Jack London; the calling that led him to embrace life in all its singular variety and transform human experience into high song? With the hunters he would certainly have an experience out of the ordinary, a savage life and a bitter struggle worthy of him. But for how long? The mob would soon spy him out. He would be tracked down, surrounded. He would resist to the last, rifle in hand, shouting in defiance or roaring with laughter . . . "If I had been alone," those are his words. The question haunting me since our reunion comes back more forcefully than ever: "Might I be a hindrance to him? Are we a hindrance to each another?" I am about to mutter something when Haolang stops me short. "I can guess what's going through your head right now. It is unfair and useless. *I* am not alone; *you* are not alone. The two of us are not alone." He looks me in the eye, and the last rays of the setting sun highlight the scars on his face. I say nothing. The one time my friend has decided to broach this subject, I am determined not to interrupt. "Something terrible has happened on this earth;

something terrible has happened to us also. Why us in particular? I don't know. What are we supposed to do? I don't know. One thing is certain: our finding each other here at the ends of the earth is something of a miracle. You have pointed that out; Lao Ding once said the same. Rather than talk of miracles, I would say that our reunion is the result of our doing what we had to do. From now on, it is up to us to do what we have to do. What that is exactly, once again, I don't know. Not yet . . .

"That blasted Lao Ding—he upsets me when he says that achieving the Three on earth is not one of man's privileges, and that is why our Ancients, who understood things, put the middle Void between the *yin* and the *yang*. Then he talks of Yumei's absence being more present than her presence, of that absence one day being filled. How can he be so sure? And how can I envisage that, I who do not believe in Heaven? One thing at least I'm sure of, since it depends on me alone: as long as you are here, I shall do nothing that does not include both of us, and why not say it? The three of us. As long as I am here, I would like to see things clearly, if only for a brief second."

Our adventure with the hunters cannot last. Their appearances become increasingly rare, and by the following summer, we no longer see them, except for one last time in June. They pass through on horseback. "We aren't coming around here anymore. Those soldiers are real bastards. They hunt by firing their machine guns, they throw grenades. Everything is upset on the plain, in the water. . . . They accidentally hurt one of our men. . . . Here's some venison. It's starting to spoil; but it's still all right. Boil it up in water and put in whatever you can find." They turn around and ride off, horsemen of the Apocalypse. Suddenly the one-eyed man looks back, and calls out: "When the times turn bad, you can't do a thing. Famine, believe me, we know all about it. If you're going to croak, you're going to croak." Looking first at me, then Haolang, he adds, "Him, I don't know if he'll make it. You for sure won't die."

18

HIM, I DON'T KNOW!" But *I* know. The season of calamity having arrived, those who are going to perish are going to perish; there is little chance I won't be among them. Is there any incompatibility greater than that between my damaged stomach and the wretched nourishment the famine forces me to gulp down? In the mess hall, the daily rations get smaller and smaller. With rice unavailable, they serve our vegetables with a kind of dumpling made from the coarsely ground husks of corn, millet, and other grains. After a while these solid, hard balls cause constipation that no laxative can relieve. We resort to introducing into one another's anuses makeshift devices to dig out the fecal matter piece by piece, an operation causing extreme pain. The events related to undernourishment sicken a great many. There are a fair number of deaths, prisoners passing away from "natural causes." Others succumb to the cold that arrives far too early the second year. From early October a heavy shroud covers the land, blocking doors and windows. Phantom without pity, the blinding whiteness claims its daily share of human flesh. Despite all the extras the Friend supplies me, I can only succumb to the hardships: violent coughs that make me sick as a dog, horrible stomach and intestinal pains that induce repeated hemorrhages. Like so many others, I am put in a truck and taken to the divisional farm whose infirmary has been enlarged for the current situation. I owe my life to the devotion of one nurse, a woman in her forties. Since my return to China, it is the first time I have had the good fortune to enjoy the sweetness of woman. (No, one does not "enjoy" amid moaning beds, dirty dressings, and expectoration. But it is the only word one still clings to when a little respite comes.) With no medication available when I am racked by pain the nurse makes do with massaging my stomach or simply resting her hand on it. A sure, plump hand hoarding all the treasure of a body, a hand with the knack of calming me awhile. As I burn with fever, I am reduced to hoping for the crises—not to mention feigning them— that are the harbingers of my furtive rendezvous. When the hand is here and I feel its pulse beating, I cut myself off from its sticky heav-

iness. She who provides the relief responds to my look of gratitude
with a sad smile that seems to indicate she too is finding relief from
pain.

The dead are removed from the infirmary discreetly, then quickly
cremated. One day, a cryptic message is put in my hand: "You will
not die either." The scribbled sheet has come from another ward; the
writing is Lao Ding's. What is he saying? What does he mean by
"either"? Could he know what the hunter said? Unless he's referring
to himself? To himself! If the worn-out old man is in the infirmary,
the worst can be feared, more than it would be for anyone else. I
know that he has a lingering chest cold and is gradually wasting
away as the famine continues. We brought him extra food in vain;
despite being exhausted by fits of coughing, he has always refused to
eat more than others, passing out the food to those around him.
Indeed, he has come to the infirmary to die. There is no doubt that
he has insisted on choosing his hour. That is his only freedom, but
sovereign, but superb. His death, quiet as it may be, is distinguished
by a mute scorn for those who have stripped him down to the very
bone. Before I am well enough to drag myself to his ward, one
night—one of those nights when the wind howls so fiercely that even
indoors we must shout to be heard—the nurse brings his last communication, an envelope in which I find a small flat tin box and a
thin pamphlet no bigger than the palm of the hand. I recognize the
box, for in it Lao Ding kept his needles and thread. He would often
take them out to patch his jacket or sew on buttons for comrades.
And the pamphlet is not unfamiliar either. It is one of those little
booklets that I used to see missionaries distribute in the streets of
Nanchang when I was a child. Passing by one day, I chose several, in
various colors, as playthings: that was before I knew how to read.
The old man had probably carried the tract with him secretly, sewn
into his jacket maybe, during all his travels from one camp to
another. On the cover, I read four characters that are translated as
"The Gospel According to Saint John." Didn't I read extracts from
this Gospel, in France, in Gide's *If It Die,* and in Mauriac? Now, hiding under my blanket I peruse it in Chinese and soon find myself
transported elsewhere, disoriented. Will I ever be able to figure out

the message of this translation into an odd idiom, which is Chinese without being Chinese, a language with puzzling neologisms, a syntax at times wobbly, a rhythm that is jerky? I think of the Buddhist texts I once copied for my mother, they too studded with expressions and forms that put you off balance or make you dizzy, texts that the Chinese spent centuries assimilating. How can a Word that is so very different penetrate you, upbraid you, blast you? How can this Word delight you or violate you profoundly and permanently to such an extent that it becomes your voice and gesture, your flesh and blood? To such an extent that one day a Lao Ding trusts absolutely in this truly unbelievable statement: "He who loves his life shall lose it, and he who loses his life in this world shall have eternal life."

19

THE FAMINE is over. Along with many others, Haolang and I find ourselves aged but alive. Hunger, gone on too long, has damaged the organs; cold, gone on too long, has frozen the marrow and eroded the bones. The skin, loose and flabby, has darkened. There is not a movement of the body that does not arouse some of the accumulated aches and pains. Not a movement of our bodies, however, that does not reach toward the mad desire to exist anew. We have become half savage, like this land to which we remain inevitably tied. No longer do we imagine ourselves living in some other region, perhaps under the thumb of an even sterner dictatorship. Tied to the soil of the Far North, without attachments elsewhere, we have finally been won over to this space, whose mineral flintiness has become for us a symbol of purity and splendor. The camp staff, themselves tested, do not try to restore the iron discipline of prefamine days. Our camp now bears the inoffensive name "collective farm." We share a room. The pigsty has been moved to an animal husbandry facility run by a different crew. Other than participating periodically in collective endeavors, we have only to take care of the vegetable gardens . . . and, alas, as always, the latrines, somewhat improved. That is the price for our independence. With a little more time to ourselves now, we can indulge in other pursuits as long as they are "correct." Near the camps and around the market towns, villages have begun to grow up, populated by the families of craftsmen and former soldiers and by newcomers to the region. Fertilized by the blood and sweat of the pioneers, the Far North has become exploitable despite its hostile climate.

The spring of 1962 is like every spring in this Chinese Siberia where nature, impatient at the overly long winter, splits the ice and explodes with all its repressed energies. The horizon widens incessantly, pushing its boundaries ever further, beyond the flights of wild geese and beyond the drawn out, promising clouds. Everywhere the bursting of flowers through patches of snow, an echo of the magnificent surge of the animal world. Yet we seem to be experiencing this inaugural season for the first time, our first spring as a pair, as we quiver with some indefinable anxiety. Only as a pair? Neither one of us has for a moment abandoned the one without whom we would not be here. Without whom we would not be bound to each other for life, like the right arm and the left arm of the same body, fulfilled by a friendship so vital that it is—one wants to believe—of the same stuff as love. This being, the Sister, the Lover, we do not often name during these years of struggle, but not out of forgetfulness or neglect; we are simply no longer in the habit of speaking of her as a third person because she has become the most intimate, the most vivid, part of our existence. We no longer see her outside us, or even right in front of us. She is here, more present than we ourselves; she is here, in the innermost realms of our consciousness, in our sleep and when we awaken. She becomes our thoughts, our gestures, our expressions, our voices, our monologue that is dialogue, our silence that is unbroken song. She is no longer the object of our desires; she *is* our desires. She exists, weighty and substantial like a breast swollen with milk, and at the same time, lighter than dew or mist.

A long winter and a short spring bring obligations. We have to confront the exhausting tasks that come one after another, at a faster and faster pace: plowing, planting, repairs around the fields and in the dwellings. When spring has passed seamlessly into summer, we finally enjoy a short break once the hoeing is done. We have a strong desire for escape, not forgetting the prescribed limits. I am drawing again, thanks to supplies left by the commandant's son, who departed for Peking at the height of the famine. The need to "work from nature" provides ample justification for my outings, especially since my watercolor landscapes have found a certain favor among the staff and their wives, some hanging them behind their desks, others in their homes. We gradually encounter less and less resistance to our requests for leave. Whenever we can, we explore the surrounding countryside on foot, thus reviving the memory of our long trek across Sichuan.

I wonder if others have known with such intensity this boundless exultation rarely granted in life; this reliving with exactly the same sensations a blissful experience of the past, not through the efforts of memory, but physically, through all the fibers of the body, in all the secret recesses of one's being? We relive Sichuan with luminous cognition, or to be more precise, with total recognition. Each step, each stop, each thirst, each hunger, and the very fatigue that seeps too quickly into our weakened limbs all contribute to the reconstruction of a present eternally lived before, to be eternally reborn. Under our feet, everything seems to be regained, yet everything remains to be discovered. Just as its flora and fauna reveal an unsuspected richness, this half-tamed, half-wild landscape, seemingly monotonous, offers more varied configurations than one would imagine. Once beyond the cultivated fields, we come upon occasional stretches dotted with flourishing meadows, capricious streams, conifer-covered hills, and rocky ravines. Sticking the whole together is a ground of black clay brightened by great clusters of flowers of every sort. Here where there are no roads, to go from one point to another we make long detours around the marshes. The only sounds that seem natural over the constant humming of the wind are the calls of birds and the sudden scattering of animals. Human voices are dulled by the wide open spaces and fade away into the sands, incongruous. Yet, in the heart of the limitless, the idea of sheer loss is not always excruciating. At the hour when shadows fade, finding ourselves exhausted at the top of a hill, we let the immense void take over and we become ever so briefly the most silent and motionless part of the universe.

One day we head for a place the hunters used to talk about. After a forced march begun at dawn, we arrive in unknown territory. We cross a dry riverbed to enter a wooded area where the trees are tall and the air is saturated with buzzing insects and the perfumes of resin and moss. A pristine nature reveals to us its inviolate mystery. At the far end of China we are already in a world beyond; in this spot we have the sense that we are beyond the world beyond. Our goal a distant clearing, we follow a vague path, probably made by the occasional hunter working his way through the choking thickness of the trees. As we walk along, a heavy branch cracks and falls; an animal flees, breaking the bars formed by the sun's rays. Where a stretch of water glistens, a flock of geese flies away with noisy wings and strident cries. Then everything grows calm, recovers. Suddenly there is a passing breeze, and the air turns blue. Without hesitation I recognize the Place and the Presence. "Yumei!" A mute cry from deep inside. The Friend, up ahead, turns around, freezes. He too sees. The outline is clear, the smile intact; poignant ecstasy in a gaze that is boundless . . . Boundless, the duration: a flash, a lifetime? But already that within reach is out of our grasp; already the bedazzled air regains its clarity. And now Haolang begins to run, a giant stag struck between the eyes. He runs as fast as he can, for fear of being overtaken by sadness and longing. He runs, with raucous cries, a savage caught up in a ritual dance. Out of breath, he staggers, then collapses into the dry leaves, arms outspread, face to the sky. I join him and lie beside him, taking his hand in mine. I am aware of his panting and of the heart pounding in the familiar body weighed down by ten years and more of physical ordeal. Lines buried deep in memory rise to my lips:

When nostalgia overwhelms you
Drive it off, to the far horizon.
Wild goose cleaving the clouds
You carry in you the dead season
Frozen rushes, charred trees

Bent low beneath the hurricane.
Wild goose that need not tarry
Free now for flight, or death . . .
Between natal soil and welcoming sky
Your sole kingdom: your own call!

Haolang listens without a word. But I can just feel the pressure of his hand, now so tight that it hurts, crushes my bones. A long moment passes. I rise to help my companion to his feet; his face is streaked with tears, smudged with dirt. His injured left leg is covered with blood.

This is a turning point. That very night, in the room adjoining the old pigsty, Haolang is unable to sleep. By the light of the candle that supplements our failing lamp, frenetically he puts to paper the words that rush from his fingertips: he writes all night. I sleep fitfully. Whenever I wake up, I hear the pencil going up and down on the paper, and I smell singed hair: an odor from our high school days when tired heads would bend too low over their candles. At dawn there is a pile of blackened sheets on the table: fragments of sentences and poems. When I glance through them, I am accompanying my friend on his journey through hell. I recognize the salient and the private moments of his agitated life. Nothing has been skipped over. Friendship and love mingled, in these pages everything is accepted and exalted like a fateful mystery. On one of the last sheets, two lines in larger, more regular characters:

Now comes the day, memory and forgetting over,
They meet the beloved in the bright wood.

20

SURELY THIS IS what we have left: writing. Others have done it, even at the height of repression hurriedly committing to paper spur-of-the-moment ideas or obsessive thoughts or a last will and testament. Is there any other route for the shackled if they still want to transform this whole mess into moments of life? It is all that remains within reach. What to write? Wouldn't it be simplest to recount the details of everyday life? But is it that simple? Some have harbored such lofty dreams that when struck down, they are stupefied, incapable of describing day-to-day existence. In order to write, they require events as dramatic as the ones that struck them down.

As the days go by, Haolang keeps writing: he is just beginning. Passage after passage, he goes over his scribbled drafts, waging a veritable battle. It is impressive to see. No, there is neither rage nor aggression in him, nor any trace of the nonchalant grin he sometimes affects deliberately to fool himself. The expression on the anxiously concentrating, sternly uncommunicative face simply denotes dignity regained, the look of a man who, facing utter ruin, suddenly comprehends what he has to accomplish. Looking at him—rarely do I have the chance to gaze at him like this, at length and at leisure—I see that despite appearances, in him something invincible has had time to grow. Behind his battered but untamed face, reminiscent of myriad intransigent faces from over the centuries, those who would reduce him to silence no longer exist. They will vanish. They have merely been giant obstacles in his path, forcing him to retreat into himself and turn to the essential. They will vanish. Haolang's revenge could not lie in thrusting a penknife into the back of some petty leader, nor in fleeing to some wild region. He is here, confronting himself at last.

But as I look at him, questions arise in my mind, one after another. What is my friend doing? Giving a second birth, through song, to a story inextricably of three? And is the story in any way unusual? Maybe it is up to him to make it so? Maybe it is up to him to transform a series of reverses into a series of revelations that would be redemptive? Revelations of what? The poet himself probably doesn't know. He only knows that despite all that has been lived and said, nothing has really been lived or said. He who thought he would become the great bard of life is reduced to recounting its minor events. But are there any minor events? Isn't every minor event tied up with major ones? His personal history was so tied up with history on the grand scale that the two came to be hopelessly entangled. In his struggle for survival, he ended up forgetting the only weapon he possessed: writing. Now he has found it again. As long as he is here, beside the candle, within these mildewed walls, his uncompromising weapon is at hand. No one—not even the most cynical of tyrants—can keep him from saying all. No one can keep him from saying of what he has to, up to the very end. The end? Here again I am assailed by another string of questions. Where is it, the end? Does it even exist? Is it enough for the poet to bring to life what he thinks he experienced? Can that alone make everything meaningful? Indeed, saying is what the poet is given, but isn't true saying a quest whose impact cannot soon be measured, whose conclusion cannot yet be predicted?

Except for some general remarks and a few questions about specific details, Haolang remains silent as to the progress of his tale, either because he can't sum it up in a few words or because he is being tactful: so much of what he is recalling involves me. I respect his silence. I do not want to offer help as an excuse to interfere. Strangest is that during these days, once the tiring routine tasks are done, I stay here, right here. I cannot do anything else, caught as I am in the concentric movement of the waves emanating from the tense, inspired body of my companion. I sense that I should not stray from the scene: a voice is here, so near, so distant, speaking to us both. I am sure that my own listening is indispensable for this voice to remain loud and clear. Yet, in these hours when the energy of despair has come to our rescue, I wonder whether Haolang and I are hearing the same thing.

When I ask myself that, I realize how different we are yet how incomplete we are without each other. Haolang is molded of earthly clay and faces life straight on or soars as high as he can, however heavy the cost, however great the wounds he might inflict on himself and others. That is his nature. I on the other hand am from somewhere nebulous and far away, and life in this world never ceases to shock me. Yet at the same time I have an infinite capacity for astonishment and wonder that wells up from some mysterious inner longing. That is my nature. The voice casting a spell on us now can only be Yumei's. She loved both of us deeply; she understood only too well that we were very different and that we were not complete without each other; in fact, that is why she needed both of us. But I repeat my question: When we listen to her voice, do we both hear the same note, the same words? Probably not. Haolang must hear an earthly creature calling him, while I am stirred by some indefinable echo that is not of this world.

When I hear Yumei's beloved voice I also hear the muffled thunder of spring and other voices murmuring their truths. Voices all merged into one, the voice of Woman, who springs from an unknown compost, her true source the mythic realm. But as I sort out my thoughts, do I find the word "mythic" perplexing? Not really. Since my stay in Dunhuang and my visit to the Campo Santo of Pisa where I saw the frescoes of the Master of Death, and since Yumei's becoming the most inward and inaccessible part of us, I have come to believe that only a mythic vision allows mankind to assume control of what cannot be fully verbalized. Who among us can claim to take the measure of real life, to know how deep it sinks its roots, how far it extends its branches? Can we be content with merely recording the bits and pieces of what we think we have heard and experienced? Every life, once it has uttered its first cry, will continue to make noise, echoing a Call that comes from that life itself yet goes far beyond its limits. How is the Call expressed? Is there a specific, definitive formula? Out of necessity, we turn to mythic figures to make up for what cannot be fully verbalized. And the object of the quest, woman—maybe we should speak of the feminine mystery rather than of woman—is a presence enigmatic above all others, enigmatic even to herself; whatever her source, the Vixen or the White Serpent, the Cloud or the Lotus, in this life or any other, is she ever willing to remain static? She does not want that. "Woman of unfulfilled destiny, where you go, I shall join you. From life to life, it is your uncertain steps that trace the surest path," I say to myself. I do not forget that since my long-ago visit to the room of the hanged woman in the family home, I have been in league with this path of migration; I do not have to fear possible perdition.

"But it's not too late, we can still do something!" Yumei's cheerful words echo in my ear like a final injunction. I know that I too can still do something. Even in my shameful degradation, something shall be born of my hand, a figure, a beloved figure, as like Yumei as possible and yet very different.

<h1 style="text-align:center">21</h1>

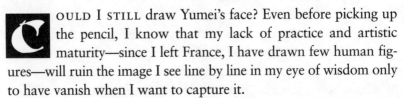 OULD I STILL draw Yumei's face? Even before picking up the pencil, I know that my lack of practice and artistic maturity—since I left France, I have drawn few human figures—will ruin the image I see line by line in my eye of wisdom only to have vanish when I want to capture it.

The human figure. Once I felt the urge to capture Véronique's image. It happened in the birch wood beyond the vegetable gardens, the grove where Lao Ding's ashes had been scattered. Walking among the trees as their pale green and light gray foliage glittered in the gentle breeze to create a rustle in the surrounding air, my eyes were drawn to the slender outline of one birch trunk in particular. The fine crazing of its silvery bark revealed the sap within. Suddenly I thought of Véronique, of her milky body appearing before my astonished eyes each time she uncovered it, with neither haste nor false modesty. My own body, so weak, dried up by years of deprivation and coarse fare, began to swell with sudden desire. I pressed myself against the tree and rubbed against the fleshy trunk as long as I could until I had emptied the little semen left in me. I flopped down at the foot of the tree, on the thin mat of dry leaves. I felt rather ridiculous, yet I took comfort in the thought that I could still quiver, that the sap of life could still rise in me. The next day I came back to the wood and lingered awhile, like a murderer returning to the scene of the crime. I tried to reproduce my vision of the previous day by sketching a woman who would show through the trees. I couldn't make that figure real and I gave up on the idea of a human presence, focusing my attention on the birch itself, trying to discover what had inflamed my imagination. I ended up with a picture in ink, enhanced

by a few discreet touches of color. There was the birch in its dignified radiance and, set back, a second tree. Did my rendering say all I
felt? By the same token, had Van Gogh said all when he spoke
through a cypress or an olive?

And now I am faced with the same dilemma as in Italy. The
ancient Chinese avoided representations of the human figure,
entrusting to landscape—or to the elements that make up a landscape: tree, rock, spring, et cetera—the task of signifying their inner
world, their spiritual impulse as well as their carnal impetus. To
paint one individual this way, a fortiori a woman, seemed to them
somehow artificial, devoid of profundity. The West doesn't to have
the same doubts: it has a long tradition of representing woman, especially the Virgin, with all the symbolism that surrounds her. Rich in
this material recognizable to all, the artist can put on his canvas the
characteristics of a dear, familiar being, while at the same time ele-
vating them to an idealized form endowed with multiple meanings,
thereby going beyond the goal of a simple portrait. Thus, Lippi or
Raphael could paint the Madonna through the figure of the beloved,
Della Francesca through the figure of his mother.

Recalling Della Francesca helps me overcome my dilemma. I am
taken back to the Monterchi Cemetery, droning with light, and to
the tiny white-walled chapel, its cool darkness lit only by the sole
presence of the Virgin, with her calm expression and skirts wide
enough to shelter the whole living universe. I am suddenly gripped
by an irrepressible desire to create a fresco of my own Virgin, my sister, my mother, my Lover, they who are my most remote longing, my
only longing, never satisfied. Well, when? But starting immediately!
Well, where? Alas! nowhere . . . I have no choice but to accept that
nowhere in this despoiled land under total surveillance do I have an
open patch on which to leave a mark.

I disclose my plans to Haolang, and he is immediately full of
enthusiasm. An unused storage shed, a rock spied in the forest one
day, caves mentioned by the hunters—in our search for a place, we
consider every possible spot, all the while knowing it will be difficult
to carry out any project without the authorities' finding out. We are
ready to give up when we remember the carpenter. The guardian

angel of the damned whom destiny, in its game of dice, has cast upon this soil, he is nothing if not ingenious. After hearing us out, his face breaks into the warm smile of the sturdy craftsman:

"At my house."

"At your house. But how?"

"Come and see my workshop. I've enlarged it by adding a room in back. I need to put all my books in there, and my tools and finished projects will go in front of them. Then, all I have to do is divide the workshop in two with a portable screen. That way, you can paint on all the back walls, which get light from a little window right under the roof. Behind the screen you can work at your leisure. There's only one thing: you'll have to come and stay in the village."

And as encouragement, the carpenter even offers me suitable materials: he knows how to thin his paint down so I can use as much as I please.

After my visit to the carpenter, I am obsessed by his three empty walls. I think of them as a cavern promising treasure, only it is I who must supply the treasure. One day I picture in my mind the mausoleums I saw in Ravenna, especially that of Galla Placida, its interior lined with mosaics—their main colors golden green and dark blue—rendering the enclosed space as luminous as a starry night. No more is needed to kindle my fire of creativity. I shall create my own mythic dwelling. It makes no difference whether it is a tomb, a chapel, or an open ruin someday. Haolang's work is progressing well, and he is as excited as I am at the prospect of a fresco in this secret place. He is sure that the images born of my hand and sensibility will inspire him, carry him beyond his own vision.

The watchful eye of Party cadres is no less present in the village, but it looms on our horizon as the Promised Land all the same. We know that staying in a village to participate in local life is sanctioned by the authorities. To ensure their approval, however, we wait until autumn harvest season to present our request, and we provide an additional reason: to depict peasant life in art and writing.

In the meantime, I concentrate on preliminary watercolors. Through a variety of sketches, I hunt down nature in its most secret recesses, in the interstices where the elements of the mineral and vegetable world pass from visible to invisible and vice versa. Through these fragments, an overall vision of the fresco emerges in my mind. I have a vision in which living things, including people and animals, emerge from a background marked by the hues of spring and autumn as well as those of day and night; marked by all that hovers between real and unreal, between accepted event and unexpected advent. All the elements of the composition, each of which possesses its own space, are borne on the same current and converge on a central figure that has against all odds become the crux of my life, the crystallization of all my murkiest desires and wildest dreams. The Lover.

But when I try to sketch her, however familiar, however internalized she may be, perhaps too familiar, too internalized, I realize helplessly that she refuses to be set down on paper, or rather that I cannot pin her down on paper without betraying her, without smothering her.

One morning I have the courage to take out the drawing Yumei left me upon her death. Long folded, the paper has yellowed over the years: many lines are obliterated, leaving only the draft. An oval outline drawn in a manner still awkward—quite exact though, for it was intensely felt and fussed over, with all the tenderness my seventeen years could muster. How did such a tenuous imprint survive so many ordeals? And it was with this that a despairing Yumei spun a web across the abyss of earthly life. In sketch form the features are all the more visible and moving because they retain their virtuality. Now I understand the message of the Lover: not to fix her features, not to imprison them in a single expression. To depict her face and her body so starkly, so laconically—precisely the essential but essentially precise—that they live and evolve, revealing all that has been experienced or dreamed, and leaving themselves open to the breaths that bear them aloft.

The moment finally arrives for the two accomplices to take up residence in the village. Haolang has the tiresome obligation of cranking out some suitably worded articles on peasant life. He tries not to sell his soul and attempts to uncover the humanity hidden in each person he meets. His warm personality and innate friendliness soon create a connection with the local people, not to mention the bronze warrior body that disturbs the sleep of more than one young woman.

Except for a few odious characters, narrowminded or fanatical, we find in the inhabitants the generous spirit of the old rural race we know well, though here they are more uncouth, since most have emigrated to this harsh region following disasters in their native provinces. When it is time to do portraits, I am especially drawn to the youngest and the oldest. Many of the adolescent girls still have foreheads wreathed in dreamy mists; many of the wrinkled old women are silent with resistance and resignation. As for the men, most of the young males have an animal instinct expressed in their muscles; they find it hard to repress a brute strength that comes about naturally in a region populated by animals of every sort— four-footed, reptiles, raptors. With primitive means—sticks, picks, axes, stones, ropes, hooks, et cetera, either for fun or as a challenge, they hunt these creatures down, stunning them, cutting off their heads in one fell swoop, breaking their necks with a cracking of bone, poking out their eyes—all this done with mingled pleasure and fear. Only the great law of the vegetable kingdom can subdue these youth, domesticate them; with age, they come to resemble their fathers and grandfathers, who walk slowly, limbs gnarled like old stunted tree trunks. These men know the patient growth of plants, from the roots anchored in the ground to the tops exposed to sun and wind, thunder and frost. Extreme fragility, yet the renewal of the miracle of life. Well acquainted with the disasters and tempests sown by death, the old peasants keep their faith, each year uniting their flesh more closely with the living clay. They bring to mind the Hebrew prophets who remained ever faithful to their God despite the incomprehensible trials he visited upon them.

It is among these people that, behind my screen and before my three blank walls, I take on the work of my life.

Having overcome my initial hesitancy, then some technical blunders, I feel the work is progressing well and that the gods and spirits are behind me. Forms gradually emerge, almost as in my vision, but not without retaining all their capacity for metamorphosis. Absorbed in my work, I forget about the stifling heat of the room. My brow and my bare chest are often dripping with sweat, but so what! Provided that the project goes forward, that it takes shape. Do I just have to keep going, confident? But I know that in focusing my efforts on the indispensable details, I run the risk of upsetting the overall movement, of bungling the unity of the whole. Until the very end I shall be in the clutches of this tension mixed with fear.

One day I enter the secret hideout more keyed up than usual. It is the day I am to place around the figure of the Lover the particular blue finally hit upon after a number of tries, that clear and bottomless blue I saw both in scenes of the adoration of Buddha at Dunhuang and in the paintings of Simone Martini.

Before laying on the color that is to crown my fresco, frightening yet decisive gesture, I hesitate a long while. Then, hand trembling slightly, I surround Yumei's face with the blue long ripened in my mind. An accident of brushwork leaves the expanse of blue with one colorless streak—a shooting star? a swallow's flight?—that I do not alter. To break the tension I put down my brush, sure in my heart of hearts I have it right. Yumei's face, even if hardly finished, takes on a singular relief and seems as if incarnate. A face with precise contours and indefinable features, hesitating between mark and nonmark, scarcely face and more than face, being the face of all the others who instinctively turn toward it. Central, the figure of Yumei is all the more the crux of the overall movement in that she does not impose herself, is ready to efface herself at any moment. Free and mobile as she is, not at all fixed, she appears by turns serious or smiling, molded by grief or ecstasy.

That afternoon we are to attend a political meeting where the local Party head will announce the harvest work schedule. Haolang has come an hour early, to meet me. His entrance into the hidden cubbyhole coincides with a ray of light falling heavily from the high shutter, like a sword piercing a curtain. He who ordinarily offers a spontaneous opinion on the work in progress stands silent in the shadows. He has before him at last an almost total vision of the fresco. Visibly moved, as we leave the room he says simply: "That's it."

22

LET TIME DO its work; let the thing do its work. How well I know the old adage. Once the gardener is through, let plants and fruits effect their own ripening; let a manual skill or an acrobatic technique guide the body practicing it. Non-activity is not so much doing nothing as it is doing the essential and then not interfering. Ah, don't interfere! No more interfering! I hide behind this sage advice and, for the time being, do not go back to see the result for fear of being disappointed and losing the courage to continue. Confirmed by the Friend's "That's it," my intuition tells me my last work session may have marked the attainment of an equilibrium—precarious but sufficient—even though the fresco is not quite done. The slightest blunder, one little gesture too many, and it could well be ruined.

Sticky-rice broth with eight vegetables, a dish my mother made so skillfully and had so patiently taught the Lover to prepare, how smooth in the mouth, how subtle its taste . . . "Wood ears," earth vegetables, bamboo shoots, Chinese cabbage, chives, lotus roots, water chestnuts, et cetera—each ingredient of this broth, while blended into an harmonious whole, retains its own flavor. The trick is to add the vegetables separately, each at a specific point in the cooking, then be mindful not to lift the cover of the earthenware pot again, even for a second, before the cooking is finished; the soup does not simmer long and continues to cook once the fire is out. As if these vegetables that know one other and confer with one another can be trusted, the cook leaves them to work their alchemy free of outside interference. This substantial broth, concentrating all the perfume of my native soil, became my favorite dish; it would line my stomach like a soothing salve. My mother used to make it when I was sick or run down. Yumei also prepared it whenever she had the chance. Emerging exhausted from my struggle with the fresco, I think longingly of this broth. All the more so because unconsciously I harbor the naive notion that if I apply the "non-activity" method in cooking it, from afar I might be encouraging my fresco to do the same, to finish up on its own. Be that as it may, to allay the anxiety of leaving my work aside, with Haolang's help I gather the ingredients for the broth as a special treat for the peasant family putting us up, northerners unacquainted with this kind of food. Since not all the vegetables grow in the region, we have to make do with some substitutes. Our long hours of exploring nature's odorous nooks and crannies almost reconcile us with the vast plant world that has cost us such pain and sweat, a world of wild grass to be burned and uprooted, of vegetables to be tended through every kind of weather, of rice seedlings to be set out one by one, of grain to be sickled armload by armload and transported bag by bag. With our positive outlook, the broth cannot but succeed. The steam rising about the weathered, toothless faces provokes exclamations and laughter too long repressed.

The autumn harvest is upon us and I can wait no longer: I resolve to take a good look at my creation. A first sweeping glance over the three panels convinces me that nothing must be touched, that it must be left as is, that the incomplete is to be its form of completion. Instead of the embarrassment or disappointment I expected to feel, I am struck by something apparently simple emanating from the depths of the fresco, a sort of irradiation or surge of energy that surpasses my original conception. I realize that the whole I time I worked so intensely, so beset with doubts, I was in a state of grace. And I shall not come upon that state again.

In the painted space, through their postures of inspiration, the human figures merging with the natural elements appear to be carried aloft by a rhythmic breath and swept into a virtual dance, the same dance that brings about the round of the seasons, the alternation of day and night, the conjunction of heavenly bodies in the universal rotation. Here the dance transcends the distance separating these humans, each immured in his or her drama, transcends the terrestrial gravity holding them prisoner.

Initiated by Haolang's writing, in return how much will the fresco affect the poet in his work? I could not say. Still tactful, Haolang leaves it up to me whether to read his effort, so very close to both of us. In any case, I see my friend has gone back to his long poem with renewed ardor, neglecting the articles he is supposed to turn out for a local newspaper. When he finishes this second plunge deep into his world of imagination, he agrees to put his pen aside, knowing that he too should let his song pursue its path unfinished. For my part, I am sure that this song, this quest, would not resound with its echoes of the infinite had the poet not infused the last section with a new dimension that has to be called mythic.

When the earth has drunk the deluge
The arrow shot from the rainbow
Strikes the doe full in the face

Trailed by all and the two-antlered stag
Slow moving she reaches the barrow
Pure offering: fountain of blood

And the fresco, what will be its fate? We shall not know. Already it has escaped from our control, from our sight even. After we leave the village, the carpenter cannot resist showing it secretly to some of the residents, who develop a strong attachment to a work in which they recognize themselves. Inevitably, the fresco's existence will be betrayed to Party cadres; they do not dare destroy it, however. The informer is a disagreeable sort, a fanatical fellow who detests us and is infuriated when he hears his wife and daughters praise us. By order of the camp authorities, the two clandestine creators find themselves forbidden entry to the village.

23

URING THE famine years, many of our fields lay neglected. Now we have to start all over. More serious, countless trees were cut down for firewood and other uses, with no reforestation. Now, as they look ahead to renewal projects, the camp leaders don't want to deplete further the little clumps of forest scattered over the vast plain. Accordingly, in early fall of 1965 they organize an expedition into the high mountains on the Far North's northern frontier. Unusual undertaking for fall. Ordinarily they send men into the wild to fell trees only in the depths of winter, never giving a thought to the harsh living and working conditions. After all, that is the season when prisoners are idle and when sleds—horse or tractor drawn—can easily haul logs and men.

A crew of fifteen is selected. Its mission is to establish a base in a previously unexplored area of the high mountains and amass the largest wood supply possible. A minimum goal is set. As we rather expected, the role of foreman falls to Haolang. Incontestably, he is one of the most experienced. Didn't he spend his entire first year in the Far North in the mountains, sawing wood, quarrying rock, doing the toughest tasks? Besides, everyone knows he is an excellent hunter, on essential skill for surviving in the wild.

I am not to be on the crew; I am not up to it physically. But I ask to be assigned to the small quartermaster team, preparing meals, supplying water, seeing to the tents, et cetera. Tasks no less harsh, I shall discover to my sorrow. I'll also learn the truth of a saying popular in the camps of the Far North: "They can give them all the fancy names they want, but every job's a killer." From the moment the truck leaves the crew near the mountains, the humble quartermaster has to face the same ordeals as his companions: hacking out a narrow passage through virgin forest with his axe; enduring the assaults of giant mosquitoes and ants just as big; arming himself against the snakes and wolves that lurk about; eating and drinking unheated rations during the day; and at night, drawing a last bit of strength from a body riddled with sores so he can set up a few makeshift tents. . . . Then once the base camp is set up, adjusting to the primitive life, entering the skin of a savage; letting his hair and beard grow; moving about in the tent naked when the fire is roaring; being out in rains that last for days; drinking muddy water that tastes of decayed branches; plucking, cutting up birds and beasts, their blood still warm. Then, replacing two seriously injured comrades and sawing felled trees.

The felling of trees. To men transformed into brute force, the matter seems simple enough. Of course, they know the unflinching will of these silent, heavily aromatic presences, forest giants that do not give an inch. Under the woodsmen's pitiless blows, the trees keep their dignity to the last; they fall in one piece, with never a hint of submission. Their crazed bark and bleeding pulp attest to a stubborn existence, lived deep in the soil and high in the sky. There is no doubt that these pillars of an invisible temple are the guardians of some solemn law of Creation. And each time one falls, its trunk detached from its roots to lean slowly at first and then plunge precipitously to the ground with a thunderous roar, there is a sense of sacrilege. But the men who confront the trees could not care less. They are subject to another law, the law of destruction. They themselves have been destroyed, body and soul. They must use the remnants of their life-force to carry out the express order: destroy.

Like construction, destruction is a trade. Except for Haolang and two or three others, the apprentice woodsmen have to be taught everything. By not respecting the proper angle at which to aim the axe and the right direction in which to push the tree, two of our comrades are seriously injured by a heavy trunk that rebounds as it falls. Their lives are saved by two passing hunters who administer first aid. Impressed by the incident, the apprentices become meticulous. Humbly they learn the most elementary skills: how to drag trunks to the cleared area, how to operate a saw according to a special movement and rhythm. Movement and rhythm nonetheless punctuated by scrapes and wounds.

This life could be without constraint; it is constraining. It is up to Haolang as foreman to impose discipline on the crew, however repugnant he finds the task. Before winter we have to reach the quota agreed upon by camp leaders. We start early in the morning and stop late in the evening. Even in early fall, the nights are already cold. The work day is broken up only by meals and a short rest period. It is a hard, grubby life, but these forced laborers like the break from work in the fields. Many even hope their stay can be prolonged. Unconsciously they put their trust in the mountains, as did the Chinese of old, who would often flee there to escape imperial tyranny and a restrictive society. For hermits, too, the mountains were once a favorite hideaway, for they saw in them the meeting place of the breaths of Heaven and Earth.

As the days go by, our crew of political prisoners and common criminals establishes solidarity without too many clashes. The most discordant element is Yang the Sixth, a former soldier sent here for committing unlawful acts—robbery and rape. A quick-tempered brute, he does not accept Haolang's authority, frequently picking quarrels with him, and with others, too. The common criminals who were tempted to go along with him have now distanced themselves. "Son of a bitch . . ." "Son of a tortoise . . ." Using these expressions non-stop, the former soldier thinks to show his superiority. This particular day, in a foul mood, he deliberately piles his logs where they are in everyone's way. There is invective between him and others, intervention by Haolang.

"Put the logs where they belong, and let's have a little quiet if you don't mind."

"You can take your quiet and shove it, you son of a bitch!"

"In the new society we do not use foul language, comrade."

"New society, new society! But we're the ones, us tough guys, who built it! We fought with our fucking rifles. It's ours, the new society!"

"For the moment, I am in charge. I forbid you to use such language in my presence."

"You forbid me? Better watch it, son of a tortoise! I'll show you how they forbid me . . ."

With a kick, he sends his pile of cut logs rolling. He retrieves a big forked branch and brandishes it, threatening.

"Put it down," says Haolang." Fight like a man, with your bare hands."

The two men set to and have their scrap. A rain of blows, sharp and heavy. Those struck by Haolang seem better aimed, their target the face, the shoulders, and the chest of his adversary. Long years in the penal colony have not blunted the force of his fists; in fact, all his repressed rage has only increased the accuracy of his punches. With everyone watching, the other cannot very well launch the low blows—to the genitals—in which he excels. Haolang is ready to quit, when a flying kick gets him on the chin. His mouth is bleeding. His indecisive response only elicits another kick. This time he is on his guard and he grabs Yang the Sixth's leg, repelling it with all his strength. The enemy falls backward on the ground, his left arm scraped and bleeding. Haolang approaches, puts out his hand. "Okay, let's say I won this round. The next time it might be you." The defeated soldier cannot refuse his hand. He gets up, attempting to keep his composure, and mumbles, "Yes, next time . . ."

"Hurrah! hurrah! Let's have a drink!" The onetime actor, always cheerful, scurries into the tent, comes out with our bottle and some rabbit legs. In the mountains, away from the iron yoke, the men give rein to their need for rowdiness. Soon, a bit stupidly they see their loud talk turning into loud laughter. Only the surrounding trees are silent, barely shuddering at the capricious sport of men. On fine days, their work done, their bodies tattooed with scratches and insect bites, some go to the cave for water, others cook around the fire. Still others simply coil up against a tree and look at the distant sun which, suspended like them between heaven and earth, toys with the mist one last moment before bedding down for the night. Now only the silent flights of crow and eagle are woven in the air above. We have become mountain men and cannot imagine any other life. Very relaxed one evening, Haolang starts reciting, then intoning, Wang Wei's poem:

In middle life, devoting myself to the Way,
I chose to dwell under the Zhongnan.
When fancy strikes, I go alone to the mountain,
And alone I delight in views beyond words.

I walk to where the source runs dry,
And seated, I wait for the clouds to rise.
Sometimes I meet a hermit on the path,
We talk, we laugh, no thought of the trek home.

The intoning is followed by a long silence. This poem of questionable ideology, which we would not dare recite in the camp, is rapidly taken up by the crew, becoming their hymn. They often ask the poet to recite it, as children will demand a favorite lullaby at bedtime.

24

HE DAYS GO BY; more and more overcome by injuries and fatigue, our woodsmen for a season are unaware of the change in the weather. Awakening in the tent one morning to the chill north wind that blows here in the fall, amid the smell of frosty humus and cut wood I discern another odor, far away, long forgotten but buried deep within me, the indefinable odor of a vast presence. As a man of the North and a child of Harbin, Haolang too can identify the odor. Almost simultaneously, the two us say: "It smells of the river!"

This is too unsettling for us not to try to solve the mystery. We have to go to the top of our mountain at any cost and see what is hidden behind it. After two days of preparation, Haolang has collected the necessary equipment for an ascent through brush and bramble, and we undertake the hard trek up the mountain, even harder because there are only the two of us and I am not always a good helper. Before we go, Haolang entrusts the unit to one of his staunch supporters and claims he is off to explore possible lumber camp sites. We leave before dawn, carrying a little food in case we get lost. After eight or nine hours of relentless struggle, faces and limbs covered with scratches, we reach the summit exhausted. Standing on an immense rocky surface crowned with wild plants, we see another mountain in the distance and are discouraged although it is not as high as the one we have just climbed. It is already late, almost three in the afternoon, and we rest on the rock, trying to decide whether it would be better to return to the base or continue our adventure. After surveying the scene a while, we spot a hunters' refuge at the foot of the south slope of the second mountain. The tiny structure attracts us like a blue shadow on a desert horizon. What can we do but go? We are aware of the risks we take by deciding to pursue our path: they may worry back at the camp; we may be rebuked and bullied later. Yang the Sixth or somebody else will be quick to betray us. We disregard all that. By dint of being reprimanded for every trifle, we have become habituated, hardened. Like any con, we know the saying: "When you're stuck in a camp, the worst can't be any worse than what it's like now."

After a few minutes thinking thoughts of our bivouac, we are making the descent into the deep valley below. A descent nearly as hard as the morning's ascent. Clearing away brambles, gripping tightly to the rock, sideslipping—our poor bodies take the measure of the interminable slope, more abrupt on this side of the mountain. Now we have bruises to go with the deep scratches acquired earlier. Besides the physical challenge, there is the apprehension felt by anyone facing the unfamiliar and forbidden. The sun seems in a hurry to withdraw, like a servant bowing as he backs away from the angry faces of his masters: having a tête-à-tête at this hour, the haughty peaks do not suffer intruders well.

It is night when we finally arrive at the refuge. Two dead weights, we collapse on the two wooden beds. Covered with animal skins we find hanging on the walls, we spend the night in the relative mildness of the south slope of the other peak.

But physical exhaustion has not put my mind to sleep. A little past midnight, I hear the call of the night. Am I awake? Am I in the middle of a dream? No need to find out: in the depths of night, all is connected, undifferentiated. The night is my compost, my cradle. All my life I have been hearing this gentle, poignant call. Since the night of the woman crying out for the soul of her dead husband; during the night with my father atop Mount Lu; on the night I gazed secretly at the Lover asleep after her lustral bath; then the starry night on the Dunhuang road; and the night in Assisi when, worn by fatigue and rejection but fulfilled by terrestrial beauty, I dozed atop a rampart on warm stones scarcely cooled by the moon; and that of the fire when I found the Friend among the lifeless, struggling against death.

Through the opening that is our window, beyond the space that let in the sporadic cries of nocturnal birds, I see a few stars, constant and changing. Drawing ever closer, they betoken the limpid blue-black of the Source and alert me to the presence of a giantess with a body of sandalwood and myrrh. Instinctively my body opens wide to receive this other body that takes possession of mine, and I feel holy fear mixed with unmistakable familiarity. In slow sips I drink the milk flowing from the matrix breast.

I finally fall asleep again, awakening several hours later. Being a light sleeper, it is up to me to rouse Haolang, a heavy sleeper—the same duty as in our high school days and on our trek across Sichuan whenever we decided to set out before sunrise. Whether it was hot or cold, whether it was fleas or other bugs nibbling us, Haolang would always sleep like a log, as unmovable as a statue. I had to pull his body bit by bit from the abyss into which it had sunk . . .

This morning, once on our feet, we rub ourselves, we pound ourselves to get warm. Then we breakfast on a few *mantou* washed down with the lukewarm tea in our thermos.

The ascent of the second peak is less arduous: from the refuge there is a path, although overrun in places by brambles and wild grass. We are relieved to reach the crest before the morning is too advanced. A look around, another disappointment. Not because we have sighted a third mountain rising in the distance to thumb its nose at us. Worse: there is nothing. Only a whitish expanse. Mist? Fog? Smoke? A blend of impalpable substances, scarcely of this earth. Sitting on a little hillock, the cold wind stunning us, we cannot doubt that we are on earth. And the odor risen from the depths of the earth, from the depths of memory, coming in gusts, lashing our faces. Odor of leaves before a thunderstorm and of cracked soil soaking up rain, odor of hair wet through and of laundry drying,

odor of a fleshly presence so long familiar. We are here, like two wid-
ows turned to stone from waiting.

A siren cleaves the opaque invisibility and we jump. The howl
that stirred the blood of the child of Harbin on the Songhua and the
child of Mount Lu by the Yangzi, the howl that thrilled both in the
port of Tchoungking. The piercing sound, slow to fade away, awak-
ens another beneath it, the sound of a great current of water, a sound
so omnipresent and so diluted in the fragrant air that we do not hear
it right away, just as a man does not notice the breathing of the
woman asleep beside him, whose vitality is simply the very air he
inhales.

Now, we have only to wait. Wait for the wind to tear aside the
fog, wait for the naked river to stretch out before us. And it is not
just any river. The Black Dragon! The River Amur! It is worth having lived an entire lifetime to be here at this moment. It is worth having dreamed an entire lifetime not having dared dream of such an
encounter.

These two solitary beings, displaced and distraught, at the ends of
the earth, at the edge of the sky, on this unknown peak, in this
unknown hour. "The river below! The river below!" They shout, no
sound issuing from their breasts. Can the sight before them be real?
Are they themselves real? Are they in a state of dementia, like very
old people who have lost their memories, forgetting the present and
living in a distant past? In the moment of their past when they stood
on the hot clay of Sichuan in wartime and tried so keenly to picture
the far reaches of Siberia after their reading of Tolstoy and Dosto-
evsky. . . . But their vision of the river is filling in: there is a boat, followed by the sound of a horn; there are flights of gulls crossing the
river; there is a wide ink-colored stream flowing east. Soon they can
see all the way to the opposite shore, and there are scattered isbas,
and a wooden Russian church that reaches high as if to make its
presence known; and beyond, there are open fields, swollen, brownish or grayish, with scattered patches of fresh or ancient ice, and a
look-out tower in the middle . . .

As we used to do in our Sichuan days, shouldn't we be rushing
intrepidly down the mountain to dip hands and head in the river

water—and why not—dive in or even swim across? Hasn't the other side always been a source of fascination for us? And this time the other side is the very dream we dreamed in our youth. But we do not stir. This time our days are numbered. And the cold brought by the penetrating wind immobilizes us on our frost-covered summit. We do not stir, knowing it is necessary to preserve the vision intact: we must leave it at that. Yes, one step less, and we would have seen nothing. Now, on the mountaintop, we have been given this ultimate vision that connects with the initial vision of our lives.

Without knowing where we were headed, all our years of bad luck, pain and suffering have pushed us to the limit and brought us to this far edge! Here we two damned creatures join all the damned of the earth. For the Amur River is one of the experimental sites of the spirit of Evil: on both its shores the humiliated and offended are deep in a hell created by men. Here we are at the ends of the earth, not the North Pole, but the pole of human misery, where individual suffering meets universal suffering. No point in going any farther. We have gone from river to river to this last river. The loop of destiny ends here, of that we are certain.

But it is not for us to know how and where the Great Loop will end. Will the blood, sweat, tears, and other human secretions that have fed the rivers from the beginning evaporate to become cloud? And after their life in the air, will they condense and fall to earth again as rain, watering a different land? And in the same way, will wandering, floating, scattered souls return to the Body and be as one? And will the departures, all the departures—forced or desired, in happiness or in heartbreak, precipitated by a harsh blow or delayed by a beloved hand, of whole groups amid hideous fumes or one at a time deep in a vile cellar—be borne aloft by the circulating breaths and finally arrive at the Great Return?

For now, we have to hurry back to the camp and all the unpredictable consequences of our trek.

25

ALWAYS THE SAME astonishment at still being here. And just
where is "here"? Sunk in reality up to the neck? Or soaring
in a sphere that is totally unreal? There is the material
world, obstinate as a wild boar, tough, ferocious, a world ruled by
the laws of man and climate, imposing relentless struggles.

There is the body, penetrated by odors of manure and animal
vomit, eaten up by leeches, horseflies and giant mosquitoes, a body
with bones ground down by hard work and cold. If a touch of
breath or spirit remains in what is left of the body—permanently
weakened, given over to pain—something is bound to happen. And
something is happening. At the slightest favorable breeze, a mist rises
from the tops of trees frozen to their roots, a mist as light as the coils
of smoke that rise from a stick of incense.

Here we are at the limit, at the edge, much as our own Far North
is on China's edge. But even here, can't we still hear the call? Can't
we once and for all turn away from the horrors of the real world to
the realm of the inconceivable, which is more real than reality?

The two damned men are privileged to enjoy a state they cannot
name, since they have not sought it. A state of half-sleep, as when
the depleted body lets go after making love. A state that seems to
remove them from everything earthly. A state of emptiness, and with
it the near certainty that nothing is finished but all is accomplished;
that the breath continues to circulate in a space without partitions;
that what they desired has crossed the barriers of time to come
together, making any further request or expectation seem pointless.
Here and there zones of longing and regret still hover. But when they
enter these, they lose themselves in a presence. A presence as palpable as water or light. Warm and snug inside that presence, they no
longer see it. They are part of it. It is here, you are here, I am here,
an indivisible center, shining forth eternally. Three in one. One in
three. "Yumei-Haolang-Tianyi," "Tianyi-Yumei-Haolang," "Haolang-
Tianyi-Yumei." Echoes of the lark in the waterfall. Flame of the lark
in the smoke. Well, when? Well, where? Here! here! here! United at
last. One at last . . .

The two friends are privileged to experience a felicity without name. For a while, for all time, they have become like those who, according to the Taoists, "Feed on clouds and sleep among the mists."

26

OWN LOWER, much lower, below the sphere outside time, black clouds gather over the world, but the two fulfilled beings do not see them coming.

In 1966 China is precipitated into an upheaval of unprecedented magnitude. This occasioned by the return of the man who has spent his life fashioning the destiny of several hundreds of millions and who cannot conceive of a life without such power. After the great famine the principal leaders of the Party, frightened, had removed him from the center of decision-making by granting him highly honorific titles with little power. After some time spent pondering the movement of History and ideology, he reappears, a figure both familiar and new. China has every reason to believe he has undergone a profound reversal in his thinking. The supposition is not gratuitous. For his ultimate reform, is the man not describing of a radical revolution in human culture? How salutary this Cultural Revolution might be, if it were genuine! Isn't just what the world needs, a world stifled by arrogant wealth on the one hand and intolerable poverty on the other? They deserve to be honored, the scrupulously ethical adherents to the principles of the Cultural Revolution. It is apparent, however, that such an all-embracing dream is not yet within humanity's reach. As time passes, the dream will degenerate and the reality prove to be other than what is promised. Against a background of merciless struggles and continual shocks destined to last ten years, this tragic retaking of power will lead the entire country into a madness served by cruel and base instincts and will produce several million victims. All of this will end only when the instigator dies.

But long before, at the beginning, the instigator envisions a project on the grand scale although of limited duration. He cannot foresee that he is caught in a mechanism soon to be out of control, that his action is going to arouse all the demons of division and arbitrariness lurking in a society still anchored in feudal tradition. He proceeds as planned, his first step to make sure he has the secret support of one branch of the army, in the person of its commander. Ostensibly, he is acting through the Red Guards, made up of all young people fifteen or sixteen and up. Interrupting their studies, overnight these youngsters find themselves invested with the right to topple everything. Dumbfounded by such outrageous license, they are thoroughly delighted to strike down those they dislike, starting with their immediate masters, unbearable examiners, and school officials. Huge herds of youth, traveling by special train, are universally hailed as the new conquerors. Armed with slogans and red insignia, not bothering to acquaint themselves with history or the current situation, they plunder everything in their path, even the treasures of the past. They know nothing about the experiences of the people they're after; they simply set themselves up as judges and claim the right to punish, their penalties often extreme: they smash the hand of a famous pianist guilty of playing Western music; they break the leg of an old revolutionary at the very site of his war wound. . . . They drive others to suicide. Their acts reveal a new line of justice lovers and petty bosses. A short-lived line, however. For they are actually directed and totally controlled by a secret authority that consults with the Leader, who tries to keep the situation in hand. Any faction that becomes too powerful is brought down by counterbalancing it with another. The factions proliferate, and their rivalries and conflicts lead them to quarrel so much that they cancel one another's influence. Soon countless young people are swelling the ranks of far-off work camps, including those in the Far North. Thus, these youngsters, so pure in their early idealism, so fragile and malleable, will be doomed to vain battles and sacrifice before they even reach adulthood.

According to the strategy of the man who is calling upon all the resources of his dialectical genius, what works with the Red Guards is also good at a higher level. The commander of the army, with whom he has been in collusion, becomes so powerful there is a danger of his taking over. Now the Leader must form another group to put down the commander. It is done. But the new group is not entirely trustworthy, even though headed by a prestigious figure from the old team; soon or later it will be necessary to rely on other forces.

Nearly a decade goes by. The man, alone, searches the horizon and observes that it is sparsely populated, maybe even say empty. One after another all his old companions have been liquidated, sent to prison, or exiled. Enfeebled by Parkinson's disease, weak-limbed, slack-jawed, and drooling, he now trusts only his wife—but he is wary of her, too—and two or three young stooges who obey without question. Wielding absolute power and using the Red Guards as she pleases, his wife passes out prison and death sentences. She is profiting from her position to settle personal accounts, of which she has an amazing number. Accounts to settle with important Party cadres who, back in the Yan'an days, disapproved of the Leader's remarriage: they thought he should not repudiate his legitimate spouse, who had followed him during the Long March, to wed a failed Shanghai actress seeking adventure in Yan'an. And there are accounts to settle with Shanghai theatrical and film circles, which include onetime lovers, of whom she vows to wipe out every trace so as to restore her virginity. Then there are scores to settle with hundreds from the artists' groups created during the Sino-Japanese War, whose members always managed to escape her control, thus thwarting her ambitions to reign over the nation's artistic activity. Accounts with the unlucky women obliged to become the Leader's short-term secret mistresses after he had taken a shine to them, . . .

A lengthy blacklist of targeted persons and their families is drawn up. Secretly, the order is given to hunt them down all over China and seize them. No official death sentences are necessary. Relentless persecution is enough. Suicide, an untreated illness, or long decline in some hidden jail will do the rest.

All of this, however, has to do with future developments. At present, the endless nightmare is only in its first phase, and we are in the

Far North. How long will our land of banishment be safe from the infernal flood of events?

27

A UTUMN 1968. Life in the camp is turned upside-down; the Red Guards have arrived and are in command. The non-military camp directors, relieved of their duties, are themselves about to be put on trial.

For better control over the cons, the Red Guards turn them out of the dormitories and regroup them in large halls reminiscent of wartime refugee centers.

Because of the heavy schedule imposed by the new arrivals, we are on the qui-vive every minute of the workday. Personal needs and meals are speedily dispatched. We still tend the livestock and work in the fields, but as fast as we can. Most of our time is devoted to endless political gatherings: we study passages from the *Little Red Book,* we perform what are styled "loyalty dances" as we shout "Ten thousand years, ten thousand years, ten times ten thousand years of life to the supreme leader!" Sometimes we are awakened abruptly in the night by the loudspeaker; we jump out of bed and assemble on the square to hear the latest orders from Peking.

After looking over the files on this cursed population that has spent so many years in the Far North, the apprentice revolutionaries are overjoyed to unearth a rare pearl in the person of Haolang. The latter soon finds himself with a glorious title, that of "the most ancient and most stubborn rightist," granted by those who could not have been more than two or three years old back in the days of the Hu Feng affair and who have never had the opportunity to read a single line of said writer. Haolang ends up among those housed in rooms called "cowsheds," all located on the opposite side of the square and kept under strict guard.

Although unaware of the details, we know what is in store for these prisoners. Each is isolated in his cowshed, where the only lux-

ury, apart from the straw-covered bed, is a table. The table is important; around it, the man in solitary receives his guests, for he holds
perpetual open house: at any time of the day they may arrive to
interrogate him. They ask him to recount his past and his "errors"
orally, then in writing, all this repeatedly, for various bands take
turns visiting, some more violent than others. One group is headed
by a leader who wears a heavy metal-encrusted belt, a man known
for his cruelty and aggressiveness. More and more frequently these
interrogations take place in the open at a general meeting. The
square is then transformed into a stage on which a perverted humanity performs a cruel comedy. Those packed into the large halls on
this side of the square, their daily tasks done, can come out and
watch the show for entertainment and see what they cannot avoid
seeing.

I too see. What I see, I shall never stop seeing; the end of my
earthly life will not change that. Haven't I spent that life overcoming
fear and remorse, training my eye so it can take in at least once,
straight on, the vileness of this world, not excluding what I, myself,
Tianyi, put on view?

I see the collective interrogations on the square, with the accused
lined up on a long bench and the assembled Red Guards facing
them. The overexcited young militants, shout appropriate slogans to
support the accusations the ringleaders are hurling at the accused.
From time to time, all the enthusiasts raise arms that end in a flower
bed of little red books in bloom. Standing out from the other
accused because he is so tall: Haolang. Seated on the bench at the
first such session, he is the only one who doesn't lower his head,
despite the efforts of the strapping lads around him to keep his neck
and shoulders down. Furious, they finally grab him by the hair, a
gesture that brings to mind the death of historian Wu Han, the first
victim of the Cultural Revolution, who, among other atrocities suffered, had tufts of hair pulled out. . . .

The Friend becomes the favorite target of the budding revolutionaries, for at subsequent sessions they always see him on his feet,
standing alone before the crowd. Unkempt, unshaven, obviously
deprived of sleep, he remains dignified as he replies in ringing tones

to all the questions posed, which actually allow no answers. Thus he further unleashes the fury of his accusers. After one such session, he is walking away when one of the leaders hits him from behind with a belt, aiming several blows at his legs. He falls, tries to get up. They drag him to his cowshed. At the following sessions, it is a limping Haolang who comes before the judges. Always on his feet, the long rip in his trousers more noticeable each time, he no longer speaks. His head is slightly tilted, his look mocking.

I see the bonfire blazing on the square and the Red Guards furiously tossing in all the writings, books, and papers snatched from the dormitories. The Friend's manuscripts are among the materials feeding the flames that send bits of burned pages floating in the air. (Henceforth, the passing on of his poems will depend on those who have learned them by heart.) The sinister celebration is in full swing; the racket made by these people from elsewhere is louder than ever. Atop the pile of books, as if to crown it, they place larger items, made of heavy paper; even from a distance, I easily recognize my pictures. They are only landscapes and portraits. But in the eyes of these apprentice sorcerers who feed only on the magic potion of the *Little Red Book,* a landscape lacking peasants bent to the task is not a landscape; a person without raised eyebrows or a steely glance is not a person. I painted my pictures on durable cardboard so they would last. It turns out they are more exposed to oblivion than a piece of straw.

I see truckloads of Red Guards returning to camp after a day of raids in the region. Before dinner, a whole group of fanatics led by petty bosses, everyone drunk on wine and power, seeks to discharge its remaining energy on the tough enemy within easy reach. The men hurry toward the cowshed. And now the enemy steps out the door, a long spade in his hand, one of those spades with a sharp cutting edge for breaking the frozen ground of the Far North, a tool that can lop off ten heads in turn (it was with such a spade he stunned the wolf so long ago). He advances slightly, limping, stands resolutely on his good leg, pulls himself up to the full height of a man of Manchuria. He utters the long cry of the wild animal at bay, a cry heard in all the surrounding structures, a cry that stops the group in its tracks. Brief astonishment. Then the stone-throwing begins, and the Friend is struck on the shoulder. A little shaken, he raises his spade as a shield. The stones keep coming. Suddenly, a red star on his forehead, another on his left temple, this one streaming blood. The heavy body collapses. Several Guards break away from the group to jump on him. Another group intervenes to keep things from going too far. (Eventually these groups will be doing each other in. For now, killing in cold blood is not in their plans.) In no time the square is empty. An unusual silence falls on this ghostly universe.

I see Tianyi: I see myself—but is he whom I see still myself?—a ghost among ghosts, going toward the square, toward the one lying in a pool of blood. A few other ghosts join him, courageous comrades, medics. They improvise a stretcher and carry the body to the infirmary. Hasty cleaning of the wounds, dressings for the head, their white soon scarlet. Muffled death rattles of a beast with shattered flesh, sounds gradually turning into a heavy, more regular breathing. Late at night, the eye not blinded by blood opens, recognizes the face of a friend, smiles faintly, as on the night of the fire: smile of a fallen angel with charred wings. Now the rusted bronze mask can close up. The final death rattle and spitting of blood will not change its form, set at last.

.   .   .

I SEE Tianyi, doubled over with stomach and intestinal pain, carried to the town's clinic. I see him a few days later, escaping from his room and heading down the corridor at every opportunity. He runs in the open fields until exhausted. When they find him, he is barely recognizable and his pockets are stuffed with horse dung. Brought back to the clinic, he flees outdoors again and looks for dung to fill his pockets. Why do these yellowish balls fascinate him, why does he want to chew and swallow them? Do they really remind him of the cardboard he once used for his painting, appropriately named "horse-dung cardboard"?

Finally I see Tianyi taken by military truck to an enormous building, an asylum for the mentally ill and the physically handicapped, in the city of S. From now on, he is without identity. They do not treat him; they just give him mind-numbing drugs. They leave him in peace. In peace, if you can call it that. He is unceremoniously thrown among discarded humanity, broken creatures, misshapen, repulsively dirty, but strangely free. Free to shout, to bang on things, to obey their every impulse or to lie prostrate all day long. I see Tianyi clinging to thick rolls of all-purpose paper as if they were a lifeline. He writes day and night on this coarse paper that smells of grass and earth, letting each roll unwind and unwind under his hand like an endless river, like an ancient scroll painting entitled *The Yangzi River over Ten Thousand Li*. He puts down in writing all he has lived and seen on earth, an earth incredibly destitute, incredibly rich.

IT IS THUS POSSIBLE for the miracle—often awaited, often experienced—to occur one last time. It could not be otherwise. For Tianyi, so ordinary and so unique, is reconstructing bit by bit the happenings of a lifetime; in so doing, he lets the flowing water connect the separate events of his life, which were actually all of a piece; lets the breath retrace the twists and turns of his path, which actually led him straight ahead. As he writes and writes, he is certain that life—real and intact—is still with him in spite of everything; now that he has gotten to the end, real life is just beginning. He, Tianyi, learned about life through a borrowed body; now he will learn about life through himself. Since pain engenders a shudder ever more intense and joy engenders a joy ever more concentrated, might not what could happen be as real as what has really happened?

Really happened? Who could verify that, when things are in such a tangle? So many dreams, hopes, dreads, longings are added to life's happenings. After all, Tianyi the wanderer—from the start dispossessed and careless—no longer possesses any document, any certificate. What does he himself know for true? Does he know that in the beginning, without the meeting of the three, there would have been no story? But how many times has he asked himself whether the three, once together, were ever separated? Did Tianyi ever leave and return? Did Yumei ever quit this world? Was Haolang ever lost in that faraway land? Would he believe someone who came along and suggested that all of it might have been imagined? That in the end all of it could resume, in a different way. If he calls Yumei, he will hear, again and always, the cheerful voice: "But it's not too late; we can still do something!" And if he merely speaks Haolang's name, his ear will echo, again and always, with the sound of the energetic steps that will transform the landscape into rhyme and meter. A trifle, and once again they will trod barefoot the warm red clay and the bright, sweet-smelling meadows. From circle to circle, time will resume its faultless, immemorial rhythm. The faithful blue smoke will mount on the horizon, where the sun sets and gives way to the moon. The nocturnal earth, crystal clear in the moonlight, will await the unforeseeable start of a new cycle. Eternity should be enough time for the tree of desire to grow again. It will grow again; for certain, it will. If not, why have they been here, tormented by such fierce hungers, such inconsolable sorrows? They only have to know how to wait.

While waiting, with nothing more to lose, all tears choked back, Tianyi the witness has only to grip his pen and not interrupt the course of the river. The invisible breath, if it is indeed the breath of life, cannot forget what it has known on this earth, furors and savors both. The breath carries within itself enough unsatisfied longing that, like the river, it will return—when it wishes, where it wishes.